CW00622005

Nick Bleszynski was born in Scotland
eastern Africa. After returning to th
Anglia University, he went into televis
has worked as a writer, producer and director for some of the
world's biggest broadcasters. This is his second book, following on
from the success of *Shoot Straight You Bastards!: The Truth Behind
the Killing of 'Breaker' Morant*. He is married and lives in Sydney,
Australia, with his wife, Jill, and son, Stefan.

To contact Nick or to find out more about his books log on to
www.blackrosemedia.com.au.

This book is dedicated to my son,
Stefan Peter Bleszynski,
and the two Peters he never met:
Peter Grant Harvey (1910–2000) and
Peter Harvey (1942–1999).

Be as a tower firmly set;
Shakes not its top for any blast that blows.

Dante Alighieri

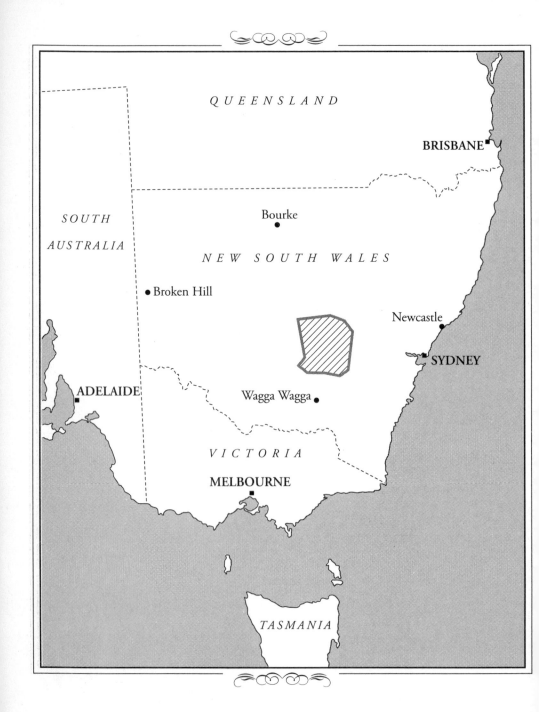

BEN HALL IN NEW SOUTH WALES

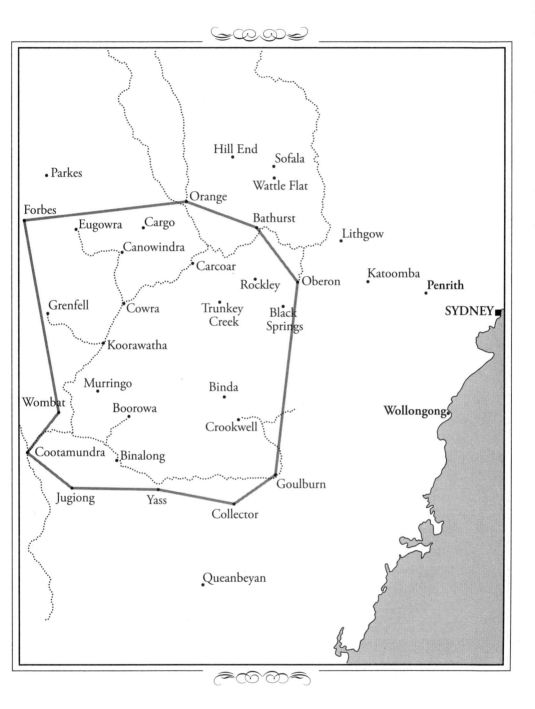

BEN HALL IN THE INNER WEST OF NEW SOUTH WALES

BEN HALL COUNTRY

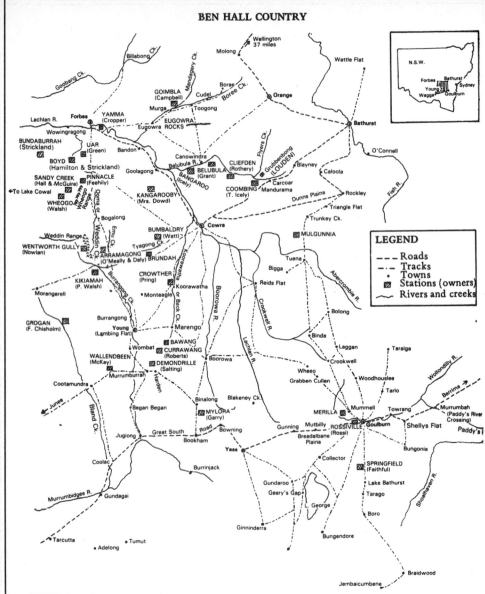

NOTE: Locations are approximate.

Sources:

1. N.S.W. Counties Maps: Monteagle, 1875; Forbes, 1867; Bland, 1896; Argyle, 1862; Bathurst, 1859; Harden, 1864; King, 1865.
2. N.S.W. Parish Maps: Weddin, 1902; Kikiamah, 1909; Brundah, 1904; Coba, 1902; Wheogo, 1904; Eualdrie, 1903; Bogalong, 1903.
3. Balliere's N.S.W. Gazetteer 1866, accompanying map.
4. John Sands new atlas of Australia. Sydney 1886.
5. Map of bushranger landmarks, prepared by Grenfell Historical Society.
6. H.E.C. Robinson. Map of N.S.W. showing pastoral stations 1911.
7. Royal Australian Survey Corps maps 1:250,000 — Forbes, Narrandera, Canberra, Cootamundra, Bathurst, Goulburn.

* Reproduced from *Ben Hall: Bushranger* by D.J. Shiel with permission of University of Queensland Press

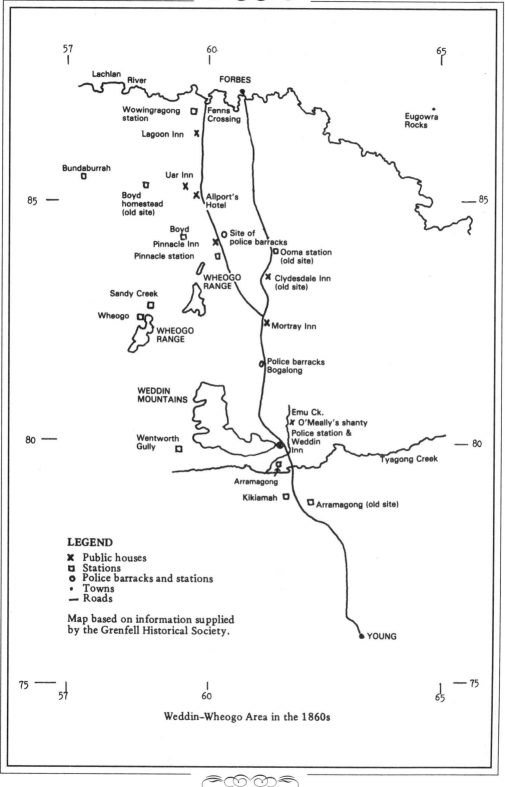

57 60 65

Lachlan River

FORBES

Wowingragong station · Fenns Crossing

Eugowra Rocks

Lagoon Inn ✘

Bundaburrah ◻

Uar Inn ✘

85 —

Boyd homestead (old site) ◻

✘ Allport's Hotel

— 85

Boyd Pinnacle Inn ✘ · Site of police barracks

Pinnacle station

◻ Ooma station (old site)

WHEOGO RANGE

✘ Clydesdale Inn (old site)

Sandy Creek ◻

Wheogo ◻

WHEOGO RANGE

✘ Mortray Inn

○ Police barracks Bogalong

WEDDIN MOUNTAINS

Emu Ck.
✘ O'Meally's shanty
Police station & Weddin Inn

80 —

Wentworth Gully ◻

— 80

Tyagong Creek

Arramagong

Kikiamah ◻ ◻ Arramagong (old site)

LEGEND
✘ Public houses
◻ Stations
○ Police barracks and stations
· Towns
— Roads

Map based on information supplied by the Grenfell Historical Society.

· YOUNG

75 — 57 60 65 — 75

Weddin-Wheogo Area in the 1860s

* Reproduced from *Ben Hall: Bushranger* by D.J. Shiel with permission of University of Queensland Press

Prologue

The warmth had barely left my body, but already they have my obituary written. It's been waiting in the drawer of John McLerie, the Inspector-General of the New South Wales police, for the past six months.

They brought me into town on the back of a donkey, like Jesus, paraded along the main street of Forbes on the way to the police station up on Barrack Hill.

It takes a lot to bring the busy main street of a prosperous gold-mining town of twenty thousand people to a halt, but the sight of my raw, bleeding, bullet-riddled body was enough to silence idle chatter and still the ponderous tread of the beasts of burden that plough a furrow up and down the wide, dusty street day and night.

Ignoring the foul gases erupting from my body, the trickles of urine and strands of bloody flux running down my legs, staining the ochre dust, the traps dragged me by the boots into a cool, dark room lit by a single shaft of yellow sunlight. Roundly cursing because the rigors had set in, making their task more difficult, two strapping Forbes constables raised their batons high above their heads and brought them down with sickening cracks to ease the stiffness in my joints, knees and fingers. Grunting and sweating they forced me upright on a stretcher in the corner of the room, forced a pistol into my dead hand and, with greasy thumbs, gouged my eyelids open to reveal what the newspapers called my 'mad, wide-eyed stare'.

Their work done, they shuffled off for breakfast and a woman called Mary came in and washed the dried blood from my face, hair and hands with a cloth and warm water. Though she couldn't hear or see me I leaned close and thanked her softly for her kindness, and wondered if her other name might be Magdalene, like that other

Mary who had performed the same service for another poor bastard who hadn't deserved the end he'd got.

When the rattling dice in the back room had decided the fate of my saddle, gun and holster, the black curtain at the doorway was swept back and the 'viewing' commenced. The big Irish constable, with pork fat from his hurried breakfast still glistening on his moustache and the mist of a celebratory whisky still on his breath, began collecting pieces of silver from his customers with a well-practised backhand. Soon the room was full of whispering shadows; the ghouls, the morbid, the curious and the souvenir hunters, come to ogle at the bullet-ridden corpse of the notorious bushranger Ben Hall as though it was some kind of carnival curiosity. But any reverence for the dead was soon forgotten. The whispers became chatter and then clamour as they tore strips from my bloodied shirt, souvenired locks of my hair and some 'Doubting Thomas', a rat-arsed weasel of a bloke with baccy-stained teeth and a squint eye, stuck his fingers into my bullet wounds to make sure I was really dead.

A flash of powder lit up the room momentarily, as a photographer recorded the grisly scene for posterity and, no doubt, profit. As the smoke settled the Irish constable called 'time', but before the ghouls skulked back through the black curtain into the burning sunlight and gritty dust of Forbes, one or two peered into my dead, unseeing eyes as if trying to winkle out of me that last terrible secret that I had taken with me beyond the grave.

What is it that brings to the surface the terrible, malevolent forces that live deep in the souls of men? And what measure of good and evil must a bucko battle with before he's forced to ride out along with his devils? Learned men at Melbourne University are looking for the answers inside 'Mad' Dan Morgan's empty, decomposing head, sent to them in a hatbox by the good folk of Wangaratta. Even a man with no schooling knows the criminal tendency has nothing to do with the shape of the head, or the size of the brain. It is determined by the measures of betrayal, guilt and vengeance that seep into a man's life and dictate his actions and destiny.

I came to the sad knowing of this even as I watched through my own dying eye my bloodied, torn, bullet-riddled body being hoisted up by the New South Wales police and tied to a tree. 'You'll never take me alive,' I once told Inspector Norton, and they took me at my word.

Their voices, still hoarse with the unholy joy of their success, decreed that death was not punishment enough. They were seeking vengeance for all the times the Ben Hall gang brought ridicule and disgrace down on their heads and for the comrades that we killed. So, drunk with power and Irish whisky, they used my cadaver for target practice. Only after a hail of bullets had ripped my flesh and bone asunder and their gunsmoke dispersed along with the early morning mists would any kind of satisfaction have a ghost's chance in Hell of stilling the pounding of those bastards' cruel hearts.

My life was one crowded hour. I was the most notorious bushranger in Australian history. I was with Darkie Gardiner when he pulled off the biggest-ever armed robbery at Eugowra Rocks and led the gang that bailed up banks, towns and more citizens, coaches, shops and stations than any other bushranger.

I was betrayed, gaoled, shackled and shot. I declared war on the squatters and the New South Wales police. I took on their curses, their guns, their native trackers and dogs and survived. But along the way I also buried and grieved for good men who lost their lives. I never killed anyone, nor did I ever set out to, but men did die, though not by my design.

Fate also played its mysterious part in turning me from selector to bushranger. It brought me to the people and places that influenced the road I took. Did my story turn out as God intended, or did meddling hands change the course of my destiny?

From my vantage point, high up in the rafters, I watch the local undertaker, Mr Toler, heaving my stiffened cadaver into a rough wooden shell with as little care and ceremony as the Forbes constabulary. As I look upon his grim doings below, I am strangely reluctant to depart for the Great Hereafter. As I see it, I must be already there, or nearabouts, anyhow. But before I discover the great mysteries of the afterlife, I have a story to tell, and as is usually the case, a life less ordinary began in very ordinary surroundings.

Part 1

LIFE

Chapter One

'Push now, Liza,' said Mrs Beaven in her urgent baritone. Our ma just grunted in reply. The exchange reached the dusty patch outside our hut where the steady traffic of feet had worn away the thick wallaby scrub during the ten years or so we had lived in the village of Haydonton, near Murrurundi in the Upper Hunter Valley. Over the years we kids had seen enough new arrivals to feign boredom, but our da with his constant pacing and puffing at his pipe was skittish enough for it to be his first, not his eighth child.

Early that morning our ma had taken our stepbrother, Tommy, by the hand and said gently, 'Go tell Mrs Beaven to come, it's nearly time.'

The formidable Mrs Beaven, the large, blowsy local storekeeper's wife, had arrived mid morning riding side-saddle on her man's big bay gelding. I'm sure she had a proper name, though I never heard anyone, even our parents, dare call her anything but Mrs Beaven. She was no midwife, but had given birth to six children herself and knew how to deliver one.

'Get that fire going and the water on,' she commanded as our other near neighbours, Mrs Knowles and Mrs Schmidt, arrived. The mysteries of childbirth were the realm of the womenfolk and Mrs Beaven had shooed us from the hut like chooks with a knowing look in her eye and the words 'it won't be long now' following us out the door.

I know babies all come out as blue and purple as a big bruise, which is little wonder as the minute they're born they hoist them up by the ankles, all bloodied like a skinned rabbit, and give them a good skelp on the arse. Four years ago our ma had what was called a 'difficult birth' with my brother Henry. She screamed so loudly that I thought she was dying. Being only seven at the time and not knowing better, I burst into the hut, my eyes all tearful, just as

Henry was being dragged out of my mother. We were almost at the same stage again judging by the sounds coming from the hut.

'I can see it,' Mrs Beaven's firm voice reassured our ma who let out one last anguished scream. Then there was a pause as the newborn filled its lungs with that first breath of new life and announced the arrival of another little Hall into the world with an insistent, high-pitched wail.

There was another nervous wait as hot water was fetched and the women made our ma decent for visitors. Finally, Mrs Beaven opened the door and allowed a hint of a smile to crack her flinty features as she said to our da, 'You've a lovely wee girl.'

Our da led us all in, held up his new daughter to the light and cooed, clucked and marvelled at her every tiny perfection. She would be the apple of our da's eye until he'd lose patience with her and then she would become a nuisance, just like the rest of us.

With the arrival of Ellen, as this little mite was named, I now had seven brothers and sisters in all. Tommy Wade was the oldest at eighteen and was born to his namesake in Parramatta in 1831, before our ma and da ever met. The Hall brood started with Mary, or 'Polly', as we called her, in 1833. Bill followed a year later, Edward two years after that, me the year after, then there was a five-year gap to Robert in 1842, Catherine followed the year after, Henry two years later and another four-year gap to wee Ellen born this day in 1850.

'That's the last, Ben,' our ma rasped from the bed where she lay, her hair all wild and sweat-drenched and her face still flushed from the tribulations of childbirth. In a rare show of obedience, our da just nodded.

We were all native-born Australians, but our ma and da were both convicts ripped from their kin and transported here by the English who made their criminals serve their sentences either working for the Governor or the rich squatters.

On those rare occasions when it rained on our patch all work stopped. The downpours, which were mostly short and violent, couldn't penetrate the hard pan of the sun-baked earth and would come skidding under the rough slab door of our hut and puddle in the middle of the floor where our feet had worn a little hollow. We kids would perch on chairs, with our feet tucked up under us like cats for warmth.

'Tell us a story,' we'd demand. In preparation for a long yarn our da would carefully pack his clay pipe with tobacco with as much care as an explorer about to venture out across the vast interior of this sunburnt land. Whatever his faults, he could tell a good yarn.

'It was July 1825 and I was just eighteen when I was dragged up in front of the dishonourable Judge James De Villiers who sat resplendent beneath a coat of arms bearing the legend *Mon Dieu et Mon Droit*, "My God and My Right", with a lambskin wig on his head,' he would always begin. We had heard the story a hundred times, but our kin were all faceless people in faraway lands we could not even picture. These stories were all the history and ancestry we had to pass down to our children and as we could neither read nor write we committed it all to memory in moments like these.

'De Villiers was a skinny runt, as old, dried and withered as parchment, as if his vocation had sucked all the juice and joy of life out of him,' our da said with a shake of his head. 'The purpose of the law was not truth or justice, but to protect the property of the rich from we common people. There were 223 capital crimes on the books and I heard it said they hung children as young as eight for stealing a spoon.'

Fortunately for our da, transportation to Australia was favoured over hanging, branding, gibbeting or pillory, and for stealing a few items of clothing De Villiers sent him 'Bay side' for seven years.

When he was maudlin with the grog he would tell how he had the presence of mind to look up, one last time, into the pale blue eyes of Sarah Jones, the girl he was engaged to before two burly policemen dragged him from the dock, down the stairs to the cells. He'd sit in that little slab hut of ours, just about as far away from home as he could possibly get, roll up his sleeve and show us a crude SJ he had tattooed on his left arm with a pin and blue ink. As the years passed the tattoo faded, but in his mind's eye, she became softer, younger and more beautiful than perhaps ever she was. Every time our da happened upon a Somerset man he would ask them if they knew a Sarah Jones, but it was a common enough name and he never did find out what became of her.

'In December they put me on a transport ship called the *Midas*, a four-masted bark bound for Botany Bay,' he would continue. 'There were one hundred and fifty men in one section at the stern of the ship where rows of hammocks had been slung between the bulkhead beams. We were stowed below the waterline and knew if she was holed going round the treacherous Cape of Good Hope there would be no escape.'

They were luckier than those who went before them, but only because the ship's owners were only paid for those they delivered alive. A transported convict was worth around £30 in 1826, less than a darkie slave who fetched £45 to £50.

They'd been cooped up in her stinking innards for two days before the tides and a favourable breeze finally conspired, and the bosun used every profanity in the English language to get the crew to unfurl the sails more quickly. The rising wind and the crack of heavy canvas sails drowned out the bosun as the *Midas* took the mighty elements in harness. There was no teary farewell to the mother country.

'Tell us about the sharks,' piped up Henry.

'Well, son, it was off the coast of Africa that we first spotted those grey fins, curved like an Arabian dagger, knifing towards us through the warm, green waters of the Indian Ocean. As every drop of drinking water had to be rationed, we cast buckets over the side on the end of long ropes to collect salt water to wash our bodies and clothes. The fins disappeared and four or five long grey shapes, about twelve feet long with ugly flat heads, began circling the bucket.' He would twirl his finger round and round to draw out the yarn, then, clapping his hands together he would pick up the thread of the story again.

'Without warning, one of the creatures snapped at the bucket with its great jaws and began thrashing it from side to side. It almost took the six fully grown men who were hanging to the other end of the straining rope over the side.' Lifting up his pinkie finger he always finished the story by sending a shudder through us.

'The bucket, made of stout English oak, was scarred by great tooth marks up to a pinkie deep.'

'There's no sharks in Australia, are there . . . da?' Henry would wail.

'No, son, not hereabouts anyway,' he'd reassure him with a pat on the head.

None of us had ever been to Sydney or even seen the sea, so our da always finished his story with a description of how they arrived in Australia.

'On February 15, 1826, two months, three deaths and two births later the Australian continent suddenly hove into view off the port side and we caught our first glimpse of New South Wales.'

Lush green vegetation tumbled down from tree-covered hills to the shoreline where tall, exotic palms, inhabited by a profusion of quarrelsome, highly coloured birds, lined the coast, which seemed to be one long stretch of white, sandy beach. There was no sign of human habitation until the day they saw the thin wisps of white smoke rising into the peerless blue sky.

'Them's savages,' said one of the guards.

Another redcoat appeared next to the first, flashed a broken-toothed smile and added, 'They know we're shipping "white meat" and they'll be building up 'em cooking fires.' Enjoying their fear and uncertainty he continued, 'If any of you buggers are thinking of making a break for it, remember they're out in the bush waiting for you with spears and sticks.'

'Eat the whole lot, they do,' chimed in the first redcoat.

'Every last bit!' confirmed the other with relish.

The *Midas* dropped anchor in a bay off Port Jackson and fired its gun to let the authorities know they'd arrived.

They got their first taste of convict rule when the soldiers came aboard, did a name check, put light irons on their legs and handed them their prison uniforms, ill-fitting canary yellow suits of Indian cotton with arrows painted on them, which they were told were called 'Devil's claws'. Anything that had a government mark on it was referred to as belonging to the Devil.

The history of Australia was a short one and its population numbered only around 10,000 by the time our da arrived, but it had already seen more rebellion, uprisings, mutinies, hangings and flog-gings than many much older nations. The unruly convicts formed half the population and the fear of rebellion was so great that the Captain of the shore detail warned them when he came aboard that 'any prisoners attempting to escape will be shot'. He need not have bothered.

'We staggered ashore, blinded by the bright sunlight and could hardly walk. After months in a confined space with little exercise, our leg muscles were all wasted.

'They marched us up the hill from the harbour, past the residence of Governor Darling to Hyde Park Barracks where we were to be billeted for a short time. Each convict was interviewed and the particulars of our previous employment taken. As I was a groom with a seven-year sentence for a lesser crime, and the horse was essential to the functioning of the colony, I was spared the "chain" and the road gangs and assigned to Mr Alexander Brodie Spark, a Scot as industrious as his name suggested.'

We would then turn to our ma for her part of the story. Unlike our da, our ma, Eliza Somers from Dublin, had been spared exile twice for thieving from shops, probably on account of her young age. But the British were keen to get as many Fenians out of Ireland as possible, by starvation, emigration or transportation, so her age did not save her a third time, though her crimes were petty and done out of necessity not wantonness.

'When I arrived in Sydney aboard the *Asia* in January of 1830, four years after your da, the clothes we left Ireland in were taken and we were given brown serge dresses that marked us out as convicts. As we came ashore at Circular Quay, a large mob that seemed to have worked itself up into some state of excitement were waiting for us. At first we feared we might be set upon, but soon found out they had come for quite another purpose.'

The First Fleet landed with a cargo of 552 convict men and 190 convict women and by the time my ma had come ashore, there were eight men for every woman in the colony. Whenever a transport ship docked, men rushed to the docks and bayed like animals for the women to be brought off. Some got proposals of marriage, but most got propositions of another nature. Some craven creatures even grabbed at their dresses hoping for a quick handful of sinful pleasure.

Our ma was transported upriver from Port Jackson to Parramatta and marched up the hill to the Female Factory situated in four acres of rolling hills and farmland, just downwind of the Governor's fine mansion and across the way from St James' church, the ministry of the infamous 'Flogging Parson', Samuel Marsden. Despite its attractive setting it was still a prison, a three-storeyed whitewashed building surrounded by a sixteen-foot wall, which was as much to keep the men out as the women in. It held 500 transported and local convicts, who were divided into three classes.

The first class were women who were awaiting assignment and had committed no crime in the colony, including unmarried convict women with children abandoned by the father. They were engaged in spinning and carding wool and paid a proportion of the profits from their labours.

The second class were criminals awaiting trial. They performed the heavier, more menial tasks and received less pay and rations.

The third class were the drunks, prostitutes, thieves and trouble-makers who had no hope of salvation. They were given the worst rations and performed the dirtiest tasks for no pay.

'I was in the first class and quickly discovered that there was a certain type of man who would use all his influence to get a Factory girl assigned to his home or business so he could use her like a chattel,' our ma continued. We kids weren't too sure what a 'chattel' was, but supposed it was something bad as more than once our ma was forced to flee her place of employment.

The first few months of her sentence were spent being assigned, absconding and returned to the Factory where her sentence started all over again. She would always pick up the story with a sad little smile.

'Finally, I did the only thing I could and chose a suitor to protect me. His name was Tommy Wade and he was a decent, gentle man, but he didn't want the responsibility of a family and disappeared when he found out I was carrying his child. I went back to the Factory where I gave birth to your brother, Tommy, who I named after his father.'

My sisters, who were now old enough to have that natural female fascination for anything romantic, would nag our ma for the last piece of the jigsaw, the story of how she and our da first met. We boys rolled our eyes and feigned boredom, but were soon hanging on her every detail. Our da was no romantic, except when he was drunk and on the side of the angels. Bit by bit we pulled the story out of him.

'By 1832 I'd served out my seven years and continued working for Mr Clift, the station owner I'd been assigned to near the end of my sentence after I absconded from Mr Brodie.'

'Where were you headed?'

'Back to Sarah Jones in England?'

'Nah, China,' our da chuckled.

'China,' we all chorused. We had no schooling, but from what was said in our presence we knew China was a faraway place where all the chinkies lived before they came to Australia to be cursed by the diggers for stealing our gold.

'The Irish believed that one hundred miles northwards of Parramatta lay a river that separated Australia and China,' our da explained. 'China was a Shangri-La inhabited by a copper-coloured race that treated convicts like kings and no work need ever be done. It's human nature to cling on to hope of something better. We believed it enough to try and find it, but didn't get further than the nearest pub. Mr Alexander Brodie Spark didn't want me back, so they assigned me to Mr Clift for the last six months of my sentence.

'I'd saved up some money, built up a small herd and told Mr Clift I'd like to get married and start a family. He cautioned me: "Women are as rare as rainfall out here and cause about as much excitement as a good downpour," but told me I might find a wife at the Female Factory down at Parramatta, where all the convict girls were kept. They had "courtship days" where suitors could meet the girls and, if both parties agreed, they could marry that day in St James' church across the road.

'After a week in the saddle, I arrived in Sydney and marvelled at how fast it had grown in the years since I staggered off the *Midas*. I read in the newspaper that Tuesday was "courtship day" and at the appointed time I stood outside the Female Factory, looked up at the lines of narrow cell windows and thought there must be one here for me.'

Da would often miss out what happened next, but he followed a line of smartly dressed men filing through a side gate into a large, dingy ground-floor store containing sacks of grain and large piles of potatoes and pumpkins. A guard, or turnkey, as they were known, directed him to stand in one of the three lines of ten men that had already formed.

Mr and Mrs Bell, the gravely faced Matron and Master of the Factory, inspected the ranks as if they were royalty. As far as finding a wife at the Female Factory was concerned, they wielded absolute power. They looked the suitors up and down as you would a horse or cow and examined the letter our da had obtained from Mr Clift saying he was a fit and proper person to have a wife. Not all the suitors were deemed acceptable. Any man who'd stopped in for a nobbler to steady their nerves, or anyone they didn't like the look of was dismissed. The redcoats, brandishing sturdy polished wooden billyclubs, removed any dissenters and weren't too fussy how they did it.

They all waited in the gloom until the clock of St James' tolled three times. The Master nodded to the soldiers and the sturdy, studded double doors that led into the high-walled courtyard swung open.

Blinded by the sudden burst of bright sunlight, the men moved forward instinctively and as their eyes became used to the light again they saw the one hundred and fifty women who had consented to be present lined up along the whitewashed walls. Those with land, property or prospects ran along the line cutting out the prettiest ones, whilst others of more modest means were less bold.

Our ma giggled like a young girl when she recalled how she spied our da shuffling along the gallery of faces in his Sunday best, nodding as he went, avoiding the attentions of the old trollops still living 'on the hip', who would brazenly wink at the passing men.

'I think he had just about given up hope of finding anyone suitable when he spied a shy-looking lass who none of the bolder men had yet approached. Pretending to stop and light his clay pipe, he used the distraction to sneak a proper look at me.'

Our da chimed in, 'The first time I laid eyes on her she was not much over five foot, but had shoulder-length dark hair and was pretty enough. She had small, delicate features that reminded me of an elfin. I guessed she was Irish. I felt the sweat on me brow and me heart hammering against me ticklers, but pretended to be calm and collected.'

Our ma remembered it differently and probably more reliably.

'He walked up to me, doffed his hat, smiled and did a half-bow all at once. He opened his flycatcher to say something, but couldn't find words to put in it, so he clamped it shut.'

Still smiling at the memory of it all these years later, our ma said it was the one and only time she saw him lost for words, so she spoke first.

'Hot the day isn't it?' she remarked in a thick Irish brogue.

'I'm sorry?' he replied anxiously.

'Ye've sweat on yer brow,' she elaborated.

'Sweet?' came his perplexed reply.

'Nah, sweat,' she said wiping her brow with her open palm to aid translation.

'Oh, *sweat*, yes summer. A bit hotter than Somerset.'

'And Dublin, for that matter,' she agreed.

Seeing a procession of matched couples pass close by reminded him he'd come to find a bride. Now they'd finished the small talk, it was time for him to declare his intentions, but, as usual, she beat him to it.

'You ever been married?' she asked.

'No,' said our da, thinking better of mentioning Sarah Jones. After all, they were only engaged to be married. 'Have you?' he shot back.

She took a sharp breath and answered honestly, though she feared the consequences. 'No, but I have a child out of wedlock.'

'I see,' was all he could muster.

She thought he looked a bit downcast, but resolved it was better to be straight with him now. There would be no more wasted time in her life, no more rash promises made in the throes of passion that melted away with the darkness and the footsteps on the stairs.

She continued, 'The father wanted no part of it. He left as soon as I fell pregnant.'

He just nodded. This was more than he had anticipated, but from what he had seen there were few other options. She had been honest about her situation, a virtue he suspected was a rare commodity in such a place.

'What's yer son's name?' he asked, indicating that her sudden revelation had not put him off.

'Tommy, Tommy is his name. He's just over a year old now,' she replied, her voice full of fresh hope.

He smiled shyly, 'I've always wanted a son.'

Her heart leapt, but she kept her emotions in check and fixing him with a hard stare reminded him again, 'But he's another man's son.'

Our ma hoped her calm exterior would mask her secret desperation. Children of unmarried convict women serving sentences at the Factory were taken from them when they reached the age of four. They were placed in government orphan schools until aged ten when the boys were apprenticed and girls put into domestic service. Like any decent mother, she didn't want to lose her son and the only way to keep Tommy was to get wed. Our da looked thoughtful for a moment then nodded, 'Aye, I understand that and I'm keen to have a few of me own too.'

Our da said he paused and looked down, fearing he'd said too much, but when he looked up she was smiling. 'I took all the courage I had in my two hands,' he recalled, 'reached into my pocket, pulled out me handkerchief and, as tradition dictated, threw it at her feet.'

By bending down and picking it up our ma accepted his proposal. That last bit always made my sisters sigh and afterwards they'd be outside swooning and throwing scraps of cloth at each other's feet.

Sadly, such moments of togetherness were few and far between in the Hall family. Our da was not a kind man. His tongue was as rough as his hands and I often felt the full force of both. Just because he had given me his name, it didn't follow that he gave me his favour. All his children were treated the same. Neither a hard day's yakka, nor a job well done pleased him. The slightest irritation was cause enough for him to unbuckle his belt and administer punishment. For a man who had lived in constant fear of the 'cat' as a convict, you'd think he'd be more sparing with the lash. Had his youthful indiscretion been treated less harshly then marriage and children might have made him into a good father and subject. But the squatters in Australia had need of his unpaid labour and the memory of what was taken from him had rotted and festered in his guts until it soured his once gentle nature.

If we thought that the Hall family had finished its great journeys, we were sadly mistaken. About six months after Ellen was born, our da's good mate, Johnny Chisholm, a Somerset man who worked as a turnkey at the local court, came racing in from Murrurundi, a concerned look on his face. We were all shooed outside as Johnny and our ma went into conference. We heard crying and raised voices. Ma wouldn't say what it was all about after he'd gone, but quietly started packing our clothes and crockery into boxes.

The mystery ended when our da arrived home just after dark and announced that we were leaving Murrurundi and moving out west to the Lachlan district that night.

He had purchased what he said was 'the finest piece of land in the district' and made it sound like some sort of biblical Promised Land, 'a place where a man could still breathe clean air'.

I had my doubts about that immediately.

I had heard the local cockatoo farmers, or 'cockies' as they were known, say many a time that all the best land in New South Wales had already been carved up between twenty-nine people who belonged to just four families, our 'new colonial nobility'. There had been much uproar in the colony a few years back when the squatters got the British Parliament to overturn Governor Gipps' *Land Act*, which would have freed up large parcels of squatter land for poorer selectors. The squatters, led by the treacherous William Wentworth, got a fourteen-year lease on the land they held with the option to purchase at £1 an acre. Anyone seeking to buy their land had to pay the full market price. This was called the defeat of the common man and forced poor people like us to move further west, out beyond the limits of white settlement set by the Governor. He should have known you can never legislate for man's restless spirit.

As always, our da got his way and that night we loaded up our dray, hitched the oxen to it and slipped out of Murrurundi under the cover of darkness. Our cries of anguish and tearful questions were ignored by our tight-lipped parents.

During the slow 300-mile wagon trip west, which took about two weeks, towns became villages and then distant stations. Tall gums and wattle became stunted and stringy and then disappeared as the land opened out into wide plains covered by the aptly named wallaby scrub over which large mobs of their larger, grey brethren ranged freely. The heat, which also seemed to be increasing as we went west, meant we needed to find fresh meat every day. We occasionally saw large mobs of ungainly looking emus kicking up a dust storm in the distance, but they were much too skittish for our da to ever get off a shot at them. Besides, they didn't look too appetising, though I'd heard many swear there was good eating in those long legs. During our great trek we mostly lived on a diet of kangaroo meat. Whenever we saw a mob of roos bounding through the bush or lying in the dappled shade with their young, we'd send up a shrill cry, much too urgent for the sluggish pace of bush life.

'Roos, roos, roos!' By the time our da pulled the cart over and unslung his rifle, they had hopped off, stopping some distance away to rest on their powerful hind legs and stare curiously at us.

'They're quick,' I observed rather needlessly.

'Aye lad, but I've never seen a roo outrun a bullet yet,' said our da dryly. I learnt that there was always one a bit bolder or more careless than the rest and that's the one he aimed for. He brought up the rifle, squinted down the barrel and pulled the trigger.

They thought they were out of range, but a blast from our da's double barrels showed them different. We watched them bounding off into the distance, through the veil of gunsmoke, their great tails wagging behind them, all except the careless one. He had taken one of the barrels and was thrashing about in the long grass about thirty yards in front of us. Seizing me by the arm, our da said urgently, 'Come on, boy.'

Although not sure what I could do, I stumbled after him towards the wounded roo. Even though the animal was mortally wounded, our da was still cautious. Stomping down the grass around it he pulled me closer. I could see its wild-eyed stare and the dark blood pooling beneath it. I felt a hand on my shoulder as our da said in his soft, rolling Somerset brogue, 'Careful, boy, we got him good, but he's still a mean, dangerous bastard. See them nails on 'is back feet? Could rip a man's guts out and them claws on his front paws could slice through saddle leather.'

As he moved in closer the wounded roo used its tail to lift itself up and slashed at him with muscular back legs. Our da picked up a heavy ironbark branch, raised it high over his head and charged into the grass where the wounded animal hissed angrily. There was a crunch as heavy wood met bone and the hissing gave way to a high-pitched squealing, which was almost human.

The thick grass thankfully hid the grisly details of the roo's dispatch. All I saw was the rise and fall of the heavy cudgel, which was painted bright red with blood. Eventually, the squealing stopped. Our da straightened up breathing heavily, his clothes, face and hands covered in gore. The sound of my sisters' piteous wailing came drifting across the swaying grasslands, riding in on the waves of shimmering heat that rippled the air. As our da knelt down again to examine the roo he swore loudly.

I averted my eyes from the roo's head, which was little more than a bloody stump, and saw our da pull a skinny little joey from the roo's pouch. Unaware of the grim struggle for survival going on around it, it stared up at us all sleepy-eyed and innocent. There was no tenderness about our da, who was as hard as that ironbark branch both outside and in. Holding it upside down by its back legs, he pushed the wriggling creature up at me.

'Here, get rid of it.'

'What, me, kill it?' I stammered, my stomach churning with sudden fear. I had never killed a living thing before. My eyes misted and the tears came suddenly. I brushed at them with my bare arm, embarrassed that our da saw them.

'Stop yer snivelling and break its bloody neck,' he snarled. I looked up at him pleadingly, but there was no pity on his blood-spattered face. Hoisting the joey up higher he insisted, 'You'd be doing it a kindness. It won't last without its mother's milk. His mob's long gone and the dingos will sniff him out before darkness. That's the way of nature, boy, and you'd best learn that quick. Too bloody soft, spend too much time with yer mother.'

If he was hoping I'd prove him wrong by seizing the roo and snapping its neck, then he was sorely disappointed. I turned and ran, leaving our da to deal with it.

A few minutes later he came to the dray to fetch Tommy to help him butcher the big roo and to tell our ma to get the fire going. His eyes bored into me but I kept looking straight ahead even when he leaned close to snarl in my ear.

'That's right, you stay there where you belong, with your sisters.' Now I knew, beyond doubt, that I, the son bearing his own name, was a sore disappointment to him. This had been a test, a chance to win his trust and I had failed him, but I suspected it wouldn't be the last time.

If I was a disappointment to our da, it was nothing compared to our selection. We all groaned inwardly when we saw it was nothing but a wide, flat expanse of sunburned wallaby scrub and sky, broken only by a few yellow box gums and the distant, brooding rise of Mount Wheogo. The thirsty cattle lowed at the creek that had dried to a precious trickle. We were on the edge of nowhere, halfways to nothing and drought, flood and disappointment would be something we would become well acquainted with in the years that followed.

Out in the bush a new kind of man, an Australian, was being forged on the anvil of the land, his backbone straightened like tempered steel by the heat and hard yakka. Amongst the gnarly roots of stunted gums and wisps of knotty, sun-bleached grass that clung doggedly to this miserable, fly-blown wasteland that stretched for as far as the eye could see, we gained a purchase by building a hut to live in.

The walls were made from red river gums, which we felled at the creek, split into thick slabs an inch thick and drove into the ground close together. Thick clay mud from the creek was pressed into a small wooden box with a loose bottom called a stock, and baked in the sun until hard to make bricks for the fireplace and chimney that would stand at one end of the hut. The roof was made of long, straight branches lashed together with greenhide and covered over by lengths of three-quarter inch thick ironbark, which we carefully stripped from the trees and fastened to the frame.

Inside, sacking curtains covered the windows instead of glass, and various lengths of heavier, floral patterned curtain material were suspended from the rafters by a spider's web of taut greenhide string. By day our hut was one big room where we lived and cooked, but at night the curtains could be pulled across the room at various angles to divide it into sleeping areas with a little privacy.

As well as helping with the building, we had daily chores to perform. The nearest school was over a hundred miles away in Bathurst, so our days were spent milking cows, turning the handle to churn the butter, hunting, planting or weeding the potatoes and pumpkins, and scaring off the birds who tried to ruin whatever we planted. My sisters helped my mother with the cleaning, washing, cooking and the baking of the daily damper. As most of our work was done in the cool of the early morning, or late afternoon, there was time in the middle of the day to go off exploring on the horses we'd cut out of the wild and broken for ourselves.

The Dalys, Nowlans, O'Meallys, Thurlands and Walshes surrounded us on all sides. Mostly Irish, they seemed fine enough people, but our da reckoned they attracted the traps like 'flies to a cow's arse'. Mind you, our da was every bit the rogue he thought they were. When he decided to start a butchery, every station in the district did a muster on the day he opened for business.

During those innocent, carefree days, I first met the sons of our neighbours. There was big, snub-nosed John O'Meally, with his rotting, broken teeth, twisted grin and close 'county crop' that made him look like a felon. Dan Charters was picture pretty with his blond curls and blue eyes. He always spoke 'nice' and was always dressed in what looked like our Sunday best. Then there was the tough little nugget, Mickey Burke, whose dark-eyed determination and fearless bareback riding made up for his lack of size. Our playground was the Weddin Mountains, which rose dramatically out of the scrubby flatness of the western plains. Mickey would career at breakneck speed down its slopes weaving in between tightly packed trees to claim the title of best rough rider and the attentions of the watching girls, who always kept their kisses for the winner.

As children do, we imitated the heroes of our day in wild, make-believe adventures that always ended in a great battle in which the evil wrongdoer and all his disciples are slain.

As we lived in a country that did not send its young to war and had no Drakes, Nelsons or Wellingtons, we worshipped the early bushrangers known as 'bolters', such as Michael Howe, the 'Governor-General of the Woods', 'Bold' Jack Donohoe and the local boys Scothcry and Witton. They appealed to men like our da who had been freed from penal servitude, but never from the taint of convictism, and to whom the New South Wales police were a real source of grievance. Modelled on the hated Royal Irish Constabulary, they behaved more like an army of occupation than a police force. 'Tis a noble calling,' our da would declare, 'to show the squatters and the traps that they can't have it all their own way.' But it was not just the Irish and the traps that raised our da's ire, God and the government did their bit too.

'Bloody do-gooders,' he growled, rustling the pages of his newspaper to signal his displeasure. Whenever he went to the store or town, or met a traveller along the way, he would scrounge a paper and spend long hours behind its tall pages. Unlike our ma, our da got five years of schooling in Bristol and learned to read and write, but he did not pass on this gift to his children. 'No amount of reading will prepare you for a life in the saddle,' he'd tell us whenever we'd ask him to teach us.

'The powers that be in Sydney are fretting that there's a generation of "bush bastards" breeding out here in the heat like rats without the influence of God,' he muttered irritably. 'Mark my words, if we let God in the door, the government will be close behind him.'

Most Lachlan folk were Irish Holy Romans of convict stock who had come to these wild, untamed margins of white civilisation to escape both God and the government. Like Governor Lachlan Macquarie, who gave this district its name, they fiercely believed in freedom and that once a man had paid his debt to society he should be left in peace. At least on that our da and our Irish neighbours were agreed. God might live in Sydney, but out here, in what the natives called the Never-Never, he was barely on nodding terms with the people.

Whenever a drought started to bite, the cockies would go out into their paddocks and lift their faces heavenwards. It was not to God that they directed their prayers, but 'Hughie', the Australian pagan god of rain. 'Throw it down, Hughie!' they would roar into the firmament. In Australia, God had to play second fiddle to Hughie. The newspaper said a minister had been dispatched from Sydney to save our savage souls, which caused much amusement.

The old nag our saviour arrived on looked as much in need of retirement as he did. With the patience of Moses the kindly, white-haired old Scotchman trotted from hut to hut telling anyone who'd listen in his singsong voice that, 'the rock of my faith is unshakable', until he turned up at O'Meally's shanty. A local wag interrupted his sermon with a puzzling observation.

'It's a bloody good job that the Bible was set in Arabia and not Australia.'

'And why would that be?' asked the preacher innocently.

''Cause the Three Wise Men would have realised it was a fool's earn by page three and detoured to the nearest shanty.'

That was the last anyone saw of him and his old horse.

Final proof that God had abandoned us like the old Scotch preacher had come with the sensational news that gold had been discovered at Ophir, near Bathurst, which was about a hundred miles away. Some locals rushed east to stake out their claims before the hordes arrived from Sydney, but most, including our da, pre-ferred to bemoan their misfortune and curse God for not blessing the Lachlan with that same good fortune.

On the question of God, it was neither the good folk of Sydney, the Scotch preacher nor our da who had the last word, but our ma.

Our da, like most people out here, was angry with God and didn't want anything to do with the church or the Bible. Our ma hid the one given to her on the *Asia* by the good ladies of Elizabeth Fry in a nook behind the meat safe as she knew he'd burn it if he ever found it.

God may have turned his back on the Lachlan, but the government never would. Now we had taken up our selection and our da had started his butchery, Her Majesty wanted her share. The Crown Commissioner came round once a year to collect the tax on our land and the animals.

Word went round the district as soon as he and his police escort were spotted and our da would go bush for a few days with some of our stock. I was certain it had more to do with the real reason we left Murrurundi in such a hurry, but our parents said it was to lessen our taxes and to remove any duffed cattle from our run.

Our da was a cattle duffer, but who wasn't in these parts? Raking the surrounding gullies, flushing out feral cattle and branding any 'cleanskins' as your own were practised by everyone, from the richest squatter to the lowliest cocky.

No sooner had our da faded into the horizon than ma got Tommy to hitch the bullocks to the dray and drive us into Bathurst. Each year, one of us was secretly baptised by Father Timothy McCarthy at St Michael's. 'None of my children are going to meet the Holy Father as heathens,' she told Father and received a blessing right away. She swore us to secrecy, made us cross our hearts and hope to die. Just in case, she gave us a precious sixpence, which we were allowed to spend on toffee.

Our ma decided that I was to be the first baptised, although I was never quite sure why. I protested that I wasn't the oldest, or youngest, but maybe she felt I was in the most peril on account of me having the same name as our da, or maybe it was just a mother's instinct. But sixpence bought a lot of toffee and the ugly looks on the faces of my brothers and sisters warned me what to expect if I came between them and their treat. My resistance broken by threats and bribery, I was delivered to the House of God.

St Michael's was the grandest church in Bathurst. We all felt a sense of awe when we saw the stained-glass windows and the rows of strong-smelling incense candles that sat at the foot of the cross with Jesus on it. Our ma knelt and crossed herself, something we were not to do until we had been baptised and cleansed of sin. Our ma told me to go over to the confessional and tell Father McCarthy all the bad things I'd ever thought or done.

'*All* of them?' I exclaimed a little too loudly and was hushed.

'Yes,' she said firmly and then told me there was a screen between us so he'd never know who was confessing their sins.

I argued that as we were the only people in the church and I was the only one being baptised Father McCarthy would know it was me. Sometimes a child's logic cannot be faulted, but our ma had an answer for everything.

'It's tradition,' she hissed and pushed me towards the confessional.

As I entered the booth, I could see the shadowy outline of Father McCarthy's head on the other side of the screen. He told me to close the door and sit down and then asked, 'Is this your first confession?'

'Yes, Father,' I repeated dutifully, as our ma had instructed me to.

'Do you have any sins you'd like to confess, my son?'

'Yes, Father,' I said again. I thought if I started with all the big sins, like peeping at my sisters whilst they were in the bath, that might be enough for him.

'Is that all?' he said with an edge of disbelief in his voice that warned me he knew there was a lot more to come.

'Well, there was the time I put a goanna in my brother Edward's bed,' I admitted.

'Is that all?' asked the patient voice again, and so it went on. He kept pulling more and more out of me until I'd run out of small sins and finally gave up the one I'd been holding back on, 'I helped our da duff some cleanskins out at Mount Wheogo.'

He must have known that was the really big one because he now seemed satisfied that my soul was empty of mortal sin.

'Do you understand that these are sins and that you must never do them again?'

'Yes, Father,' I intoned and he told me to go back into the church, kneel in front of Jesus and say five Hail Marys. Five seemed a lot and I wasn't sure if that meant that I had committed a lot of sin for a boy of twelve.

After I made atonement for my sins Father McCarthy gathered the family, read a blessing, pulled my head over a foul-smelling font, tipped some holy water over my head and urged me to 'renounce the Devil and all his pomps'. Our ma was very pleased. That was one son spared from eternal hellfire and damnation and in another seven years, she'd have saved us all. I think I spoiled it by asking, 'Why weren't we all done at once?'

I received a slap across the head from our ma who reminded me indignantly in her thick Irish brogue, 'It's a holy font, not a cattle dip.'

I also received some sharp elbows in the back and sides from my brothers and sisters who wanted another outing to Bathurst and more toffee next year. As I hobbled away from St Michael's I had some idea how our Lord Jesus suffered on that cross at Calvary. But it mattered little that someone died on the cross because no sooner are we forgiven our old sins than we find new ones to take their place.

When our da returned from the bush we finally completed our hut. The floor, a mixture of hard-packed cow dung and clay mud, was the last thing to be laid.

We all tumbled outside to admire the rough but serviceable hut we'd built with our own hands just as the last long shafts of golden light arrowed in from the distant horizon and the cockatoos were settling the last territorial disputes of the day in the boughs of our big gums.

The evening light turned the rough wallaby scrub the colour of gold and picked out the long-necked silhouettes of curious kangaroos and the stealthy creep of other more predatory figures that preferred to remain on all fours. The hour before sunset and sunrise were the best times of the day in the bush. These were rare periods of calm when nature's creations were between sleep and stir and you could enjoy the cool air and vivid colours. Turning towards our new home, our da said, 'Well, it'll have to last us at least forty years.'

A frown creased our ma's brow as she asked, 'And why's that?'

Unable to restrain his mirth any longer he exploded, 'Because I told that bloody Scotch clergyman that Moses only spent forty years in the wilderness, but we Australians will be out here a lot longer.'

We shrieked with laughter and ran about like demented creatures in the fading light until darkness extinguished the last embers of the dying sun and the needle-like stings of the humming mosquitos finally drove us indoors.

Chapter Two

Betrayal, guilt, vengeance, the 'unholy Trinity', first crept into my life at the height of summer, 1851, when I was thirteen. At least the betrayal and guilt did, the vengeance took a little longer.

It all began when a mob of tall Abos with thin, bird-like legs, wild woolly hair and barely enough to cover their modesty, appeared in the paddock next to our hut. There had been a bad drought that year and they came around looking for food and water, but the history of this colony meant that the arrival of Abos with long spears and curved boomerangs always inspired fear and suspicion.

They were from the Wiradjuri tribe, who had lived on this land for hundreds, maybe thousands of years before the first white man came to the Lachlan district twenty-five years ago. The uneasy peace was short-lived and before long they were shooting and spearing each other over accusations of land and cattle theft. The British ended the hostilities by imposing martial law, but fear and mistrust still lingered. Commonly, the squatters would shoot over their heads to drive them off, but our da and the other poor selectors could always use an extra pair of hands and the Aboriginals would work for a bit of tucker or some stores.

Such is human nature that we need to be able to look down on someone and feel there is still someone worse off than ourselves. The English squatters looked down on the selectors, who looked down on the freed convicts, who looked down on the ticket o' leavers, who looked down on the convicts, who looked down on the Irish. The only people that we Halls could look down on were the Aboriginals. That was the order of things in this time of our living.

The blackfellas were camped in a gully near our creek. They did a bit of fishing then put up the round, low houses we called 'humpies', which were a framework of branches bent to make a rounded shape and covered with leaves. I noticed a young bloke about my own age looking over at me, so I went over and said, 'What's your name, mate?'

'Billy,' he replied with no hint of the usual timidness displayed by his kinsfolk.

'Billy what?'

'Billy Dargin.'

I didn't think that sounded very Aboriginal, but our ma said because their own native names were too hard for us to say, they often took the name of the whitefella they worked for, or, if they had been saved, the one given to them by a missionary.

Say what you like about them, but Billy and those blackfellas showed my brothers and me how to find bush tucker like geebung fruit, the sweet native grape that grew in sheltered gullies, and how to spear opossums and wallabies. The Abos were very keen on their spears and could nail a wallaby at fifty paces. Our da went out with his fowling piece and just let rip till he hit something. We mostly ate what were called 'bush meats', which meant anything that came within range of our da's fowling piece: kangaroo, goanna, opossum, bush pig, or any kind of bird. Before it could be cooked our ma had to pick out all the shot, which clanged into the metal dish, punctuating her dark mutterings about our da's marksmanship.

Billy also showed me how to find water during summer or the 'hot time', as they called it.

The large toads that kept us awake at night with their insistent croaking stored water in pouches attached to their bodies. You could prick these with sharp sticks and suck out the water. This horrified my family who cringed at the idea of touching a toad, far less sucking on one. It was another matter the day I brought home fish, which my brothers and sisters thought only came out of a tin.

'Where d'ya get 'em?' our da demanded suspiciously.

'I hunted 'em–'

'You hunted 'em?' he sneered.

I poked my chin out defiantly at him, 'Yair, the blackfellas showed me how.'

The strange sight and smell of the fish brought my curious brothers and sisters crowding around and I was the centre of attention, which didn't happen often in a large family like ours. They were all on for a yarn and I spun them one like a seasoned bushie.

'First, you cut a branch from the ti tree, the straggly ones that grow down by the billabong. Then you put it between your teeth, take a deep breath, dive into the billabong and swim to the bottom.' I paused, scanning their faces. All eyes were on me, intent on every word.

'Next, you push the branches into crevices between the rocks and swim back up to the top. After a bit the fish just float to the surface like they're dead, except they're only under the influence of the "jungle juice" found in the ti tree.'

There were gasps of amazement and I lapped up the admiring glances of my sisters, the jealous stares of my brothers and the tight-faced contempt of my da. I left out the fact that it was Billy who had performed all those heroics. What they didn't know wouldn't hurt them.

'Fish is my totem. My mother dream about fish before I be born and give me that fella sign,' Billy had said as he pushed the mass of fish towards me. 'Take 'im home. Good whitefella tucker,' he'd added, grinning for all he was worth as he turned up his nose and showed me a row of white teeth.

My da was glowering like a spoiled kid. Our hunter and provider didn't much like being upstaged by kids. 'Bloody Abos,' he snarled, but had his share of the fish all the same.

Billy also taught me all about signs and portents. Unlike the white-fella, who considered everything in the world was put there for his use, rocks, animals, trees as well as people all seemed to have their special place and meaning in the world of the Aborigines.

One day we were sitting together in a clearing and Billy explained some of these signs to me. My blond hair was plastered down with red river clay, my face was transformed into a mask of bright colours from the dye in the roots and berries we had collected. I had my eyes closed as I repeated back what he was teaching me. This lesson was all about the importance of messages from different birds and animals.

'An opossum means someone is coming,' I intoned. 'If the curlew calls three times, he's telling that death is coming. The little black and white Willy Wagtail, who is a big *jengwallah*, is listening to everyone's business and goes about the place gossiping.'

'What else 'im be?' Billy quizzed me patiently. I grimaced and squeezed my eyes shut as I thought hard.

''E's also a "death bird". If he raises his wings and stretches 'em out like the sign of the cross, then it means someone's died.'

Billy clapped his hands together and congratulated me with a dazzling show of white teeth and a slap on the thigh.

'You catch it. You bush boy now. Mebbe you go through the rules like us blackfellas.'

To seal our friendship and celebrate the fact I had graduated from Billy's school of bushcraft, he took me deep into his ancestors' country.

'Where are we goin'?' I asked curiously.

'Special place,' was all he would say and pointed at the distant outline of the Weddin Mountains. We went way beyond the slopes where me and the other farmers' sons knew every rock, track, gully and cave that pitted its sides. The deeper we went, the darker and more sinister it felt, the thick stands of trees blocking out most of the light. We stuck to the forest floor, but up above I noticed caves gouged into the craggy outcrops of red rock by nature's fearsome hand.

We started climbing until we arrived at the mouth of a small cave. Outside was a circle of ceremonial stones blackened by many fires and in amongst the grey ash were bones. Billy must have sensed my apprehension because he patted his belly and explained, 'Have big corroboree here an' big feed of tucker. Them bones was some whitefella's bull.'

Billy ducked his head, crawled inside and motioned for me to follow. I did and immediately I felt some sort of strange presence, like the times we went to St Michael's in Bathurst.

'This sacred place of ancestors,' said Billy proudly, pointing upward. I looked up and as my eyes adjusted to the low light I saw hundreds of red handprints of all sizes all over the cream-coloured walls and ceiling. There were also rows of single marks and some stick figures of men.

'Who do they belong to?' I asked running the tips of my fingers over one of the handprints.

'To ancestors. This place for memories. We come here to remember our ancestors.'

'What do they mean?'

'This say I was here, we are from Wiradjuri people and this is our land. Bring brother and family this place.'

I realised that this was a grand gesture of friendship, something reserved for special people met along life's path.

'What do we do?'

'Like this,' said Billy going over to a ledge where a trickle of runoff water seeped into the cave. Cupping his hands together, he held them open under the dripping ledge until he'd collected enough for a small mouthful. He took a small lump of what looked like red clay and popped it into his mouth. He nodded at me and I copied him. It tasted chalky. He began chewing the clay, and moving the water from cheek to cheek so he wouldn't swallow it. Quite quickly the clay became soft and began to turn to liquid.

Billy placed one of his long thin hands on the rocky wall of the cave, spread his fingers wide and then spat the red chalky liquid all round his hand. He held it there a few minutes until the warmth of his hand caused the clay to start caking. He pulled his hand away to reveal the red outline of his hand. He took my hand, placed it next to his and urged me to copy him. I spat, but not as well as Billy. After a few more sprays, I managed to do the whole outline of my hand.

As we stood back and admired our handiwork, Billy nodded at my smaller, fatter handprint and said solemnly, 'Look your hand. Whitefella hand different. People know whitefella come here with blackfella mate. Hands stay here for long time. You never forget Billy and Billy never forget you.'

Tears lay close to my eyes, though I never let Billy see them.

I was on my way to meet Billy one afternoon when I bumped into John O'Meally, Dan Charters and Mickey Burke. Mickey had brought along a new kid, Henry McBride, who was straight off the boat from Ireland. He had the reddest hair and whitest skin I had ever seen. Since I had become mates with Billy, I hadn't seen much of them.

'What've you been up to?' O'Meally asked. He had broadened out since I last saw him and the spots on his face served notice that he'd begun his journey to manhood well ahead of the rest of us.

'Oh, this and that,' I said evasively, not keen to share my new world of discovery with them.

'Where you off to?' pressed Mickey Burke. I looked at their eager faces and thought that maybe I should introduce them to Billy. We could all become blackfellas together.

'I'm off to meet these blackfellas who live down by the creek. Got a mate called Billy.'

'Abos!' butted in O'Meally, and they all looked at each other, held their noses and yelled 'poo'.

'What are you doing with them?' said O'Meally with more than a hint of disgust in his voice. 'Your own kind not good enough for you?'

'They've been showing me things.'

'What things?' demanded Charters.

Again O'Meally was quick to the punch.

'How to wipe his arse with leaves, I reckon.'

The image drew laughter from the others, but the minute I pointedly brought up the long thin stick I'd been using as a staff, and rolled it in my hand, it was a different story. Before O'Meally had time to blink I used it as a spear like Billy had shown me. He took one look at the spear quivering in the papery bark of a eucalyptus a couple of feet from his head, and his face went white. Not finished, I leaned over and plucked a bunch of the jewelled red berries called *lilly pilly* off the lower branch of a nearby tree.

'See them?' I said. Having had it drummed into us that native berries are poison, a gasp of horror did the rounds as I opened my mouth wide and popped in the whole bunch.

'Ben!' breathed Dan Charters, his big blue eyes were wide with astonishment.

I chewed the berries, rubbing my belly and moaning in pleasure. 'That's what they've been showing me,' I said proudly with the bitter tang of *lilly pilly* still bursting in my mouth. From that moment, I began to see blackfellas in a different light. They might have no knowledge of our world, our habits and the contraptions we'd built, but they knew their land and how they fitted into it in a way we could never properly understand.

'Jesus!' said Mickey Burke, his mouth open.

'Can we come with you?' said Charters, his eyes now shining with excitement.

'Aye, I'm in,' said Henry McBride, raising his hand, unaware he was making the biggest mistake of his short, uneventful life.

'Sure,' I said casually. They fell in behind me as I picked my way through the bush. O'Meally, feeling upstaged, trudged after us a little way behind.

We stopped when we came to the gully where the Abos were camped. A thin haze of wood smoke from the big cooking fire drifted over the dozen or so shell-like 'humpies'. Bare-breasted gins dug in the ground with sticks as they searched for yams and others sat cross-legged in the dust singing and stirring their pots, while a group of naked piccaninnies ran around in circles trailing a big goanna on a piece of string.

'Stone me,' said O'Meally, speaking for the whole staring lot of them, who were now standing with their flycatchers open like explorers who had just discovered the Lost Kingdom. As we scrambled down the bank and passed through the camp I waved and shouted to those I knew, enjoying the knowledge that the others would never dare come here on their own for fear of being eaten or speared.

At last we came to the cool cover of the trees by the river where Billy and some other boys were crowded round.

'What are you fellas doing?' I asked.

Billy flashed me his wide, white-toothed grin, 'We be gettin' some bush tucker.'

We watched in horror as one of the other boys lay on the ground next to a big snake hole. Billy and the others sank down on their haunches, he motioned for us to do the same and brought a finger to his lips. Once everyone was completely still, the boy slowly put his hand down the hole until it was almost buried up to his shoulder in hard, red earth. Then he laid his head on the ground and was very still for about twenty minutes, though we could see by the muscles twitching in his shoulder that his hand was doing something in the hole.

Minutes passed. Then more of them. Just as we were all beginning to doze off in the stillness and heat, the boy began to withdraw his arm very slowly.

I watched, mesmerised by the sight of his long, thin arm covered with a film of fine, red dust mixed with sweat streaked across his black skin like ceremonial paint. If any ritual or rite of passage was deserving of such an accolade, then this was surely it – raw, primal and dangerous.

With a delicate little flourish, the boy lifted his shoulder, bent his wrist and pulled out his hand. Flashing a brilliant smile he showed us his treasure, half a dozen white eggs the size of marbles.

We sat there in dumbfounded silence, which was broken by the well-spoken, cultured voice of Dan Charters.

'Don't you know the Devil lives down there?' he said, shaking his blond, curly head in disbelief.

I doubt Billy understood a word he said. Instead, he demonstrated what had happened down in the hole by tickling the palm of one hand with the two middle fingers of the other and explaining to us, 'Yeah, but we make big magic. We tickle 'is belly till 'im all sleepy and take out 'is eggs all nice and slow like.'

Dan shuddered and shook his head again. Billy and the rest of the blackfella boys shocked us more by sharing the eggs, popping them into their mouths and sucking out the juice with relish before spitting out the soft shells.

'Good tucker,' said Billy rubbing his stomach and smiling at the thinly veiled horror on our faces.

On the way home, no one said much. We were still in awe of what we'd witnessed. O'Meally finally piped up, 'It wasn't that good. I don't reckon there was even a snake down there.'

Henry McBride, who had done very little, except watch in open-mouthed amazement, finally spoke, 'An' have ye the guts to put your hand down there?'

You could almost see O'Meally's hackles rise as he glared at the doubter. 'Course I have. Us Australians know all about the bush, not like you "croppie" boys.'

Henry reddened right down to the roots of his carrot-topped hair, but came right back at him, 'Ye're full o' shite, O'Meally. Ye're da was sent out here a convict and is as big a Mick as we are.'

It was John's turn to blush. 'Right, let's see,' he said and started looking about for a snake hole.

'Come on, boys,' I said, sensing things were turning ugly. 'We're not blackfellas. Billy and his mates were shown how to do that by their elders.'

Reason is always the first casualty in moments of great passion and the O'Meallys were very passionate folk. John continued to look about on the ground until he found what he was after. The black snake hole stared up at us – a portal that reached down to Hell itself. Rolling up the sleeve of his shirt O'Meally knelt down beside it.

Now I was really alarmed. 'No, John, don't,' I said. This was dangerous folly.

These were the stagnant waters of ancient evil seeping into Australia. When there were no English to fight, the Irish turned on each other. I believe they could find a corner in a circle to put their backs against. And in a scene that had been doubtless repeated down through the ages, an O'Meally faced down a McBride. Their blood was up and they eyed each other like two fighting cocks.

John fixed Henry with a malevolent glare and yelled, 'See ya in hell, ya bloody Mick.' Before anyone could stop him, he thrust his arm down the hole.

'No!' cried Charters, turning away hardly able to believe what he was seeing. We all went quiet as we watched John.

'Come on, John, you've made your point,' I said.

'Take your arm out now,' said Mickey Burke anxiously.

John left his arm there for what seemed like an age and with a wild-eyed look of triumph finally pulled it out, waving it around to show us he hadn't been bitten.

'See, we can do anything the Abos can do.' Pointing at Henry he leered, 'Your go, Paddy.'

Mickey Burke, who had brought Henry along and was supposed to be looking out for him, was very alarmed. 'Don't do it, Henry,' he said, his voice full of dread.

'You'll never be an Australian,' countered O'Meally, 'you'll always just be red-headed, pale-faced Henry the Hibernian.'

We all held our breath as Henry slowly put his arm down the snake hole.

'That's enough, Henry. You've gone as long as John,' I said.

But Henry wasn't listening. His and O'Meally's eyes were locked together in a battle of great wills.

'That's it. You've lasted the longest,' I said again, hoping a quick declaration of victory would end the madness.

A slow smile played across Henry's lips and a look of triumph shone from his green eyes. He started to withdraw his arm.

We all relaxed and gave a sigh of relief. Except O'Meally who let out a roar of anguish mixed with anger. Enraged at not only having his bluff called but bettered, he started dancing on the spot, lifting his knees in some wild, primitive dance, drumming the ground with his feet as if he were trying to summon up the Devil. Whether that was his intention or not, he succeeded. Henry's arm was almost clear of the hole when he stiffened and let out a single piercing scream. A feeling of dread tightened in my chest. O'Meally quit his prancing and his face lost its colour. In a rare show of emotion he yelled, 'Holy Mother! Help him somebody, will ya?'

Mickey Burke looked as if he was going to spew. He cast his eyes around wildly, looking for a way out. 'Me da will fuckin' kill me for this, not to mention Henry's. Oh, Jesus, Jesus.'

Henry was rolling around on the ground, howling with pain and clutching his hand.

The spit had dried in my mouth. I knelt down by him, grabbed him and said urgently, 'Let me have a look.'

'No, no, it hurts,' Henry wailed, rolling into a ball and clutching at his hand as though he didn't want us to confirm what he already knew deep in his heart. He was going to die.

'Hold him,' I called out to the others, who stood rooted to the spot. 'Hold him,' I roared. The second command shocked them out of their stupor. They came forward, rolled Henry onto his back and held him down. Except O'Meally who stood sullenly in the background, chewing at his nails.

There were two fang marks in the meat just below Henry's thumb. Little beads of deadly venom oozed from the wounds and the skin around them was already red and puffy.

'Bleed the wound and suck out the poison,' repeated Mickey Burke over and over as he fought back mounting fear.

Even I knew that was an old wives' tale. The only thought drumming through my brain was *our da will know what to do, our da will know for sure what to do*. Our hut was the nearest and I knew the only sensible thing I could do was to get help. I was on my feet and yelling.

'Stay with him. I'm going for help.' I raced off taking a shortcut through the bush. All the way home I pleaded with God to save Henry McBride, accepting the sharp twigs and branches that raked and bloodied my face and arms as part of my penance. As I plunged out of the trees, I was never so glad to see my da in my whole life. He was sitting outside the hut, smoking his pipe and reading the paper. When he saw me sprinting across the paddock he jumped to his feet, sensing something was wrong.

In between gulping down great lungfuls of air I told him what had happened. Cursing fit to bust he saddled up the horse and a few minutes later I was holding onto him like grim death as we galloped back through the bush.

My da shouted back to me, 'Did you see what colour the snake was?' Not having told him exactly how Henry came to be bitten I just shook my head and said, 'No.'

In the end the colour of the snake didn't matter because by the time we got there Henry lay stone dead on the ground. A big, ugly V-shaped vein stood up on his forehead and his eyes bulged in a glassy-eyed stare. I stared down at him. I'd never noticed that his eyes were such a vivid emerald green. A rivulet of white foam trickled from the side of his mouth, ran down his chin and collected in a clear pool in the little hollow at the base of his throat. Mickey and Dan were huddled together their eyes and cheeks flushed red from crying, but O'Meally just slouched against a tree, a sullen, guilty look on his face.

My da knelt down, put his fingers on Henry's neck and felt for a pulse, then gave a great sigh as his shoulders slumped in defeat. Gently he passed a hand across Henry's face, closing his eyes. Getting to his feet he looked around at us all, then asked, 'What happened?'

No one spoke, but eventually between great heaving sobs Mickey Burke explained, 'After Ben left Henry started fitting and choking and then just went still.'

Etched into the earth around the body was the evidence of those final, terrible moments. As the poison took effect poor Henry had raked the ground with the heels of his hob-nailed boots and clutched blindly at dead leaves and grass, which now hung in limp bouquets from his tightly bunched fists.

'Best we get him home,' my da said softly and started wrapping Henry in a blanket he always carried in his saddlebag in case he had to 'bush it' in a hurry. I noticed that he handled Henry's body with a rare tenderness. He worked quietly and steadily, and it was only after he'd slung Henry over the saddle that he turned back to us.

'How did it happen?' he asked.

There was a silence as we looked at each other, except for the sound of clicking as Dan rubbed the nails of his middle finger and thumb together. O'Meally was quick off the mark, covering Dan's nervous tic with a shrug of the shoulders and a suitably vague explanation.

'It happened so quickly. We were just messing about when the bastard came through the grass an' got Henry on the hand.'

O'Meally's lie became our cover story, for a short time.

Chapter Three

I may have been spared the anguish of having to deliver the news and Henry's body to his parents, but not the lash when the truth came out a day or so later. I had no idea who turned us in but our da came galloping home and caught a hold of me by the collar as I was splitting shingles at the back of the hut. He spun me around and threw me to the ground.

'You lying little bastard,' he roared. All the pent-up rage he had been carrying back from the McBrides' exploded out of him. I don't think I'd ever seen him so mad at me, except for the time I refused to kill that joey he found in the pouch of the roo he'd shot.

'Is that why you came running for help? Were you the one with the guilty conscience?' he demanded. The commotion brought our ma running out from the hut, her arms white to the elbows with floury damper mix.

'What in the bejesus is going on?' she demanded.

'This son of ours has told us a pack o' bloody lies,' seethed our da, his face flushed. 'It was his fooling about with them damn blacks and sticking their hands down snake holes that got Henry McBride killed.'

Our ma's face crumpled in anguish. 'Oh Ben, we told you stay away from them snakes.'

Her quiet disappointment was far worse than his fizzing rage, which he took out on my bare arse with his belt in the butchery. After our da had finished with me, he mustered our three kangaroo dogs. He and the other men from the nearby selections were planning to get even with the Abos, whom they blamed for Henry's death even more than me. Before he left, our da looked down at me from the saddle of the horse, his face and eyes still showing his red anger. He'd never approved of me being mates with Billy and now was his chance to teach me a lesson.

'God made whitefellas and blackfellas different for good reason. Each should keep to their own, see?' With that he dug his heels into the horse's flanks and rode off.

Our da returned a day later with eyes as red as the Devil's and his clothes smelling of wood smoke.

'Burnt the bastards out!' I heard him tell my ma through the window as he washed his hands in the wooden pail standing by the door.

'Tell me you didn't kill anyone,' she pleaded.

'Henry's da was out for blood, but by the time we got there, them blacks had edged it. We had a look about, but there wasn't even a footprint. It was as though they'd never set a bloody foot in the place.'

I heaved a sigh of relief. My mind had been full of the stories I'd heard about places like Wattle Creek, north of Bathurst, where white settlers pushed forty Aboriginal men, women and children over a gully to their deaths. I was glad they were safe, but sorry I'd never see Billy again.

It later came out that Dan Charters broke down and confessed everything to his mother. He was different to the rest of us. He came from squatter stock and enjoyed an easy life. His private tutor had taught him Latin, French and all about the Kings and Queens of Great Britain, but nothing about the bushranger's code of silence and never turning in a mate.

There ended my first lesson in justice. It seemed to me that as long as someone is punished, justice was said to have been done. It would not be the last time I would have cause to curse the name of Dan Charters.

That was the end of my innocence. I knew when I felt the first arrow of vengeance hit my heart. You see the world differently after that.

But that wasn't the end of it. Henry had to be buried and our da took, or, should I say, dragged me, over to the McBride house where Henry's body lay in the back room in a rough, wooden shell for everyone to look at and pay their last respects.

Like most boys of my age, I had never seen anyone laid out. I held back, but our da got a handful of my shirt and forced me into the room, in front of him. Despite the brilliant sunshine outside, heavy black drapes kept the house dark. The only light came from incense candles like the ones they had in St Michael's. They gave off a spicy aroma, which, in my limited experience, meant one of two things – sin or death. Old women sat rocking back and forth in chairs near the coffin, 'keening' as it was known in Ireland.

I stood in front of the coffin, but kept my eyes on the shiny brass handles they would use to lower Henry into the hard, dry ground.

'Go on, look!' said our da, angrily, fetching me a slap across the back of the head. When I lifted my eyes I could see Henry. His hair was still the reddest I had ever seen, but his pale white skin was as waxy as the candles that lit the funereal gloom, and had a purple mottled tinge. My stepbrother Tommy told me that meant he had begun to rot inside with the heat. I felt sick.

Another whack from my da.

'I'm sorry, Henry,' I said in a low, trembling voice. All that I could manage.

I doubt anyone had heard me, but my da announced my shame to the four corners of the room.

'It's too late to be sorry now, boy,' he boomed.

Bowed heads were raised as people looked reproachfully at the man who dare raise his voice in the presence of the dead and disturb their grieving, but no one said anything. They knew better than to come between a man and his son. Life was a tough trot and a backhand now and again would stop him straying from the straight and narrow.

I ran from the room, past Henry's maudlin, bleary-eyed relatives, who were all in black, with our da's harsh words nipping at my heels.

'See what your damned fooling has done?'

My aching heart thudded heavily against my sides and I was close to breaking. I stumbled out through the door, tears of humiliation and regret running down my face. Blindly I ran down the sun-baked yard past fidgeting horses and out into the bush, finding sanctuary in a clump of banksias. Away from prying eyes, I let rip and howled my eyes out. Just as I had finally reached the bottom of my deep well of tears, I was startled to hear someone beside me.

'Don't be taking too much notice of your da, Ben.'

Wiping the back of my hand over my dirty, tear-streaked face, I looked up to see the black cassock and robes of Father McCarthy, the priest who had baptised me. He sat down beside me, unconcerned about getting the dust and dried seed cones on his clothes. He had come down from Bathurst to perform Henry's service. His presence was a comfort to me in my present predicament.

Being shamed for the death of a mate in front of everybody, and by my own father at that, was the lowest point of my entire life. That clump of banksia became my confessional booth, but this time I needed no invitation to give up my greatest sin.

'I killed him, Father,' I insisted, trying to keep looking him in the eye.

Father McCarthy held up his hand and smiled sympathetically, 'No you didn't, son, the snake did. It was just an accident–'

My need to confess was so great that I did the unthinkable and cut him off. 'After the snake bit Henry I asked God to help him, but he didn't.'

Father McCarthy sighed and smiled wearily. Even after thirty years in the priesthood, he knew of no way to explain why God saves some people and lets others die, especially to the young.

'God hears all our prayers–'

'He didn't hear mine,' I interjected rudely.

'I'm sure He did, but you see He has a grand design for all of us . . .'

'What design?'

'Well, Ben,' said Father McCarthy, 'If I knew that I'd be the wisest man in all the world. He wanted Henry near Him and we must trust that He has his reasons.'

'He'll hate me now.'

'No, He won't.'

'But Henry died . . .'

The sanctuary was rudely disturbed with a rustling of leaves and scuffing of feet in the dirt. One of Henry's relatives had come looking for the priest. On the other side of the bush was a short, dark-headed man clutching his sweat-stained cabbage tree hat respectfully in one hand. He murmured, 'It's time for the Mass, Father. We have to lay the boy to rest.'

With a gentle nod he motioned to the house where Henry's grief-stricken mother was being held up by her husband.

'Tell them I'll be along in just a moment.' Father McCarthy turned back to me and the man withdrew. I remember thinking that it must be grand to have people obey you like that. He ended my confession by putting his right hand on my head, in blessing, but also so I would take heed of what he was about to say. 'Maybe God wanted us to know that life is a precious gift we must not take for granted and preserve it if it's within our power. Did you mean for Henry to die?'

'No, Father.'

'Did you try to help Henry?'

'Yes, Father.'

'Then you did your best. Henry is safe in God's hands.'

I gave a final guilty glance towards the house, thinking of my father's anger that was no doubt waiting for my presence.

Father McCarthy gave my head one last pat, then got to his feet, brushing the dust, seeds and bits of grit off his black cassock. Then, in a way that told me clear as day that he could read my thoughts as well as save my soul, he took hold of my elbow, his kind fingers were strong.

'Your friend's waiting for his Mass to be said. You'll come with me, for it wouldn't be fittin' for you not to be there to help him on his way to Heaven, would it?'

I couldn't speak for the lump the size of an emu's egg in my throat. Our da would be no match for this man.

That was how it ended. Well, almost.

Chapter Four

When Father McCarthy told me I should preserve life, I don't think he counted snakes. I took my vengeance on those fork-tongued devils every chance I got. I chased them through the bush on horseback, and with a single, flowing movement would unfurl my long greenhide whip, bring my arm around in an arc and take their evil heads off with one clean snap.

Mulgas, red bellies, death adders and eastern browns, I did the lot. As I watched the headless bodies stop twitching I would say, 'That's one back for Henry McBride.'

Revenge on snakes wasn't enough. My da pinning the blame on me once too often still rankled. He was falling from my heart.

A few months after Henry's death there was a spate of horse thefts in the area. We heard the traps were visiting the surrounding stations to check brands and what stock they had about the place.

One day, when my brother Bill and I were out doing our most hated chore, fetching water from the creek in big wooden buckets, we saw a couple of blue jackets riding across a distant paddock. Bill's eyes had a worried look.

'It wouldn't surprise me if our da wasn't at the back of that.'

I dumped the buckets on the grass to rest my aching arms.

'What d'ya mean, Bill?' I asked.

'Nothing,' he said too casually, moving past me, pretending to keep an eye on the level of the water in the buckets.

Pausing to shade my eyes against the bright sunlight, I peered after him. 'Come on, Bill, you can't just leave it like that.'

'It's nothing,' he shot back over his shoulder, but he never was any good at lying. Running after him, I pulled down on his shoulder, causing him to spill some of the precious water we'd just carried half a mile.

'Hey, watch out!' protested Bill, knowing if the bucket was less than three-quarters full he'd be sent back again.

'Tell me,' I insisted, keeping a hold of him.

'No, I can't,' he groaned. His downcast eyes confirmed my suspicion that he knew more than he was letting on. He tried to move past me with his buckets again, but I jostled his shoulder and the thirsty earth soaked up another splash of water.

'Tell me or I'll tip the whole lot over and you'll be back to the creek.'

Rubbing his hands, that were already chapped red raw from the rough wooden handle on the bucket, he looked back across the dusty paddock in the direction of the creek, past the haze of shimmering heat. He sighed and put the buckets down.

'All right, but you can't tell anyone else.'

'Promise.'

'The reason we left Murrurundi and came out to the Lachlan in such a hurry was because our da and Patterson, a lanky idiot of a mate of his, had been running a horse racket, which the traps had caught onto.'

'I knew our da's scheming was at the back of it,' I exclaimed and sat down in the paddock to hear the rest. I think the secret had been gnawing away at Bill and he was glad to get it off his chest.

'The scam was to steal pregnant blood mares, keep them out of the way at a secret pound we built out at Doughboy Hollow until they'd given birth. We'd kill the mare and sell on the foals as yearlings. That way the owners could never trace the horses. Unfortunately, some of the horses belonged to Messrs Bell and Abbott.'

'Stupid bastards!' I snapped. Archibald Bell and JK Abbott were the founding members of the Scone Association for the Suppression of Horse, Cattle and Sheep Stealing.

'They put pressure on Chief Constable Johnston and our da was worried they would be onto us, but nothing happened for a bit and our da thought the danger was past.'

'What happened that day that Johnny Chisholm came out to see ma?'

'Our da thought it was safe enough to go back into Murrurundi and took me with 'im. We happened past the courthouse on warrant day and stopped in to see Johnny. Well, when he saw our da coming up the steps Johnny removed the clay pipe from his mouth, stood up and looked at our da as if he was a ghost and hissed "What in the bleedin' 'ell are ye doin' 'ere?"

'Our da spread out his arms and shot back, "Well, that's a fine welcome for an old chum. What d'ya mean?"

'Johnny pulled us into his tiny key room, closed the door and told da, "There be a warrant out for ye, me old mate. Sworn the day by the Magistrate. They're after ye for liftin' all them nice gentlemen's 'orses."

'Our da thought he was off the hook, but the Chief Constable put the screws on his daft mate Patterson and he gave 'em up. They also found all them 'orses they had penned up out at Doughboy Hollow.

'Our da started fidgeting about like an opossum in a sack. There were traps standing outside talking, traps on horseback on the street and traps coming out of the courthouse. Then our da remembered a bloke in the pub spruiking some land he owned out west and went to buy it off 'im.'

Suddenly it all made sense. Convict blood being as thick and red as that of any family, Johnny Chisholm came out to see our ma right away. That's what all the commotion was about and why we left Murrurundi that night and not a moment too soon, according to Bill.

'The very next day, the New South Wales *Government Gazette* offered a ticket of leave and the Scone Association a reward of £10 for "the apprehension of Benjamin Hall, a notorious horse thief and cattle stealer".' No wonder the old boy went bush every year when the Crown Commissioner came to collect the taxes. He didn't care that we were marooned out in the middle of nowhere, halfway to nothing. With a warrant out in his name he welcomed, even craved it. He probably thought if he laid low for a few years it would be forgotten. Little wonder he fretted about our Irish neighbours attracting the attention of the traps.

I repeated my promise to Bill to tell no one and as we started for home the buckets now seemed lighter. I was still smarting from the way our da had treated me over Henry and I turned the information over in my mind and wondered how I might use it to get even.

A few weeks later those evil serpents – betrayal, guilt and vengeance – must have known what was in my heart because the past our da was so anxious to leave behind in Murrurundi suddenly caught up with him.

Late one evening, Edward, my brother, came running into the house to tell us someone was coming down our fair beaten track. A visitor to our dry patch was a rare event and we all raced outside to see who it was. Even at a distance, with the sun just a coppery smudge on the distant horizon, his dark blue jacket and kepi cap were a dead giveaway. It was a lone trap.

Our ma lifted her hand to her eyes and grimaced, 'What in the blazes would he be wanting?' Her brogue thickened, as it always did when she started worrying. 'It can't be the taxes, the Crown Commissioner was here not three months ago.'

The trap didn't hurry. He just came slowly, puffs of fine, powdery dust coming up off his horse's hooves. As he neared, we saw he had his pistol drawn as if he was expecting there might be trouble. Our ma hustled us inside as he dismounted and told us to draw the curtains. We overheard the conversation between them as she met him at the door.

'Good evening, Missus,' he said with that same singsong Celtic lilt, though it was softer than our ma's.

'Constable Kennedy,' said our ma in reply, and although they were fellow countrymen, her greeting carried no warmth. It was bad enough that he was a trap, but an *Irish* trap. 'You won't be needing that,' she said sharply, nodding at his pistol. 'There are only women and children present and you're not in Ireland now.'

Kennedy's face flushed as her well-aimed dart found its mark, but he blundered on, 'Your husband wouldn't be at home at all?'

'He's been out the whole day.'

'Will he be back tonight?'

'Later perhaps. And what would you be wanting with him?'

Still smarting from her earlier comment, Kennedy puffed out his big chest like a warring cockatoo and announced, 'I have a warrant for his arrest.'

'On what charge?' said our ma with anguish, already anticipating the worrying years ahead bringing up a young family with no man to put food on the table.

'Horse stealing.'

'He's stolen no horses,' cut in our ma, but her voice sounded ragged.

'Not here, perhaps, but this warrant was issued in Murrurundi. We came across it when we were investigating a recent outbreak of horse thieving and saw that it has never been served.' He pulled a folded document from inside his jacket and our ma's brave front crumbled in the face of the Royal crest and the letters 'VR'.

'But that was years ago,' was all she could muster in defence.

Unmoved, Kennedy shook his head. 'It makes no difference. A crime is a crime for as long as there's a warrant out for him. I'll have to wait on him, Missus.' Kennedy was a big, solid man, well over six foot, and had to stoop as he stepped into our humble hut. Once over the threshold, he planted his fat arse on our da's 'throne'. That little joke was one of the few small ways my brothers and I could get back at our da, although by the looks of Kennedy, the 'King' was about to be dethroned.

Listening and peering from behind the curtain, my heart leapt. I didn't have to use my secret, the old goat had brought it on himself. Of late, he'd lost his fear of officialdom and was forever in court for obscene language or for disputing the ownership of a horse or a cow with the neighbours. Somehow he always got away with it, once even convincing a judge he paid for a horse he'd stolen. This was our chance to be rid of him once and for all.

Kennedy looked over expectantly as ma prepared our supper. 'Smells good, Missus,' he said, dropping a broad hint. Our ma grimaced, but it was not in her upbringing to be rude to a visitor, whoever he was. She ladled out some wallaby stew but wouldn't serve him. She left it to me to take it over with a piece of damper to soak up the gravy. I decided that a little bit of lip service was a small price to pay for our freedom.

'A fine stew, Missus,' he said appreciatively patting his ample girth. 'As only the Irish can make. Where is it you said you're from?'

Our ma was having none of his blarney, 'Nowhere you'd know,' she said, cutting him dead.

'Fair enough,' he said coolly, but couldn't resist trying to justify himself. 'I'm only doing my job, you know.'

'Aye, that's what the Royal Irish Constabulary said an' all,' said our ma bitterly.

That reference to those hated persecutors of the Irish, with whom the New South Wales police were often compared, stopped Kennedy dead. He turned his attention to us kids. From where he stood he could see our eyes glistening in the darkness like opossums ready to scurry back behind the curtains that divided our one-roomed hut into bedrooms.

Kennedy looked a decent enough sort of man. He had mutton chop whiskers and a kindly looking face that had grown red with the warmth of the fire and the hearty stew. Like a magician, he produced a fancy-looking package and held it out towards us. He unwrapped it slowly, but none of us moved.

Inside the paper was proper cake, not johnnycake, the dried fruit damper we were used to. He broke it in half and sniffed the air as a tantalising smell of dried fruit soaked in sherry drifted across the room. He held it out again, but we kids stayed well out of his reach. He may have offered us a taste of Eden, but his uniform belonged to the Devil and that made his cake forbidden fruit. He popped a piece in his mouth, rolled his eyes and made moaning noises as if he was being pleasured. He held out a piece to wee, curly-headed Ellen, who would normally curl up in anyone's lap like a cat.

Even though our mouths were watering with the thought of that cake, there was still no movement from us, so he shrugged his shoulders, said 'please yourselves' and popped the rest into his great, whiskery maw.

A full belly and the warmth of the fire soon sent him to sleep and he snored loudly, his head lolling to one side. Fearing what would happen when our da came home, we lay in our beds and waited. This fat Irish cove in front of the fire could be our saviour, if only he would wait long enough to take away our da.

All of a sudden, he stirred and consulted his fob watch with a watery eye.

'Perhaps he won't be back tonight, Missus,' he said as he stood up. I couldn't believe it, he was leaving! My thoughts of revenge had been too hasty. He rubbed his hands and pushed his open palms towards the fire taking a last warm before the long ride home. I wanted to shout that he mustn't leave, that it was his duty to wait and arrest our da so we could be free of his bullying ways. But I knew I couldn't because that would have hurt our ma. I looked around, wondering what I could do to keep him here. It was time for desperate measures, so I peeled back the calico from the window between Bill's bed and mine as our ma saw Constable Kennedy to the door.

'What are you up to?' hissed Bill as he watched me go out the window headfirst. He didn't get an answer as I dropped onto the ground, ignoring the pain as the rough wooden frame raked the skin off my shins. Staying in the shadows, I crept down the side of the house towards Kennedy, who was now framed by the dull yellow candlelight that filtered out through the open door.

'Goodnight, Missus,' he said tipping the visor of his cap with his greasy fingers.

'Goodnight, Constable,' said our ma with as much civility as she could muster. The door closed and my heart pounded against my sides like a beast hell-bent on freedom as I realised it was now or never. Constable Kennedy was in the saddle and just about to pull on the reins and turn towards home when I called out.

'Constable, wait!'

He stopped mid-action and frowned as he tried to make out the shape that hovered uncertainly at the side of the house. Pulling his pistol and cocking it he called, 'Who's there? Show yourself.'

I stepped out of the shadows and he relaxed when he saw I was a mere boy. Lowering the pistol he frowned and asked gruffly, 'What do you want?'

'You can't go yet.'

'There's no point in my staying. Your da ain't goin' to turn up, not this side o' midnight anyway.'

'Speak to Billy. He knows all about them horses that our da stole in Murrurundi,' I said urgently, making Kennedy's face crease into a suspicious scowl.

'What's all this about, son? Seems like ye're wanting me to arrest yer da?'

I didn't answer so he licked his lips and said, 'I suppose ye'll be wanting to "go whacks" on the reward. There's still ten quid on his head.'

My heart had slowed to its normal rate and I was no longer afraid of what I was about to do. I looked Constable Kennedy straight in the eye and shook my head.

'Nah, I don't want yer blood money. Gettin' shot o' 'im will be payment enough.'

Kennedy paused, as if weighing up the odds, pursed his lips, nodded and dismounted again. I turned and ran back up the side of the house and was through the window in time to hear a rap at the door and our ma exclaim, 'Constable Kennedy! Have you forgotten something?'

'Is there a Billy here?'

'Bill. Billy? He's my son,' answered our ma with alarm in her voice. 'He's only a boy. Surely you can't be after him?' Kennedy, uncomfortable in the face of our ma's increasing distress, hurried to reassure her.

'It's nothing like that, but he may have witnessed the theft your husband is wanted for. I need to speak with him.'

Bill was sitting on our bed, his feet dangling over the side. Tears were falling from his eyes and plopping onto his legs like the big drops of winter rain that soak you through when a shower catches you out on the paddocks. He looked up at me, his face showing all the shock and hurt he felt in his heart.

'You told him!' he hissed.

I said nothing as I climbed onto the bed next to him, put my arm round his shoulders and whispered in his ear, 'Bill, you've got to go in there and tell the trap that our da made you help them steal all those horses.'

'I can't,' he said looking at me, shaking his head and biting down hard on his lower lip.

'Why not?' I pressed. 'He did steal the horses, so it's not as if you'd be telling a lie.'

'But da says we should never snitch. All pimps come to a bad end,' Bill snivelled, drawing his finger across his throat for emphasis.

'Do you want him to keep coming back all full of grog and making our lives a living misery?' I hissed.

Bill wouldn't meet my gaze and kept staring at the floor.

I continued, 'I would do it myself, believe me, but I'm not old enough to go to court, you are.'

Without a word, he got up, walked through the curtain and came face to face with Kennedy, who had taken his hat off and was holding it under one arm, while he warmed his fat arse by the fire.

'Billy is it?' he asked, pinning my brother with his eyes. 'Son, I've come to ask you a question and I need an honest answer. Nothing will happen to you, your ma or your brothers and sisters if you tell me the truth.'

Though this little speech turned my stomach, I just wanted him to take our da and be off. Bill stood in the middle of the room self-consciously looking at his feet, unable to look up at Kennedy. Taking a few cautious steps forwards Constable Kennedy carefully reached out and pat Bill on the shoulder.

'Bill, when you was living in Murrurundi did you see your da steal some horses? Yes or No?'

In the deathly silence that came on the other side of Kennedy's question, there was only the hissing and spitting of warring opossums in the branches of the nearby eucalyptus to be heard. Ma's face had gone several shades paler than usual and the eyes of the other kids were the size of saucers as we all waited for Billy to say something.

Bill kept staring at his feet.

Feeling the heat of the fire, Kennedy moved away, dabbed at his brow with his handkerchief and repeated irritably, 'Bill, I'll ask you again, son. Did you, or did you not see your da take those horses?'

Bill's eyes bulged out of his head and he was breathing heavily as if he was about to expire from the tension. He jerked his head up, looked at Kennedy and blurted out, 'He stole the horses in Murrurundi and he made me help him.' He looked at our ma's distressed face.

'S–s–sorry, ma,' he cried, then turned on his heel and ran. He tore his way back through the curtain and then came the muffled sound of sobbing. Kennedy had his witness now. He would have to wait until our da came back.

True to form our da showed up hours later much the worse for wear, his drunken rendition of 'The Rose of Tralee' waking our guest from his slumber.

Warning us to stay behind our curtains, Kennedy took up his position behind the door. As our da staggered over the threshold, Kennedy caught hold of him and quickly got him in a good grip, twisting one arm up behind his back. There was a momentary pause while our da tried to work out what was happening. Judging by the stream of oaths, I imagined, with some satisfaction, that the look on his face was one of pure disbelief.

'What in hell is going on?' he roared drunkenly. 'What's a

fuckin' trap doing in my house? You bloody bastards! Can't you leave a man in peace?' I lay there with my brothers and sisters, quiet as mice, as we listened to the grunting, groaning and heavy boots raking the earthen floor, furniture going over and plates smashing.

Our ma screamed, high and piercing, 'Don't you hurt him.'

Suddenly, there was silence, save for the rhythmic ragged breathing of two men long past their fighting best. We heard a low groan and a metallic click as Constable Kennedy clamped the darbies on our da's wrists. The grunting and scuffling resumed as the fat trap dragged our da, still gamely resisting, outside.

Squinting through the gaps in the slab walls of our hut we watched Kennedy lash our da's hands to the pommel of his saddle with a short length of greenhide rope while our ma wrung her hands and looked on helplessly.

Finally there was the soft drum of hooves as Kennedy set off for 'the logs' at Forbes and a scratching as our da fought to keep his feet on the uneven, muddy ground beneath him. The soft sobbing of our ma and sisters overtook the sound of hooves receding into the distance.

I crept out of my bed and put my arms around her and said with all the conviction I could muster, 'Don't worry, ma,' I said. 'We'll manage, you'll see.'

It rained hard that night and I thought of our da, soaked to the skin, his boots full of water, stumbling through every puddle between here and Forbes.

My last waking thought that night was of Bill drawing his finger across his throat and bubbling, 'We should never snitch. All pimps come to a bad end.' We'd been brought up to hate the traps, but they'd done me, us all, a good turn tonight and I didn't hate them. I pulled my flour sack blanket tighter around me. For once, I didn't mind its coarseness on my chin. At least it was dry.

By my reckoning, it would have taken the troopers the best part of a week to take our da back across New South Wales to Murrurundi to face the court. As luck would have it, Mr JK Abbott, the man who put up the reward and who could identify the stolen horses in question, had died two years before. In the end, the court went soft on making Bill testify against his own da because he was a boy of tender years and, to my horror and disgust, they acquitted him for lack of evidence. But that didn't stop the traps from keeping our da in the logs while they investigated some other crimes they suspected he was involved in. As they put it, he was 'a very old offender' and 'a reputed horse and cattle stealer'.

Bill, Tommy and I picked up some seasonal work mustering and tailing cattle for our neighbours and we sold some of our ma's cows to one of our da's butchery rivals.

I also found a seller for our cheese. During a business trip to Sydney an enterprising Forbes salesman persuaded a swanky grocery store in George Street to take a few rounds of what he called, 'a popular country cheese'. When asked its name, he hesitated. At that moment a horse and cart went past and with the image of those whirling spokes in his mind's eye he turned, looked at the grocer and said, 'We call it wagon wheel cheese.' That off-the-cuff invention gave birth to a new enterprise that helped keep many a poor selector from ruin. Wagon wheel cheese became much sought after and the profit from just one round of cheese would pay a farmhand's wages for a week.

With regular money coming in, it was a golden time for us. In those long, hot summer days the younger boys took it in turns to crank the handle of the butter churner as my sisters came running in from the fields with posies of wildflowers for our ma. When all the work was done, she rewarded us all with a spoonful of golden syrup or 'cocky's joy', as we called it. It was one of the few times in my life I could say I was truly happy, but I had played dirty and knew I would have to face the consequences of my betrayal when our da returned. I constantly scanned the blue horizon and gave thanks for every day that it remained empty. He was not just being detained at Her Majesty's pleasure, but mine too.

Our da eventually returned after five months in the logs. Close up he looked older, greyer, and his skin, which had not seen the light during all those long months, was as pale and transparent as goat's milk. A spell in the logs might have worn him down, but it had not improved his temper. Without so much as a greeting, our da called me outside into the front yard. He was onto me, but I feigned innocence. He had the sly look of a dingo on the prowl about him, a dangerous expression that we boys had come to know brutally well over the course of our short lives.

Jabbing a finger hard into my chest he bailed me up, speaking in a quiet, menacing voice so our ma wouldn't hear, 'I know it was you.'

'What?' I replied hoping to brazen him out. I should have known better.

His strange Somerset drawl, which sounded completely out of place out amongst the wallaby scrub, gums and kookaburras, became more pronounced whenever he got excited or lost his temper. He shouted, 'I knows you put Bill up to it, boy. He spoke the words, but you put 'em in 'is gob.' Our ma had appeared, followed by Bill and Edward. Bolstered by their presence I continued to state my innocence.

'I put Bill up to nothing.'

He moved towards me, forcing me to take a step back. Our ma, sensing he was about to blow, tried to intervene.

'Ben, what's this all about? Come in, your dinner's on the table.'

We were almost toe-to-toe and however much growing up I had done while he was away, I still only came up to his chest. The rank smell of stale body odour mingled with the peaty toasts of whisky bought in his honour down at O'Meally's shanty. His eyes, red-rimmed from the dust and squinting into the harsh sunlight, bored into mine.

'You're a grown man and if you is intending to live the three score and ten that the Good Lord has apportioned you then you needs to learn that snitching to the traps is a dangerous line of work.'

He then demonstrated my lack of worldly experience by punching me full in the mouth with his clenched fist. I never saw it coming. I was brought back to the land of the living with a shock of cold water sloshed over me by Bill. From what seemed like a great distance away I could hear our ma shrieking, 'You've killed him, you've killed him.' As my eyes managed to focus, I could see her rabbit punching him, whilst he stood over me glowering.

I could taste blood in my mouth and as the numbness in my lip wore off it was replaced with a sharp pain. The ritual humiliation of the family traitor wasn't over yet. Unable to get up, I could only watch as he sprayed my face with all the snot, foul-smelling tavern whisky and tobacco-tainted saliva he could muster. 'That'll learn you to turn dog on your own da, ya little bastard!' he warned, which earned him another flurry of blows from ma.

Bill and Edward helped me sit on a felled log near the well. Our da, still muttering about betrayal and treachery, went inside to sit on his throne and waited for our ma to wait hand and foot on him. To soothe our da's anger ma would bring out her secret supply of grog and by nightfall he'd be laughing, singing and the storm would have blown over, till next time.

'Bloody bastard!' spat Edward. 'I'll kill him one of these days.' Bill and I had our ma's milder character, but Edward took after our da and was fiery with it.

'Forget it, Ed, he'll only take it out on ma,' reasoned Bill.

'Let it go, Ed,' I echoed.

But Ed wouldn't be silenced. 'I'll give him a dose of his own medicine, see if I don't,' muttered Edward, bunching his fists.

At that moment I was more concerned with the damage to my lip, which I poked at gingerly with my finger and tongue. It was already swelling.

Ed confirmed my self-diagnosis with a simple understatement, 'She's not good, mate. Your bottom teeth have sliced through your top lip and chewed her up a bit.'

'Not good' in bush language was better, at least, than 'not too good', which really meant you needed a doctor. Mostly, you only got the doc out if you were 'bad', which meant you had a serious injury, or were dead, in which case he did a post-mortem to make sure you hadn't been murdered. As the nearest doctor was a day away and there was no money for luxuries like medical attention, you'd have to grin and bear it, settle for a dab of Holloway's ointment or a native remedy like hop bush leaves, used to soothe everything from fever to a toothache.

I got by with a dab of Holloway's and eventually my lip healed. However, it curled back whenever I smiled and gave the appearance of a villainous sneer. This little trait was a godsend for a young man just starting to 'feel his oats' with young girls, especially those who had an eye for men with a hint of danger about them. I'd never felt my father's hand in kindness and I supposed I never would, but who said that nothing good ever came from a crack in the mouth?

As a result of my falling out with our da I came to man's estate early, which was common enough for boys brought up in the bush. I was going on fifteen when I decided to begin that 'life in the saddle' our da had long promised us. One night I took a walk across the paddocks with Bill.

'I've had my fill of this blind hole of a place,' I announced suddenly.

Bill said nothing, so I continued. 'Things between our da and me will never be right again. I'm going off to get a start as a jackeroo. Thought I might give Mr Green out at Uar station a go. Seems like a decent enough bloke.'

Bill thought for a moment and said, 'Yair, I'll join ya.'

The day we left, our da stood in the doorway looking daggers at us as we fixed our swags to our saddle and kissed our tearful mother.

As we started off he spat into the dirt. 'Bugger off! Good riddance,' were his parting words. I vowed there and then that whatever happened I'd never be the son of the father, I'd be a better man than him.

Chapter Five

I was seventeen years old when news came in of the terrible slaughter of diggers. It happened at Eureka on the Victorian goldfields, outside Ballarat, a few weeks before Christmas, 1854.

The source of the tension was the unfair and corrupt licensing system, which the Victorian Governor, Sir Charles Hotham, refused to reform, and the corrupt system of justice, which allowed a friend of the police to go free after killing a digger.

The diggers, led by an Irishman called Peter Lalor, built a wooden stockade and raised the Eureka flag, a white cross and the five stars of the Southern Cross constellation on a blue background. Lalor knelt in the sand beneath their standard and declared, 'We swear by the Southern Cross to stand truly by each other and to fight to defend our rights and liberties.'

The troops charged at dawn on the Sabbath morning of December 3. The buckshot, pikes and scythes of the diggers were no match for their cannons, rifles and bayonets and in just fifteen minutes the rebellion was over. Five soldiers and twenty-four diggers lay dead, with many more wounded on each side. The diggers lost the battle, but won the day. The hated licence system was reformed. It was only years later that I understood its importance.

As Australia was coming of age, so was I. After the turmoil of leaving home, I was enjoying a rare period of calm. Mr Green gave Bill and me a job and tried to give all us young blokes who worked on the station some guidance. Most were already larrikins and wasted their wages on grog, flash clothes and their donahs. Having seen what the grog did to our da, I had no taste for it, but I did like clothes and at least God had seen to it that I never had to pay for the company of a doxy. Dances, flash clothes and a bit of 'heels up' with the local girls were the extent of my horizons. My introduction to the pleasures of the flesh came on my sixteenth birthday. I got a knee-trembler up against the back of Morris' store at a dance in Binda after we'd finished droving some cattle down to the market at Goulburn.

I don't recall much about her, only that she was a country girl about my age called Daisy whose breath smelt of sweet sherry. When she'd heard it was my birthday she came over to give me a kiss, but things moved along quickly once we got outside.

She let me put my hand inside her dress, which I quickly slipped over a full breast and started kneading it gently, as Patsy O'Meally, John's younger brother, had told me to. She gave a deep, contented sigh when I tugged gently at her teat and, not knowing anything about woman's breasts, was surprised when I found that it had stiffened in my hand.

She hitched up her dress and I pulled my strides down. I could feel her heavy breathing on my neck and I launched myself between her legs like an untethered bullock, all thrusting energy, but no direction. With her back against the weatherboards of Morris' store, she pushed down on my shoulders, lifted herself up, squirmed and twisted against me and then suddenly I was inside her. The sudden heat and silky sensation, as she took my full length, left me breathless for a moment. Then, responding to natural instinct, I started driving at her, trying to keep my balance and support her weight while she clung to my shoulders.

'Wait, wait!' she laughed as she freed herself from the untidy tangle of limbs. We tried again, this time with a bit more direction, and we soon had the weatherboards behind us rattling like a dray on a rutted track. Patsy had also warned me that if I wasn't careful it would be over in a minute. He said I should try to think of something else like counting mokes into a stockyard or something like that, but I couldn't hold on. There was an almighty rush as I let go inside her and in that rapturous moment I discovered why men are prepared to cross oceans and scale mountains for the love of a woman.

Panting and puffing, sweat pouring off the both of us, we stood up laughing and straightened up our clothes. Resting our aching backs against the weatherboards, we stood there a minute, enjoying a little breeze that had kicked up on the darkened plains, but before

I could find out anything more about her, a female voice came sailing through the night, 'Daisy, you there?'

'Coming, Maggie,' she called back. Even though I couldn't see her face I could make out that she was looking at me, then there was a bump of noses, that taste of sweet sherry again and the sound of her retreating footsteps. Later, I went back to the dance and looked about for her, but no one had ever heard of a Daisy. That was the first and last I ever saw of her.

But Daisy gave me a taste for women and along with John O'Meally, Dan Charters and Mickey Burke, I travelled far and wide to weekend dances to play the field.

Dressed in an elegantly tailored blue suit with a purple velvet collar, white shirt, thin ribbon tie and elastic-sided Cuban-heeled boots, Dan was more a city dandy than a stockman as befitted a man of his wealth and position.

O'Meally and Burke were flash jacks with their long, oiled hair, cravats, loud vests studded with jewels, buckskin trousers, polished boots and leggings, long-cut sac coats and red sashes round their waists.

I was somewhere between the two. I favoured a moleskin shooting coat, flashy waistcoat, cord trousers tucked inside Napoleon boots and all topped off by a red ribbon, which I wore around my low-crowned cabbage tree hat.

Dan, with his boyish charm, blond curls and big blue eyes was always a great favourite with the ladies, but the rest of us didn't fare too badly either. I had no desire for a serious attachment and we dealt with sex as we did with most things in the country in a more casual way.

My work became as intermittent as my love life. I left Uar and flitted from station to station wherever there was a job to be done and a pound to be earned, but my gallop ended the summer I started working for our old neighbour John Walsh. Though he'd come from Ireland as a convict he'd 'done good' in Australia and now owned a sixteen thousand acre run he called Uoka and over five hundred head of cattle.

While working there I met John 'Jacky' McGuire and Bridget, or 'Biddy', Walsh. She was old man Walsh's middle daughter. He had three girls and a boy called John, who became known as 'Warrigal' after the wild Australian dog who roamed the bush.

I was put to work under McGuire, who was Walsh's head stockman.

'John McGuire's me name, but me mates call me Jacky,' he said with a wide, white-toothed grin. Though he only stood a little over five and a half feet tall, he had a lean, muscular build and his thick black hair, full beard and nut brown tan gave him the look of the tough Australian outdoorsman.

He was four or five years older than me, but we became great mates right away. Jacky was a lively, talkative rogue who sat easy in the saddle and who could spin out a yarn for a whole day as I discovered when I asked him where he was from.

'Might take a bit of telling,' he replied with a broad wink, 'but we've all the time in the world out here.'

'Sydney boy, are ya?' I pressed.

'Born in Sydney to a convict father assigned to the Reverend Marsden, "the flogging parson". Our da was broken on the chain, happy to live out his natural quietly after he got his ticket, but I took to the road when I was eight hell-bent on a life of adventure.

'I went to work for a stockman who later decided I was more hindrance than help, so he abandoned me in the bush to fend for myself. Some wild blacks found me wandering in the wilderness, brought me up as their own and taught me secrets of the bush, which I've put to good use as a stockman.'

I told him about our da and his warrant, about Billy Dargin and how I got even with our da.

'Best not get on your bad side, then,' Jacky joked in his easy way. 'Worked here long?'

'I've worked for old man Walsh for years. Slowly built up a couple of hundred head of cattle of me own. Lightning struck the old boy in a great storm a few years back and he never fully recovered. Since then, I've been running the place.'

'He's got three nice daughters, all good-lookers,' I observed.

Jacky tapped the side of his nose and gave me a wide grin. 'Ah, well I've been courting the eldest one, Ellen, in secret mind. Not a word to Mrs Walsh, or you'll be doing my job as well.'

'Doesn't she approve of you and her daughter?'

'Their natural mother died when they were all still quite young and a couple of years back old man Walsh married Sarah Harpur, an Irish widow of advancing years like himself. The new Mrs Walsh thinks Ellen's too young to be courting, but what she doesn't know won't hurt her.'

At the time, I was sweet on a girl called Betsy, a barmaid at the Harp o' Erin down in Forbes. She had a trim figure and was free enough with her favours, but I gradually found thoughts of the middle Walsh girl, Biddy, creeping into my mind.

She was a beauty, the pick of the three, and at sixteen was as spirited as the brumbies that we chased through the Weddins on moonlit nights. Like her sisters, Ellen and Kitty, she was small but nicely proportioned and well aware of the effect her svelte figure, long dark hair and sparking emerald eyes had on the men about her.

I quickly found myself studying her form and learning her routine so that when she was out doing her duties I could happen past and exchange a greeting or tip my hat to her. We progressed to polite conversation and to teasing each other, both sensing a romantic development, but not hurrying the courtship dance. Jangling nerves and a fluttering heart began to accompany a strong sense of anticipation whenever I planned one of our 'casual encounters'. She would greet me with a surprised expression.

'Why, Mr Hall, you seem to have a great sense of timing.'

'That would be right, Miss Walsh, but as you know when rounding up cleanskins or brumbies, timing is everything.'

Feigning annoyance she put her hands on her hips, furrowed her brow and exclaimed, 'I trust, Mr Hall, that I am not being likened to cattle stock or horses?'

'Of course not, Miss Walsh, just making conversation.'

'Well, I'm sure there are plenty of cattle to be tailed and brumbies to be broken.'

And so it continued like a two-step, quick, quick, slow, slow, but although I was regarded as a good-looking fella and had no shortage of admirers myself, I was on the shy side and a little wary of approaching her, on account of her stepmother. She kept a sharp eye on her three flighty stepdaughters, and, as Jacky had told me, made clear her feelings about girls who married too young. But what was meant to be will be, whatever the rules.

Now and again, we'd go bush and corral a mob of brumbies, break them in and sell them on. Once tamed, brumbies became excellent rough riders – strong and sure-footed on the wooded slopes and gullies of Mount Wheogo or the Weddins. Us young fellas from the station, who had been round horses all our lives, would act as buckjumpers and compete for the job of breaking the most spirited horse. We brought in a mean old brumby who got caught up in a mob of younger ones. No one was game enough to take on that yellow-toothed old bush rooter who flailed his great hooves viciously at anyone who came within cooee and earned the nickname 'Slasher'. He had a bit too much white in his eye for the folk around the place.

'I reckon I'll have a crack at old Slasher this arvo. Time someone showed that bugger who's boss,' I announced casually at lunch one day. Part of the attraction was the kudos of riding a real rogue horse, but it would also give me a chance to show off to Biddy. I was never one to let an opportunity go by. Not having the poet's way with words, we country boys had to resort to shows of strength and bravery to attract a mate. In the bush there was nothing guaranteed to capture the female attention quicker than a dashing horseman.

Word soon got round the station that I was going to have a dance with the Slasher and all other work was forgotten or left half-done as the station hands clambered up on the rails of the pen to get a good vantage point. The pen was a fenced-off area where we broke the brumbies we cut out of the wild. It was a hundred yards square of hard-packed red earth pounded flat by boot and hoof and baked in the sun until it was as hard as rock.

Once I was sure Biddy was in the crowd, I came strolling out of the big barn to hearty applause. I doffed my hat and took a good look at old Slasher, who just stood there, pretending not to notice the fuss.

He was a dun-coloured stallion with a bit of white dappling, a striking blond-coloured mane and stood about seventeen hands high. His coat was dull and careworn, and he was a bit bony around the ribs and shoulders, which told me his best years were behind him. Despite this, I approached him carefully as you don't get to be that age surviving in the bush without knowing a trick or three.

On my signal, the boys threw a length of greenhide round his neck and Slasher showed he was still as spirited as a yearling. He reared up on his back legs, flailed his front hooves like a boxer and forced the stockmen to pull back.

'Give us a hand down here,' called one sweating bloke, the muscles in his arms popping as he tried to hold Slasher down. A couple of stockmen threw more ropes around Slasher's neck so that they could pull him back down to earth. They managed to steady him long enough for two other blokes to come out with a blindfold and saddle.

'She's ready to go, Ben!' shouted one bloke as he ran from the pen and clambered up onto the rails. Slasher appeared to have been tethered and I came in from the side ready to mount him. When you come at a brumby you need to have all your wits about you. Distracted for a moment, I glanced over towards Biddy who was looking at me anxiously. Slasher chose that moment to twist against the greenhide and kick out with his rear hooves, one of which caught me full on the right leg, just below my knee.

I never saw it coming, but I sure as hell felt it. I heard a sharp crack as my shinbone shattered, followed by a searing burst of pain. The sky was spinning above me as I fell and I tasted the rustiness of blood mixed with dust. As I writhed in pain, I was dimly aware that Slasher's hooves were still pounding around my head. My last memory is of Biddy shrieking my name above the cacophony of cracking whips, yelling men and my own agonised screams. My stomach heaved as I felt myself plunging down into a deep pit of darkness. I tried to turn back towards Biddy's voice but couldn't.

I'm told it was two days before I finally stirred. When I tried to move the jolt of pain that shot through my leg confirmed that it was not all a bad dream. The first person I saw when I awoke was Biddy. When I saw that she had not seen me stir, I watched her through half-closed eyes.

Biddy was sitting by my bed looking out of the west-facing window bathed in the soft light of late afternoon. The dull, orange glow illuminated one side of her face revealing a coppery tinge in her dark mane.

Every so often, she would get up and lean over tenderly to mop my fevered brow with a damp cloth, looking concerned. I caught a whiff of her scent, a heady brew of lavender water and salty sweat.

I decided it was time to re-join the land of the living. When Biddy saw me stir, she grasped the hand I held out to her. Fighting through my headachey haze, I succumbed, under her serene gaze, to unconsciousness.

Waking the next morning, Biddy was still by my bedside. She smiled and put down the piece of needlework she had been working on. As I tried to pull myself up and prop my back against the wall, a fresh stab of pain shot up my leg forcing me to grimace, lie back and take a few deep breaths.

'Mrs Strickland came over from Bundaburrah and set your leg,' Biddy explained.

'Broken, is it?' I asked with a dry croak.

She nodded her head sagely.

'That bad,' I said and Biddy smiled serenely and returned to her nursing duties.

Whilst I was resting up I had plenty of time to think about my feelings for Biddy. I had no doubt that my thoughts had gone way past mere flirtation. I'd have been more at ease cutting out a good horse, than a woman, but Biddy was different to the other girls about the place.

She was a good looker, of country stock, well used to the hardships in the bush and its strange ways. Betsy was a 'townie' and not a good match for a country boy who made his living off the land. I wanted to get married and raise a family that would work on the station and inherit what I built. That was the order of things in the bush and women were in short supply. There was a saying round these parts, if you find a woman worth marrying, marry her quickly before some other bugger does. Love? That was something that would come in time.

Many times, as she sat at my bedside, I thought about declaring my true feelings, but as I had never told a woman I loved her I was worried that it might come out wrong and spoil things. I decided on a less risky strategy; let things take their natural course. There was a certain comfort in not forcing the issue. It allowed me to go on looking forward to her visits, which broke up the long days in my stifling, airless room.

Each day she would bring me meals, which were typical station tucker – damper, pickle and meat. The only difference between the three was the way the beef was cooked and whether it was served with potatoes or a convict-style barely gruel our da used to call 'smiggins'. Each evening she would sit in the fading light and read to me from a book whilst I watched the night gather in around her.

Seven weeks after the accident, the local doc, Doctor Sloane, stuck his cheery, windblown face around the door.

'Ben, how are ye, me boy? I was on my way over to the Thurland place and thought I'd look in.'

'A lot better than the last time you saw me,' I grinned.

'That's grand,' he said. Looking at Biddy, he added with a sly wink, 'And the private nursing has no doubt helped yer recovery. Now, sit up and let's have a look at that peg o' yours.'

After poking, prodding and bending the offending limb, he announced, 'I'd say the bone has knitted nicely, but even for as good a job as Mrs Strickland did, that old bastard will leave ye with a permanent limp. It'll not hinder yer in the saddle, but it's the end o' yer dancin' days. There'll be a bit o' stiffness an' soreness on cold mornings.'

It was another month of slow and painful progress before I could walk any distance. Each evening, after supper, Biddy would accompany me along the rutted station track as I tried to build up my wasted leg muscles. I soon tired of the same walk and one evening I suggested taking a detour down to the creek.

'Are ye sure about this, Ben?' Biddy protested. 'It's a steep run down and the ground is treacherous.'

'I have to test out the leg sometime,' I said, smiling at her motherly concern.

'Well, wait for me,' she said coming over and tucking her arm around mine.

'I'm as safe as houses now,' I said as we set off. We negotiated the first part with no problem, but as we got nearer the creek, where the ground was softer, my heel caught on a clod of earth. I lost my balance and went down on my arse, dragging Biddy with me.

Rolling over with a look of alarm on her face, she said, 'Ben, are you right?'

I flexed the leg a bit and said sheepishly, 'It's fine.'

She was so close I could feel her warm breath on my face. I looked into her startling green eyes and neither of us broke the stare. My heart was drumming against my sides and I realised our moment of truth had arrived. I raised myself up on my elbow and kissed her full on the lips, hoping she'd respond, but also wondering if she didn't whether I could withdraw quickly and make it look like a gesture of fondness. I needn't have worried.

As our lips met, she opened her mouth and allowed me to probe its warm, slippery recesses with my tongue. Her arms went around my neck as she drew her body into mine and I felt her soft, unfettered breasts crush hard against my chest. With a reckless haste, born out of the sudden flowering of passion, I slipped my hand under her skirt and found she was ready for me. And there, in a bush clearing, with all of nature as our witness, the courtship that would bring me my greatest joy and despair began.

Just as I started stepping out with Biddy, McGuire confided that he had asked Old Man Walsh for Ellen's hand, but her stepmother had refused saying Ellen was too young to be wed.

'What did you say?'

'Nothin'.' I didn't have Jacky down as a man who took no for an answer and with a twinkle in his eye he added, 'But there's more than one way to skin a possum.'

I had a feeling he was about to add another colourful yarn to his bulging swag.

Displaying all the native cunning of a man brought up in the bush by the Abos, a week later Jacky picked a stupid argument with the old girl about cattle feed and got sacked. He left the farm, drove his cattle to Bathurst, sold them and made all the wedding arrangements. He then returned to Wheogo and camped out in the bush, well out of sight.

Ellen came to meet him, as arranged, and they eloped to Bathurst where they were married a few days later. Realising the deception much too late, Ellen's stepmother came after them, interrupted their honeymoon and threatened to have Jacky charged with abduction, rape and all sorts. But the newlyweds stood their ground and in the face of their defiance Mrs Walsh relented. With typical Irish pragmatism, they healed the rift over a few drinks, returned home together and Jacky resumed his old position at the helm.

I was smitten and decided that I wanted Biddy for my wife. My leg healed and I returned to my duties as a stockman, but despite the closeness we shared during my convalescence and the free, passionate love we'd made under the canopy of the heavens, Biddy seemed to have gone cool on me. She became very flirty around other blokes and I rose to her bait. At one of the local dances I followed a jackeroo, Johnny Russell, outside and warned him to leave her be. He finished his piss with a nonchalant shake, buttoned up his fly and turned to face me.

Arrogantly hooking his thumbs into his leather belt, he looked me straight in the eye and said, 'I don't reckon you've got any claim on her, mate.' Russell was square-jawed and broad-chested with a reputation as a fighter.

'We've been stepping out for a couple of months,' I said, explaining myself.

'Looks like the lady's changed her mind,' he sneered looking round at the gathering crowd with a confident grin. As he turned to head back inside the hall he deliberately caught me in the chest with his elbow. Quick as a flash I caught his arm, spun him around and saw the surprise in his eyes. He knew picking fights at dances wasn't my style and realised there was thunder in my blood.

A stand-off quickly becomes a full-on blue because like a bush-fire the sparks set light to everything around it. It had sucked most of the crowd out of the hall and into the circle that had formed around us.

The days of chivalry must be well behind us because Biddy was not at all impressed by my defence of her honour. Seeing Johnny and I standing toe to toe, she guessed she was the prize and stormed off home in disgust. With Biddy gone, the tension receded and after a bit of growling and sparring everyone drifted back to the dance, although my blue with Johnny warned off the other young bucks who might have similar ideas. I couldn't fathom her behaviour and decided it was time for a manly yarn with the one bloke I could rely on for straight-up advice.

The next day I found Jacky in the long barn sharpening a scythe. As my eyes adjusted to the darkness, after the harsh sunlight, I watched angry red sparks flying off the long blade as he turned the handle of the grinding stone. Seeing me standing there with something burning holes in me, Jacky removed the blade from the spinning stone, tested the keen edge with his thumb, eyed me up and down and listened to my woes.

'I want to marry her, Jacky,' I said firmly. He shrugged his shoulders and got those powerful arm muscles working on the handle again and as the spinning stone built up momentum he looked at me straight as an arrow and said, 'She's testing you, mate. She wants to know if you are just a young man feeling his oats, or if you have more serious intentions. Spit it out. Don't keep the girl waiting, but remember you're marrying a Walsh. They're as thick as thieves. Read one, read 'em all.'

Before I could ask what he meant, he was expertly working the blade across the stone, sparks flying again, his head bent over his work.

I'd done some damn fool things in my time; ridden rogue brumbies without a saddle, and gone rough-riding down the side of Mount Wheogo in the dark, but my stomach had never turned over the way it did the day I decided to speak to Biddy.

Biddy was feeding the skinny chooks at the back of the house. She half turned that head of long dark brown hair as I approached to see who was coming, but when she saw me, she turned back to her fly-blown birds.

'Biddy, can I have a word?' Sensing the tension in my voice she turned away from the squawking chooks, folded her arms and gave me the benefit of the doubt.

'I'm sorry for that carry-on with Johnny Russell. I didn't mean for it to turn out like that.' My mouth was as parched as a summer paddock, but as Jacky had counselled I came right to the point.

'But I couldn't watch him take away the girl I want for my wife.'

When Biddy heard those words, all the hardness melted from her expression and she smiled. 'Ah well,' she sighed, 'as you've scared off all other possible suitors for miles around, I've no choice but to accept, or die a lonely, old spinster.' She came into my arms and I took this to mean 'yes'.

Mrs Walsh gave me a wry smile when I went in and told her and the glassy-eyed Mr Walsh whose expression never altered whether the news was good or bad that I'd like to marry Biddy.

'Well, son,' she said, her Tipperary burr as rough as sandpaper, 'if I said no, you'd likely run off to Bathurst and do it anyways. As she's turned sixteen and seeing as you had the decency to ask, you have our blessing.'

My joy only lasted the time it took to tell my parents. Our ma was pleased but as expected, our da had nothing good to say.

'I'll tell you straight, they're too bloody flighty, those Walsh girls. Wild as cats wi' more than a bit o' the Devil in 'em. And I'll have no truck with the Irish, the Holy Romans at any rate. Filthy Fenian bastards,' he raged.

Usually our ma let his tirades wash over her, but this one was too close to home. She put down the knife she had been using to skin the fat grey opossum I'd brought as a peace offering, and faced him squarely, hands on hips.

'Is that what you think of me?' she said sharply. 'Your own wife's naught but a Fenian bastard?'

Realising that he had said too much, he blustered on.

'Aye, well you're different,' he said impatiently. 'You're not all religious and moral like that stupid old woman Walsh went and married. Bloody do-gooder.'

Muttering under her breath, our ma went back to skinning.

Our da shot me a warning look.

'Mark my words, boy, you'll rue the day, see if you don't.' With that, he settled back in his throne to indicate that the audience was at an end.

In defiance of our da's wishes, on February 29, 1856, at the age of eighteen, I married Biddy Walsh at the Mortray Inn, just off the Bathurst to Young road. Father McCarthy, who I had last seen five years before at Henry McBride's funeral, married us.

Before the service, as he did with all his young grooms, he poured me a nobbler of whisky to steady my nerves. Smiling, he said to me, 'I'm glad to see your fortunes have improved since I last saw you.'

I lowered my eyes as I remembered, with some embarrassment, that I told him that God hated me. I hoped he'd forgotten it, but priests are said to be like mothers-in-law, they never forget a slight.

'I was grieving for Henry, I didn't know what I was saying,' I mumbled by way of explanation.

Father McCarthy put me at my ease with a smile, and said, 'I'm sure God understood. Now He's brought you together with this lovely girl who is going to share your life, perhaps you can see He doesn't hate you and that you have been blessed.'

That day I did feel blessed. My older sister, Polly, and my brothers Tommy, Edward and Bill all came, bringing best wishes from our ma. Our da had refused to come and it would never have done for a woman, who was not a widow, to have come on her own. I understood and vowed that he would not ruin our day. In the end, I did that myself.

As night follows day, religious ceremony gave way to revelry. When the fiddler and a man with a box accordion arrived someone declared, 'We've waited a decent hour since last invoking the Good Lord's name and it's high time we broke open the grog.'

We pushed the furniture into the corners and let the fun begin. Persecuted and on the outer we may have been, but there was always drinking, dancing and music. Mindful that I would be expected to perform my conjugal duties later, I vowed to stay away from the grog, but had the misfortune to fall in with that pack of bastards otherwise known as my best men; Jacky McGuire, Mickey Burke, Dan Charters, John O'Meally and a new chum, Patsy Daly. They patted me on the back, ushered me to the bar, and told me not to worry because Biddy would make a man of me once she got me home.

It was all a blur after that.

Shortly after first light the next morning, I woke in a ditch, blasted out of my drunken stupor by the mocking call of a kookaburra. It was customary to deposit a drunk on a cot in the 'deadhouse', a spare room at the back of the pub, where he can sleep it off. My mates thought it would be a better idea to drop me out in the bush five miles from home, without my boots.

I had plenty of time to repent for my sins as I walked home in the rising heat with a thumping headache and was met on the threshold by my new wife and had to brave a torrent of tears and recriminations. She retreated to the bedroom where she lay with the curtains drawn, sobbing her heart out. After a couple of days she came out and our married life began. All seemed to be forgiven and we got around to consummating our marriage, but it went deeper with her than it did with me. It always does with a woman. A girl's first sorrow never leaves her. She may fight it down and carry on, but they're never quite the same again. I later saw that the moment I lost Biddy's heart was right there at the very start.

Within a year, I found myself riding through the darkness to Dan Charters' place to bring him and his mother over to help Biddy deliver our son, Henry, named after the one that was lost.

'Still think about him?' asked Dan as we stood on the veranda in the still, warm night puffing on our celebratory cigars as the women fussed over the bairn inside.

'Sometimes,' I admitted, shrugging my shoulders. 'It won't ever make things right, but as we took one Henry away I thought we should put one back.'

I looked over at Dan, whose finely chiselled facial features were illuminated by the dull orange glow at the point of his cigar.

He nodded and said, 'You're a good man, Ben.'

We left it at that. We both stared out into the darkness, trying to banish all the bad memories and feelings we wanted to forget.

At first, Biddy seemed to take to motherhood, delighting in each stage of Harry's rapid growth from baby into a little boy. But the constant round of domestic demands and having to spend days, sometimes weeks, on her own soon made her restless. I knew she was young and flighty when I married her, but was sure she'd settle down once she understood the responsibilities of family and children. Only when you live with a woman do you discover her true nature, trust a woman for that. She'd always been comfortable and carefree at Uoka and nagged at me to take her to Bathurst and Orange to go dancing, shopping and to 'see life'. I kept agreeing, but such fun or frivolity didn't square too well with a man intent on securing a future.

Charged with the twin responsibilities of marriage and fatherhood, I vowed we would never live a hand to mouth existence on the fringes of the law, not knowing where our next meal was coming from. I was prepared to work hard, build up my own stock, get a parcel of land and start breeding up.

I decided to go back to Mr Green, who gave me my first start at Uar station. On my first day he gave me a late wedding present, a fine three-year-old stallion that stood at about seventeen hands, with a grey and white marbled hide.

'You can't go wrong with this fella,' Green said as he handed the reins over to me. 'He's part brumby for rough-riding, and part thoroughbred racehorse for the straight sprint at the Wowingray-gong races. He's a real galloper.'

I smiled, little knowing how grateful I would be for both those qualities in the coming years.

'You're a fair rider,' he said with laconic understatement. 'Might put a few bob on you myself.'

'He's a stunner, the finest horse that ever stood on legs. I don't know what to say–'

'Thank you will do, son,' he said waving away any difficult show of emotion with his hand, which he offered to me instead.

I was about to lead the horse away when I turned and asked him, 'What's he called?'

He flashed me a toothy smile, 'Ah, my grand-daughter calls him Willy the Weasel, but you'll probably want to call him Flash Lad or Thunderbolt or something the like.'

I thought a moment then replied, 'Nah, I like that. Willy the Weasel will do me.'

During the next couple of years, I worked hard, saved my money and looked to the day I would have my own station. Mr Green let me keep the cleanskins I cut out of the herd during the musters to help me build up a herd of my own.

He also helped me learn the letters and write my name, something that I'd like to have done earlier. My marriage certificate was the first official document I ever had to sign and I had to make do with an 'X'. I was a willing student with plenty of long evenings and Sundays off to practise. Within a year, I was able to read a newspaper, though there will always be some words lost to me. Through my reading, I started to become a 'man of affairs' able to find out for the first time what was going on in the world beyond the outback.

The issue of land was still close to the hearts of the common man and in 1859 Henry Parkes, Jack Robertson and Charlie Cowper were elected to the Legislative Council on a ticket of fixing the system of justice and opening up agricultural land tied up by squatters to the legions of small selectors.

By 1859 I was twenty-two years old and had saved enough to take on a lease with Jacky McGuire, who, like me, dreamed of having his own spread. On our own we didn't stand a chance, but together we could do it. Between us we leased Sandy Creek, a run of around fifteen thousand acres that would support six hundred and forty head of cattle. We each owned a half-share, which we could sell any time we wanted, and built our houses a couple of miles apart.

Sandy Creek took its name from the meandering, mud-coloured trickle that wormed its way across the bottom of our lease. This was where we resolved to put our stockyards and butchery. Our run was situated about twenty miles from Grenfell on the flat plains that lay between the imposing silhouettes of Mount Wheogo and the Weddin Mountains, which dominated the western horizon on either side of us.

Jacky, Ellen, Biddy, Henry and I stood out in the paddock that first evening as the sun slowly died in the western sky, the golden shafts of light like a halo around its crown. We just stood there breathing in the 'clean air' my da had boasted about all those years ago when he dragged us across the country from Murrurundi. Jacky cracked a bottle of Old Tom. Before he took a pull, he raised the bottle high in a toast and said, 'Here's to the landed classes.'

It was true. We were off the bottom rung of the ladder and were now landowners. I had a suck of Old Tom and looked away down the hill that led to the long, flat plains that ran uninterrupted all the way to the far horizon, all the way to the future.

Or so it seemed in that golden, unforgettable moment.

Chapter Six

Our world changed forever one day in June 1860 when a wild-eyed bullocky, going by the name of Jack Mills, burst into O'Meally's and breathlessly announced, 'They've found gold out at Lambing Flat.'

Just as Sydney had been struck dumb a decade earlier when Edward Hargreaves announced he had found gold at a place he called Ophir after the legendary Old Testament goldfields of Solomon and the Queen of Sheba, Mills cut dead the cursing and idle rambling that flavoured the atmosphere like the beer and baccy. At any time of the day, you could cut through the thick fug of blue baccy smoke and beer fumes that crept into every nook and cranny of O'Meally's dingy, low-roofed shanty from its sawdust and spit-stained floor to its grimy, rough-hewn rafters with a knife. A rare moment of silence fell over this house of ill-repute and the rough crowd of duffers, sharpers, bushrangers and stockmen just stood watching delicate swirls of smoke arcing upwards in a shaft of light. It was like some biblical fable as though God had just delivered us from the wilderness. We were no longer on the edge of nowhere, halfways to nothing.

The peace lasted no more than a few moments. Chaos reigned once more at O'Meally's as Mills was surrounded by yelling, pushing, bleary-eyed men all demanding information about the location of the strike at the tops of their voices.

'They made the strike out at Burrangong Creek on James White's run. Looks like rich pickings,' were the only words anyone who was there that day heard over the urgent clamour that followed.

I went to see Jacky a few days later and told him straight, 'It's a godsend. We've just taken up the lease on Sandy Creek and we need to find new customers for our beef. They'll need mobs of cattle to feed the thousands that are going to come to try to grab up that gold.'

Jacky wasn't so easily convinced. '*If it's true*. We've all heard the yarns about the first gold rush and how the city folk deserted their jobs, homes and half-eaten dinners to come out bush to live in a slab hut, and grub about in rivers and dustbowls in the hope of striking it rich. Few did and maybe people won't be so easily led as they were ten years ago.'

'I reckon we go out there and have a look,' I said stubbornly. Jacky shrugged.

We rode out to the large area of rough pasture sixty miles south of Forbes, which was known as Lambing Flat because the selectors put their sheep up there for winter and left them there until the spring lambing.

When we got there a few hundred prospectors, fearing thousands more were about to come trooping over the horizon, worked feverishly to mark their claims with wooden stakes or mining tools, but there were nothing like the numbers I'd been imagining.

Jacky shook his head, 'Ah well, never mind.'

A dull, distant clanging caught our attention and turning east we saw a cloud of dust on the horizon. It looked as though a huge mob of cattle was headed our way. As the procession appeared on the horizon and started towards us through the shimmering heat, we realised the ragged symphony was thousands of tin cups, kettles, pots and pans banging against each other. Carpenters, blacksmiths, bank clerks, ships' captains, storemen, bakers, butchers and stonemasons were coming towards us in carts, on horses and on foot, some with no more than a shovel, swag and reckless hope in their hearts. For a licence fee of 30 shillings a month they had the privilege of working their guts out on their chosen strip of dirt, even if they found no gold. Within the year some would look heavenward in gratitude, thank God and declare this the 'lucky country', whilst others would fall exhausted upon their empty tailings, declare it Hell on earth, trudge back to civilisation and ask for their old jobs back.

'Well, bugger me,' said Jacky smiling broadly, 'Looks like we're gonna be rich after all.'

Jack Mills was dead to rights about rich pickings. Gold, both nuggets and dust, was found in numerous remote little creeks and gullies that ran into Burrangong Creek. According to those old prospectors who had run the rule over many such fields, that pattern meant the mother lode was nearby and that the search was spread out over a dozen different locations within a fifteen-mile radius of Lambing Flat.

But it was not only those with a pan or a cradle that were getting rich. Over the next few months Jacky and I spent most of our waking hours driving mokes from Sandy Creek down to Lambing Flat, buying more at market and driving them up to Sandy Creek to be fattened. Best of all we could command whatever price we asked as the thousands that were now arriving weekly consumed everything in their wake.

Within a few weeks of the first strike, the stands of tall, strong gums and ironbarks that lined the river had been reduced to stumps, plundered for building materials and firewood. An assortment of the crudest shelters imaginable had also sprung up along both banks of Burrangong Creek. Most consisted of little more than a length of calico stretched across two poles, crude bark huts or Aboriginal 'humpies'. Their appearance was of little importance. They were just places to cook and fall into an exhausted sleep between long, hot days of sinuous labour.

This same rough standard applied to the wild-haired, mud-spattered creatures that seemed to have emerged like some lost civilisation from the ugly red gash gouged into the earth by pick and shovel in the desperate search for riches. They wandered around for weeks in the clothes they worked, ate and slept in, eyes reddened from exhaustion and the pall of wood smoke that hung over the settlement day and night to ward off the bitter winter chill that frosted the grass and froze them to the bone each night.

Turbans, skullcaps and the straw coolie hats bobbed rhythmically amongst the native cabbage tree hats and strange accents and faces from America, Germany, Scandinavia, Ireland and Asia floated in and out of the chaotic din. They may have been speaking different languages, but they were all talking about one thing – gold.

Well-worn yarns about gold nuggets found under wattle trees, men stubbing their toes on rocks with the telltale shine on them, and great finds like the 'Welcome Nugget', which weighed in at 2,217 ounces or 158 pounds and fetched over £9,000, were repeated over and over round camp fires. Every story of good fortune was salve for aching muscles, split and bleeding hands and red raw sunburned necks.

But a man can only endure so much honest sweat and toil before his mind turns to sin. I'd give the most god-fearing man a month in that purgatory of dust, sweat and calluses before his spirit is in need of jollification, his throat of lubrication and his body of gratification by way of fornication. In and around the goldfields of Burrangong and Lambing Flat there was no shortage of willing hawkers, gin merchants and whores ready to cater to their every whim.

Arriving hard on the heels of the storekeepers was a colourful caravan of sly-grog shops, gambling dens, brothels, opium tents, and the circuses with their strolling musicians, tumbling acrobats and exotic animals. Priests roared about sin and fornication from their pulpits and the gold commissioner sent in the traps to tear down their flimsy weatherboard shells, but the next day it would all begin again.

The gold also attracted another race of flash characters called bushrangers. I was raised on the romantic legends of the early convict 'bolters', men who could no longer 'stand the steel' and took to the bush to 'have a go', make some easy money and enjoy whatever time the Good Lord had portioned to them. Bushrangers were a different breed. They were local larrikins, hardened criminals and failed miners fed up with hard yakka, low wages and the lack of excitement. They took to the roads and took up 'the game' or went 'on the cross'.

The most infamous in the Lachlan area was the Gardiner gang, which started operating around the Burrangong goldfields in 1860. The leader, Frank 'the Darkie' Gardiner, was from the first generation of 'Currency Lads'. Jacky was worried as he'd taken to bailing up everything going in and out of Young and we needed to make sure we weren't caught with our takings, which sometimes amounted to £1,000.

'Who is this mongrel?' I asked Jacky.

'No one knows for sure. He answers to the name of Gardiner now, but it seems he's also had convictions under the names of Clark and Christie. Some say that he's Francis Christie, son of a Scotch free immigrant who bedded an Aboriginal girl called Annie Clark and produced a son.

'They lived together like man and wife in a "kangaroo marriage", until Christie's real wife arrived from Scotland. Annie mysteriously disappeared and the Scotch wife didn't want a bar of her husband's half-caste bastard. So, aged about ten, Frank took to the bush and lived with a mob of wild blacks who taught him bushcraft.

'As a teenager he fell in with some horse thieves who called him "the Darkie", on account of his swarthy skin. They were caught in Victoria in 1850 and he was given five years hard labour under the name Frank Clark. Having no need of a degree from that academy he quickly went over the wall only to be arrested again in New South Wales for stealing horses, this time under the name Frank Christie. This time he got seven years hard labour in the quarry on Cockatoo Island.

'They let him out after five for good behaviour and he went straight back on the game at the Kiandra diggings up in the Snowy Mountains. He teamed up with a young Canadian larrikin called Johnny Gilbert. The traps scared him off, so he came up here and started a partnership with some butcher. He duffed the cattle and the butcher slaughtered and sold them. The traps lifted him for duffing under the name Frank Gardiner, but couldn't make the charges stick, so he got bail and skipped town. Now, he's out there in the bush with Gilbert.'

'A hell of a yarn,' I said with a shake of my head.

'A hell of a bushranger too, by all accounts, but let's hope we steer clear of him.'

The name Darkie Gardiner was soon on everyone's lips again after news of a dramatic shoot-out with the police at a hut out on the Fish River was splashed in vivid colour across every newspaper in New South Wales with no detail spared. Gardiner and the owner of the hut, William Fogg, had been partners in that crooked butchery business at Lambing Flat and the traps suspected that he might pay his old mate a visit. Their suspicions proved correct when a snitch reported that Mrs Fogg was seen putting out a red shirt on the washing line, a signal to Gardiner that the coast was clear.

On July 15, 1861, the Police Magistrate at Carcoar dispatched Sergeant John Middleton and Constable William Hosie out to Fogg's. As they made their way down into the green, wooded valley where Fogg's modest slab hut nestled, a lazy wisp of white wood smoke rising from the chimney, they heard the mournful caw of a currawong, a sure sign they'd been spied. Sure enough, when they arrived an anxious-looking Fogg was waiting on the doorstep for them insisting he'd not seen Gardiner for months.

'So, you'll have no objection if we look around then?' demanded Hosie.

Before Fogg could protest Middleton was through the door where he found the butcher's wife and children standing by the table. Jerking his thumb over his shoulder, he commanded sharply, 'Outside.'

As his eyes adjusted to the gloom, he noted the warm glow of an inviting fire that crackled in the hearth, a faint, earthy whiff of cow dung from the newly laid floor and the homely smell of bush stew wafting from the pot-bellied cauldron simmering by the fire.

There was no one inside and nowhere to hide in the hut's single room. The only sound was a moth beating its wings against the calico screen on the window in a futile effort to escape and Fogg still protesting his innocence outside.

Middleton was just about to turn and leave when out of the corner of his eye he saw the calico screen that stood in one corner of the room twitch slightly. As he moved towards it, the muted light from one of the small windows revealed the outline of someone standing behind it. Pulling out his pistol, he shouted loud enough for Hosie to hear him outside, 'Are you there, Gardiner? Come out now or I'll shoot!' But there was no reply.

The moth's frantic drumming only increased the policeman's anxiety. His mouth was dry, he dared not breathe and his eyeballs were burning. Such was the reputation of his quarry that he dare not blink, in case the Darkie used that split second to come out and plug him.

Taking his life in his hands Middleton crossed the floor in one bound, flicked back the screen with the point of his pistol only to find himself looking down the barrel of the Darkie's Navy Colt pistol. Instinctively, both men fired at the same moment. Miraculously, the ball from the sergeant's single-shot .66 Tower Enfield pistol seemed to cannon off Gardiner's forehead without even breaking the skin. To many, this was proof that the Darkie possessed some sort of supernatural powers and that the traps would never hold him or kill him. The only injury Gardiner sustained was a powder burn to his face, which would tell you just how close they were standing to each other when they fired.

However, the new Navy Colt suffered from no such deficiencies and Middleton took one bullet in the mouth, which knocked him backwards and another through the hand and leg before he had a chance to re-load. With his nostrils and eyes burning from the gunpowder smoke and blood pouring from his wounds, the sergeant staggered out of the smoke-filled hut desperately calling on Hosie to stay outside.

The constable bravely rushed inside and traded bullets with Gardiner. Once again he missed the elusive Darkie but the constable took a bullet himself. Despite his wounds, Middleton re-joined the fray coshing Gardiner across the head with the leaded handle of his whip when he tried to barge his way out of the front door. The struggling bushranger went down under the ferocity of Middleton's attack and lost consciousness.

When Gardiner came to the darbies were round his wrists. Middleton remarked grudgingly, 'Well, Gardiner, you're the gamest cove I ever saw,' but had not bargained for just how game the Darkie was.

With both traps wounded, Middleton ordered Fogg to ride to Bigga for help, but the butcher shook his head. 'I'll have no part of this caper. I've got a family and know better than to take sides.'

'Are you refusing to help the New South Wales police apprehend a wanted criminal?' Middeton roared at Fogg.

Realising he was treading on very dangerous ground Fogg held up his hands in protest. 'No, I'm refusing to put a noose round my own neck!' Pointing at the bloodied figure of Gardiner he continued, 'This ruffian forced me to harbour him, then you arrive, turn my house into a shooting gallery and ask me to help bring him to justice. But I wanted no part in any of this.'

With that Fogg turned his back on the lot of them. Middleton decided it best if he went to get help and left Hosie in charge of Gardiner.

No sooner had Middleton left than the Darkie threw his cuffed hands around Hosie's neck when he was getting a drink of water and wrestled him to the ground. Gardiner broke free from his captor and got over a picket fence and headed for the Fish River, which ran across the front of Fogg's property, whilst Hosie ran back to get his pistol.

Realising that even he couldn't outrun a bullet, Gardiner picked up a stout stick and ambushed Hosie as he plunged blindly into the bush after him. Once again the Darkie defied death when the trap fired at him and missed from less than ten feet. A vicious hand-to-hand struggle followed under the cool, dark shade of the river gums during which the two men bashed each other with cudgel and pistol butt. Both men crashed to the ground bloodied and exhausted. Hosie, none too keen to resume the battle, shouted, 'Go to hell, Gardiner! Get out of here,' before collapsing onto his back.

The attempted murder of two policemen sent the traps into a spin. There was a rumour that the Darkie had a squeeze in the Weddin area. Police patrols started combing the area and turning over houses, mostly of the Irish selectors suspected of being sympathetic to Gardiner or in his pay.

Needless to say, the Walsh place got a visit, but all they got was a gobful from the Warrigal who had grown into a big, 'roaring boy' of fifteen with hands the size of shovels. He already looked the world square in the face and was afraid of nothing or no one. I tried to warn the young hothead off.

'Be careful, Warrigal,' I said seriously, looking him straight in the eye. 'Cut across them blokes and they'll make yer life bloody difficult.'

But he just came right back at me in a brogue as thick as Irish stew, 'Don't be worrying about me, Ben. I've got their measure.' *Aye, and I thought I had the measure of the Slasher*, I thought to myself. If I could take time back now I would have tried harder to turn him round.

Though the bushranging menace was the talk of the district, it always seemed a distant concern, just something we read about in the papers, until that is, the day we were returning from yet another hot, dry cattle run to Lambing Flat. We were met by one of our stockmen who brought the shocking news that Jacky McGuire's place had been stuck up by bushrangers. Racing home, we found a tearful Ellen sitting on the doorstep, shaken but unharmed.

A mob of four blokes had come when we were away and bailed up Ellen and the few station hands we had working about the place. They got about £20 out of a jam jar in the kitchen and her wedding ring. To add insult to injury the bastards had the cheek to make her cook them supper before taking off into the blue with a couple of Jacky's good horses.

Bushrangers were romantic figures from our childhood who modelled themselves on the gallant 'Tobymen' of old England who robbed the rich and gave to the poor. We were hardly rich squatters and saw no reason, especially now, to side with these mongrels.

A few weeks later, we heard the traps had got wind of the Darkie and were staking out a nearby hut, so Jacky and I took them some tucker.

As the daughter of an Irish convict, Biddy had also been brought up with the belief that the traps were the enemy and wasn't best pleased that we were hob-nobbing with the traps, but I told her straight, 'We're landowners now and free of that old convict taint forever.'

Jacky seemed on very good terms with Sir Frederick Pottinger, the big, bluff Englishman with the military bearing and colourful past, who'd arrived recently to take command of the Lachlan district.

The son of Sir Henry Pottinger, a distinguished British soldier and civil servant, Frederick joined the prestigious Grenadier Guards straight out of Eton where his father's money and social connections got him a commission. He was set for a career in the army, until the sudden death of his father. Young Frederick became a reckless gambler and frequenter of London's notorious rakes clubs, gentlemen's dens where all manner of debauchery was the order of the day, and squandered his father's estate with alarming speed. He went through about £100,000 and left his family almost destitute.

Disowned by his mother and unable to live in the manner of an officer and a gentleman, Pottinger was forced to sell his army commission and used the proceeds to purchase a modest ticket aboard a leaking hulk bound for the Antipodes alongside other ne'er-do-wells and remittance men.

Pottinger arrived in Australia almost penniless and tried his hand at the gold diggings. That gamble also failed and as a last resort he joined the New South Wales police as a constable under the alias of Frederick Parker.

I did no more than shake his hand that night, but had I suspected the kind of cove he'd turn out to be, I'd have kept my hand in my pocket.

When Jacky introduced us, he studied my face as if searching for something, but didn't elaborate. It was an odd reaction, but I supposed that being a trap it paid to be suspicious of everyone.

'Any luck?' I said nodding at the thick canopy of trees where they suspected the Gardiner gang were hiding out.

'Not as yet,' he said sharply, as if defending himself. 'It would help, though, if people round here didn't harbour and supply these brigands with food and fresh horses,' he added haughtily as if he took personal offence from it.

'We won't be doing that, rest assured,' I said to him. 'Anything we can do, just ask.'

He looked at me strangely again and I thought it a curious reaction to an offer of help, but something else had caught my attention.

Amongst the throng of white faces, his black skin stuck out a mile. Until recently, the sight of a blackfella would have been an unusual sight in such exalted company until Inspector Pottinger started the controversial practice of using blacktrackers. Though the notion of using blackfellas to run down whitefellas did not sit well with everyone, it was a sensible measure if the traps ever hoped to keep up with the bushrangers who knew the lay of the land.

The tracker drew my eye, not just because he was the only black-fella in the patrol, but because he looked familiar to me. He was older and heavier and his features had lost that piccaninny softness I remembered. His skin seemed darker and his nose had broadened and flattened out, but I was pretty sure it was him. As I moved in closer to get a better look he pulled the cabbage tree hat down over his eyes, turned on his heel suddenly and I lost him in the crowd.

I walked over to one of the troopers who was hobbling his horse. 'Who's the blackfella with ya?' I asked, gesturing with a thumb back in the direction of the blackfella.

'Billy Dargin,' said the trooper squinting up at me. 'Bloody good tracker, been with us these past few months.'

I didn't hear the rest of the yarn as I searched the crowd trying to pick him out again amongst the milling police and horses. I'd been right. It was Billy.

After all we put him through, perhaps I wasn't surprised he'd chosen the path of justice.

After receiving information that the Darkie had been seen in the area, Pottinger's patrol dug in for a while. One of them, a trooper called James Taylor, came up regularly to fetch water and to collect some of Biddy's freshly baked bread and a leg of ham or beef. As I was away attending to business at Lambing Flat I only saw him now and again, but he seemed a decent enough cove, married himself and knew a fair bit about cattle and horses.

In hindsight, I was much too trusting, too caught up in my own grand schemes and didn't see what was happening under my very nose. It is an unfortunate truth about treachery and affairs of the heart that the victim is always the last to find out and usually only by accident.

Chapter Seven

'Get in there! Go on,' I yelled as I dug my spurs into Willy's flanks, moving forward to help manoeuvre the river of cattle through the stockyard gate. I watched with weary satisfaction as the thundering hooves of fifty sleek, brown and white beasts, urged on by the crack of a stockman's greenhide and a nip on the ankle from a tenacious cattle dog, stirred up a cloud of dust. This would be the second delivery this week to Lambing Flat, or Young, as it was re-named, after the terrible rioting against the Chinese which ended in an orgy of looting and killing on Sunday, July 14, 1861. No digger was ever brought to book for those shameful events and it was a dark stain on the reputation of all Australians.

In the town of Young, all the tents and humpies had given way to more permanent stone and weatherboard structures and now boasted a population of forty thousand. The demand for our meat and produce was a boon for Jacky and me who could now ask and get £20 a head, seven or eight times what we were getting a year ago. The huge demand had turned our dusty little holding into a busy cattle station.

I looked over at young Henry, who was now almost four. He was growing up fast and already eager to get into the saddle. When I looked to the future, I could see him growing from boy into man and vowed that by the time he was ready to take over, Jacky and I would have built up a fine spread.

For some reason Biddy didn't seem to share my joy at our improving fortunes. As with most marriages, the first flush of passion had passed and things had settled into a routine that was all too comfortable for Biddy's liking. She didn't seem to understand that this was the normal order of things. Money must be made when things are good because fortunes can change very quickly.

Drought always follows rain in the bush. She was surly and foul-tempered these days and constantly nagged me to take her to Forbes or Sydney for a taste of the bright lights and to indulge her craving for shopping.

I always agreed, to keep the peace, but kept putting her off until 'things quietened down'. I had been spinning her that yarn for three years and should have realised that it would lead to trouble.

'Come out from under there, Henry,' I ordered, for the third time, as I bent down and peered under our bed. He looked out at me, mischief in his eyes. He had inherited my blond hair and grey eyes, but there was no doubt he had his mother's stubborn nature.

'Your ma will be home soon and if you're still under there we'll both be in big trouble.'

'Where's Ma?' he asked, rolling onto his back, and sticking a finger up through the bedsprings.

'Over at Auntie Ellen's,' I said, trying to keep the impatience out of my voice.

'She's always over there,' he complained, turning his head in my direction. His thumb found its way into his mouth.

'Well, she needs company too.' I heard my voice saying the words that I didn't quite believe. 'Now, if you come out I'll take you for a ride on Willy before your ma comes home. Quick now.'

A ride on Willy the Weasel was a ruse that always worked and Henry came shooting out from under the bed on all fours.

'Good boy!' I said, reaching out for him, intending to tidy his rumpled, dusty clothes. I frowned when I saw he had what looked like a bundle of well-read letters clutched in his sticky hands. The letters were tied loosely with a yellow ribbon, which I recognised as one Biddy sometimes wore in her hair.

'What's that you've got?' I asked, gently prising the bundle of letters away from him. At first I thought that they might have belonged to Biddy's late mother, but the paper of the letters in my hand looked recent, not yellowed by age or heat.

A worm of apprehension began to wriggle around in my belly. The longer I looked at the bundle of letters and the yellow ribbon tied around them, the more they took on a different complexion. I couldn't think who would be sending her letters. I'd never seen any letters around the place and she'd never mentioned anyone writing to her.

There was an impatient tug at my trouser leg and Henry pleaded, 'Are we going to see Willy now?'

'In a moment, mate,' I replied distractedly. I carefully undid the ribbon and opened one of the folded notes. My blood ran cold as I read the spidery scrawl. They were not the words of a poet, but I can still recall them:

My darling Biddy,

It has been two days since I last saw you and it feels like an age. I have asked myself over and over if it can really be true. Did I really hold you in my arms and kiss you?

Sweat prickled my brow. I could scarcely believe my eyes. I let the note fall to the floor and fumbled to open the next one. Again there was a tug at my strides.

'Daddy. Willy! Willy.'

'In a moment,' I promised. I felt a hot flush come to my cheeks and now the sweat trickled down the side of my face. My heart quickened as my eyes feverishly scanned the note I had gripped in my hand. Written in the same hand, it said:

The smell of your hair, the feel of your skin and your sweet, sweet lips.

Another plaintive plea drifted up from my son. 'Mummy will be home soon.'

'I know, Henry, I know.' Any thoughts of a ride on Willy had gone right out of my mind. My head was pounding, a mixture of pain and rage hammering in my brain. I screwed the letter into a ball, tossed it aside, peeled off another letter, determined to see it through to the end:

Biddy, I have fallen for you . . . I know you're spoken for, but I must know, is there any hope for me?

Who in the hell was writing love letters to my wife? My eyes snaked down to the bottom of the page:

With all my love. Until we meet again,
Jim.

Jim? Who in hell's name was Jim? I racked my brain, trying to think. *I don't know any Jim. Where did she meet him?*

The sudden shock took its toll. I slumped down on the bed and sank my head into my hands as the uncomfortable truth swept over me in a wave of gut-churning rage and humiliation.

My wife had taken a lover behind my back, whilst I was busting my guts out building up this station. I launched myself off the bed and started pacing the room, pulling at the curtains and peering up the track to see if there was any sign of her coming home. I wanted her here to explain what the hell was going on, to reassure me I was mistaken, to tell me who Jim was. *Where is she? Damn her!*

Though he was still a child, Henry knew something was wrong. He would never understand the enormity of what he had discovered, or that taking a ride on Willy was out of the question. He stood looking up at me, anxiety written all over him.

'Dad!'

'Not now, Henry!' I said, my impatience boiling over into anger.

'But, Dad . . .' he insisted

'Go to your room!' I growled

'But you promised.'

I wasn't thinking straight. Those letters had shaken me to my very core.

I roared at him, 'NOW! I'VE CHANGED MY MIND!' I fetched him a slap across the head to send him on his way. There was a moment of silence and a look of bewilderment on his reddening face, before the hot tears broke over his cheeks.

I never lifted a hand to him before that day or after it.

Fearing there was more on the way, Henry ran crying from the room.

At that moment my anger made me oblivious to the hurt and pain I'd just caused. I marched out to the shed, fetched the long-handled axe and despite the gathering chill, stripped off to the waist. I set to work on the mountain of logs I had stockpiled for winter. As I landed each blow, I grunted, 'Jim', and pretty soon I'd chopped enough to see us through the whole of the coming winter, and the next one too.

The light had dimmed to a cold, steely blue by the time I heard the sound of horse's hooves coming along the track. Biddy came around the side of the house and was surprised to find it in darkness, and equally surprised to see me standing in the gloom leaning on the axe, a fierce look in my eye.

'Ben, what are you doing? Why isn't the fire lit?'

I had no words for her. I just stood there, the sweat dripping off me, my chest heaving from the exertion. Her face registered shock as she realised something was wrong. Her first instinct was Henry.

'Henry! Where is he? Ben, what's happened?' Always quick to tears, she was off the horse and in the house shrieking.

'Henry! Henry!' He met her at the door with great heart-rending sobs. Taking him by the hand, she brought him back to me, brushed away her tears and asked, 'What's wrong? Why are you like this?'

I looked straight through her.

She had never seen me like this before and pleaded, 'Ben, what's going on?'

I took a deep breath and reached into my back pocket, producing the bundle of letters and thrust them out towards her. Her face fell when she saw the trailing yellow ribbon.

'This is what's wrong,' I said, barely able to contain my anger.

'Where–'

'*Our* son found them under *our* bed,' I said, heaping on the guilt, wanting to make her feel ashamed for betraying both her son and her husband, wanting her to hurt, wanting my own tears to start flowing.

Biddy opened her mouth to speak, but thought better of it as I slowly advanced towards her, the letters in my outstretched hand. Curling my dirt-engrained fingers round those clean, fragile sheets, I slowly and carefully ripped a handful of them to shreds and scattered the pieces to the winds.

'Ben.'

'Who is Jim?' I asked, cutting through her weak protest. My voice was trembling with rage. The name stunned her into silence. Her downcast eyes and the red blush of embarrassment confirmed what I'd hoped wasn't true. She really did have someone else. And what was more, things had gone further than I'd ever expected.

Keeping my eyes on Biddy, who still couldn't look at me, I said quietly, 'Henry, go wait inside.'

Realising that the raised voices had something to do with the bundle of letters he'd found under the bed, Henry started crying again, but did as he was told. I waited for an answer. There was nothing, just the sound of my uneven breathing.

Feeling the anger rising again, I took my final revenge and ripped the rest of the letters into shreds and sprinkled them over her head like confetti. I taunted her as she brushed the debris off her hair and dress.

'What's the matter, Biddy?' I said mockingly. 'I thought you liked being a bride.' I grabbed her chin and brought her head up, but she turned her eyes away from me.

'You're hurting me,' she said in a tight voice. I leaned in close forcing her to look at me. I said softly, 'That's nothing compared to what you've done to me. *Now, who is Jim?*'

Shrugging her shoulders she said, 'Jim Taylor.'

'I don't know any Jim Taylor.'

Biddy crossed her arms impatiently,

'You'd know him as James Taylor.'

The realisation of who my wife had been cavorting with hit me like a kick to the guts.

'You went with a trap, a *bastardising* trap?' I was rendered almost speechless by the sheer impact of it.

The sullen tone of her voice mocked my outrage. 'You're the one who said we've lost that convict taint and brought them here and fed them,' she said impudently. But her words passed over me as I frantically searched for his face in my memory.

Once I found him, I nodded, 'It all makes sense now. He was never away from the door for one thing or another, pretending to be collecting rations or interested in the station.' I slammed a punch into the weatherboards that shook the house and startled Biddy. 'That mongrel, I'll settle with him.'

'Don't hurt him,' she pleaded.

Seeing panic on her face and enjoying it, I roared on, my injured pride as raw and painful as my white, skinless knuckles that were now smeared in blood. 'Hurt him? I'll kill him. Why shouldn't I?' I demanded. 'Don't I provide for you, don't we have a wonderful son, a house, a good going station?'

Though stunned by the force of my initial attack, Biddy wiped away the tears and began to fight back.

'Yes, but you've no time for me,' she countered bitterly

'No time for you?' I thundered back. 'Why in hell d'ya think

I work both early and late. For you and Henry, that's why, you stupid–'

'While you're off to Forbes and Lambing Flat with your cattle, I'm stuck here on my own with Henry, day in, day out.'

'But you're his mother, where else would you spend your days?'

She brought her hands down from her face and looked at me, her eyes blazed not with guilt, but with defiance and hurt. Clenching her fists and shaking with emotion, she went straight to the heart of her grievance.

'Ben, I'm still only twenty. I don't want to spend my life boxed up out here, I want to go out dancing and "see life", before I'm an old woman.' She paused and took a few deep breaths, clasping and unclasping her hands in agitation. 'I was bored and Jim, Jim was kind to me. He listened to me.' She looked at me pleadingly, hoping that my anger had faded. 'I didn't ask him to fall in love with me.' The question that had been gnawing at me since I found the letters hung over us, poised like a dagger.

Barely able to think it, let alone say it, I accused her, still refusing to accept the possibility.

'Did he *touch you?*'

Shaking her head and wiping her eyes with the back of her hands, Biddy quickly denied it, maybe a little too quickly.

'No, no, he never touched me, I swear,' she insisted, her index finger tracing the sign of the cross over her heart. I didn't believe her. Virtue comes easily to those who don't fear the consequences of their lies.

'Why did you keep his letters then?' I snapped.

The tears started falling again and Biddy raised her hands to wipe them away.

'Because they were nice,' she blubbered. 'Because no one ever wrote me letters like that. You, you weren't even around on our wedding night. You were drinking with your mates and I went to bed alone.'

That was a bullet I couldn't dodge.

'Why didn't you tell me?' I asked, the harsh edge disappearing from my voice. My rage had been blunted by her hurt. At that moment, even if she told beautiful lies, I so much wanted to believe them.

'You were always busy, tired. It didn't seem important.'

I sighed. 'Of course you're important, Biddy. You should have said what was ailing you. How's a bloke to know if you don't let him in on it?'

Her little arrows of guilt had found their mark and doubt began to replace the anger in my mind. *Maybe I was away too much. Maybe I was partly to blame.* My anger spent, I said wearily, 'Let's go inside. Henry needs his supper.' I gently rested her head on my shoulder, a truce that she gratefully accepted.

I stayed close to home for a while and honoured my promises. Needing a break from the routine that had caused so much pain, Biddy, Henry and I went to Forbes and up to Bathurst to 'see life', and the hurt and pain of our falling-out seemed to have re-kindled some of the fun and passion of our courtship days. With relations between us seemingly on the mend, we didn't speak about Taylor or the letters again, but I hadn't forgotten him. The thought of him festered, biding its time.

When I was next in Forbes, I stopped by the police station fully intending to give the mongrel fair warning to stay away from my wife, only to find he was a step ahead of me.

'He hooked it,' the sergeant told me after I'd made inquiries about his whereabouts. 'Taylor was a crooked cove, always on the grog. We were about to get shot of him anyways. No room for the likes of him in the new police service.'

The *Police Regulation Act* of 1862 had taken local control of the police away from corrupt district magistrates and placed it in the hands of the Colonial Minister, Charles Cowper. The word in the district was there was little hope they'd be any less rotten, as many of the old faces were still there and the men they brought in were no better, even when they dressed them up in nice blue jackets and hats.

I put it around the Harp o' Erin and O'Meally's that when Taylor came out of hiding I would settle up with him. Slowly the memory of Taylor and that terrible night passed, and things seemed to have returned to normal. Or so I thought. Biddy appeared to be in much better spirits and I looked after Henry some afternoons so she could visit her sister Ellen.

'Come on, boy,' I said, urging Willy on through the bush. The sun had already slipped behind the pudding-shaped mound of Mount

Wheogo and I was anxious to be home before dark having just finished a cattle run to Goulburn. I had kept close to the station for a couple of months, but recently mine and Jacky's stockyards were full to bursting and we agreed to do a run to the markets. I had told Biddy we'd be back in under a week, but unfortunately the Belulbula River had been swollen, which cost us a day as we searched for another crossing. There was a glut of beef cattle and prices were down at the market, another half-day was lost haggling a decent price out of the cattle dealers.

When I finally got home, I opened the door, dusty and weary, but keen to see Biddy and Henry again. There was no one there, the place was empty and silent, except for the ticking of the wag-at-the-wall clock.

Probably at Ellen's again, I thought to myself, heaving a sigh. It wasn't until I was fixing some damper and tea that I spotted the envelope on the table. It was propped up against the fancy sugar jar Biddy had bought on our trip to Bathurst. My name was written on it in Biddy's neat hand. I suspected nothing. It looked innocent enough. I opened it expecting that it was a note telling me where they had gone. Nothing could have prepared me for the few short lines she'd written:

> *Dear Ben,*
> *I have gone away with Jim Taylor and taken Henry with me. I love him and cannot live without him. Don't follow us as I will never return.*
> *Forget me, Ben.*
> *Biddy*

The shock buckled my knees. I slumped into a chair, felled by a raw, savage pain like being cut with a knife. First there is a sharp sting as the blade slices through the skin, then the pain recedes to a dull, throbbing ache as the blood begins to flow. The same cold, sick feeling that twisted in my guts when I found Jim Taylor's letters returned.

Finding my feet I ran through the house, hoping to find proof that it was all a terrible mistake, but the bedrooms confirmed the truth of her letter. All their clothes, every item they possessed was gone. All that was left were my clothes, the furniture, the pots and pans and dishes, some food in the cupboard, and me. This was not some impulsive act, carried out on the spur of the moment. It was neat and methodical, something she'd planned carefully. She'd lied.

All I could think of was getting over to Jacky's. He would know what to do. Dazed, I left Willy behind and stumbled two miles through the wallaby scrub until I reached Jacky's spread.

As I came through the back door, I saw Biddy's sisters, Ellen and Kitty, in the kitchen. Kitty looked away quickly as if I had just staggered in with a great gaping wound in my chest. Jacky was sitting in a chair smoking his pipe, comfortably wreathed in smoke, oblivious to the fact that Biddy had consigned me to Hell.

'Ben! How are you? Come in–' he called cheerily. I walked past him and fetched up in front of Ellen who busied herself stirring the pot of stew that was bubbling on the fire.

'She's gone. You know where she is,' I said, but like her bitch of a sister, she couldn't look me in the eye.

'I don't, Ben. She never told me a thing,' protested Ellen.

I wasn't having it.

'You're a lying bitch!' I stormed. 'You're her bloody sister. She would have told you first.'

'Jacky!' Ellen called in alarm at my change of tone. Jacky stood up, his face clouded in puzzlement and annoyance.

'Ben, what the hell's up with you?' I turned to face him and his expression softened as he saw the anger and pain in my face. He stepped forwards and clapped me on the shoulder, 'Jesus, mate, I'm sorry.' He looked beyond me to his stern-faced wife, who was attending to the dinner with a care not normally warranted by a simple bush stew.

'Nell, what do you know about this?' he barked. Keeping her eyes down Ellen shrugged her shoulders.

'Nothing,' she said, her voice tight with suppressed emotion. She took refuge from the truth in a woman's last resort, bursting into tears. Jacky steered me through to the front room. After the heat and fire of the kitchen it was cool and dark, a balm to my tortured nerves.

'Sit down, Ben,' he ordered, pouring me a stiff nobbler of illicit whisky, in the hope it would quickly take the edge off my worries. 'I'm sorry about Biddy, Ben. I thought you'd patched things up.'

'You and me, both. Never said a word, Jacky, she just went. She wrote me a letter, said she was never coming back.'

Jacky poured a glass for himself and asked, 'Took Henry, did she?' Noting my hollow-eyed stare, he nodded, then raised his glass in salute. 'You were good to them, Ben. They never wanted for anything.'

He meant it sincerely, but was small consolation in the circumstances.

'What did she see in that bastard Taylor?' I lamented. 'Even the traps were about to throw him over.'

Jacky sighed and took a hefty swig of the whisky. The fiery brew made its way down his gullet drawing a gasp out of him as its venom spread through his chest and throat. 'God knows how their minds work,' he said.

I drained my glass without it having any visible effect and poured myself another.

'Do you remember what you told me when I came to ask your advice about proposing to Biddy?' I asked.

He looked up quizzically.

'"Them Walshes are as thick as thieves." You were dead right. That's how it is with the Irish, family first, everyone else second,' I said bitterly. 'No woman would run off without confiding in another first, it's not in their nature.'

Jacky stood up and nodded in the direction of the closed kitchen door.

'Let me work on her, mate, I'll see what I can find out.'

Jacky and Ellen's murmuring, punctuated by the odd raised voice and choked sob, filtered through the kitchen door.

I sat in the dark downing nobbler after nobbler of the strong-tasting grog. The cruel words Biddy had written kept going around in my mind like swarming bees, stinging and driving me mad with their poison. *I love him and cannot live without him. Don't follow us as I will never return. Forget me, Ben.*

A half-hour later the door opened and Jacky's shape appeared in the half-darkness. He sat down opposite me with a heavy sigh.

'Bad news, mate. It seems Biddy had been meeting Taylor secretly. She was meeting him when she told you she was over here seeing Ellen, same old trick as before. He asked her to go with him and she waited until you went on a run before she left, wanted a head start.'

His words stunned me, even through the thick, numbing filter of grog. The deception had been going on while she was still sharing my bed and reassuring me all was well between us.

Though I had been with other women before I was married, I had little experience of their wiles. I wondered miserably if you ever know what's in a woman's heart, even when you're married. Maybe you only really find out when they leave you.

Jacky warned me he didn't want any more trouble, but he needn't have worried, the grog and the confirmation of Biddy's betrayal had knocked the fight out of me. I let him lead me back to my place like a lamb. He sat me down and lit the fire.

'Thanks,' was all I could manage. Biddy's leaving had put the stuns on me. I stared into the fire, not wanting to look at him, not wanting him to see my pain. I didn't even look up as the door closed. All I could do was clasp my hand around the bottle Jacky had left and draw it towards me. Time was the only cure for my ailment, but whisky was the best medicine.

To lose your wife to another man is a bitter blow, but the loss of a child is something that no man can tolerate. Any man who has looked into the face of his child and, by that wondrous miracle of nature, seen his own reflection staring back will understand what I mean. Biddy and Taylor had robbed me not just of the present, but the future too. I raised my fists to the heavens and asked why God had visited such misfortunes on me. I remembered there was no God in Australia. I lowered my hands and placed the blame on that bastard Taylor, let vengeance enter my heart and started plotting my revenge. Those serpents had risen again.

By sunrise, I was guiding Willy up Sandy Creek road towards the main road. I searched for my family for three or four days, tried to pick up their trail, stopping at every shanty and hotel between Sandy Creek and Bathurst. Angry and dispirited after my futile search, I returned home, but couldn't bear to be in the house. I threw everything left in the hut out onto the ground outside, but the sound, smell and memory of them still filled every room.

Finally, my own company wore thin so I rode to Forbes and took a room at the Harp o' Erin where there was plenty of activity. I sought solace in all the wrong places – the grog and an old flame called Betsy, who worked as a barmaid in the Harp and was still a fine-looking woman. She'd been hurt when I threw her over for Biddy, but took no satisfaction from my misery. A grieving man brings out the mothering instinct in a woman and that night she offered me her breast for a pillow, but it was a kindness, I regret to say, I did not return. When someone breaks your heart, you're never the only one who gets cut on its sharp, jagged edges.

Later, I rattled her narrow, metal-framed bed taking my frustration out on Betsy's body. I didn't even bother to undress her. I tore open her blouse and corset, suckled greedily on her teats before I pulled her legs apart and took my pleasure, such as it was. I gorged myself on her, but cared nothing for her. I just wanted to get even with Biddy. *I could be unfaithful too. I could caress, and undress and fuck, fuck, fuck.*

'Ben, Ben, BEN!' The faraway voice calling my name grew louder until I jerked violently back to reality and saw Betsy's sad, tear-stained face looking up at me. She realised what I was doing and said softly, 'Stop, you're hurting me.'

After I rolled off her, she turned away, brought her knees up to her chest and started sobbing softly. I saw that my unshaven chin had rasped her soft, white neck and breasts raw.

I let out my breath sharply as I caught sight of my naked self in her long mirror; crouching over her in the gloom, drool running down my chin like some hideous Bunyip. I was unfit for human company. Knowing that it was too little, too late I mumbled, 'I'm . . . I'm sorry, Betsy.'

I hastily pulled on my clothes and took my leave, quietly closing the door behind me.

About the last man in the world I wanted to run into was our da, but the next morning as I was making my way up the main street of Forbes, I spied him coming down the front steps of the Club House Hotel. He was a dab hand at finding other kindred spirits, men of less refined tastes to do his drinking with and they were 'on the burst' already. He was a bad drunk, the worst kind, and on this day he was running true to form.

'Ahha, the prodigal son returns at last!' he trumpeted, almost falling down the last few steps. He turned to his two mates, whose names he'd obviously forgotten and, throwing out a careless arm, slurred an introduction, 'Boys meet my son, Ben junior, the worst little bastard his mother ever spat out.'

The two bushies eyed me with suspicion. One was a toothless, worn-out old lag with a grey beard and dressed in dusty, threadbare clothes. He was the type of nameless, friendless sundowner who'll be found dead in a ditch.

The other was ages with our da, a tall, dark, wiry fella with a long, pointed chin, hidden by a close-cropped beard. He looked as sharp as a knife and just about as dangerous. His mean, little feral eyes were full to the brim with malice and the raised knuckle of bone in the middle of his hooked nose boasted that he was no stranger to a blue.

'Bloody kids,' he growled. 'Left mine for the dingos.' I didn't doubt it for a moment.

'Lost yer wife, I hear. She was a no-good Irish whore, I told you that from the start,' our da taunted, searching for my weak spot.

I brought my knees together as a signal to Willy the Weasel that it was time to move on, but our da was a man who enjoyed his sport.

'Never knew what you saw in her,' he sneered, 'but I hear she likes to come into town for a good night out, so I expect we'll all find out by and by.'

That cruel jibe drew a belly laugh from his cohorts, but the smiles came off their faces when they saw me dismount and start towards them, my stock whip in hand.

I allowed the greenhide to uncoil at my feet in the dusty, pot-holed main road. Constant handling and hard work had burnished its sleek, oiled length. Our da, fortified by strong drink, threw back his head and roared with laughter. He looked at me, face flushed red, and waved a finger in my direction, 'You haven't the guts, boy. I gave you my name, but bugger all else.'

I had never done another man any serious harm, but that day I discovered that every man has a black place where vengeance and other dark feelings live. In some it lies just beneath the surface, but with others it's buried more deeply.

With a flick of my wrist, I let fly. The greenhide fairly sizzled through the air and caught our da a crack on the meat of the upper thigh slicing through his thick moleskin trousers like soft butter. The agonising pain took a moment to cut through the filter of grog, but then his growl turned to a howl of agony. His dull-witted mates roared with laughter thinking it hilarious to see their new mate hopping around clutching his leg, but their jaws dropped open as the whip came down for a second time. Our da tried to grab the greenhide, but I pulled it back sharply and it wrapped around his wrist with a crack drawing blood as it unwound. As I moved in, his mates decided to hook it. Hobbling, one hand up to ward me off, our da began to back away.

'Ben, son, no.'

I didn't hear him then, my mind was lost in the past. Each time I heard the bat-like swoop and the sharp crack of the greenhide, an image flashed into my mind.

CRACK ... Ten years old, my brother Bill holding onto a bucking gelding in the rainstorm with raw, bleeding hands. CRACK ... my da holding up the joey for me to kill on the road to the Lachlan. CRACK ... dragging me by the collar to look at Henry McBride's cadaver as he lay in his shell. CRACK ... the smack in the mouth he gave me the day he got out of gaol.

The sound of sobbing brought me back to reality and I found him cowering in the dust in front of me. His trousers and jacket looked as though they'd been through a threshing machine and he was covered in angry, bleeding welts. Pain and nausea contorted his face and tears rolled down his unshaven cheeks, which were now flecked with white. He reached up a hand to ward off the whip, a drool of bile running down his chin, pleading in a ragged voice that I had never heard him use before, 'For pity's sake, son, enough.'

The old softness that had always defeated me in the past had gone, replaced now by a cold, hard detachment like a lump of rock lodged in my guts. I looked around at the shocked faces of the locals who had rushed out onto the veranda of the hotel, thinking they were just going to see a bit of Saturday afternoon sport between father and son, which was a common enough sight.

I heard someone in the crowd say, 'I didn't reckon young Ben Hall was like that–'

'Got his da's temper,' observed another.

My father's ragged, wheezing laughter startled me. 'Well, boy, you're not so different to your old da now, are ya? Found that mongrel at last.'

Without a word, I coiled my stock whip round my hand and climbed back up on Willy the Weasel. Blindly heading in the direction of Sandy Creek I felt a tightness in my chest. *Have I become the son of the father?*

When our da was away droving or hiding in the bush I remember my mother reading to us from the Bible. Unlike her husband and wild brood, her transportation to Australia, and the ordeals she had endured and survived, served only to fortify her faith and belief in some divine power. Something that always stuck in my mind was a passage she would recite to us as we drowsily sat round the fire on biting cold winter nights.

'Remember this in difficult times,' she'd tell us and I heard her voice clearly now, as the miles slipped away beneath Willy's hoofs:

For man also knoweth not his time:
As the fishes that are taken in an evil net,
and as the birds that are caught in the snare;
So are the sons of men snared in an evil time,
When it falleth suddenly upon them.

My 'evil time' was about to begin.

Chapter Eight

Eighteen sixty-two was not only a time of great turbulence for me, but the whole district. The *Land Act*, sponsored by good old Jack Robertson, Secretary for Lands, came into effect and it looked as though ordinary folk would finally get a fair go. Selectors could now select two and a half thousand acres of land anywhere they chose without survey.

More local lads had taken to bushranging. Travellers and coaches were being bailed up every day. Johnny Davis, Johnny Connors and Johnny McGuiness, known as the 'Three Jacks', the Darkie's apprentice, Johnny Gilbert, and John O'Meally, my child-hood chum, joined forces under Darkie Gardiner. It came as no surprise to me that O'Meally ended up in the game.

My own journey from law-abiding citizen to bushranger began the day I found a six-chambered Navy Colt revolver on the Forbes road. By what quirk of fate did this tool of the Devil come into my possession? Did it fall from some unsuspecting traveller's belt, or did some fiendish hand leave it there for me to find?

I thought nothing of it at the time and a few hours later I walked out into a sunlit paddock with my brother-in-law, Jacky McGuire, and aimed the loaded pistol at a row of empty grog bottles. I had never fired a pistol before as I had never had any cause to. I normally used an ancient fowling piece to bag a rabbit or an opossum for the pot. Holding the pistol felt different. My heart started thumping a bit as I felt the cold, smooth metal slip easily into my hand, and I adjusted my stance to counter the foreign weight.

After showing me how to load and prime each of the chambers with percussion caps, Jacky showed me how to sight a target down the barrel.

'Now, squeeze the trigger, don't pull it,' he urged, but in my eagerness I jerked at it, causing the gun to jump as it went off. The ball fizzed well over the row of bottles, unseating a mob of sulphur-crested cockatoos that were perched in some branches overhead. They took off in a flurry of white and yellow, sailing into the blue sky and, amid much indignant squawking and territorial displays of their yellow combs, re-convened in the higher branches of a neighbouring blue gum.

Jacky threw back his head and roared, 'You missed the bottle, but you sure scared the shit out of them cockies!'

I had plenty of time to practise. During the past few months, after my adventure in Forbes, I had brooded quietly at home, pining for Biddy and Henry, reliving every word and action, praying she'd tire of Taylor and return so I could do things differently. The only thing I didn't regret was the whipping I'd given our da.

Every so often I'd go out to O'Meally's shanty, where I'd get drunk and wallow in self-pity. I'd developed a taste for a rough native brew called Weddin Mountain Dew, which O'Meally himself distilled using a mixture of water, opium, laudanum, vitriol and tobacco. The potent brew dulled the senses quickly, the best salve for a broken heart.

Willy the Weasel would often turn up at Jacky's with an empty saddle and stand patiently while Jacky mounted him while cursing me. Willy would lead him back to where I was lying, snoring my head off after having tumbled out of the saddle. Jacky would sling me over the saddle like a slaughtered sheep and bring me home. Over a few pints of strong, black coffee, he'd try to talk some sense into me.

'You're a mess, Ben. We need to get back to work and replenish our funds, they're getting low.'

I was always sorry and promised to reform my ways. I'd do a few days work and the whole process would start again. My heart wasn't in the work anymore. I'd lost the reason for building up this station.

With its broken rails, overgrown paddocks choked up with burdocks, wild oats and crowsfoot that came up to my chest, empty whisky bottles, rusting tools and the rotted remains of furniture still lying about in the yard, Sandy Creek was looking as neglected as I was.

Gone was the flash young cove. Sporting a ragged beard of biblical proportions I now went about the place in dusty, stained moleskins, a buttonless shirt frayed at the collar and sleeves, my sun-bleached hair long and greasy.

Word around the district was that I was 'a ruined man'. I'd heard it said about the sad, old sundowners and scourers that sat alone in the corners of pubs and cattle stations, staring off into space, lost in the glories of their younger days. Wife died on him . . . wife went off with another man . . . gone to the bad . . . gone to the grog – the reasons varied, but there was always a woman in there somewhere. Being 'a ruined man' was like being stuck down a smooth-sided well. There was no chance you could climb out and most never tried. Might as well sit back and accept your fate and for a while I did too.

Despite all the grog and practice, the art of pistolry still did not come natural, and I swear I used more gunpowder than Guy Fawkes before I finally popped a grog bottle. I practised until the slap of the pistol grip in my palm, the weight of it in my hand and the vicious recoil became as familiar to me as my own well-worn pigskin saddle.

One afternoon I was out doing a bit of target practice, using the plentiful supply of empty whisky bottles lying around the station, when a voice interrupted my concentration.

'Ahhh, great shot, Ben. Careful, or the Darkie will be after your services.' I turned around to see Jacky's face grinning at me.

I frowned at the thought.

'That mongrel. Haven't the traps run him down yet?'

'Ah, he's not as bad as he's made out to be,' said Jacky mysteriously.

'And how would *you* know?' I asked taking aim and exploding a bush melon from twenty yards, sending the succulent flesh to the four corners of the paddock.

'Oh, I've met him,' said Jacky with a casual nod.

'Bulldust!' I said lowering the gun. 'Where did an old soak like you meet someone like Darkie Gardiner?'

'Right here,' he replied pointing to the very ground we stood on. Sensing he might be serious, I changed tactics.

'How come?'

'I'd met him once or twice before, when we used to supply cows to that butcher fella Fogg at Spring Creek?'

I drew my brows together in surprise. 'What, you mean we were in partnership with Darkie Gardiner?' I exclaimed.

Jacky looked sheepish, 'I didn't know they were partners at the time and Fogg was straight enough with us.'

I shook my head in disbelief.

Before I could come to terms with the fact that we'd been up to our armpits with Gardiner all along, Jacky dropped another surprise on me.

'Well, strike me dead if he didn't bloody well turn up here, out of the blue, a few days back.'

'Gardiner?' I asked, my eyebrows now disappearing into my hair. 'You mean Frank Gardiner came *here*? What the hell did he want?'

'You won't believe it, mate, the Darkie has gone an' taken up with Kitty Walsh.'

I frowned.

'But she's married to John Brown.'

'So what?' countered McGuire with a wolfish grin. 'When did matrimony ever put a Walsh off?'

'Bloody Irish bitches, always on heat,' I muttered, darkly alluding to Biddy's painful infidelity. 'I suppose that means we're more or less related to him as well now?'

McGuire shrugged his shoulders nonchalantly.

'Distantly. Would you like to meet him?'

'Who?' I asked distractedly, still harbouring thoughts about Taylor and what punishment I'd hand out.

'The Darkie, ya idiot!'

I shrugged my shoulders and tried to stay detached but the idea of consorting with the most wanted criminal in New South Wales was an intriguing prospect. I didn't think of it as taking a step towards the other side, just a bit of curiosity, that was all. And what young bloke wouldn't like to boast that he'd met Darkie Gardiner – the scourge of the squatters?

'Okay, yer on,' I told Jacky.

A few days later McGuire invited me for supper. Sitting at his rough kitchen table, trepidation mixed with excitement as we waited. Hearing the clip-clop of horses' hooves on the sun-baked ground outside I raised myself out of my chair and glanced quickly out of the window in time to see Jacky pull up outside and dismount. With him was a man on a black mare. The animal was magnificent, its gleaming hide soaked with sweat, looking as though it had been carved out of fine ebony by a craftsman. Gardiner called it Black Bess after the famous mount of highwayman Dick Turpin. Its master dismounted in one easy movement, the red dust settling around both rider and mount, delicate swirls trapped in the soft orange glow of sunset.

The fact that no one knew for sure who he was only added to his air of mystery. I'd never seen a Scotchman that colour, but what did it matter where he came from or if he was Christie, Clark or Gardiner? The Darkie had a rare dash and style that set him apart from all the other bushrangers of his day.

Footsteps sounded on the wooden veranda, the back door opened and Francis 'the Darkie' Gardiner swept into the room.

He was about five foot ten, a powerfully built, striking-looking man. As he came towards me with a wide, confident stride, I studied him closely. His longish mane of dark, curly hair was fashionably swept back and he had a short, neatly trimmed beard and moustache, all which lent him the swarthy look of a Spanish pirate.

If clothing made the man, the Darkie clearly felt himself the equal, if not the better of the squatters he took delight in looting. He was immaculately dressed in Bedford cord riding breeches tucked into fashionable 'v'-topped Napoleon boots, and a blue, velvet-collared duck coat. The only concession to his true nature was a highly coloured waistcoat of reds and blues. He had what my da would call 'a bit o' the flash and dash' about him.

Jacky did the honours.

'Frank, meet my brother-in-law, Ben Hall, one of the finest horsemen and best shots in these parts.'

'Nice to meet you, Ben,' said the Darkie. His handshake was firm, his black eyes dancing with mischief as they met mine.

'Likewise,' I said, meaning it.

'Sit down, boys, let's have a drink,' said Jacky, plonking a bottle of Old Tom on the table and shoving a couple of chairs in our direction. We toasted each other's health, several times.

As we laughed and drank, I caught myself staring at Gardiner, and struggled to keep my eyes off him. I guess it was his reputation that fascinated me.

Someway into our second bottle of Old Tom I staggered outside for a piss. I was looking out across the surrounding countryside to the distant hills, which were all lit up by moonlight, when I heard the heavy tread of footsteps fetch up alongside me.

'Ahhhh,' said the Darkie as he stood next to me, surveying the scene. 'Ben, your brother-in-law tells me that you've had a rough trot.'

I breathed in a draft of cold, clear night air and gave a little chuckle.

'Well, you might say that. The wife left me, ran off with a trap and took my son.'

The Darkie nodded in the half-dark. Without preamble, he came straight to the point.

'And was this before or after you helped the traps to hunt me down?'

I glanced over at his dark frame and decided that I'd better come clean, say it straight.

'Aye, well, that was just after some shady mongrels bailed up Jacky's wife and before I knew the true nature of the New South Wales police. They'll get no welcome at my door in the future.'

'That's fair and honest enough,' he said, clapping me on the shoulder. 'If I hear of the whereabouts of that cove Taylor, you'll be the first to know. I'll need your word that you'll not tell them about me and Kate.'

'No, Frank, your secret's safe with me.'

My heart leapt in my mouth as the Darkie reached inside his jacket, but instead of the pistol I expected, he produced a jar of clear pochin or 'grapple the rails' as the Irish call it out here. Catching the look of apprehension on my face, he gave me the trademark Gardiner grin, then called up to the house.

'McGuire, get yer fat Irish arse out here and drink a toast to those three Irish witches who have stolen our hearts and led us astray.'

Jacky came out and the three of us stood under the bright clear eye of the full moon, passing the jar from one to the other, raising a toast: 'To the Walsh Witches of the Weddin Mountains. May their shadows never grow shorter.'

'See this pochin?' gasped Gardiner. 'Made from the finest Irish potato.'

'A fine vintage,' I coughed and spluttered feeling my face turn red.

'Thanks, Frank,' I said, after I got my breath back.

'For what,' he asked, his teeth flashing white.

'For helping me make light of my troubles. Sometimes a man can do too much thinking and not enough drinking.' I was still sober enough to say it straight without sounding maudlin.

'It's not me, mate,' said Gardiner. 'It's the grog, the finest salve for a broken heart known to mankind.'

'I'll drink to that,' I said. I felt my worries drain away as the clear fiery liquid burned its way down to my stomach.

Over the next few weeks I saw quite a lot of the Darkie, and I'll not deny he had an easy way and a certain charm about him. Always flush with money, dressed in smart clothes and with that little minx Kitty Brown hanging about him.

As open and seductive as he could be, there was a dangerous, ruthless side to him, which came to the fore as events in the Weddins began to move apace.

The 'Three Jacks' finally ran out of luck. They were drinking at Brewer's shanty, over at Lambing Flat, when the traps got the drop on them, albeit by accident.

A police patrol happened to be taking a few prisoners they'd captured to Lambing Flat in a coach when they pulled up at the shanty for refreshments. Davis, Connors and McGuiness, seeing there was a mob of them, ran for it. The police gave chase and exchanged fire. Johnny Davis got hit in the thigh and was deserted by his mates, who rode off and left him where he fell. Davis kept firing gamely, but was forced to give up once he'd used his last ball.

Gardiner went mad when the news reached O'Meally's shanty. Banging his fist on the bar he yelled, 'By God, that's not how a bushranger behaves! You never leave a mate behind, never!' Taking their actions as a personal slight on what he saw as a profession with standards like any other, he saddled up and went out looking for the rest of the gang. As we knew from the old bolter tales, loyalty was paramount in the bushranging game, betrayal meant death.

Gardiner intended to let his 'telegraphs', his informants, the pimps and the police know that he took the issue very seriously and show what happened to those who broke that sacred oath. The next thing we heard was that Johnny McGuiness had been shot and

Johnny Connors' body was found out on a lonely plain. The rumour that it was all the Darkie's doing raced around the district.

Shortly afterwards a letter appeared in the *Lachlan Miner* alleging that the Darkie took silver and even the boots off travellers he bailed up. In bushranging terms, this was tantamount to a charge of 'conduct unbecoming'. The Darkie was the self-styled Prince of the Tobymen and in keeping with that tradition he did not harm or menace ladies, and never took silver coins or personal items of clothing, such as boots or coats. Also, it was seen as a gesture of decency to hand back items of sentimental value or to leave travellers enough money to complete their journey.

Gardiner dropped into the offices of the offending newspaper and perched on the editor's desk. He dictated his reply, which he wanted published in the following day's edition of the *Lachlan Miner*.

'My good name has been impugned and I demand redress,' he demanded.

'I'll see what I can do,' said the editor distractedly, one eye on the bulge of the revolver in the bushranger's jacket, as he hastily marked up the copy for the next day's edition.

The Darkie sighed theatrically, 'They say the pen is mightier than the sword, but I don't hold with that myself.' In one smooth action, Gardiner casually pulled out his piece, cocked it and pushed the cold metal into the cheek of the terrified editor, causing him to drop his pen and raise his ink-stained hands above his head. Although the smile never left the Darkie's face, he lowered his voice and spoke softly, an edge of menace in his words that told the quaking editor that they weren't to be taken lightly.

'You'll do better than "see", you damned cove. If my reply doesn't appear tomorrow, you'd best give some rapid thought to your epitaph. Now pick up that bloody pen and take down the following . . .'

His letter appeared the next day. It stated clearly that it was one of his rules never to take silver from travellers and whilst one of his men did steal some boots, the Darkie had immediately dispensed with his services. He signed his letter, 'The Prince of the Tobymen'.

You had to hand it to him, the man had class. The best part of ten years in prison, and five of those spent on the dreaded Cockatoo Island, had not broken his spirit or altered his principles.

*

Whether by accident or design, April 14, 1862, was the day I became tangled in Gardiner's web. That was the day he bailed up two drays on the Forbes to Young road, near Uar station where I once worked as a stockman.

I had the misfortune to be riding to Forbes that day with a stockman called Jack Youngman when we happened upon the Gardiner gang bailing up the drays in a gully flanked by thick bush. The Darkie approached us with pistol raised. Even though he was wearing a comforter pulled well down over his face, I still recognised him, but didn't let on that I knew him.

'G'day, Ben. I wonder if you and your mate would wait over there until we finish up here.'

We waited in the bush along with two other travellers whilst the gang unloaded goods from the dray, stuffing them into saddlebags slung across the packhorses.

He then brought over two packhorses, laden with booty, and asked us if we'd hold onto them. We did, not in the commission of a crime but in the hope that the Darkie would finish his business quickly and let us all move along. I thought nothing more of it and said nothing to Jacky. However, it was that incident which caused me to make the acquaintance of Inspector Frederick Pottinger, for the second time, two weeks after Gardiner bailed up those drays.

Although Wowingraygong was grandly called a racecourse, it was no more than a large area of flat, rough paddock that had been cleared at the edge of the Stricklands' Bundaburrah station, about five miles west of Forbes. Dipping down into a flat hollow and surrounded on all sides by a thick growth of eucalyptus trees, it was a natural arena. Every year the New Year and winter races were hosted there, which gave the locals an excuse to load family and friends onto their drays and drive out of town a few miles to have a drink and drop a few bob on a spicy nag.

As Mr Green had promised, Willy the Weasel was a galloper. I had just run him a close second in the all-comers race and was enjoying a celebratory glass of grog when Pottinger came swaggering up, whip in one hand, cigar clamped between his teeth. He asked my name, as though we'd never met before.

'Ben Hall, is it?'

'As well you know, Mr Pottinger. You and your men have availed yourselves of my hospitality in the past.' My tone was dry.

He smiled, but there was no warmth.

'This isn't a social visit, Mr Hall. I'm here to take you into custody,' he said in his smooth, clipped English tones.

'For what crime?' I protested in surprise.

'Robbery under arms,' he said, raising his voice and making sure everyone within earshot heard the charge.

I stared at him in disbelief. The buzz of comments and intrigue was building up around us, along with the crush of avid spectators.

'What the hell are you on about?' I demanded. 'I've never been involved in a crime, any crime, in my whole damn life. You've got the wrong bloke, mate.'

'You were recognised as one of the bushrangers who stuck up Bill Bacon's drays on the Forbes to Young road two weeks past.'

'I had nothing to do with it!' The words sounded weak and unconvincing as they left my mouth.

Pottinger remained impassive. He jerked his head at the two burly blue jackets who now flanked me. One of the traps was Kennedy, the one who took our da.

'You'll have your say in court. Constables, if you please.'

For a brief moment Pottinger's eyes met mine. They were a peerless blue, and as pretty as a girl's, radiating an unshakeable calm and self-assurance. The British Empire was built by blue-eyed, blue-blooded men like Pottinger who thought the world, and everyone in it, was theirs at a nod.

'Hold on a minute, there ...' I shouted, but Pottinger had already turned on his heel. As I moved to follow him, Kennedy jabbed me savagely in the ribs with his baton, while the other constable twisted my arm behind my back and shoved me down onto the grass. As they were clicking the darbies on me, people started crowding round.

'What's this all about, mate?' demanded one of the stockmen, a big fellow with swinging horny fists the size of a prize fighter's. 'What do you mongrels want with Ben Hall?'

'Nothing to do with you lot. Piss off!' snapped Kennedy, aggressively turning to face him, raising his police baton, holding down the man's stare. 'Unless any of you want to come with him,' he snarled.

No one moved and Kennedy, relishing his moment of superiority, growled, 'I thought not.'

As they led me away, a voice shouted. 'You're a dirty mongrel, Kennedy!'

' Kennedy proved the man right by starting in on me, again digging me viciously in the ribs to emphasise the depths of his rancour.

'I pinched the father and now the son who turned him in. Who would've thought it?' he said with a smirk. 'You're a flash jack, Hall, fine clothes, and that grand horse of yours. How did the likes of you afford that?'

'Hard yakka, mate,' I spat back.

'You'll be doing plenty of that where you're going. Like father, like son, eh?'

That sly dig was beyond the pale, and I took great exception to it. To the cheers of the onlookers, I lowered my head and charged him. We ended up on the ground, where an out of kilter wrestling match took place, due to my hands being manacled behind my back. Nevertheless, I still managed to inflict a bit of damage on Kennedy by head-butting him in the face.

A roar of 'Go on, Ben!' went up from the crowd, but Kennedy soon spoiled their fun. Even with blood gushing from his busted nose, he kept me on the ground and they had their way. One kicked me in the ticklers a couple of times before dragging me back to my feet then booting me on my way.

Jacky came running when he saw me being led away for the second time.

'Ben, why in the hell are they pinching you?' He eyed Kennedy's gore-spattered shirt and grinned at me, hissing a 'well done, mate' out of the side of his mouth.

'I'm buggered if I know,' I said, putting a defiant face on it all.

I did know. It was that day on the road to Forbes. Gardiner and his bushranging business, calling me by my name in front of the unfortunate civilians being robbed, getting me to hold the pack-horses. It looked bad. Nobody was going to take my word for it that both Jack and I happened to be in the wrong place at the wrong time, and had been roped in as unwitting accomplices.

The Forbes lock-up was a crude, stockade-like building made from the stout trunks of tall trees. As the traps pulled open the door, the smell of stale sweat, tobacco and an overripe slops bucket greeted me.

'Hope the accommodation is up to your usual standard, Hall,' sneered Kennedy as he shoved me through the door. I hit a wall of logs, rattling me to my very bones, then bounced off and ended up on my arse on the floor.

The darbies were replaced with a leg iron attached to a length of chain, which fed through the ringbolts driven into the wood.

The door slammed shut, leaving me to feel the full extent of every bruise, welt and scrape I'd collected along the way. As my eyes grew accustomed to the dark, I saw I was in a dark, damp earthen-floored space, roughly twelve feet square, with benches around the walls. Two small barred windows cut high in the ceiling, scarcely large enough for a small boy to wriggle through, offered the only ventilation and light. The bucket in the far corner was to be shared by everyone held in here. I groaned when I realised it was barely reachable at the end of my chain, a deliberate ploy that added to the humiliation of being locked up. The atmosphere was, at best, gloomy in this blind hole of a place. The dark, the smell and the fluctuating temperatures, stifling by day and freezing at night, were all designed to break the will of the unfortunates who landed here.

A rustling and surreptitious cough from the far corner of the cell told me I wasn't alone. A pair of red-rimmed, bleary eyes blinked at me owl-like through the gloom.

'Got any grog on ya, mate?' This request was followed by a blast of stale booze and a whiff of the great unwashed.

I stared at the heap of rags for a long moment wondering whether I should dissolve into great guffaws of laughter or just slump down in the other corner, put my head in my hands and howl like a dog.

I just shook my head and said, 'Sorry, mate.'

I spent an uncomfortable first night in the logs. I studiously ignored the feeble entreaties of my one companion, who wanted me to listen to his long, tough yarn. I had enough troubles of my own to be going on with. Eventually he gave up and fell asleep, snoring loudly. During that long night I went over and over the set of circumstances that had brought me to the present state of affairs. Sure, I was guilty of the stupidity of not getting my arse out of the way the minute I realised what Gardiner was up to. But robbery? Never in a million years.

The next morning, still shackled, I was escorted through the police station into a bare room with dirty, whitewashed walls and sat down at a rough wooden table.

A few minutes later, a burly sergeant showed Jacky in. Instead of leaving us to it, he pointedly came in, closed the door and stood with his back against it.

'Inspector's orders,' he announced sourly, in answer to our accusing stares. There was nothing for it but to conduct our interview in low whispers.

I had noted no reassuring smile on Jacky's face when he arrived, and pretty soon it was obvious why.

'I went to see Pottinger,' he said slowly, not quite meeting my eye. 'And he confirmed they dropped on you for taking part in a robbery under arms on the Bacon drays.'

'But I wasn't in it,' I insisted, trying to keep my voice down.

Holding my stare, Jacky finally asked me straight up.

'But you were there, weren't you, Ben?'

'Yes, but I didn't bail them up, I only held the packhorses–'

'Yeah, carrying the stolen loot,' interrupted Jacky in a fierce whisper, slapping the side of his head to show how stupid I'd been. 'Ya need that head examined, boyo.'

'But I wasn't, I'm not part of the Gardiner gang,' I insisted.

Again Jacky interrupted me slapping his palm on the table, making the sergeant jump.

'Jesus, Ben, there are no half-measures in these things. As far as the traps go or any sodding court in this colony, you're either in or you're out, guilty or innocent, there's no halfway with them,' he hissed.

A couple of days after my arrest I was even beginning to miss the drunk, who had been dragged out cursing and kicking the morning after my arrival. He had been neddied good and proper by the two traps outside the door.

Alone, I huddled into the old campaign coat Jacky had brought me and settled down for another fitful, freezing night.

Being a 'man of affairs' and having nothing better to occupy my time, I sat and listened to the grievances of the local men who passed through the lock-up. Most of their crimes concerned the main currency in these parts – livestock.

Thanks to the new *Free Selection Act*, the squatters and selectors were now much closer neighbours and there were endless squabbles over lost, stolen or strayed animals. With no fences to stop them, stock roamed at will across other people's runs. The newspapers were full of notices offering rewards for their return, and described animals that had strayed and been impounded until the settlement of all damages. If the police found a stray animal belonging to a squatter on anyone's land, they would be charged with duffing and thrown in the logs.

If the neighbours or the police weren't at you then it was the local pound keeper, a man almost as despised as the traps. Every town had a pound where stock that strayed onto common ground was kept until claimed by their owner and a fine paid. As these were often working animals and money could not be found to pay the fine until work was done, this led to more hardship for the poor selector.

The sound of someone snapping back the metal bolts ricocheted round the enclosed space like gunshots. A shaft of pale light, a welcome draught of cool, rain-filled air followed by a rough hand on my shoulder brought me to with a start.

I knew better than to ask the armed troopers, who were removing my chains and hauling me to my feet, what was happening. However, one of them obliged as he pushed me through the narrow door.

'You're up in court today.'

I also refrained from asking him what day it was. I had lost all sense of time as the days and nights merged into the eternal gloom and stench of my prison cell. I only knew from the direction of the sun, which was rising behind the trees, and the freshness of the air that it was early morning, not evening. The short walk round the corner from the logs to Forbes Police Court was a welcome respite.

The court was laughingly referred to as the 'theatre' because we criminals got to play a brief part on its stage. On that day, there was one fine actor treading its boards and playing the part of the victim, the portly, white-haired figure of Bill Bacon. I stood in the dock and listened to Bacon swear under oath that he'd seen the Darkie and me bail up the drays, which were carrying tobacco, gin and an assortment of other goods. Despite the fact he was fully two hundred yards from me at all times, that Gardiner's boys had all worn comforters and I'd never set eyes on the man before, he swore that he knew me well and had drunk with me in Forbes.

This was also confirmed by the driver of one of the drays, a cove named Ferguson, who said he'd seen me at Feehily's bar at the Pinnacle station. Though this had the smell of a fix-up, I was on strict instructions from Jacky through much glaring and head shaking from the public gallery, to keep my own 'counsel' and bite my tongue.

I was refused bail and ordered to stand trial in the May Quarter Sessions in Orange, so-called because every three months they flushed the flotsam and jetsam out of the prisons to receive their punishment. At least my fate would be decided by a jury of ordinary people of my own kind.

Although they were sure of my identity, Bacon and Ferguson were not so sure about Jack Youngman, who had only been standing next to me during the robbery, and he was released on a surety of £50, which Jacky put up for him. Although I understood why he had little faith in the New South Wales judiciary, the mongrel cast further suspicion on me and put Jacky's bond at risk by skipping town. It was a folly that Pottinger exploited to the full. Shortly afterwards, he published the following notice in the *Police Gazette*:

Found in the possession of Benjamin Hall, bushranger, a light chestnut gelding 16-1/2 hands, branded 'BB' near the shoulder, small star.

Also a saddle and a double-reined bridle, Colonial made; the seat and kneepads in hogskin.

The above are now in the possession of the police at Forbes.

This none too subtle accusation was designed to blacken my name and influence the outcome of my forthcoming trial. I bitterly regretted any help I ever gave the traps – making my brother Bill turn in our da and sheltering and feeding them when they were after the Darkie.

It was true I consorted with vagabonds and criminals, but then, who didn't? They were so thick in the district that if you cast a stone there was a better than even chance of hitting a horse-stealing, cattle-duffing, pilfering bastard of some description than an honest man. But association alone does not make a man guilty, not that the traps gave a hoot about that. In a case of mistaken identity, a poor bugger could spend months in the logs awaiting a court appearance where they would finally be released for lack of evidence and re-arrested on a similar charge a short time later. By this method, the blue bellies could punish anyone they had issue with for months, or even years in some cases.

Back in the perpetual gloom and stink of the lock-up, I resolved out loud, 'If that's Pottinger's game, then it's gloves off, no Queensberry Rules. I just hope he remembers who started it.'

There was a chuckle from the opposite side of the room from an old lag who was evidently well known to the traps and had been jugged for the past week on a charge of dishonesty. Unlike we young blokes who were desperate to get out, he was happy to sit there, smoke his pipe and let time pass. He had a wizened face so weather-beaten and lined that it might have been carved from the stump of an old tree.

'So, you're not too happy with our new Inspector?'

'Some might think him "a fine example of an English gentleman", but he's nothing of the sort. He's never slow to berate us for being of convict caste, but at least our fathers and mothers stole clothes and other necessities from strangers and never stooped to stealing from their own families to feed their vices,' I said sourly.

'That's not the half of him,' said the old lag tapping the side of his nose.

'Have you heard more?'

'I get to hear all sorts of things. The traps are so used to me they forget I'm there. I happened to hear how the good Inspector came by his new commission, if you're interested.'

'I'm interested,' I said making myself as comfortable as my reduced circumstances would allow. He spun every rumour, whisper and yarn that he had gathered from various sources into an elaborate tale of lies, treachery and favouritism.

Going by the name of Frederick Parker, Pottinger hid in the ranks as a lowly trooper, where he distinguished his uniform by getting involved in bar brawls and yet more gambling troubles. One day late last year, Inspector-General John McLerie suddenly summoned Parker to the headquarters of the New South Wales police in

Sydney. As no explanation accompanied the summons, Parker climbed 'the gallows', the two flights of stairs leading up to McLerie's office, fearing the worst.

He'd heard that Inspector McLerie liked to dispatch them himself.

He stopped at the top of the stairs and straightened his tunic before knocking hesitantly and opening the door to McLerie's lair.

He half-expected McLerie to be waiting to pounce on the other side, but found the door opened to a large seemingly empty office. Tastefully furnished in dark, heavy furniture, the far wall to his right was lined with rows of official-looking leather-bound tomes, and a portrait of the young Queen Victoria dominated the wall to his left.

After he checked his fob and fumbled with the telegram to make absolutely sure he had the correct time and day, he looked around at the door and made to leave when a voice with an accent as thick cut as a Scotch fillet came out of nowhere, and asked, 'Trooper Parker, is it?'

Startled, Pottinger whipped back to the right to find that a balding, heavyset man had materialised by the bookcase.

Now in his mid-fifties, John McLerie had emigrated from Ayrshire in Scotland twenty years before. With a thinning, greying mane of black hair, thick black eyebrows and mutton chop sideboards that ran down to ruddy, windburned cheeks, his was the most distinctive profile in the colony's police force. At no more than five foot seven, Pottinger understood why he'd heard the words 'gritty' and 'nuggetty' used to describe him.

The Inspector-General's face broke into a smile, 'Sorry if I startled you.' By way of explanation, his hand went to a hidden lever. There was a loud click and the heavy bookcase moved sideways revealing a dark recess in the wall behind it. 'Might come in handy if the Fenians rise again,' he said with a hearty chuckle. Unsure of how to interpret this moment of levity, Pottinger said nothing. The man briskly crossed the room, his cool grey eyes raking over the man in the doorway.

'Take a seat,' said McLerie, taking Pottinger's outstretched hand in a firm handshake and gesturing in the direction of two over-stuffed armchairs by a solid, cast iron fireplace. Pottinger balanced himself uneasily on the edge of one of them, his eyes fixed on

McLerie. 'Whisky?' inquired the Inspector-General busying himself at a lacquered sideboard. Pottinger nodded like a man in a dream as he accepted a thick cut crystal glass.

The peaty tang of a mature malt whisky assailed Pottinger's tastebuds. He was used to short, sharp justice. *What way was this to dismiss a man? Oh well, at least I'll enjoy the whisky,* Pottinger thought to himself as he allowed the earthy taste to linger on his tongue. Looking down at his own glass approvingly, McLerie confided, 'The Gaels call it *uisge beatha* – the water of life and little wonder.' *Let's hope it's not the kiss of death*, thought Pottinger grimly. Strangely though, he could detect no underlying anger in McLerie's relaxed expression.

The Inspector-General leaned forward suddenly in a conspiratorial manner and said, 'Now, as I've told you one of my secrets, I'd like you to tell me one of yours.' The cool grey eyes pierced the blue of Pottinger's own, keeping them a prisoner under their force. *Here it comes*, thought Pottinger, and braced himself for the bullet.

Not for the first time that day McLerie surprised him by holding up a letter, which he then handed to Pottinger for his perusal. A red stamp, which bore the Queen's Majestic likeness, identified England as its origin. His heart leapt when he saw it was addressed to 'Frederick Pottinger Bart' in a stately scrawl he immediately recognised as his mother's.

Giving the man calling himself 'Trooper Parker' a moment to let the discovery of his true identity sink in, McLerie bored on, skewering the luckless Pottinger with his piercing gaze. 'Tell me, Trooper *Pottinger*,' the Scots burr paused a moment to let the full implication sink in, 'how did the son of an English aristocrat come to be working as a lowly constable in the arse end of the New World?'

Pottinger was staggered, unable to believe what was happening. He shot a rueful glance at his Inspector-General. *Good or bad? Hard to tell*. He decided to take the risk. His capricious past lifestyle had, if nothing else, taught him how to spin a plausible yarn without a blink of an eye.

Sighing and running his hand through his thinning mop of wiry black hair and looking suitably contrite, the words and the sentiments came easily to him.

'Well sir, it's a long story.' Staring fixedly at the royal blue carpet below his feet and pausing as if he were wrestling with some great, unspoken secret, he stammered, 'My father–'

'Sir Henry Pottinger,' interjected McLerie.

'You've heard of him? Well, to put it delicately, he was something of a philanderer, a man too fond of brandy and the fair sex.' McLerie nodded sympathetically and allowed him to continue. 'When he died, debts and death duties swallowed up most of his estate. To cut a long story short, sir, I no longer had the means to maintain my commission in the Guards.' Pottinger broke off as if overcome by the memory of it, then gamely rallied and carried on with his deception making sure that he displayed the full set of emotions to the eagle-eyed McLerie. 'My choices were limited in England,' he said looking the Inspector-General in the eye, 'and Australia offered a clean start.'

Although it was a barefaced lie, the loss of his army commission still pained him, so maintaining the right degree of *gravitas* required no effort.

Not wishing to prolong Pottinger's discomfort, McLerie held up his hands to indicate he'd heard enough. He chewed his lip a moment, as he searched for the right words, then replied, 'Thank you for your candour. I must confess I find myself in a delicate position. I rank above you as regards the police force, but you hold the social rank.'

Pottinger, now luxuriating in the whisky's warm current, which he knew would carry him to tranquil waters, had guessed correctly.

McLerie then announced that it would never do for a man of his social standing to continue as a mere constable. In short, now that he had been revealed to be a Pottinger, and no mere Parker, he was to be promoted to Clerk of Petty Sessions at Dubbo forthwith.

'Can't have a man of your stature and breeding milling about in the ranks,' said McLerie, filling up Pottinger's glass again. 'A toast to your promotion. We need more like you out here, show this rabble what's what, eh?'

The old lag clapped his hands like a magician releasing me from a spell and I returned to the gloom and the overripe bucket of the Forbes logs.

'Very interesting . . . I'm sorry, I never asked your name.'

'They call me Scabby Harry, on account of my bad skin,' explained the darkened figure. 'Any time you need information, let me know. I hear all sorts of things of interest,' he said simply.

Later, Scabby Harry told me more about Pottinger's rapid promotion through the ranks, which was nothing short of astonishing. He quickly advanced to become a Magistrate, an Assistant Superintendent and recently an Inspector, based at Forbes, on a salary of £300 per annum. McLerie had made a man with no bush experience or appreciation of the people he held sway over, second in command of the whole Lachlan district. Spread over some two hundred thousand square miles, Pottinger's new command stretched across Bathurst, Dubbo, Orange, Mudgee and Rylstone. All in all a perfect example of how things are done in the gentleman's class.

The Inspector of police is the biggest man in the district, but will not prevail, unless he can win either the fear or respect of the people. Early on in his command, Inspector Pottinger led a raid on a selector's hut looking for a Fred Lowry, a local bushranger who had two harbourers in the area. When Fred wasn't at the first, they headed over to the second. A few miles along the road, a young barefoot boy, riding bareback, went powdering through the bush past them clinging to the neck of a roan gelding.

'He'll be gone by the time we arrive,' muttered one of his more experienced troopers.

'How can you know that?' snapped back Pottinger, whose military training made him intolerant of defeatist talk.

'Because Fred is just about to receive what is known in these parts as a "bush telegraph",' reported the trooper, pointing at the rapidly fading figure of the young horseman.

'A what?' asked a bemused Pottinger, peering through a cloud of fine red dust that came drifting back towards them.

'A message telling him we're on our way delivered in person by that young lad that just ripped past us.'

'I see,' was all Pottinger could muster.

Pottinger's dirty tactics eventually rebounded on him, as they were fated to do so often during our eventful relationship.

At my trial, held in the grand courthouse in Orange complete with ornate stone frontage and decorative arches, William Bacon soon caved in under fierce cross-examination from Mr Lee, the barrister Jacky had secured for me. He insisted that he'd seen me participating in the robbery, even though the bushrangers who robbed him were wearing comforters over their faces and he was never closer than two hundred yards to me. However, he did admit, contrary to the statement he made in Forbes, that he did not know me personally at all and had only ever seen me a couple of times going about my cattle business in Lambing Flat.

The prosecution's case began to buckle, but when Ferguson changed his original story and finally admitted that I had *not* been present at the robbery, it collapsed altogether. Ferguson was one of the drivers and much closer to the action, which made him a more reliable witness than Bacon.

Pottinger's trump card turned out to be the joker.

To make matters worse for the prosecution, the two travellers who had been held up at the same time as the dray also failed to show. So, why did Pottinger's star witness change his story?

I later heard that the traps had spooked Ferguson into implicating me, but between my court appearances in Forbes and Orange he had been paid a visit by Gardiner himself. The Darkie had come up behind Ferguson as he sat at his supper, putting a couple of long-tailed notes next to his lamb chops. As Ferguson studied Her Majesty's portrait, Gardiner advised him to have them 'for afters' because they'd settle better in the stomach than a ball of lead. The traps were not the only ones who could spike a witness.

My barrister directed me to make my one and only statement. I stood in the dock, with traps on either side of me, and told the court my side of the story. 'Had I been allowed to call witnesses I would have been able to prove I was not one of the bushrangers,' was all I said. It was a tactic designed to cast doubt in the minds of the jurors, but by then it was a mere formality. Pottinger's conniving had already done our work for us.

The Judge went through the formality of dismissing the case against me, due to a lack of evidence, much to the disgust of a red-faced Pottinger who barged out of the courtroom. Through the heavy door he could be heard thundering out oaths and profanities, which did not announce him as the gentleman he claimed to be.

Outside the court, my brothers, Bill and Tommy, were there with Jacky to greet me. As I shook Jacky's hand solemnly, I felt a bit choked up. He had been a good friend throughout. 'Mateship' is what they called it at the diggings, but, as is the way with Australian men, you keep it simple. A handshake was enough to cover everything from a simple favour to the saving of a life.

'Thanks, mate,' I said.

'You'd do the same for me,' he said, his usual smile fixed to his face. As we headed to the Commercial Hotel for a drink, I realised he was no longer keeping step with me. Wondering where in the devil he'd sloped off to, I spotted him on the other side of the street stalking the ample figure of a stunned William Bacon. Catching up to him, Jacky whispered something in the fat man's ear, which caused him to behave in a highly agitated manner.

When Jacky returned, I threw the obvious question at him.

'What was that all about, then?'

'Oh, I just put the fear of God in him,' he said casually. '"Bacon," I says, "you are well named. One dark night we'll be round to fry yours."'

We all had a good laugh at that one.

'Aw, bugger it,' chuckled Jacky, wiping the tears of mirth out of his eyes. 'I couldn't help myself. That bloody pimp no more saw you there than we'll be seeing the Virgin Mary after we all get grogged up tonight. Come on, I've a thirst on me that would tempt the Pope.'

Unfortunately for me the matter didn't end there. A couple of days after my acquittal Jacky took me aside to warn me about the latest gossip doing the rounds.

'The traps were overheard in the pub saying that you had somehow tampered with the witnesses.' He looked at me, with a serious look in his eye. 'A crime they regard as far worse than the robbery, Ben.'

I felt the starch go out of me as that moment of truth hit me hard. I was not in the Gardiner gang, nor ever had been, but as far as the forces of law and order were concerned I was in it up to my armpits. I remembered what Jacky had said to me when he first saw me in the logs, 'There's no half-measures in these things. You're either in . . . or you're out.' I would have to make that decision very soon.

A few weeks after my release I had a visit from the Darkie at Sandy Creek. He sat with me on the veranda, put £50 on the table and held out his hand.

'That should cover your court expenses. I'm sorry you got dragged into this, Ben. It was not my intention.'

I took his hand and we shook on it.

'No hard feelings, Frank. But next time they'll have something to arrest me for.'

That comment caused him to pause, and look me straight in the eye.

'Then join us, Ben. Get even with those fuckin' traps and we'll lead them a merry dance into the bargain.' That rakish grin was so wide it filled the room, and the twinkle of Celtic devilry in his eyes made it seem as if we were just boys getting up to mischief rather than grown men putting nooses around their necks.

Although I shrugged my shoulders, trying to seem casual, I had already decided to throw my hand in with the Darkie. I was now out for revenge. And who better to go looking for it with than Darkie Gardiner. I grinned.

'What the hell. What better place to meet the man who ruined my life, than at the end of a gun.'

That night, I swore an oath of allegiance at McGuire's hut.

When I arrived, the Darkie, Gilbert and O'Meally were playing cards. The room was illuminated by a single tallow candle, whose flickering yellow light threw shadows onto the faces of the three men seated around the table. I knew every inch of my childhood mate, the broad-shouldered, crop-headed, scar-faced John O'Meally, but I had never met the Darkie's 'Lieutenant', the Canadian Johnny Gilbert, before that night.

He was about my own age, though with his boyish good looks, smooth, hairless face and long, girlish hair, which reached down past his collar, he could pass for someone much younger. He was slight of build and no more than five foot seven tall, but despite this he had a reputation as a rare fighter. Mind you, he'd have to be to dress as flash as he did, a habit he'd picked up from the Darkie.

Clothing was not only a symbol of personality and recognition amongst fellows, they were a way in which people could distinguish class. Being some years older, the Darkie preferred to dress like a country gent, me the flash stockman, and Gilbert was the city dandy.

He liked single-button silk jackets, white shirts, ribbon ties, which he combined with moleskins and highly polished Napoleon boots that, along with a cabbage tree hat, were his only concessions to the practicality of living in the bush – though, like me, he had decorated his hat with a red ribbon.

I watched as they silently dealt hand after hand of the Devil's picture cards, winning and losing without joy, loss or any kind of expression or comment, just accepting whatever hand fate dealt them, but still having the nerve to use a weak hand to call or bluff and take a big pot. I expected this was an indication of the profession I was about to enter and by joining them I was putting my soul and my destiny on the table and would have to play with the hand I was dealt. I looked round the table and asked myself why the rest of them were in the game.

That first night at Jacky's the Darkie told me he was in it because he had been betrayed and abandoned by his family. He felt the world owed him something and that he 'intended to take it any ways he had to'.

From what I knew of him, Johnny Gilbert could find no fault with the world. He was just an adventurer, a knight of old, born late. Long ago he might have been one of King Arthur's cavaliers. To him, the Darkie was made of the same chivalrous stuff.

I quietly asked O'Meally and, as always, when matters of pride or honour were mentioned, a strange, wild light appeared in those green eyes.

''Cause I was born Irish,' was his answer. As I guessed, he'd grown up with the burden of history weighing heavily on his soul. 'When I was a young fella, I used to lie in the grass outside our da's shanty and listen to the men singing all the old rebel songs. Used to bring a tear to me eye.'

Our da had spoken about such occasions. Although he maintained that he hated the Irish, on the first day of September every year he toasted the anniversary of the shooting of 'Bold' Jack Donohoe at Bringelly in 1830 and sang the old songs like a Dubliner. In New South Wales a man could be locked up for singing so-called 'treason ballads' and O'Meally's could have lost its licence, if it ever had one in the first place. It never had a licence and the seditious words of Francis MacNamara, or 'Frank the Poet' as he was known, were spoken with gusto to the trill of an Irish whistle. The Irish and the convicts had few enough champions and the bushrangers and their songs gave voice to the frustration of small people against the police, the squatters and the law. That bitter spirit had kept the Irish going for centuries and would ensure Australia would never be another England.

The Darkie looked up at me and smiled, as though he had heard my thoughts ricocheting round in my head. He broke the silence.

'G'day, Ben, you come to join us?' he said evenly shuffling the cards without looking at them, his fingers cutting and splitting the deck as deftly as any cardsharper. My Jack of Hearts was about to join O'Meally's Queen of Clubs, Gilbert's King of Diamonds and the Darkie's Ace of Spades in the great revolving pack. He called me to sit down and showed he meant business by staring straight at me and speaking so I might understand clearly what he was saying.

'Mate, this is like joining an army. We need to know we can trust each other and that if any of us ever squeaks to the traps the consequences will be dire.'

He left that threat hanging, but he knew we had all heard the rumour that he shot Johnny Connors, one of the 'Three Jacks' gang, for leaving Johnny Davis behind during a hot go with the traps. The Darkie had tasted the bitter fruits of treachery, cowardice and deceit and didn't hold with them.

The oath, in itself, was simple schoolboy stuff, but that night the hut bristled with menace and it was clear to all that simple though the words might be, they carried a deadly intent, if ever the oath was breached.

This was no game.

'I swear to be faithful to the Gardiner gang, to never run from a trap, to never leave a mate in trouble and to never give him up. If I do, I know the punishment and will accept it as just.'

With the razor-sharp point of his Bowie knife, the Darkie traced a bloody line down the inside of our palms, parallel to our life lines, to symbolise the new life we were beginning. Gardiner waited until a decent trickle of claret had run down his hand and pooled between his fingers before he looked me in the eye and held out his bloody hand.

'Welcome to the brotherhood, Ben.'

I looked at his outstretched hand for a split second or two, my mind racing. I knew I could still back away, but that once I took the Darkie's hand and repeated the oath I would lose my soul forever to the bushranging game and whatever devils had created them.

The tallow candle hissed and spluttered as rivulets of wax spilled onto the crude, wooden table. I looked into the Darkie's eyes. I knew I had reached the point of no return. I gripped the Darkie's hand hard, pressing my own bloodied palm into his until I was sure our blood had mingled.

That's how I got my start in the game. That June night at McGuire's in the year of 1862, Frank Gardiner and I joined hands, mixed our lifeblood and took a vow. Simple as that. Ben Hall, son to Ben and Eliza Hall, one-time farmer, husband to Biddy and father to Henry, disappeared.

In his place stood Ben Hall the bushranger. Part of a new family, a new brotherhood.

Part 2

DEATH

Chapter Nine

The Darkie was keen to blood me like a fighting cock. It was as though he was afraid I might change my mind. I might have been new to the bushranging game, but I was fair set on getting revenge on Pottinger who had branded me a criminal without justification. I also wanted to make enough money to start a new life in California.

To us Currency Lads, California was what China had been to the Irish bolters, except it really did exist. I knew the shipping lists and schedules off by heart. Ships left Newcastle bound for California almost every week and the passage was £25. The price of the ticket and enough to buy a bar were all we needed.

'I hear it's a grand place. Lots of our blokes went out to the Klondike and reckoned that America was the Promised Land, a place with no frontiers. A man can ride for weeks across green, fertile land, stake out his claim and live without hindrance. No traps come asking your name or accusing you of wrongdoing on account of your da's bad name. In fact no one knows your name,' I explained.

'Aye, and them Yankee boys saw the British off,' said O'Meally holding up a clenched fist, always the true Irish rebel.

'Even at this very minute they're fighting to stop the slaving,' added Gilbert.

'Well, if they've room for the blackfellas, they've room for us,' concluded the Darkie.

As most of our fathers had been slaves of a sort, there was a natural sympathy for that particular cause. The room went quiet as we all painted our own pictures of the paradise that awaited us over the sea in California.

We never had much schooling, but from newspapers and the well-read ne'er-do-wells who now wandered the Australian bush, we knew the Americans and French enjoyed liberties, such as equality and protection from unjust arrest and detention, denied to us by the British.

Having placed this vision of a new start in the forefront of their minds I put my idea to the 'council' that consisted of Gilbert, O'Meally and the Darkie. It occurred to me that bushrangers seemed content to live like dingos, scavenging on the edge of towns, living off scraps and the occasional juicy morsel. I had been hatching a bold plan and I decided now was the time to let the rest of them in on it.

'We need to pull off one big job that will set us all up for life,' I started.

'Queen Victoria has too many Beefeaters round her jewels, Ben,' the Darkie quipped, drawing a round of laughter from the others.

Bugger it, I thought. Throwing caution to the winds, I threw it fair and square into the arena. 'Then, why don't we do the next best thing and bail up the Eugowra gold escort?'

Everyone went silent. There was just the sound of Johnny O'Meally sucking on his clay pipe. I did notice that the Darkie was not wasting his time on shock or even surprise. He was intent on looking at all the faces around the table, taking stock of their reaction. After a moment, he cleared his throat and fixed me with a pair of sparkling black eyes.

'Strewth, Ben! There's no half-measures with you, is there? Why pick that one?'

'Because they're digging up gold like potatoes on Lambing Flat and the escort carries the biggest swag of gold and bank notes in the whole colony. It is only guarded by four traps, one up top with the driver and three inside.'

'Been doin' your homework, hey, Ben. How do you know all this?' demanded the Darkie, throwing a guarded look my way.

'Because I went down to Forbes and had a look,' I replied coolly. 'Every Sunday, the police make a great show of loading the strong-boxes into the coach in the courtyard at the back of the Albion pub, while the townsfolk eyeball them from the balcony above. You can even hear them discussing whether the escort is a 'big' or a 'light' one.

'Stupid bastards,' said O'Meally, baring his rotten teeth in an evil grin.

Sensing I had everyone's attention, I pushed on with my plan.

'Once they're clear of Eugowra they'd be easy meat for a well-organised ambush. You could pick your spot.'

'And which spot would you pick?' pressed the Darkie.

'The Eugowra Rocks,' I said without hesitation. 'You could hide an army behind them, and the track that runs past them is pretty crook, so they'd have to slow up just as they reach them.'

Gilbert's face flushed with excitement. 'But the traps might spring us,' he cautioned.

'Then we turn tail and lose 'em in the Nangar Ranges, which start behind the rocks. Plenty of cover. And it's a steep climb. We can breast it easy, but Pottinger's mob are no rough riders and their fat, old daisy kickers will give it up pretty quick.'

'Seems you've thought of everything,' muttered the Darkie, a sour note creeping into his voice. He spread out his hands in an open gesture and demanded, 'What d'ya think, boys? Should we take it on?'

The crop-haired O'Meally was obviously still running the odds through and asked cagily, 'How much loot d'ya reckon she'll be carryin'?'

'The escort returns are printed in the local papers each week and from those it's easy to figure out that a "big" shipment will be ten thousand in notes and five thousand ounces of gold . . . twenty to thirty thousand quid, or something like it and a "light" one maybe half that.'

No one spoke for a minute, then Johnny Gilbert let out a low whistle and muttered, 'It's a big pot, but it's risky . . .'

I was prepared for such objections and chimed in, 'No more risky than bailing up travellers on the open road where the traps know we operate, and ending up with a bullet in the back. They won't be expecting this.'

'Yeah, and it would be one in the eye for that bastard Pottinger,' said O'Meally.

'Bloody oath,' agreed Gilbert.

Gardiner, to my surprise, seemed to be feeling a bit upstaged and wore a smile like a shot fox. He didn't want to give himself away in front of the others, so he just shrugged his shoulders and made no comment.

Having put my bold scheme into action I sat back and let him direct operations. He was the cock after all. Despite my flush of enthusiasm for our new plan, I wasn't likely to forget who Frank Gardiner was – and what he was capable of.

Jacky's eyes near popped out of his head when I filled him in on the daring plan.

'Rob the gold escort! Bejesus, Ben. There's a drop o' the fighting Irish in ye, me boy,' he hooted, punching my arm proudly.

I held his gaze and said, 'I've not been much good to you these past few months, but I'll make it up to you, Jacky, you'll see. It'll be one back for that peacock Pottinger.'

Jacky nodded sagely.

I walked over to the holster and pistol, which had been hanging on a hook on the back of the kitchen door since I'd last popped that grog bottle in the back paddock. Lifting the old black leather holster off the hook, I removed the Colt, spun the chamber to check it was empty, strapped on the holster, stopping only to collect the box of shells from the cupboard before heading out to the paddock for some long overdue target practice. It might come in handy.

Gardiner set about recruiting some fresh faces for the job, which would need more than four men. He had already approached another of my boyhood mates 'Flash' Dan Charters. I heard he also had a yarn with John Bow, a stockman on Wentworth Gully station, Henry Manns, a bullocky, and Alex Fordyce who worked behind the bar at O'Meally's.

A meeting was arranged at Jacky's. The Darkie and Gilbert were already there when I arrived and Jacky was packing the hired hand, Tom Richards, who had been a butcher with Gardiner and Fogg, out of the way before the others arrived. Gilbert frowned when he saw the pistol at my hip.

'Nice piece,' he said, a strong trace of the Yankee still in his voice. 'Ain't that a Colt Navy six-shooter?'

'That's right,' I said. Gilbert looked quizzically over at the Darkie, his eyebrows raised in a quirk.

'Say, Frank, didn't you used to have one just like that?'

Gardiner shrugged.

'I did, but it must've fallen out of me belt,' he said. His black eyes flickered in my direction for a moment, a strangely deflected glance that to the casual onlooker would signify nothing. No more was said. It might have been my imagination, but in that brief pause I felt a strange current passing between the three of us. *Had it been the Darkie's own hand that had deliberately left that gun on the road for me to find? Or had it been some other devilish, more sinister force at work? Had his meeting with Jacky McGuire, which had led him to me, been as fortuitous as it appeared at the time?*

If the Darkie sensed these unspoken questions he didn't let it affect his usual poise and authority. A moment later, as he began to discuss aspects of the job, I felt a bit sheepish for ever thinking such nonsense.

'I reckon it would be a mistake to tell "Flash Dan" and the other three *exactly* what we're up to,' mused the Darkie. 'They might baulk and I don't want loose lips blabbing our business around the district. We keep our powder dry till the last moment. Tell them only what they need to know. Agreed?'

The rest of the gang turned up at ten-minute intervals and agreed to help us give Pottinger 'one in the eye'. Only those in the Gardiner gang and Jacky knew what that really meant.

Before we set off, Gilbert and Charters were sent to town to buy some of the stuff we would need for the job – shotguns and ammo, a tomahawk, powder, percussion caps, blacking for our hands and faces, comforters and scarves.

We started for Eugowra on June 14, 1862, camping overnight by Mandagery Creek, a few miles from the town of Eugowra and the rocks where we would set the ambush. The Darkie woke us nice and early.

'For breakfast we'll feast on tinned salmon, courtesy of Mr Johnny Gilbert who lifted them from a store at Uar station. And after today we might be having salmon for breakfast every morning,' he added with a knowing smile.

There was a smattering of laughter and handclaps, but none except the gang knew what really lay behind his comments. Spirits were high, but still the Darkie held off telling the others any more of our real plan. The wary expression in his eyes and stern face said, *Wait*.

While they ate their breakfasts, I rode the fifteen miles back into Forbes. The Darkie had chosen me to go back to check that there were no nasty surprises, and to try to find out whether the escort was 'big' or 'light'. If it was a 'big' one, we couldn't possibly carry away five thousand ounces or over three hundred and fifty pounds of gold. Some would have to be planted in a safe place and collected later.

By the time the party of eight local traps started their Sabbath ritual of carrying the strongboxes containing the gold and money across the road from the Oriental Bank to the rear courtyard of the Albion Hotel, I was up on the balcony with a beer in hand and a good view.

Right on midday, the Ford & Mylechrane Company coach bound for Orange came clattering up Rankin Street. When it reached the Albion Hotel it turned sharp left and passed under the balcony of the wide-fronted hotel, through the archway and into the rear courtyard.

From my earlier research I knew that Sergeant Condell and the three armed constables – Haviland, Moran and Rafferty – would load the gold here with the help of the local police who brought it from the bank. I stayed as close to the balcony rail as I could and strained to hear the conversation below over the aimless chatter about cows and taxes that was going on around me.

'What've you got for us today, Constable,' called Condell as he climbed down from the box seat next to the driver and flapped at the red dust that had collected on the front of his smart, blue tunic.

'You'll be travelling light today, Sergeant,' replied a mutton-chopped Forbes constable, wiping a slick of sweat from his brow. I winced as I heard the news. I had been hoping for a big escort that would set us all up like Lords in California. Knowing I would have an hour's start while the driver and the horses were fed, watered and the gold loaded, I drained my beer and made my way back to Willy. To make sure I wasn't seen, I took the road less travelled through the country and arrived back at the camp just as everyone was preparing to move out.

The ones 'in the know' crowded around, anxious. Not wishing to attract attention I held up a beef shank and a bottle of Old Tom I had bought at the Albion to explain my sudden absence and said casually, 'No surprises. She's running on time, there's four traps with the gold, but the escort is travelling "light".'

'Shit!' growled O'Meally.

'There'll still be a good pay in it for us all,' said the Darkie patiently.

'We've come too far to turn back. We go on with it.' He turned away and called out to the others who stood around in small groups.

'Ben's back with the supplies, let's saddle up.' A sudden speeding up of my heart came with the realisation that *We were on. We were actually going to bail up the gold escort.*

We all rode the couple of miles up to the Eugowra Rocks that rose abruptly and steeply out of the gently rolling countryside. The escort would travel very close to the large rocks strewn next to the rutted road providing us with plenty of cover. In case we needed to make a quick getaway, we tethered and short hobbled the horses in a stand of stunted cypress and gum trees, a few hundred yards from where we planned to attack.

We slid down a steep slope on our arses and came out behind a smooth, mountainous lump of rock. It stood about twelve feet high, about twenty wide and was large enough to conceal our entire group. This cathedral of large rounded boulders, which looked as though they had been placed by some divine hand, was a sacred site for the blackfellas. The large rock we stood behind, which looked like a stray marble that had rolled away from the others, was called '*Coonbong*', or '*Dead Man*'. I hoped that wasn't a bad omen. I remembered Billy Dargin telling me that blackfellas believed all large rocks were sacred because the souls of warriors lived inside them. There were other smaller, assorted rocks scattered in front of Coonbong, which meant the coach would turn a blind bend as it approached us.

Having surveyed the ambush site thoroughly, we sat and waited in the dappled shade of a big gum behind Coonbong. The Darkie decided it was time to come clean about our purpose here. Dapper as always, clad in a cream Panama jacket, crimson waistcoat, sported by the Colonial gentry, white shirt with necktie, he stood up on a small rock, hooked his thumbs into his waistcoat pockets and surveyed his forces like a General before a battle. Every eye turned towards him. Pausing for dramatic effect, he looked at the ground for a moment, scuffed the red earth with the toe of his boot, lifted his head and announced in a loud clear voice, 'Boys, up till now I've been keeping you in the dark about what we're up to. It's time to let you in on it.'

Knowing he had their full attention, he carried on smoothly. 'Truth is, boys . . . we've planned a nice little surprise for Sir Frederick Pottinger, one that's guaranteed to wipe that sneer of his off his mug, permanent like. The bastard has taken diabolical liberties and needs to be taught a lesson he'll never forget.'

This brought shouts of agreement.

Holding up a hand for hush, Gardiner went on, 'Boys, today we're going to write ourselves into the history books. When those clever buggers get around to writing the annals of this colony's short history they're going to have to put in a deed so daring that they'll speak of us in the same breath as the heroes of bygone days.'

Men started glancing at each other searching for clues as to what was going on. The Darkie was full into his stride. Pulling his gold fob watch out of his waistcoat pocket, he looked at it, his brows drawn in thought. Gesturing westwards over towards the Forbes to Orange road, he said, 'In about an hour from now the weekly gold escort is going to pass this very spot.' Bringing his hands together, he smiled like a magician revealing his best trick. 'Boys, we're going to bail it up and live the rest of our lives in clover like English gentlemen!'

There was a stunned silence amongst those not in the know. Judging by their shocked expressions, they hadn't imagined for a moment that when they had agreed to help the Darkie, they had unwittingly made themselves accessories in the commissioning of a crime of this magnitude. The red-haired John Bow spoke up first. He nervously patted his thinning hair.

'Jesus, Frank, the gold escort, I don't know if I'm game for that.'

Alex Fordyce, the solid-looking barman from O'Meally's, chimed in, 'Yair, robbery under arms is a serious business. We could all swing for this.'

The Darkie nodded, as if he had been expecting objections.

'Anyone else feel like this? Speak now.'

Dan Charters raised a trembling hand, hardly able to meet anyone's eye. With a thinly veiled look of disgust, the Darkie spat on the ground.

'Ya bloody mongrels! You're no good here, only worrying about your own skins. Thought I'd picked some real men for the job. Seems I was mistaken.' Turning on his heel he flicked a finger in Charters' direction. 'Hook it. Keep an eye on the horses and let us know when that escort is on its way.'

As a grateful Flash Dan clambered up the rocks to relative safety, the Darkie fixed his stare on Henry Manns, the last of the group.

'Henry?' he said.

Manns just shrugged his shoulders, and grudgingly said, 'I'm game, I suppose.'

This was a dangerous situation. Half the gang were wavering and the coach wasn't far off. We had to hit 'em hard and finish it quick because they'd fight back, if we gave them the chance.

Slowly and deliberately, the Darkie unhooked his thumbs from the pockets of his waistcoat, unbuttoned the bottom button of his coat drawing it aside like a stage curtain to reveal a couple of pairs of pistols stuffed into the belt around his waist. He let his right hand hover near the pearl handle of his Tower pistol, almost inviting a challenge to his authority. With an ugly sneer on his face, he growled, 'I'll say this once. No one's going anywhere. The escort's on its way and we're gonna rob it. What's more, mates, every man jack of us is gonna be in it, or else.'

Gone was the amiable Darkie. We could see a man with all the attributes of his deadly calling, intent on business. And he meant every word of it.

He shot a dark glance round the silent men squatting or standing in the dappled shade. 'We're all in this together, and we don't abandon our mates. And just in case anyone has it in mind to run for it when the shooting starts, think about what happened to Johnny McGuiness and Johnny Connors.

'As you know from local gossip, those two mongrels left their mate, Johnny Davis, to be captured by the traps. I caught up with Connors on the plains outside of Forbes. He turned white as a snowflake when he saw me step out of the bush into his camp, that he did, now.'

Knowing he'd got our full attention, the Darkie looked off into the distance, seeing God knows what in the wide expanse of scrub and sun-baked red earth before him. Again, the quirky smile, the tilt of the black moustaches. Dread curling in the pit of my empty belly, I had no choice but to listen while Gardiner related how he had slain the luckless Johnny Connors.

'"*How did you find me?*" Connors asked, so I told him straight,' intoned the Darkie, narrowing his eyes against the glare thrown up from the rock hard ground. '"*As lies will catch out the liar,*" I told him, "*betrayal will catch out the betrayer.*"

'I threw him a pistol and told him to meet me out on the plain. "Fair fight, Johnny," says I . . . "man to man." So out we goes, measured off twenty paces each. Even let him fire at me first, I did. Silly bugger missed, though.' Reliving the moment, the Darkie pulled a pistol out of his belt and took aim down the barrel. Then he went on with his story. 'First shot took him right through the heart, second through the head. Left 'im for the dingos.' The Darkie eyed us for a moment or two, then announced in the same low menacing voice, 'When the escort arrives I'll step out first from behind the rock and bail it up. The rest of you follow one by one in short order. If anyone retreats under fire, the man behind him is to shoot him on the spot. If anyone fails to obey this order I'll shoot them myself.'

Having stiffened our spines with those well-chosen words, he stepped down and ordered Henry Manns to unpack the meat shank and a bottle of gin I'd bought at the Albion Hotel.

I shivered when I recalled how he'd asked me that first night I met him if I'd ever betrayed him. I was glad I'd come clean.

No one was hungry, though the Old Tom proved a good salve for our frayed nerves. Bow, in particular, was tugging hard at the neck of the bottle. There was an air of quiet tension, as we all prepared ourselves for what was ahead. After unsuccessfully trying to take a few mouthfuls of meat and bread, I lay back in the grass to take what warmth I could from the winter sun. Shading my face with my hands lest my eyes betray my thoughts, I took a few deep breaths and tried to gather my thoughts.

The Darkie's warning had reminded us that this might well turn out to be a matter of life and death. The back of my neck prickled as I thought about the possibility that if I froze during the bail-up one of our own might be ordered to pop me for cowardice.

'Penny for 'em, mate,' said a voice close by. I looked up and could make out the rough outline of a man against the bright azure sky.

'Henry Manns,' he said, as I sat up and returned his handshake.

'G'day Henry. Ben's the name.'

'Hall, I know. You're the bloke who dreamed up this caper,' he said as he sat down next to me.

'Caper, that'd be right,' I said, picking a few burrs off my clothes. 'I can't believe it was only a week ago we were talking about it and here we are, waiting for the gold coach from Eugowra.

And maybe six kinds of Hell to follow.'

Henry's slim build and smooth, fresh-faced complexion told me Manns was not yet out of his teens. I was only twenty-five, but felt like Britannia next to Henry's Australia.

'You must have done a lot of robberies?' he pressed, his eyes shining with excitement. I dropped my gaze, shaking my head as I studied the toes of my boots.

'No, just one,' I admitted. 'And that was by accident. I sort of got caught up in it, then one thing led to another.'

Nothing would dampen his enthusiasm.

'The Darkie thinks a lot of you, he's always telling me that I could be like you.'

'Does he now?' I looked over in Gardiner's direction, and there he was with that sunny smile fixed to his face, calmly watching us.

Turning back to Henry I asked, 'What about you? Is this your first job?'

'Yeah. Funny thing is I've known Johnny Gilbert since I was a boy and one day the Darkie and Johnny happened to bail up my dray. Said they admired my pluck, that they were going to give that cove Pottinger a coating and wanted to know if I was game? I didn't have a horse, but Johnny Gilbert got me one and so I tagged along.'

As Henry finished his tale the uneasy feeling that I had when I learned my Navy Colt once belonged to the Darkie again washed over me. I could see the sly grin on the Darkie's face as he handed me the reins of that packhorse on the day of the Bacon dray robbery. *Was he the great manipulator who recruits the angry and vulnerable to his cause? Did he leave that pistol for me to find and then draw me into the game, or was he some Dark Prince just granting our secret heart's desires; adventure, excitement, money and the chance to get even?*

Whatever the truth I knew it was far too late and too dangerous to pull out now. I slumped back onto the hard dry ground and put my sweat-stained bush hat over my eyes.

The escort guarding the gold consignment from Eugowra was now well into its stride. The coach, sporting the smart red Ford & Mylechrane livery, was drawn by a team of four horses and piloted by an experienced driver, John Fegan. Sergeant Sanderson sat next to him in the box seat. It had been an uneventful journey and the three traps inside the coach were dozing like cats in the warm winter sun flooding the coach. Their smart new Calisher and Terry breach-loading rifles were cradled loosely on their laps. They also had six-shot Navy Colt revolvers in the holsters strapped to their waists.

While the minutes ticked by, every sinew and nerve in our bodies straining to catch the first sound of the approaching escort, the Darkie kept us occupied by making us carefully load and re-load the guns to guard against damp powder and accidental misfires. We used revolver balls in the shotguns to ensure maximum effect from each spray.

We all changed into the shiny red Crimea shirts to help disguise our true identities. The Darkie stripped off his shirt revealing a hard, tanned body, honed by hard yakka in the quarry on Cockatoo Island, and white ribbons of scar tissue carved into his skin by blade and bullet.

Bow and O'Meally tried to blacken their faces with charcoal, but came off looking more like those American minstrels than bushrangers. It raised a laugh, in spite of the tension ricocheting amongst us.

'Bugger it,' said Gilbert, sticking out his bottom lip. 'No way I'm going to take on the traps lookin' like a music-hall turn. It ain't dignified,' he said in that quiet Yankee drawl.

We used red comforters to hide our faces. Only our eyes were visible – our noses and mouths and rest of our features distorted by the sleek fit of the woollen scarfs.

'Quiet!' spat out Gardiner, suddenly, fiercely. 'Stop yer yakking.'

He laid flat on the ground, his ear pressed to it, listening for long moments. He raised his black head, a fatal smile back on his face.

'Come on, my little beauty,' he said softly, to no one in particular.

Looking up to the smooth, rounded rocks to where 'Flash Dan' was keeping lookout we saw him windmilling his arms frantically.

Suddenly, the peace was shattered by the thunder of approaching hooves and the rattle of wheels, which sent a flurry of white cockatoos spiralling out of nearby trees, their raucous shrieks echoing alarmingly round the rocks. Even though our faces were covered, the shock was visible in everyone's eyes. A few oaths escaped from underneath the red comforters. *The bloody escort must be early!*

Hearts thumping, we grabbed our guns and glanced over to the Darkie for instructions, but he still had that smile on his face.

'Stand easy, boys! False alarm.'

Daring a peek around the corner of the huge rock, I was dumb-founded to see two drays, pulled by lumbering oxen, slowly coming down the dusty road.

The Darkie narrowed his eyes, 'Always be prepared for the unex-pected, friends. The trick is to think fast on your feet, and turn it to your advantage.' He snapped his fingers. 'Here's what we'll do. We'll use the drays to create an obstruction on the road, slow the Eugowra coach right down as it approaches. They'll never pick it as an ambush, not in a million years.'

'Johnny!' The growled command was all that was needed. Unquestioningly, the faithful Johnny Gilbert followed him. The Darkie had that effect on people.

A few moments later we heard him shout.

'Bail up!'

There was a creak as the wooden block brake was applied and a ragged chorus of 'Whoah' as teamsters slowed the steady tread of their team of ponderous beasts. We heard the Darkie order them to position their drays across the road smartish.

'But the gold escort's due . . . it's just half an hour behind,' came the cries of protest.

'Back them up! Back them up as you're bid or you're dead!'

There was an agitated snorting and rattle of harnesses as the teamsters manoeuvred the heavy carts into position across the width of the road. Amid the furore the voice of one of the drivers called out excitedly, his mouth tripping over the words as it tried to keep up with his brain.

'Bloody oath, it's Darkie Gardiner. Ye're after bailing up the gold escort, ain'tcha?'

The Darkie, annoyed that he had been rumbled so easily, growled back at the driver. 'You've got too much to say for a bloody bullocky. Move it. Try anything fancy and I'll put a plug in ya.'

Just a mile away, the escort came on unaware of what was waiting ahead. John Fegan, who'd done this run many times, had his team humming along. Its rolling wheels threw up a trail of dust as they sped down the hill, past the Fat Lamb pub and over the stone bridge at Mandagery Creek. Once through the village of Eugowra they headed due east out onto the wide brown plains towards

Orange with the green-topped Nangar Ranges dominating the horizon to the south, the rugged peaks of the House of Lords Mountains to the north.

Knowing the moment of truth was at hand, the Darkie stood up on his little rock for the second time that day and assembled us for a final benediction, which would give us the courage and fortitude to carry the day. The winter sun was setting behind him and was slanting into our eyes as he spoke. He brought out a battered tome of a Lord Byron, which I heard he always carried in his saddlebag. Though the pages looked well thumbed, I never once saw him read it, but he would recite his verse and legend to us after a few stiff nobblers. I think he fancied us as a band of the bard's Hell-bound heroes.

Turning to a dog-eared page he'd marked by folding back the corner, he spoke in a loud, clear voice:

Hereditary bondsmen! know ye not
Who would be free themselves must strike the blow?

As he spoke the setting sun touched the treetops and splintered, showering him in shards of orange light, which seemed to give his quotation a prophetic air.

But now there was no time at all to savour it, or to even consider what we would write on the blank page of history that now lay open before us. *The next half-hour would tell.*

A 'cooee' and an agitated wave from Charters alerted us. A moment later the rumble of the escort galvanised us into action.

Jumping up, we cocked our rifles and got into our rehearsed positions, my body was awkwardly stiff with dread. I pressed my face up against the rock's smooth, cool bulk, closed my eyes and silently summoned up its ancient warrior spirit, as the Darkie issued his final orders.

'Fire on my signal, boys. And, remember no bloody names. Loose tongues lead straight to the gallows.'

The rest of his words were drowned out by the clatter of hooves, the rattling of steel-rimmed wagon wheels on rutted earth and the hammering in my ears as my heart beat out a tattoo on my ribcage.

Safely crouched behind Coonbong, we were still able to hear the shouts and oaths of the driver, Fegan, as they rounded the blind bend and saw the drays across the road.

'What are these bastards up to? Move it, move out of the way! Escort coming through!'

But the bullockies, who had been ordered to lie under their drays, stayed put. Fegan cursed some more as the coach was forced to slow down to avoid running into them. He had only two choices, the first to draw the gold escort to a complete halt in front of the slewed drays while they tried to clear the road, wasting time, making the escort late, the second was to keep going and somehow to manoeuvre his way around it. There was no time to think. Although Fegan still hadn't picked it as an ambush, all his instincts and experience told him not to draw up, to maintain the momentum of the escort and its cargo and get to their destination on time.

To detour around the drays, the coach had to slow down before attempting to leave the hard surface of the dusty road and veer off left into the bush. Inside the coach, the sleepy traps were jolted out of their slumber by the yell of the driver and the grinding of the brakes.

The moment the Darkie heard the clatter of wheels and hooves change as the escort left the road and went on the soft grass, he let out a great roar and leapt out from behind the rocks and stood in front of the oncoming coach.

'Bail up, you bastards! Bail up, I tell you.'

Up in the box seat, a startled-looking Sergeant Condell immediately reached for his pistol. Inside the coach, the dazed traps fumbled with the safety catches on their carbines, but before any of them could take the initiative, the Darkie yelled, 'Fire!'

His command was answered by a ragged, but effective volley of gunfire. The force of the impact seemed to halt the coach in its tracks, and then there was a shattering of glass and splintering of wood as the bullets found their mark. One bullet took Condell in the side, and almost threw him off his perch.

Inside the three constables yelled like sleeping men who had awoken to find they had been buried alive in their graves. They felt the deadly draught of the bullets as they smashed through the flimsy wooden shell of the coach past them, showering them with razor-sharp shards of glass. The coach lurched from side to side making it impossible for those inside to stand up long enough to get out or return fire. With an agonised yell, one of the traps fell onto the floor as he took a bullet in the groin.

'Help me!' he screamed at his shocked fellow officers as he watched the red river of blood race across the floor of the coach.

The gunfire, which rumbled and rolled round the surrounding hills like peals of thunder, panicked the horses and caused them to career back across the road dislodging Sergeant Condell, who had suffered a superficial chest wound. Fegan, who felt a bullet pass through the crown of his hat and part his hair, followed him down and gamely tried to hang onto the reins, eventually being dragged across the ground.

A runaway team is hard to control and their terrified charge only ended when the front wheel of the coach hit one of the small, solid rocks scattered around the base of Coonbong. There was a sickening crunch as the impact reduced the wheel to matchwood, forcing the twisted wood and metal to plough a deep furrow into the parched ground as the momentum carried the vehicle forward unsteadily. The coach teetered then, slowly flipped over onto its side with a spectacular crash, dragging the wild-eyed horses off their feet and throwing them into a flailing heap of horseflesh.

The rattle of gunfire ceased abruptly.

'God Almighty!' Bow whistled in awe above the bedlam of the neighing and whinnying of injured horses, the shouts and curses of the wounded and of men still trapped inside the coach.

Under cover of the mayhem and a cloud of dust, the traps were attempting to re-group. Shaken by the impact, but thankful to be alive, Haviland helped the wounded Moran escape out of the back of the coach to the cover of some trees on the other side of the road. Condell opened up with his pistol as he scurried from behind the upturned coach, but was forced to dive for cover behind a tree as his fire was returned with interest.

Haviland and Moran had kept hold of their rifles and lent Condell some support, which is more than can be said of the third constable, Rafferty, who needed no invitation to take to the bush.

The tree Condell was hiding behind was almost felled by the force of the volley directed at him. Deciding things were far too hot for him, he yelled out, before crashing off into the undergrowth after Rafferty.

'Gold be buggered! I'm off, stripes and all.'

Even with their new, shiny firearms, the last two traps, realising they were now the last line of defence, decided that ten bob a day wasn't worth dying for and followed their swift sergeant's example.

That left Fegan, who had bravely stayed with his horses even in the middle of the crossfire. In spite of the danger to himself, he was trying to cut the horses free from the tangle of bridles and harness. As seven masked figures swarmed and converged on him, I could see the anxiety written large across his lean, sunburned face. He carefully stepped away from the horses and slowly raised his hands over his head.

'Don't shoot!' he pleaded.

The Darkie jerked his thumb over his shoulder, 'Go on, hook it!'

Fegan stood his ground, gestured over his shoulder with a grimy thumb towards the direction of the horses, mutely requesting time to set them to rights. A pair of the beasts were still neighing shrilly, unable to free themselves.

The Darkie nodded curtly and waved him on.

After seeing to the rest of his charges Fegan needed no more encouragement and plunged off into the bush, along with the blokes from the drays that Johnny Gilbert had turned loose, leaving us to start the plunder in earnest.

We fell upon the upended carcass of the coach like scavengers on carrion. We recovered the four strongboxes, then ratted through the mailbags as we looked for the valuables and money that were often sent in letters.

The Darkie checked our guns and the next thing I saw he was standing over the redheaded John Bow, who could barely sit upright. The Darkie lifted up Bow's rifle and snarled, 'Bastard! You didn't fire a shot.'

'I'm sorry, Frank,' slurred Bow. He'd obviously gone too hard at the Old Tom. The Darkie caught him with a short jab to the jaw, which was enough to put him on his back.

'Bloody useless, you and that other coward,' he said, pointing the gun at Charters, 'will be on short rations.'

The Darkie, while elated at our spectacular success and the speed at which we dispatched the traps, was anxious to get off the road and on our way as quickly as possible. He knew it wouldn't take the traps long to reach the nearest station and raise the alarm.

We used the little tomahawks to smash the locks of the strong-boxes and wrenched the lids open.

Inside lay small canvas bags in neat rows. They might have been compact, but by God they were deceptively heavy. One was ripped open to reveal the masses of gold nuggets and smaller grains of gold dust with which we would all prepare for our prosperous futures in California. I had seen the odd bit of gold during my visits to Lambing Flat, but had never clapped eyes on such a haul.

The magical spell the gold had cast over us was broken by a shout from Gilbert. He had ripped open some larger bags and was brandishing a fistful of banknotes all of which bore the likeness of Queen Victoria.

'God bless her!' shouted Gilbert triumphantly, and with that the cheeky Canadian planted a smacker on our sainted sovereign, then, accompanied by hoots of pent-up laughter, proceeded to fan his arse with a few hundred pounds worth of currency.

At the urging of the Darkie to 'get on with it, and stop mucking around', we passed over the mailbags and divided the rest of the loot into saddlebags. We strung them over the capable shoulders of two of the blinkered escort horses before making our way to the stand of trees where our own horses were tethered.

'I'll be happier once we get back into the woods and head for home,' said an anxious Dan Charters.

As we climbed into our saddles and prepared to move out, I turned and looked back at the carnage. In the dying light, the smashed bullet-riddled coach lay like the carcass of some great beast that had been felled in its tracks. The doors were torn off their hinges, the three remaining wheels twisted at strange angles like splayed limbs. Canvas mailbags, which had been dragged out and ransacked, were strewn across the ground like entrails, discarded letters and papers fluttered over the scene stirred up by a cool evening breeze. A heavy smell of rain hung in the air.

'We're riding in on the Devil's own tide until daybreak,' called the Darkie. 'Let's make the best of it.'

Chapter Ten

And so we rode through the rain-lashed night to Mount Wheogo, where we intended to split the rations and go our separate ways. Despite his boast that he knew the back road home blindfolded, Charters had us up and down every bluff and gully, riding into fences at every turn.

To ward off the night chill we stopped for food and a nip of the grog, which Charters fetched from his sister's station. Our perseverance was rewarded just before dawn. We stopped as we came within sight of Mount Wheogo's brooding rise, some distance away across the plains. Its pinnacle was still cloaked in the black of night, but its base was tinged with a deep blue and swaddled in early morning mist, a common feature of these parts where the dew lay heavy on the ground. It appeared as though Mount Wheogo sat in the clouds like some fabled mountain. It was our sanctuary, our heartland, our castle's keep.

From our telegraphs we learned that the exhausted traps who had fled the escort found their way to Clements' station and raised the alarm. The station owner, Hanbury Clements, rode as fast as he could to Forbes and caught Inspector Pottinger at Barrack Hill just as he was preparing for bed.

Pottinger was not often lost for words, but it was reported that his eyes glazed over and he stood like a village idiot in his state of partial undress for fully a minute before he suddenly came to life, and seized the messenger by the lapels.

'What did you say, man?'

'They robbed the Eugowra gold escort. They got the gold. It's gone,' repeated Clements wresting his clothing from the Inspector's white-knuckled grip.

'How much did they get?' Pottinger demanded, his face turning a fancy shade of red.

'According to your troopers, about fourteen thousand pounds.' The policeman put his hands to his head. The shock of the news had banished any thought of sleep from his mind. Gathering his wits about him, he barked at Clements to raise his sergeant immediately, then slammed the front door and took the stairs two at a time.

As he frantically pulled on his tunic, his blue serge trousers and leather Wellington boots, his mind raced as he tried to make a plan.

His superiors had charged him with putting these buggers down and restoring public confidence. That these poorly organised, raggedy-arsed opportunists could have pulled off such an audacious raid was hard to believe.

Who was pulling their strings? he thought grimly as he rammed his hat on his head, sweeping up his firearm on his way out.

Within an hour, a mounted patrol consisting of eleven troopers, Billy Dargin and another blacktracker, a couple of civilian volunteers and the public-spirited Clements were ready for the off.

At the same time as we were completing our westward journey, scaling the heights of Mount Wheogo, the patrol was heading east to the scene of the crime, hoping that we would have been stupid enough to hang around to gloat over our victory.

The news of the robbery was received by some in the colony with anger and dismay, with secret glee by others. The squatters' press raged and rumbled: 'Gardinerism has been allowed, by inept police work, to become a grand organisation.' But local journalists pointed out that the way in which the gold was transported was inadequate and only wondered why it had not happened earlier, describing it as 'an invitation to crime . . . a locomotive advertisement to villains to avail themselves of a splendid harvest'.

Seeking to limit the damage, and restore the public confidence in the force, the Colonial Minister, Charles Cowper, made a belated announcement stating that in future armed police patrols consisting of eleven troopers would accompany all gold shipments. Mounted police reinforcements had been sent west to help apprehend the escort robbers.

*

Whilst the authority players readied themselves for the next act, the escort coach was righted and made roadworthy. Those who saw its shell wondered how no lives had been lost.

At Eugowra Rocks, Pottinger at the head of the patrol leaned back in the saddle and scratched his beard. Heavy rain had washed out any tracks, even Billy Dargin couldn't pick up the trail.

'Sorry, boss. No good,' the experienced blacktracker said with a shrug of the shoulders. Pottinger sighed, running through the flimsy trail of hard evidence left by the robbers. The witnesses saw nothing, the bullockies, whose drays were used as a diversion, thought it was Gardiner who bailed them up, but didn't see his face.

Pottinger fumed. He knew in his bones Gardiner's lot were responsible. *Who in hell else could it be?* No one else in the Lachlan had the brazen cheek or organisation to pull it off. He shifted uncomfortably and tried to put himself in their shoes, think himself into the skulls of the damned wastrels. *These wild colonial boys had two choices*, he mused. *Either head back to the Weddin Mountains, lie low, pretend nothing had happened while the authorities ran themselves into the ground looking, or make a run for the Victorian border. Which one would he choose if he were smart, like Gardiner? Stay or go?*

His course of action decided, he lifted his arm and waved his patrol closer, the rain dripped off his hat as he leaned forward so they could hear him over the scudding wind.

'Get some rest. Provision up. We'll be moving out at dawn, five sharp. Victoria's a long way off.'

There were groans as they moved off. Pottinger had already proved he was no terror to evildoers, only to his own men. He was apt to blunder in without thinking and act with a heavy hand, as though he was still in England.

'The bloody bushrangers will be tucked up in bed, whilst we're on this wild-goose chase,' said one trap bitterly, as a fresh squall of rain forced him to draw his already rain-soaked cape tighter round his shoulders.

Meanwhile, the other patrol, led by Senior Sergeant Sanderson, headed north for the Weddin Mountains.

We chose the bosom-shaped Mount Wheogo as our rallying point because, at 1,600 feet, it offered a commanding view of the wide, treeless plains surrounding us, and its steepness made it difficult for a raiding party to surprise us. But the rain, which had followed us westwards from Eugowra, shrouded the higher reaches of the Weddin Mountains and Mount Wheogo with a thick fog. Our mistake was staying there too long after committing the biggest robbery in this colony's history.

Up on Wheogo I got to know Henry Manns a bit better. We talked about our plans for the future. We had both been nervous about bailing up the escort and were relieved no one had been killed. Now we could look forward to the future.

'I'll go down to Victoria with Johnny and his brother Charley. We're gonna buy a nice spread and raise fat cattle.'

'It's California for me,' I told him. 'The wife left me for another bloke and I reckon I need a clean slate.'

'Looks like the Darkie is havin' some woman trouble himself,' Henry ventured in a low voice nodding over at a vexed-looking Darkie.

'Well, she is a Walsh,' I muttered darkly.

Kitty and the Darkie were going off to start a new life together. She was the flightiest of the three sisters and even when the 'telegraphs' warned us that the traps were combing the area for us, she refused to leave on the back of a horse. Kitty was a lady and would only leave in a buggy. Whoever said that bushrangers only demand your money or your life, but women want both had it dead set. The Darkie refused to leave without her, so, instead of changing horses and pushing on to the safety of Terrible Hollow, we made camp on top of Mount Wheogo in a swirling, drizzly haze where we were cut off both from the outside world and all earthly reason.

Warrigal Walsh was very much to the fore fetching and carrying, as directed by the Darkie, who snared him like he did me. Warrigal was made of stern stuff, hated the traps and was fiercely loyal. He was charged with finding the pumpkin carriage that would transport Cinderella to the ball.

The Darkie kept his fidgety troops in check for two days, but on the Wednesday Gilbert and Henry Manns approached the Darkie. It was Gilbert, who knew the best and worst of the Darkie, who delivered the message.

'Frank, Henry and I want out. It's bloody madness, sitting up here waiting for the traps to come along and pick us off, an' all for a flirty bit o' skirt. Let's split the winnings, go our separate ways and lay low for a bit, just like we planned.'

In a rare display of emotion, the Darkie looked at Gilbert on the point of tears.

'Johnny, I can't leave without her.'

Gilbert agreed in his quiet, calm way.

'I know, Frank. She's got you in a twitch and you're not thinking straight. No woman's worth a man's freedom, you said so yourself. An' she sure as hell ain't worth ours. That's sayin' it plain, Frank. No offence.' The Darkie, who had listened to what Gilbert had to say, just nodded, a sullen look on his face as if leaving were some sort of a betrayal.

The mood quickly shifted from agitation to excitement as we hoisted the canvas bags out of the saddlebags. We'd not opened them since we packed them at Eugowra, as we'd been constantly on the verge of riding out.

With £3,700 in banknotes and 2,719 ounces of gold at about £4 an ounce we estimated our haul to be worth around £15,000. The escort may have been 'light', but we'd still all be off to California with a roll of soft as thick as our swags. But using a spoon and a wobbly old set of kitchen scales to measure out the rations, while being buffeted by fierce squalls of wind and rain, proved a problem. By crowding round the scales we made a fine windbreak and got a good view of the division of spoils. A stray gust of wind was a costly extravagance none of us could afford.

After much weighing and re-weighing, the split was finally to everyone's satisfaction. There were eight packages weighing 22 lbs each.

Gilbert, Manns and Bow packed their saddlebags and were soon ready for the off. I went over to Henry and offered him my hand.

'Good luck in Victoria.'

'Enjoy California.' He reached into his pocket and fished out a small photograph of himself. 'To remember me by.'

'Thanks, Henry. Look me up in San Francisco if you ever get fed up raising them cattle.' Gilbert and Manns swung themselves up onto their horses.

'Godspeed, Frank.'

'Be lucky, John. We'll have that beer in San Francisco, dandies and free men.' Gilbert reached down from his saddle and the Darkie and Gilbert clasped hands in a firm handshake, knowing that there was still an ocean and thousands of miles between them and that first sip of beer.

Gilbert then straightened up and saluted to the rest of us, 'Gentlemen, be lucky,' he said. He nodded at Henry as they put the spurs to their mounts.

For the Darkie, Fordyce, O'Meally, Charters, Warrigal and I, the commanding heights of Mount Wheogo, the fat roll in our pockets, the camaraderie and a stolen case of fine port wine gave us a false sense of security.

Four days after the robbery, the Darkie's patience finally snapped. Gilbert's blunt words concerning Kitty's selfishness had been eating away at him and he came down off the mist-covered mountain like an angry God to pay her an early morning visit.

He returned a few hours later with a face like a thundercloud.

'She won't budge an inch. She's still insisting on a damned buggy–'

We all cursed and fumed inwardly, expecting him to ask us to give her another damn day, but the spell had been broken and his mind seemed to have cleared like the sky above us.

'Saddle up, we're out of here,' he ordered with a fresh purpose in his voice we had not heard since the raid. But it seemed that abandoned or no, Kitty wasn't about to let us get off that mountain, she wouldn't let us spoil her dream.

As we set about packing the remaining ninety pounds of gold onto the sturdy packhorse, the Darkie began bemoaning the lack of proper saddlebags.

'There's two at my place,' I volunteered, 'I'll send Warrigal down for them.' But 'Flash' Dan Charters intervened.

'I don't mind. I could do with a stretch.' Charters may not have been much of a guide, but surely even he could find his way to my place and back.

He was within cooee of my house when Sergeant Sanderson and his patrol came over the rise. As soon as they saw him, they drew their weapons and called for him to stand. But instead of keeping calm and using some of that flashness he had to talk his way out of trouble, he bolted and led them back up the mountain straight to where we were waiting!

Fortunately, for us, the weather turned again and the top of Wheogo was quickly wreathed in thick mist. We could hardly make out Dan as he came galloping in all of a lather gasping that we had about ten minutes to load the gold onto the packhorse and make off before the traps arrived.

Whatever fates were protecting us were still on our side for the traps lost some more time by stopping to rake over the ashes of our fire, but once they found the red tape from the escort bags Billy Dargin had them right on our tails.

He hadn't any book learning, but I knew Billy could read our tracks as plain as print. A broken twig, a smudge in the dirt, an overturned stone, or a bent blade of grass – that was all he needed to tell Sanderson how many of us there were, where we were headed and whether our screws were fresh or tired. Squatting beside our tracks, he squinted and called out confidently, 'Five horses, boss, and one little fella with 'em heavy bags.'

'It's them all right . . . And they've got the gold! Find them, Billy!'

The thick blanket of mist thinned as we came hurtling down the mountain. Glancing westwards, I saw the sun beginning its descent behind the Weddins. If we could just keep ahead of them for an hour or so until sunset, we would lose them. So familiar were we with the lay of the land that we rode as fast at midnight as we did at midday.

But our luck appeared to be running out. For the first time, and not that far behind us, we could hear the thud of hoofs and clink of the patrol's harnesses as they rode down at us.

We would have shown the traps clean heels were it not for the packhorse, which was not made of the same stuff as the rest of our mounts.

We came flying down the side of Wheogo helter-skelter as if we had spare necks, dragging the packhorse through a thick densely packed canopy of native pine and gum.

Trees loomed up in front of us in the fast-fading light and just as it seemed we'd smack right into them we'd dodge around and continue our mad slide to freedom. I could hear the yells of the traps as they plunged after us.

Luckily, neither they nor the old screws they were riding had any experience of this kind of rough-riding and they cursed loudly as the ground crumbled beneath them, forcing them to twist in their saddles to keep from falling whilst fending off raking, outstretched branches tipped with sharp pine needles. They were rapidly discovering the true meaning of the expression 'wild country'.

But as I said, our luck was running out. In the end, if it weren't for Billy Dargin, and that crook packhorse, we'd have given them the dodge.

Gardiner cursing fit to spit ink gave the order himself. Throwing ourselves off our horses, we suddenly dismounted and dived into a copse of pines, dragging the packhorse in after us. After quietening him down, all we could do was wait and hope like hell that the patrol would miss us in the fading light.

We peered out from our sweet-smelling keep and glimpsed their silhouettes milling around in the trees with no clue where they had come from or where they were going, but Billy saw it was a blind.

His voice floated over to us, his pidgin English ringing out clear in the dying light.

'Boss, 'em fella over 'ere . . . smell 'im horses.'

The Darkie allowed a red-hot curse to escape from between gritted teeth, 'Damn that black bugger to hell. Split up! Warrigal, with me.'

We shot out of the thicket in different directions in a last bid to throw the traps off the scent. I heard Sanderson yell out, 'Follow the packhorse. Don't take your bloody eyes off it!'

I knew in that split second that unless the Darkie could pull off one of his great escapes, half of the Eugowra escort loot was lost to us. Damn Kitty Walsh! Damn her lying cheating sisters, and damn the stupidity of the men whose knees and brains are turned to mush by the likes of them. The rage and fury of it all was seething through my brain like quicksilver. I dug the heels of my boots into Willy's sides and urged him on.

The Darkie and Warrigal still had a healthy lead on their pursuers, but that old screw of a packhorse was almost used up, and was holding them back. It was foaming at the mouth, breathing heavily and the traps, urged on by Sanderson, started to gain. As the Darkie looked back over his shoulder, he saw Sanderson, who was well to the fore, lift his weapon and take aim. A tongue of fire leapt from it, followed by a loud crack. The bullet shattered the bark of a tree to the Darkie's right.

'Bastards intend to bring our corpses in with the loot,' yelled the Darkie over his shoulder. *Come on darkness . . . come on.* Like a soothsayer, he peered anxiously up at the heavens and willed the darkness to draw down and hold him in its safe embrace. There was another sharp crack of gunfire and the Darkie, who was acutely aware that his back was exposed, braced himself for the ball between his shoulderblades that would shatter his spine and send him cartwheeling over the knife-edge ridge to his death.

He thought of the lovely Kate waiting for him and the new life they had planned in California, but knew that he couldn't have it all. Not this time around anyway.

Digging his spurs into the horse's flanks, he pulled level with Warrigal, waited until he saw the gap ahead, lifted his right hand, which held the reins of the straining packhorse and, as much as it pained him, sacrificed the loot. He let go and as the packhorse charged onwards he put his left hand on Warrigal's shoulder and slued him to the left as they approached a large gum. This sudden dart to the side caught the traps off-guard and they were past them before they realised the packhorse was a diversion. Sanderson was tempted to double-back after us, but, as with all men, he found the lure of gold and the attached glory too tempting and contented himself with the minor prize.

The news of the dramatic chase was soon all around the district. Sanderson revelled in his moment of glory as he and his patrol rode down the main street of Forbes, leading the packhorse carrying the rescued gold, just four days after the robbery.

The balcony at the two-storeyed Albion Hotel, where the escort began its fateful journey, was packed as tight as a grandstand at a cricket match.

With its wide balconies decorated with intricate, *Italiene* style lattice-work, the Albion may have looked like a fine hostelry, but the characters perched up there were as rough as the land they farmed and not likely to be impressed by half a job badly done. A wag from the assembled throng called down,

'Where's the Darkie then?'

Sanderson flinched slightly as that dart caught him square between the shoulderblades. The Darkie was the least of his worries. More to the point, where on earth was Sir Frederick?

Pottinger had ridden two hundred miles in the opposite direction and, by the time he saw the telegraph detailing his deputy's spectacular success, had reached the township of Hay in southern New South Wales. Most of his troopers had already been knocked up and had been forced to drop out along the way, but Pottinger had pressed on relentlessly.

Following the news of Sanderson's triumphant procession into Forbes, Pottinger needed a long, dark night of introspection before he concluded that he'd made the wrong choice. Dispirited and knowing that only fresh ridicule from the hostile local press awaited him on his return, he decided to head for home. But he was about to experience a dramatic change of fortune.

Losing the gold was a hammer blow, but we still had our liberty and there was not a man jack of us that wouldn't have traded all the gold so long as we could go on breathing free air. Whilst most of us were happy to go back to being stockmen, bullockies and barmen, others were not. Johnny Gilbert, his brother Charley and Henry Manns, who had the good sense to come down off Wheogo first, decided to clear out of the district and take their chances in Victoria.

Three days trot from Wheogo they thought it safe to discuss buying a station across the Victorian border where they could settle down and raise fat cattle. But their dreams were ruined when they were arrested by Pottinger's mob at Merool, near Narrandera.

Although Pottinger later claimed that he had been tracking them and that his calculation that they would head for Victoria was right all along, the truth is that he bumped into them as they rounded a corner on a dusty road leading out of Narrandera.

Such was the element of surprise that Johnny Gilbert was able to escape with the £2,500 in cash he got for his gold. But Charley and young Manns, saddled with the packhorse carrying their camping gear and 215 ounces of gold, were caught.

Despite the loss of Gilbert, Pottinger was elated. He would make a triumphant return into Forbes, with not only the gold, but a few hundred pounds of the stolen money and two of the escort robbers to boot.

But Pottinger hadn't reckoned on Johnny Gilbert spoiling his parade.

Being a man who prided himself on his horses, Gilbert rode his stallion back to the Weddins like a man possessed. After a gallop of a day or more, he burst into O'Meally's shanty where he knew the Darkie would be propping up the bar.

'Bloody oath, Johnny,' cracked the Darkie, wiping the froth from his moustache, 'Victoria that bad?'

Gilbert was in no mood for small talk.

'Pottinger dropped on us. He's got Charley, Henry and the loot,' he said breathlessly.

The Darkie drained his Old Tom and dispatched Warrigal to round us all up.

It was evening by the time we were all gathered at O'Meally's. Instead of being disturbed by Pottinger's success, the Darkie was twitching with excitement. We realised he was forming a new plan of action.

'You blokes will remember the oath we all swore to each other,' he said solemnly, 'well, boys, time has come to prove our mateship, right?'

Heads nodded cautiously, every eye in the place on him.

'We're gonna rescue Charley, Manns and the gold. And leave Pottinger to take the lump into the bargain.'

No one spoke, but everyone was thinking plenty. *Was it wise to be tangling with the traps when they were out in numbers looking for the escort robbers?*

Seeing signs of wavering in the ranks, the Darkie turned to face us and looked along the line at each of us before he spoke.

'We might be thieves, but we're not without honour, no matter what Pottinger and his ilk think o' us. We've faced the guns, tasted death, and risked everything for fortune and glory. We're part of a fellowship bound by the most powerful of all ties. We're not just men; we're comrades in arms . . . Who's with me?'

Silence as the Darkie's words sank in. No one had ever put it like that before and no one who was there was ever likely to forget it.

I felt the hairs stand up on the back of my neck.

Gilbert, the tears lying close to his eyes, found his feet first and saluted smartly, 'Aye, Captain.'

Slowly each one of us stood, our throats choked with emotion answering the call with a salute and those same words.

'Then let's be away, boys,' said the Darkie.

A great cheer nearly lifted off the roof as we trooped out. You had to hand it to the Darkie, he'd use any trick to get you into the game, but once you were in, he'd lay down his life for you. He was right though, once you'd been in a scrimmage, felt the thunder in your blood and smelt the powder, you're never quite the same again.

Because we knew the surrounding country and Pottinger so well, we had little difficulty in selecting a spot on the Burrangong road to ambush him. The pompous fool continued to travel in a straight line never once thinking we'd have the audacity to strike back at a police patrol.

Having hurriedly blackened our faces with charcoal, we waited till the police party, consisting of Pottinger, Trooper Mitchell and Detective Lyons, were almost abreast with the thicket we were hiding in. Lyons was leading the horses carrying the handcuffed Charley and Manns. We charged them yelling and whooping.

'Bail up, you bastards!'

A bullet hit Lyons' horse, which keeled over trapping him underneath. Pottinger and Mitchell were quick on the rebound. Mitchell snatched up the reins of the prisoners' horses and moved himself between the pair of them, knowing we wouldn't shoot near our own gang members. Pottinger grabbed the bridle of the packhorses carrying the gold and retreated about fifty yards down the road cannily keeping the linked trio of horses between himself and our fire. When he was a safe distance away he returned our fire.

The Darkie was determined to have Pottinger's scalp on his belt. He trotted towards them, a sneer fixed to his face. Pulling out one of the six irons that decorated his belt, he discharged both barrels and as a gesture of his reckless desire to settle things, once and for all, tossed the empty guns into the dust and pulled out another.

'Come on, gentlemen,' he spat, taunting them. 'Let's have a straight run . . . you and me, one of you or both, it don't matter. Let's settle this here and now. Save chasing me all over the bloody countryside.' The Darkie had a deal too much white in his eye for Pottinger and Mitchell. Not having the moxie to hold their ground in the face of his cavalier charge, they put their spurs to the flanks of their horses and left the trapped Lyons to our mercy.

'Cowards!' roared the Darkie at their retreating figures.

Lyons' horse was now squirming in pain as its lifeblood ebbed away into the thirsty ground. The Darkie knelt down and stroked its great head tenderly, spoke to it in a soothing voice, while with the other hand he brought up his pistol and shot it in the side of the head, sparing it from further suffering.

As the Darkie gently lay the horse's head on the ground, Lyons groaned from underneath the horse's dead weight. Blood was puddling around him and the flies were already buzzing, settling and rising from their feasting.

'I've one pill left for you,' the Darkie said, pointing the piece at him. 'Might cure you of your treachery for good.'

Lifting his hands to cover his face Lyons turned his head away, begging for his life. 'Please, boys, spare me. I've a wife and a child.'

The Darkie had the measure of him and the tight, thin line that stretched across his face was more like a scar than a smile.

'You've no such thing, Detective Patrick Lyons,' he said coldly. 'I know every inch of you. You live by yourself in Rankin Street at Forbes. We could've shot you dead at your supper table, any night we chose.'

Lyons said nothing, believing the game was up.

'See how natural lying comes to these mongrels, boys, yet these men are charged with upholding the law of the land. You tell His Lordship that we're the law now.'

He aimed a savage kick at the prone figure of Lyons, then bent over him, rummaged in his pocket for the keys to the handcuffs to free our mates. Judging by the marks on their faces, the cuts, bruises and puffy eyes, both of them had suffered an interrogation the night before.

'Them bastards cattled us good and proper last night,' confirmed Henry Manns.

Charley stepped forward and pointed at Lyons, 'Lyons held a pistol to our heads and threatened to brand us with hot irons if we didn't confess.'

'Was Pottinger there?' asked the Darkie, a black scowl on his face.

'Urging him on,' confirmed Charley.

'You know what they say, Detective Lyons, one good turn deserves another.'

It was time for some good old-fashioned payback. Lyons moaned and writhed as Manns and Charley set about him with boots and fists. Even when they'd finished and were panting like cattle dogs, the trap's fate still hung in the balance.

The Darkie stood over him, blocking out the sun and Lyons shivered visibly as he felt the cold shadow of death pass over him. He was well aware of Gardiner's reputation and knew that a bashing was cheap currency in this game.

'Does he know who you are?' asked the Darkie turning to look Charley and Manns straight in the eye. 'I want the truth now, boys.'

'Nah, we gave the blue bellies a fill. We gave them the names Turner and Dacey. He knows no more than that.'

That probably saved Lyons' life. With a nod, the Darkie turned away from Lyons and mounted his horse.

Up in the branches of a gnarly old red gum the crows and magpies patiently waited for us to leave the field so they could get to work on the horse. Gardiner looked up beyond them to the yellow merciless eye of the Australian sun that blazed down from the peerless blue.

With a mocking tip of the hat in Lyons' direction he smiled, 'By the time a traveller happens along that horse ought to have ripened nicely in the heat, not that there's much to choose between a dead horse and a trap. Until next time, Detective Lyons.'

Lyons didn't utter a word of protest as we rode off and left him lying on the road.

But a dog never forgets a kick. It's a proverb we country boys know well. It was not the last we'd see or hear of Detective Lyons.

We travelled a little way along with Charley and Gilbert and then shook hands as we bade them farewell for a second time. They had decided to give Victoria a miss and try their hand at the Otago goldfields in New Zealand.

'Thanks, boys, you saved me bacon,' said Charley.

'You'll do the same for us one day,' smiled the Darkie.

After his narrow squeak, Manns decided to split from the Gilberts and go east to Gundagai to stay with relatives, a decision he would later regret.

If Pottinger thought that the return of the gold would repair his reputation, he was mistaken. Once the news of our daring rescue of Gilbert and Manns reached the ears of the newspapermen, praise quickly turned to pillory. Although the traps had recovered most of the gold, the bandits were still at large and they had yet to make an arrest.

'What must I do to get these miserable scribblers to say a good word about me?' growled Pottinger in exasperation as he crumpled one of the local papers that took every opportunity to flay his reputation.

The man who sat opposite him watched the Inspector's tantrum with interest. 'Bring me Gardiner's head,' replied the Lachlan correspondent for the *Sydney Morning Herald*, 'then, no one could argue.'

Wreathed in the smoke of one of his trademark French cigars, Pottinger nodded slowly. The man was right. *It was time to take the fight to them and to be a lot less fussy about how it was won.*

The plan that would start the war of the Weddins took shape in Pottinger's dreams. This plan would wreak untold suffering and deaths.

Pottinger awoke the next morning with a spryness and a spring in his step that he had not known for many a long day.

Chapter Eleven

Nearly two months had passed since our dramatic entry into the annals of Australian history and Pottinger had yet to make a single arrest.

Pottinger was under pressure from every quarter. He'd turned over the home of every known 'telegraph' and harbourer in the district, gave out some garnish, threatened them with dire consequences and served outstanding warrants, but still no one talked. To these people Gardiner was the Prince of the Tobymen, while Pottinger was just the Clown Prince.

Tom Richards, a solidly built former butcher, walked into Forbes police station, took off his sweat-stained cabbage tree hat to reveal a man past his prime. His once lush head of golden curls had receded to sun-reddened scalp and his work-hardened body was not as lean as it had once been. These days he earned a living making lemonade in Forbes, a seasonal venture that demanded long hours for diminishing returns. He did tailing and other occasional stock work for small selectors like Jacky McGuire. Because of what he had seen at McGuire's a couple of months back, he had an idea that it might just turn out to be the best job he'd ever taken on.

Drawing a rough, cotton sleeve across his face he walked up to the counter. A constable was sitting on the other side reading a copy of the *Examiner*, an enamel mug of stewed tea sat near his elbow.

You wouldn't think the country was in uproar to look at him sitting there, Richards thought to himself. Like most ordinary men, he had no love for the traps, but there was a reward going and 'needs must'. He leaned on the counter.

'I've come to see Inspector Pottinger.'

'He's busy,' mumbled Constable Anderson without looking up from the paper. There was nothing but the slow insistent ticking of the large clock on the wall.

Richards cleared his throat and tried again.

'He'll want to hear what I have to tell him,' he said.

'He's busy, mate, hook it!' came the bluff response from the trap, still engrossed in his newspaper.

Richards did as he was told, but as he got to the door, turned around and casually said, 'When he finishes his important business, tell him Tom Richards has got information about the Eugowra escort robbers. I'll be at the Harp o' Erin.'

The trap's head bobbed up quicker than a duck's arse, but all he saw was Richards disappearing through the doorway.

'Wait up, mate!' called Constable Anderson frantically, already halfway across the room.

The following afternoon, a genial Constable Anderson showed Richards into Pottinger's office where the man himself stood with his back to an open fire warming himself. Far from being happy to welcome this windfall, Pottinger scowled at the cove that had caused him to turn out of a warm hotel bar in Grenfell and ride through the freezing night to hear what he had to say.

'This better be good!' he growled at Richards.

'Oh, it's better than that, Sir Frederick,' Richards assured him with an oily smile, proceeding to spill his guts about what he'd seen at Jacky McGuire's and repeating, parrot-fashion, all the loose talk he'd heard about the place.

On the day of the Eugowra robbery he claimed to have been working out in the paddocks with Jacky who had checked his fob and said, 'Three o'clock, the lads will be at it now.' There was also an account of the night we had a council of war at Jacky's hut.

'And you're absolutely sure it was Gardiner?' pressed Pottinger.

Feeling very much at home now, knowing that the Inspector was hanging on his every word, Richards helped himself to another of the fancy biscuits that Anderson had brought in along with a pot of tea.

'Oh yes, Sir, Gardiner, Fogg and meself were partners in a butchery business over at Lambing Flat. I know every inch of that cove.'

Pausing to remove the top layer of biscuit with surgical precision, Richards ran his tongue down the other half rock lizard wise to remove the creamy white icing and, savouring the sticky sweetness, eyed Pottinger warily.

'Now, about that reward,' he said, the naked greed flickering in his eyes. 'A hundred quid a head, wasn't it?'

Pottinger eyed him with distaste. 'Should your information help us secure a conviction, I will present it to you myself,' he said with a forced smile.

'That's it then,' said Richards in triumph, depositing the unwanted biscuit into his saucer. 'The go is that you'll cuff me tomorrow at the Harp – in full view o' everybody, 'cause I won't make any statement till I'm safely in the logs.'

Pottinger nodded.

With that, he stood up and stuck his hand out in Sir Frederick's direction. Pottinger grasped his hand reluctantly and shuddered inwardly as he touched Richards' clammy, sticky palm.

Using his handkerchief to wipe the sweet-smelling residue from his hands, he crossed to the window and watched Richards dodge between drays and wagons as he slunk back across the road.

As a soldier, he knew that traitors were a necessary evil in the winning of any war, but it still went against the grain.

We'd have run him through, back in the Guards, he thought grimly, *but here I am promising him the proverbial twelve pieces of silver.*

Despite his reservations, the smile never left his face. The traitor's coin had just bought him his first break in a long and frustrating case.

Sergeant Sanderson opened the door leading from the side room to his Inspector's office. As soon as Richards had left, he had slipped in, and now stood there, awaiting instructions. Pottinger waved a piece of paper over his shoulder and said, 'Sergeant, prepare arrest warrants for the following people . . .'

'You're going to arrest people on the nod of that cove?' Sanderson blurted out in amazement.

Pottinger turned on him, annoyed at his apparent squeamishness. *He's already upstaged me once by bringing in the escort gold and now he's going cold on the only solid information we have.*

Realising Pottinger's dark displeasure, Sanderson hastily added. 'I mean it's *thin*. We only have the word of one shady cove that he saw Gardiner and others arriving at McGuire's. There's not nearly enough to tie them to the robbery–'

Feeling his euphoria being rapidly deflated by the pinpricks of his subordinate's scepticism, Pottinger snapped back, 'It's a start,

Sergeant. We'll give the tree a good shake and see who falls out of it.' Pointing to the list in his hand, Pottinger said firmly, 'The names for the warrants are as listed. That will be all, *Sergeant*.'

The next day, July 27, we heard the traps had arrested Fred Trotter, John O'Meally and his seventy-year-old da, Paddy.

Jacky McGuire, Dan Charters, my brother Bill and I were mustering cattle at Sandy Creek when we heard the news. We all agreed that someone was doubling on us, but because they were so far wide of the mark, it was no one in the gang. John was the only one of them in it, but was pulled because old Paddy owned the shanty where they thought the gang had been drafted.

Casting half-closed eyes up at the cloudless sky, Jacky McGuire bellowed loudly, 'Fuckin' hard, fuckin' hot, fuckin' hell!' a salutation he usually reserved for the height of summer when the mercury sat at the high end for months. Even though it was late winter, we'd been hit by a sudden hot spell, as sometimes happens when there's a long, dry summer on the way.

Our rhythm broken, we decided to stop for some tucker and a brew, but before we could finish up, we saw a dust cloud approaching fast across the plain.

'Whoever it is, they're comin' at a lick,' said Bill uneasily, knowing that no one went about the place like that in this heat, unless they'd found gold or someone had fallen off the perch. We looked from one to the other, wondering which it was.

It turned out to be neither. We were soon able to make out the perspiring figure of Pottinger coming through the shimmering heat at the head of a party of troopers.

'Act normal,' I said, knowing it was too late for anything else. We continued with our business right up to the minute Pottinger rode up to us, but we neither offered nor received any pleasantries. Nor did we make any effort to stop our work, just carried on as if he wasn't there, which got his dander up. As we continued mustering and driving mokes into the stockyard, pushing and cajoling the beasts through the gate, he held up a sheaf of papers.

'I have warrants for your arrest,' he yelled trying in vain to be heard over the thunder of stampeding hooves and barking cattle dogs. After securing the gate I eventually turned to face him, hands on hips.

'On what charge this time?' I asked impatiently.

'Robbery under arms,' he shouted over the din, his face as red as the Queen of Hearts.

'Haven't we been through this before?' I demanded, keeping up the pressure.

'And we'll do it again,' sneered Pottinger. He nodded at the familiar figure of Constable Kennedy who was behind him, the shackles ready in his hand. 'If there's any rescue attempt on the way to Forbes, you'll be shot before they take you back.'

Once again I was brought to the door of the logs. The bolts were drawn back and that familiar stench rushed out to meet me.

'Welcome home,' said Kennedy, a huge grin splitting his ugly phiz.

They might have had us, but the real prize was Gardiner, who had been jugged twice already and had no intention of wasting any more time at Her Majesty's pleasure. Like a wily old fox, he knew that it was time to move on and change his name . . . again.

The master of light, shadow and shade glanced up at the heavens and calculated that a thick bank of cloud would soon drift in front of the half-sickle moon that hung low in the sky. It would soon be as dark as the inside of a cow, perfect cover for his last hurrah on Australian soil.

A lone sentry owl hooted a warning, just as a lone rider on a black mare emerged from the undergrowth near Uoka, the Walsh homestead. But it was not just owlish eyes that watched his approach with interest. Despite the lover's tiff, which had been widely commented on in the district after our dramatic chase down the side of Wheogo, Pottinger knew Kitty the temptress would lure Gardiner back and he had resolved to be there when she did.

The Darkie looked up at the heavens and the crescent moon appeared from behind its veil of cloud, as if he had commanded it. Its soft radiance lit up the quiet, darkened countryside.

Gardiner stood perfectly still for a few minutes sniffing the air like a cautious animal, straining all his senses to pick up a stray noise or unfamiliar shape, something that would betray the presence of a crouching predator. But for once, the New South Wales police force maintained their discipline. They remained stock still in the trees, hardly daring to breathe while the Darkie's sharp eye was on them.

Suddenly, the soft glow of a kerosene lamp flickered in the window at the side of the house. Each night, Kitty had kept a lonely vigil at her bedroom window, hoping her Frank would return. When she used to sneak out and meet him for nights of passion in the bush, a light in her window was the signal that the coast was clear.

During many nights of anxious waiting, she had chewed her fingernails to ragged stumps. Frank had not been arrested with the others, but there were rumours flying about that he was on his way to California.

She could scarce believe her eyes when, suddenly, like some chivalrous hero of yore, her knight, Frank, risking his life and liberty, emerged from the darkness into the pale moonlight. It was right out of her childhood imaginings. Her heart all a-flutter and with nothing, except what she stood up in, she ran out of the house to greet him.

As the horseman approached the house, Pottinger raised the new Callisher and Terry repeating rifle he had brought with him for the job, and sighted the figure down the barrel. A rare grin split the bearded face as the figure came into focus beyond the point of his muzzle. It was Gardiner, no mistake.

'Stand in the Queen's name!' called Pottinger.

As a startled Gardiner swung round and looked right back down the barrel at him, Pottinger squeezed the trigger. But instead of feeling the satisfying slap of the wooden stock into his shoulder followed by a crack and a sharp smell of powder that would signal the end of his nemesis, there was just a harsh metallic click. Misfire! The Darkie had once again stared into the abyss and survived. He grinned at Pottinger, gave Black Bess the spurs and was gone.

Alarmed by the click of the rifle, Kitty was distraught as the black mare thundered to a halt in front of her.

'Oh Frank, you came back for me,' she cried. The Darkie reached down and grabbed her arm.

'Let's be away, the traps are close by!' He hadn't produced a buggy, but what girl could refuse the sudden fulfilment of her wildest dreams? Certainly not Kitty Brown.

With the practised vault of a Weddin girl who had sat in the saddle long before she could walk, she sprang up behind him, grabbed him round the waist and held on.

Pottinger snatched a rifle from the hands of a nearby trooper.

'Give me that–' he bellowed. Gardiner was still within range, a pale blur in the moonlight. He couldn't be allowed to get away.

But as his finger snaked around the trigger, the moon again disappeared behind the clouds and Gardiner, horse and passenger disappeared as if by magic. The musical refrain of the Darkie's mocking laughter drifted in on the gentle breeze that suddenly rippled the still night. Pottinger ground his teeth and fired some futile shots in the general direction of the retreating horse, but Black Bess carried the lovers clear.

Kitty held on tight round the Darkie's waist and pressed her face into the familiar curve of his back. She abandoned herself to the gentle caress of the warm wind that unfurled her long dark tresses as they sped away to a new life.

But the curse of the Walsh women was not done with the Darkie yet.

Denied his prize, yet again, Pottinger stormed into the Walsh home in a black fit and arrested Warrigal on a charge of being Gardiner's accomplice.

Once again he had come away empty-handed and was lambasted by the press for his failure to bag Gardiner when he had him in his sights, literally, and bringing in a sixteen-year-old boy instead. Pottinger's defence was that it was only 'bad luck' and 'damp powder' that prevented his capture of Gardiner. The *Forbes Examiner* wryly observed that these were common excuses for a lack of action in men of a certain age.

In court, it was claimed that a coat was found in the bushranger's Wheogo camp that fitted Warrigal and for that accident of nature he spent three weeks in the logs.

All the others arrested on suspicion of being involved in the Eugowra robbery suffered a similar fate. To satisfy the law, we were trotted out before the magistrate every two or three days and remanded on nothing more than Pottinger's suspicion.

The police suspected that the fifty-odd quid Bill had on him was part of the proceeds of the robbery and we needed to be held while they checked with the banks. The notes were regular and had nothing to do with the robbery, but Pottinger was keeping up the pressure, hoping for a break.

The others were held on various trumped-up allegations, the good Inspector even arguing that it was too dangerous to bail seventy-year-old Paddy O'Meally. The Magistrate agreed and remanded us all in custody.

The collusion between the Magistrate and the police was one of the prime grievances of country folk. The magistrates with no legal training, as such, were either retired soldiers or local squatters of means and some education, which was all the qualification they needed to hold sway over we lesser mortals. As a gentleman it was a given that he would act without fear or favour.

Dan Charters, a man of means, was the first to be bailed on August 6, ten days after he was arrested. A day or two later Johnny and Paddy O'Meally were set free along with Fred Trotter and Bill, who got his money back as it was proved none of it was connected to the Eugowra job.

However, Pottinger did make two additional arrests. Acting on new information received, he pulled in John Bow and Alex Fordyce from behind the bar at O'Meally's on 21 August. For police who knew nothing, they seemed to have made a pretty good stab at guessing who was in the Eugowra gang.

Finally, even the local Magistrate had tired of Pottinger's excuses and threats of the crime and disorder that would be unleashed should I be released back into society. He recommended that Jacky, Bow and Fordyce all stand trial for robbery under arms and the wounding of Sergeant Condell.

Bright and early on August 23, 1862, after almost a month in detention, the cell door was thrown open and I was more or less kicked out. No charges were laid. In the language of seasoned criminals, I had not even been in for a 'snooze', which was three months.

As I stood up to go, I looked down at Jacky's hunched figure, feeling his despair. I clasped his hand.

'Don't worry, Jacky. We'll get you out of this. You had no part in it.'

I stepped out of the Forbes lock-up, blinking as my eyes adjusted to the bright sunshine. I watched with a heavy heart as the door closed behind me, throwing a long shadow over Jacky who awaited his fate.

The fetor of the bucket still on my nose, I stood for a minute and filled my lungs with clean air. I knew I'd have to scrub my flesh raw to get rid of the stench of the place.

I caught the whiff of another familiar smell, the aroma of fine tobacco. I looked across and saw Pottinger standing at the back door of the police station, which looked onto the lock-up. He was smoking a cigar and watching me through slitted eyes. For a man who had just released most of the gang who robbed the Eugowra gold escort he had a strangely triumphant air about him. The part of me attached to my bluchers was tempted to go over and stomp on his head, but the part of me attached to my brain prevailed.

The two-mile walk along the long, dusty track to the police pound to collect Willy the Weasel gave me time to re-fill my lungs with clean air and even out my 'darby roll', the rolling gait that affects men who have been 'on the chain' with heavy irons on one leg. I resolved I would never spend another minute in that blind hole of a place again.

Feeling the need to mingle with ordinary folk and to cleanse my mouth after a month in the logs, I stopped in at the Harp o' Erin for a beer and a stiff nobbler. The first sip was barely over my throat when I saw something I wish I hadn't.

Dan Charters was in the corner with Jacky's wife, Ellen. I watched them exchange looks, smiles and touches, all the telltale signs of a rooting couple. Not to be outdone by her sister Kitty's dramatic elopement with the Darkie, Ellen McGuire had started cheating on Jacky with his friend who had just been bailed.

After the manner of Biddy's departure, I had no time for Ellen, but Jacky was a mate in trouble. I waited until Dan went outside to the dunny and accosted him. Grabbing him by the arm, I swung him around to face me. There was no look of surprise on his face, just that wolfish smile, as though he was fully expecting to see me free. I went cold as I realised in that moment that it must have been Dan who had implicated Jacky in the Eugowra robbery. *Dan was the traitor.*

'Ben, when did you get out?' His voice sounded too glib for my ears.

'This morning, and not a moment too soon by the looks of things,' I replied. 'What're you doing with Jacky's wife?'

'Just keeping her company,' he said with a sheepish look. He was up to no good.

'How's he going to feel when he hears about this?'

Avoiding my angry stare, Dan shrugged his shoulders and spread his hands out, a touch of the theatrics. 'There's nothing to tell, Ben. She's just a bit down with Jacky having been in the logs for so long.'

I noticed he kept clicking the nails of his middle finger and thumb together, like he did the day we lied to our da about the snake that killed Henry McBride. I knew Dan was lying again about Ellen.

I resolved to say nothing to Jacky. There was nothing he could do about it and he would need all his strength for the trial ahead. Getting news like that in prison would break the spirit of even the strongest man.

Anxious to be home, I soon had Willy in a pretty fair hand gallop, savouring the smell of clean air and the earthy scent of the bush. The old lags used to say that a man never truly knows freedom, till he's been 'on the chain'. I'd ended up with four hundred quid for the biggest bail-up in Australian history, not quite enough to start a new life in California, but fate wouldn't have it and there was no point grumbling.

I had resolved during my time in the logs to get out of the game and stick to the square as a cattleman.

The gold was lost, the Darkie had fled and the Gardiner gang was no more, freeing me from the pact we'd made. At full gallop, I pulled the Navy Colt from my belt and flung it into the bush. All that was in the past now and the future awaited me at the end of my journey. But I was about to learn that man does not control his fate, it is a divinity, either malign or holy, that shapes his life.

As I came along the track to Sandy Creek, a warning breeze rustled the wallaby scrub, carrying the distinctive smell of charred, burnt wood.

I gave Willy's barrel-like sides an urgent prod with my knees as we came over the rise to Sandy Creek and was confronted by my worst fears.

My hut had been reduced to a fire-blackened shell. Such was the intensity of the blaze that the sturdy foundation posts had been eaten through and the ground around the hut was completely scorched. This was no accident.

The stench of death and decay drifted in from the stockyards, which were a quarter of a mile distant. Pulling my neckerchief up around my face, I crossed the road to the stockyards. The angry frenzy of flies led me to the bloated, rotting carcasses of my cattle that had been left in the pens. The poor beasts had died with their heads poking out between the sliprails, their black, stiffened tongues hanging out for the want of the water they could smell only a few hundred yards away.

The crows, butcherbirds, dingos, blowflies, maggots and the heat had already done their worst. As a stockman, I was used to the smell of dead stock, but the overwhelming sight and stench forced me to bend over and retch until I was empty.

I staggered back to the remains of my house, looking around in disbelief. I had been hollowed out, my guts were hung out to dry.

A hundred head of first-rate store cattle had been left to perish in the two pens. They had been a mix of young bullocks and heifers, more than half fat. A prime bred mob that would have fetched £20 each at market. That was £2,000, everything Jacky and I had left in the world, money that Jacky would no longer have for his defence.

A lone rider came towards me out of the haze; it wasn't until he clapped me on the shoulder that I stirred out of my deep shock.

'Ben . . .' I heard a voice, shaking with anger and disgust. 'This must be bloody Pottinger's doing.'

I recognised Bill's voice. I looked up dazed and unable to speak. All I could do was nod. I bitterly recalled that triumphant look Pottinger had given me earlier at the gaol.

Bill sat me down, brewed a billy, and once I had taken a few mouthfuls of strong black tea laced with a generous shot of whisky, he told me the story as he'd heard it from old Murphy whom he'd met in Forbes earlier. Old Murphy, whom I had employed to look after the stock whilst I was being held at Her Majesty's pleasure, and Susan Prior, a girl I had been courting, had been staying in my hut.

About a week before, Pottinger arrived with Sergeant Condell, Constable Hollister, Billy Dargin and that slippery arse Detective Lyons, whom we should have settled with when we had the chance. Pottinger had barged in without any invitation, and told Susan and old Murphy that they had no business being there. Old Murphy was already dodging a warrant in Queensland and could only sit there puffing furiously on his pipe, but Susan, a combustible redhead, was more than a match for his lordship.

With her hands on her hips and a look of disgust on her face, she had looked Pottinger up and down and gave him the rough edge of her tongue, 'D'ya think ya can burst into folks' houses just because ye've a handle to yer name?'

'No, Miss, I need the permission of the owner for that.'

'Ben's in prison, as well you know.'

'Then, I've news for you, Missy. Sandy Creek is now the property of John Wilson of Forbes and he wants rid of everyone and everything connected to bushranging.'

'You're lying!' shouted Susan.

A triumphant smirk split Pottinger's face wide open as he produced some official-looking papers, which he waved in front of Susan. When she didn't go to take them Pottinger crowed, 'As you clearly cannot read permit me to tell you what it says. This is a warrant authorising me to destroy all buildings on Sandy Creek. Interfere with its execution at your peril. Now, stand aside, Miss Prior.' Nodding at the burly constable he'd brought with him, Pottinger barked, 'Take out what furniture there is and then burn the hut.'

Susan had refused to leave and Pottinger's stooges carried her out, flailing, hissing and spitting like a feral cat. Susan flew at Pottinger's face with her sharp claws, but he held her easily with one hand. He pushed his face close to hers and snarled, 'You tell Ben Hall this; Gardiner isn't here to look out for him, and if his convict class thinks they can have everything their own way, they're much mistaken. I'll clear this district of the lot of you, with bullets, fire or leg irons, and I don't care which it is.' Old Murphy knew it was useless to resist and saved the few sticks of furniture he could, while the traps piled wooden faggots against the hut. Pottinger tossed the butt of his cigar into the brushwood his men had piled up. It caught hold quickly. The flames blossomed and were soon licking at the roof.

Pottinger, puffed up with his own importance, drove Susan and old Murphy off the selection and warned them they'd be arrested if they returned. Old Murphy had kept on about the cattle, but Pottinger told him they were none of his concern and that they would be impounded.

Bill spat the taste of his tale out of his mouth and growled, 'Of course, the bastard did no such thing. He left them to die. I came out as soon as I'd seen old Murphy, but it was too late.'

'That double-barrelled English bastard!' I raged. 'That warrant was a blind! Sandy Creek still belongs to me and Jacky.' Bill watched helplessly as I grabbed a lump of charred wood and smashed it into a stump of foundation post. I intended to finish what Pottinger had started and kept swinging until nothing remained standing above the ground. Bill wisely stood back and let me get it all out and when I was done he came over and gently prised the wood from my blackened fingers and sat me down. We sat a while without speaking. My mind drifted back to that first meeting with Pottinger and now I knew why he was so offhand with me.

'He had a nailer on me from the start,' I said staring at the bones of my hut. 'But why?' I wondered aloud.

Bill shrugged his shoulders. 'Ben, you came a long way in a short time and you're of convict stock, the son of a well-known duffer and married to a Walsh, he figured you must be crooked, mate.'

'Bastards!' I spat, reserving equal odium for Pottinger and our da. *The only legacy our da would ever leave me was his rotten name and a reputation that stank to high heaven.*

I rose and patted Willy the Weasel on the neck, saying aloud, 'That settles it. I may as well have the game as the blame.'

The hour when chaos ruled my soul had finally arrived. The last of those great destroyers of the soul, vengeance, had entered my heart and the 'unholy Trinity' was now complete. I knew I would never return to Sandy Creek. It was poisoned land; poisoned by misfortune, bad memories and by Pottinger. My family, my wife and child were gone from me, my hut burned and my cattle left to perish and I had no money for any defence of either myself or Jacky.

'Where's Susan?' I asked Bill.

'I took her over to the Stricklands' place,' he replied, nodding towards the spread belonging to our good neighbour.

I rode to Stricklands' while my resolve was still strong. I arrived as the sun was sliding out of the blue sky, gradually softening and turning orange as if it were melting. Susan came running out, relieved to see I was alive and well. Her face fell when she saw my solemn expression. Susan was a spirited lass, but like Biddy, the tears always lay close to her eyes.

'I'm sorry, Ben, we couldn't stop them.' Her thin little frame folded into my arms.

'There was nothing you could do. Pottinger means to drive us out. Every time a moke, or a cow goes for a wander, we'll be shoved in the logs until we tire of it and leave the district. We've tasted his justice and I won't put you through any more of it.'

She broke free from my embrace, stepped away and shook her head in stunned disbelief. At seventeen, she was too young to have her heart broken like this, but better that than the life of sorrow she'd have with a marked man.

I turned to go, but the words that followed stopped me in my tracks.

'Ben, I'm with child.'

I walked back to her, reached deep into my pocket for what was in it. Seeing what was in my hand she tried to pull away, but I held her slim wrist and pressed a bundle of notes into her hand. It was my cut of the Eugowra robbery.

'Ben, it's not money I'm after,' she said, her voice cracking with sadness and confusion.

'It'll see you and the child right for a good bit,' I replied gently, watching the unhappiness flooding through her. She knew it was final, but hadn't yet resigned herself to the truth. 'It's for the best. Goodbye, Susan.'

I walked back to Willy the Weasel and hauled myself up into the saddle, but the strength had left my legs.

Sensing I was not as callous as I pretended, Susan ran towards me and grabbed a hold of Willy's bridle. Her eyes were full of tears and the blind defiance of a child. 'No, Ben I won't let you,' she sobbed. 'I'll follow you wherever you go.'

I fixed her with a straight look and put a question to her softly. 'And to Hell as well?'

She hesitated and finally understood what I was saying. Her hands slipped from the bridle and hot tears spotted her red dusty boots like summer rain. She bowed her head and sobbed: for her, for me, for the child not yet born, for the life we might have had and for the tyranny that had brought us to this moment of parting.

I dug my spurs gently into Willy's flanks. By the time Susan raised her head, I was a distant shadow moving across the darkening plains, the pale blue ribbon of sky above me broken only by the silhouettes of black trees.

*

Willy and I climbed a hill and watched the sun slip behind the Weddin Mountains. It had turned from a deep orange to an angry red and blazed a trail across the sky to match my mood.

If I thought I could cross back over the line and return to my old life, I was mistaken. Once again, Jacky's words came back to me, 'There's no half-measures . . . you're either in or you're out.' He was right about that!

The destruction of Sandy Creek was an example of everything that was wrong with the system of justice in this colony. Too much power in the wrong hands. Pottinger had no proof of my wrongdoing, yet he could still write himself a warrant and destroy my home and livelihood in the name of law and order. The traps drove men to becoming bushrangers. It was a thing that I'd heard said often enough, but now I knew it was true. I was living proof of it.

I vowed that I would push all thoughts of Biddy, Henry, Sandy Creek and Susan to the furthest corner of my mind, take up the game and continue in the tradition of the Irish legends our ma told us about. A short, but glorious life.

The final embers of my old life finally flickered and died along with the daylight and I found myself alone in the darkness cursing myself for throwing away that Colt pistol.

Chapter Twelve

I became leader of the Ben Hall gang because the destruction of Sandy Creek had given me the will to pick up where the Darkie had left off. The Ben Hall gang started with John O'Meally and Patsy Daly, who was an old boyhood chum. I knew the best and worst of them.

Patsy was a gangly, curly-headed Irish fool with a great sense of humour, a boyish, lopsided grin stuck permanently on his face. He was a few years younger than John and me, but just as brave and loyal. That he was in the game for a few bob and to impress the doxies was no secret.

'Are ye sure you know what you're getting into, Patsy?' I asked him straight, mindful that I should have done more to stop young Warrigal getting involved with the Darkie. 'It's no game we're playing. Either I'll have Pottinger's blood, or he'll have mine.'

'Suits me,' said O'Meally, answering before Patsy had a chance. He had already proved his mettle under fire, and though the question was not directed at him, John O'Meally took all such questions very seriously. He pushed up his hat and fixed me with a lazy, malevolent stare. A shaft of hard sunlight slanted through the thick cover of the shade tree we were sitting under, framing his face. A strange, wild light glittered in those cold, green eyes and they reminded me of a wild animal just before it charges you. As I learned on the day that Henry McBride got fanged, there had always been something dangerous and unpredictable about John O'Meally, but I'd rather have him at my side than at my back.

In sharp contrast, Patsy just nodded eagerly. We were a real mixed bunch, and I knew I'd have my work cut out to keep them on the narrow.

*

The Pinnacle police station was equipped with a lock-up, stables, an office and accommodation for six police. The heavy log construction had been built the previous year, on the western side of the Weddins, about ten miles from the town of Grenfell. It was positioned there so the traps could keep an eye on the diggings, which had started in the nearby Pinnacle hills, and also on the pioneer families of the Weddin and Wheogo areas whom they suspected of supporting bushranger activity. There was a police report that reckoned that out of all the families on the Blands, Weddins, Abercrombie and Fish Rivers, only five were loyal, and not connected to bushranging in some way.

As we forced open the front door of the police station at eleven o'clock one night, we felt no fear because we knew that there was no one inside. At that hour, most decent folk were in their beds, and Constable Arthur Knox should have been on watch. Instead, he was on his way to the nearby Pinnacle station to make an unscheduled house call.

As he waited for an answer to his discreet rap on the front door, he nervously ran his hand through his lank, light brown hair, feeling the short bristles at the back of his head rasp against his palm. He also hastily brushed the stray crumbs of dinner damper off the front of his blue tunic.

Margaret Feehily, a pleasant-looking widow somewhere in her thirties, who happened to be Dan Charters' sister, opened the door a crack. Though her brother had let his mates down, Margaret was a good sort and agreed to keep Knox 'entertained' while we got on with the job in hand. Smiling coyly, she pushed a hand through her long, dark hair and stood back. After a quick look right and left, he was 'up the stairs' in a blink of the eye.

This moment was the culmination of weeks of flirtatious behaviour that came in the guise of freshly baked fruit pies, scones and damper, which Margaret had taken to Knox at the police station.

As he was stepping out of his smart grey strides, we were letting ourselves into the police station and helping ourselves to rifles, powder, paper cartridges, holsters, saddlebags and a few pairs of handcuffs from the arms cupboard.

On the way out, I happened to note that Constable Knox had not registered his absence in the heavy, leather-bound station ledger. Knowing how important truthful information was to the New

South Wales constabulary, I saw it as my civic duty to keep the record straight.

Constable Knox discovered the robbery when he crept back into the station with the first light of morning. When he saw the broken door, the empty cupboard and the open ledger, a hot flush coloured his face as he realised he'd been flammed good and proper, and that his popularity with a certain widow had nothing to do with his rugged good looks. He ran sweating and cursing to the sleeping quarters behind the station to raise the alarm.

When he pushed open the door, cold, bright light intruded on the dark, cosy room, which stank of stale farts and unwashed bodies, and he was greeted with a chorus of abuse.

'Say they jumped you when you went out for a piss,' said an irritable, sleepy voice, after Knox explained what had happened.

'I can't. The miserable bastard signed me out last night,' groaned Knox.

'What?'

'Ben Hall signed me out in the ledger at eleven o'clock last night and initialled it, B.H.'

'The cheeky bastard,' came a voice from the dark. 'Where were you all night, anyway?'

'Jocking it with the widow Feehily, I'd wager,' came a second voice, bringing down the catcalls on the luckless constable's head.

'I'm fucked. The boss will roast me,' said Knox, banging his head against the wooden doorframe.

'No, *we're all fucked*,' corrected the first voice. 'Might as well get some sleep first.'

'Not if we get it all back before Pottinger gets back from Sydney,' said Trooper Hollister, his Yankee drawl cutting through the apathy and foetid atmosphere to offer the sweating, pale-faced Knox some hope of redemption.

Ten minutes later, Knox and Hollister were in the saddle and, with my old mate Billy Dargin tracking, set off after us. They caught us on the raw in the late afternoon near Pinnacle Reef. They came stampeding out of the bush and with no invitation to 'Stand', opened fire, Hollister yelling that he intended to kill me. Fortunately his aim was poor. It gave us time to get off the road and lead them down a steep slope into a wooded hollow that we were well acquainted with.

Hollister was by far the better horseman of the two, and his spicy nag was soon tight on my tail. I could hear him swearing as I weaved back and forth between the low branches to deny him a clear or steady shot. Patsy was ahead somewhere, giving Knox a run for his money.

We had a clear advantage on the pair of traps as we'd been racing around these woods since we were boys. I took Hollister hurtling down the slope towards a gnarly old gum with a huge, barrel-like girth and several low-hanging boughs. It was a long time since I'd done this trick, and have to confess I muttered a hasty prayer before I set myself to carrying it out. As I passed under the low branches, I reached up and grabbed the stoutest one, using the momentum to swing myself up into its leafy upper reaches. I felt the muscles and sinews in my shoulders and arms pop as I desperately hauled myself upwards, but with the thundering hooves of Hollister's horse close, my survival instinct overcame any discomfort.

Hollister passed directly beneath me a moment or so later. It took him another few seconds before he realised a riderless Willy was galloping away on his own. In the moment it took him to realise that he'd been tricked and to look up to the treetops I had sighted him down the barrel of my pistol.

His quick thinking saved his life. He let go of the reins and threw his hands up just as I squeezed the trigger. The ball ripped through the flesh of his right hand as if it were soft butter, splattering his face with blood, and took his horse in the ribs.

The animal died in a heartbeat, and as its legs folded beneath it, Hollister was pitched over the reins and splayed across the knotty roots of an old eucalyptus. I was on him in a flash, my pistol tickling him between the eyebrows. Instinctively, my finger tightened on the trigger. My moment of truth had arrived. Once you enter the game, killing or being killed becomes a fact of life, and each player has to decide how far he is prepared to go to.

His eyes flickered open, staring straight into mine for a long moment. Agony crossed his face. He watched me cock the hammer of my second barrel, swallowing hard he moved his lips, but no sound came out. He knew his fate rested purely with me. The man had tried to shoot me in cold blood and would do it again if I gave him the chance. But in that moment I made a discovery. I was no killer. I could kill a man in a fair fight perhaps, but never in cold blood. My nature wasn't of that make. The deadlock was broken by the shouts of his mates and the hollow clip-clop of approaching hooves.

A low whistle brought Willy trotting over to me. I pulled the pistol from Hollister's head and straightened up. Tipping my hat mockingly, I bade him farewell with a smile. 'We'll have a proper go next time, Constable Hollister, you can bet on it, mate.'

I put spurs to Willy and didn't slacken the reins for a mile or more, dodging and diving, doubling back on my tracks until I was sure I had lost them. Eventually I caught up with the others.

As we slowed to a trot, Patsy piped up, 'That was a close one.'

'How the bloody hell did that black bastard find us?' said O'Meally sourly. Remembering what Billy had told me long ago, I nodded at a small black bird with white trim, hopping about in front of us on long matchstick legs that seemed much too frail to support its plump, rounded body.

'Maybe he listened to the Willy Wagtails gossiping,' I ventured. 'The Wiradjuri say *djiri-djiri* is a gossip that listens to and repeats everyone's business.' He was also reckoned to be the bearer of bad news, so I tossed a stone, and the bird took off, trilling indignantly.

John O'Meally was in no mood for yarns. 'Bastards didn't even call for us to stand,' he seethed. 'Just opened fire.'

'If that's how he wants it, then that's how he'll get it. I'll pay Mr Hollister back in his own coin,' I replied shrugging off the reminder of just how close a call it had been.

'You should have finished the bastard when you had him, I would have,' growled O'Meally.

I shot him a warning look. 'No need for cold-blooded murder,' I said. 'I'll take him in a fair fight. Don't go putting a noose around your own neck, Johnny, there's plenty that'll do it for you.'

This was a war and, like any other, was fought by representatives, the police on behalf of the squatters and the bushrangers for the poor selectors. No matter how bloody the war, there were still rules, unwritten, and no more than a code of civilised behaviour. To depart from them was to forfeit your own right to be treated fairly. You could not shoot a surrendered or wounded prisoner, and in an ambush it was a given that you called on the other party to stand or surrender before opening fire, if they looked like refusing. I summed this up for the benefit of O'Meally, who had always operated on a short fuse.

'*I awoke one morning and found myself famous,*' was how the Darkie's favourite poet, Lord Byron, once put it. In my case, 'infamous' would have been closer to the mark.

The *Forbes Examiner* carried details of the Pinnacle police station robbery and named the Ben Hall gang as the responsible party. The paper also mentioned that I had been an associate of Gardiner's and a suspect in the Eugowra escort robbery. It went on to say that now that we had armed ourselves with weapons from the police station, citizens were advised to brace themselves for further outrages. It also reported that a furious Pottinger and Sanderson had been recalled from Sydney to take charge and that the amorous Constable Knox was suspended, pending an inquiry. The dispatch ended with the cryptic comment: 'It is trusted that all members of the service would remember in the future, that a wandering police-man can only lead to trouble.'

We followed up the Pinnacle raid with a spree along Lambing Flat road, bailing up travellers and mail coaches at will. Soon we had set up what amounted to a toll system on the main roads through the Lachlan, which the traps were not game to break. Although a mail coach might yield a nice profit now and again, ordinary travellers provided us with most of our loot.

Our routine was simple. We would choose a position along one of the main roads that offered us good views in both directions and across the countryside, wait under a shade tree and bail up every-thing that came past. We abandoned the practice of wearing comforters over our faces, as we had done at Eugowra. Now we wanted people to know that they had been bailed up by the Ben Hall gang.

As the Darkie had taught us, the game had its own rules. We never took silver, often gave back items of sentimental value and never harmed a lady, no matter what the provocation. We left those we robbed with enough money to finish their journey, unless they were rude or tried to escape. In this event we held them upside down and shook them until their money fell out. With this kind of cross work it is necessary to keep those you bail up captive until you're finished, so they don't spoil the road by warning off approaching travellers or tell the traps where you're working. Sometimes we'd have thirty or forty people waiting all day and would have to pull over a dray to provide refreshments for our 'guests'. In hot weather we'd drive the coach to a pub and treat the passengers and the customers to a few beers while we ratted the mailbags. Our cross work gave us seed money to get the gang properly organised.

I was determined to do things differently from Frank Gardiner. For all his success and dash, the Darkie had fallen down when it came to the big job. His clan was riddled with informers and cowards. It cost us the gold, our liberty and our dream of a new life in California. I vowed that this time we'd be better prepared.

We returned to the safe embrace of the Weddin Mountains and discovered a well-hidden cave buried away high in the red granite outcrops and lush canopy and established a secret lair. We stashed supplies of blankets, tinned food, ammunition and guns so we could lie doggo when we needed to. A precipitous cliff line guarded against the possibility of an attack from above, but if a quick get-away was ever needed there was a bush track down to Black Gin Gully where we spelled the horses. Several gullies ran down off the mountains so it had good grass and water most of the year.

A few hundred feet above us at two thousand feet was the Eualdrie peak, the highest point in the Weddin range. Set into the rocky outcrop was the wedge-shaped Picnic Rock, a solid stone platform that knifed out into the abyss. It offered panoramic views over the dusty green treetops to the distant plains shimmering on the horizon and fair warning of any approaching parties we preferred not to meet.

Just in case we ever came under siege, we spent a few days hard yakka setting up some surprises. Along the way to our hideouts we pulled and tied back a number of young saplings, which, when released, would whip back into their original position with enough force to knock a whole cavalry off their horses.

With great effort, we rolled some large boulders up to the mouth of the cave and placed them behind a barrier of wooden stakes we had cut, sharpened and driven into the ground. The removal of key stakes would provide a crude, but bone crushingly effective defence against invaders. Not a bad bit of earth for a clan of

'Vandemonians' as the papers liked to call us. Robin Hood had Sherwood Forest and the Ben Hall gang had the Weddin Mountains. Even with all the blacktrackers in the colony in their pay, the traps would never find us here.

At the foot of the Weddins, ten miles south-west of Mount Wheogo and Sandy Creek, lived a number of families of Irish descent. The best known of them were the O'Meallys, Downeys and Nowlans, who were all inter-related by a complex web of blood marriage, and sympathy to our cause. We knew the layout and the allegiances of every farm and the speed, endurance and pluck of all their horses. In these parts, it was much easier to be the fox than the huntsman.

I heard it often said that bushrangers robbed the rich to give to the poor. We didn't give away money, but exchanged it for shelter, fresh horses, food, weapons and ammunition. We also supported a large cast of informants, 'bush telegraphs' and 'flying squads' who were vital to our survival.

Flying squads were decoy gangs of young men who would ride to one end of the district and do a bit of road work or worry the squatters and storekeepers. Thinking it was the Ben Hall gang at work, the traps would be attracted to them like flies to horseshit, leaving us to go about our business unhindered.

We disposed of all personal items through 'Coobang' Mick Connelly. Like the Darkie, Mick was a curly-headed, swarthy-skinned, half Aboriginal who made his living from all manner of shady dealings, such as cattle duffing and fencing the jewellery, watches, gold and other precious items we collected and taking a cut for his trouble. Mick also acted as my banker, keeping my money safe until I needed it. Through these methods we took from the rich and re-distributed it amongst some of its poorer citizens. As our da used to say, ''Tis a noble calling.' There were, of course, exceptions to the rule.

One wet, drizzly evening, we were returning from a profitable day's cross work on the Young road. All day, a sullen sun had refused to lift its bright face from the grey folds of cloud, only allowing the odd shaft of weak, filtered light to break through its thick cover. There was a strange belief held by a great many folk that bushrangers didn't turn out when the weather was foul. We knew this and made a point of going out in the rain knowing our takings would be up as superstitions don't die easily hereabouts.

The mists and early darkness that closed in around us promised a wet, cold night ahead and we were anxious to be back in our crib round the fire. When we were still a few hours away from the cave, we saw a spiral of thin, wispy black smoke rising out of the bush.

We left the road and followed the trail of smoke through the wet bush to its source. As we got closer, my heart began to race as that familiar, acrid smell of burnt charcoal and damp drifted up to me, even overpowering the reek of stale piss that came off the Gidgee trees whenever it rained.

My worst fears were confirmed when we arrived in a clearing and found a woman in her middle years clutching onto a girl of about eight next to the still smoking timbers of the slabbed hut that had once been their home.

As we dismounted and walked over to them, the woman gave us a fearful look and the little girl buried her face in her ma's long skirts. There were many strange, cruel characters knocking about in the backblocks and I could see she was wondering what further indignities we were about to inflict on them.

The few bits of clothes and furniture they had managed to save from the fire were strewn in the mud, sodden through with small puddles of water forming around them.

'What happened?' I asked the woman as gently as I could. Although I already suspected from her gaunt, hollow-eyed expression that Pottinger's mob had probably glimmed her home, just as they had mine.

'The traps burnt our hut,' she mumbled, confirming my suspicions. In her voice, I heard the same defeat and pain that our ma had that night our da was dragged off by Kennedy. I reached out and laid a hand of sympathy on the little girl's head.

'Why did they do that?' As she raised a grimy hand and pushed back a strand of greying hair off her brow, trailing a streak of mud across her forehead, I noticed her hand was shaking. In a low, tired voice she explained, 'The owner wanted to sell the land, but we'd already paid our rent for the whole year and refused to go. The traps turned up a few days ago, said my husband was duffing Mr Iceley's cattle and then took him away. They came back again today and said that the owner didn't want duffers living on his land and wanted us gone.' Her head drooped in defeat, 'Then they set fire to our hut.'

'Who's the owner around here?' asked Patsy from his place at my elbow.

'Grant,' I answered dryly. 'A well-known pimp. This must be his wages.'

Since the discovery of gold, the value of land in the Lachlan had soared. The small selectors and bush dwellers were being pushed out and vast tracts sold off to bigger landowners. Those who wouldn't go quietly were being persuaded by these kind of rough-house tactics.

'Have you family here?' I asked her.

'No, sor, they're all back in Oireland,' she replied in a low voice. The tears she brushed away from her wind-reddened cheeks were mingled with dewdrops from the persistent drizzle that had fallen steadily from the leaden skies all day.

As the daylight faded around us, I knew we couldn't just abandon the woman and the child out here. I reached into my sack and brought out a roll of notes, which I pressed into her hand. 'Here, love, take it. See you and the girl get a place to stay till you can bail out your man.'

The woman blinked. She had probably never seen such a wad in her life. 'Head for Newcastle an' get yersels t' California on the next boat. I've heard it's grand there.' Still she hesitated, so I told her a lie. 'It's out of the pocket of one of the biggest squatters in this district and it's the best offer you'll get the night, Missus.'

On hearing that she seemed to regain her balance a bit and came towards me, her eyes misted over with tears of gratitude and said, 'God bless ye, sor.'

Before I guessed her game, she had grabbed my hand and kissed it like I was the Pope. I had no such power, but as the Irish say, 'If I were God, I would sort him', him being Pottinger.

Motioning Mickey off his horse, which was the only one come by honestly, I added, 'We'll leave this one for you and the girl. There's no side-saddle, but it'll get you into town. Leave him at the Harp o' Erin when you're done with him.'

I turned to leave, but she stopped me with a question.

'Can I ask yer name, sor?'

'Ben Hall.'

'Ye're the fella that has been givin' the traps a dose of their own medicine.'

'That's right.'

'Good luck t'ye and a long reign,' she said in a stronger voice, the first signs of a defiant smile twitching at the corners of her mouth. 'You'll be in our prayers the night.'

I tipped the brim of my hat before climbing back into the saddle. *Whatever they say, there was some good in us.*

But as we turned for home, it was clear that the milk of human kindness wasn't flowing from everyone. 'That roll you handed her was all our rations,' protested O'Meally as we gained the main road again.

'What's a day's rations to you lot?' I snapped back, eyeballing him hard.

'You've a fat roll in your pocket and a flash shirt for every day of the week. That woman and bairn had just what they stood in. I've stood in her shoes, John me boy, an' that's where you an' me's different–'

I cut him dead by digging my heels into Willy's flanks putting on a short spurt for home.

A little later as we all sat silently round the fire, I knew it was time I told them what was on my mind.

Taking a moment to gather my thoughts, I stood up, wandered to the mouth of the cave and looked out into the darkness until my eyes got used to it. The night was moonless, but the blaze of starlight from the heavens still threw a thin filter of pale light across the surrounding countryside. My eye followed the rolling contours of the land. It was as still as the grave, the perfect silence only broken by the yipping of dingos. I thought back to what happened in the clearing that afternoon. It was the first time that I realised there was more at stake than my grievance with Pottinger. Whether we liked it or not, we represented the grievances of a whole class of people. I turned to face the others who were eyeing me expectantly.

'Anyone who thinks he's in this game just for himself is sadly mistaken,' I started. 'Whether we like it or not they are our people and we'll live and die by them, so best we show them our good side.' My eyes flicked in O'Meally's direction for emphasis. 'That good deed we did today will be paid back one hundredfold. The old high-waymen did it and we'll do it too. If that's too big for anyone to bag in their swags, leave now, before things get serious.' I looked at them one by one, taking my time about it as well, but no one moved. 'That's settled then,' I said, hunkering down beside the fire, and filling up my bowl with another helping of stew. We never spoke about it again.

Shortly after we started operations, a bush telegraph informed us that the Darkie's lieutenant, Johnny Gilbert, had returned from the Otago goldfields. I considered him the most daring and cool headed of the Gardiner gang and immediately suggested that he join us.

We gathered at the cave and drank a toast to the return of Gilbert, absent friends and to the dream of getting clear to California, which we shared with Patsy.

'We'll whip everything that moves, make a bundle and clear out to America,' he declared with boyish enthusiasm. Raising our bottles in another wild toast Gilbert shouted over the din, 'See you in Hell . . . or in California!' It would become our catch call which we repeated each time we parted. At the start, it was no more complicated than that.

Chapter Thirteen

The formation of the Ben Hall gang took place in the shadow of the trial of the Eugowra escort robbers, which began on February 3, 1863, at Darlinghurst court in Sydney. The trial was reported in detail by the *Sydney Morning Herald* and was the talk of New South Wales. We relied on our contacts to keep us informed.

Three series of knocks sounded at the door of the Tutils' modest slab hut, which was tucked away in a gully five miles out the back of Forbes where we often lay doggo. As I pulled open the rough slab door, the single glim that burned inside threw a dull, orange glow onto the lined face of local Forbes magistrate Tom Morris. He was sympathetic to our cause and paid well to be. Now close to sixty, he was sent to Botany Bay in irons at the same time as our da, but he had worked hard, invested wisely and removed the convict stain from his name. He dressed like a squatter, but never forgot the pull of the chain, and the Devil's claws he wore on his back. He said many times that, but for the grace of God he would have taken up the game himself.

'Tom,' I said with a friendly nod and stood aside to let him in.

'I just came from the *Examiner* where them telegraph wires from Bathurst have been twitchin' like a roo's hind leg,' he chuckled, trailing a wreath of fragrant pipe smoke into the rough bark hut behind him.

He nodded at the others as he took a seat next to Gilbert at the big slabbed table and rolled an inquisitive eye towards the bottle of Old Tom that sat in the middle. I nodded and he poured himself a nobbler and started re-packing his clay pipe with tobacco from a soft buckskin pouch. He liked to get himself set for a good yarn, but he sensed our impatience and threw us a juicy morsel of news.

'Yair, they lifted Henry Manns at the Wombat diggings near Young a week back,' he announced. 'An armed escort delivered him straight down to Sydney.'

'So they tried him with the rest?' I shot back, a sick feeling in the pit of my stomach as I thought of him in a stone cell at Darlinghurst prison.

'Nah, the aptly named Judge Wise ruled he'd no time to prepare a proper defence and he'll be tried on his own.'

'So, what happened?'

'Well, after Bow, Fordyce and McGuire all pleaded "not guilty" to robbery under arms and wounding Sergeant Condell, the identities of the turncoats who had turned Queen's evidence were revealed. There was a feral hissing as the trap's star witness, "Flash" Dan Charters, was called to the stand.' I was sad to hear it said of an old chum, but O'Meally had no truck with old loyalties.

'Bastard!' he growled from the darkness to my left. 'Should've pinked him at Eugowra when he refused to bear arms.' He was silent after that, doubtless inflicting his own punishment on him over and over in the closed prison of his own mind.

Tom's pipe glowed like a beacon and he continued in his laconic way, 'His testimony was what the criminal fraternity would call a "royal spread", lies, half-truths and sheer fantasy designed to keep his own neck out of that hempen cravat. The Bible was still warm from his touch when he told his first lie. He claimed he was the only one forced into joining the gang and was brought down to Eugowra at gunpoint where he was entrusted with the vital job of securing the horses – the only means of escape and of transporting the loot. He insisted that all he gained from the robbery was a gold nugget and fifty pounds.'

'Dan was in it up to his neck,' fumed Gilbert. 'He and I went into town to buy all the supplies and then he and Manns made the bullets we used in the bail-up.'

'He has a knack of getting away with it–' I said, thinking back to poor Henry McBride who got fanged by the snake when we were boys.

'Oh, but he didn't,' interrupted Tom with a wave of his hand. 'Their QC, James Martin, nailed Dan for the difference in evidence Dan gave during the trial and the earlier statement he gave Dr Palmer at Bathurst. When he refused to say if he'd made his statement to Dr Palmer before or after he was bailed and whether it was a condition of his bail, the public knew Dan had turned Queen's evidence in return for a free pass.'

'So, why didn't he flee during the robbery, when he had the chance?' I muttered.

'Oh, he said he was scared of the Darkie,' replied Tom with a chuckle. 'Martin also nailed his other great lie that he only received fifty pounds and a gold nugget for his part in the robbery.'

'He didn't even deserve that,' snorted O'Meally. Tom paused to spit a dark stream of baccy juice into the fire and then picked up where he left off.

'Martin reminded him that in his first statement to Dr Palmer, he said that the gold was made up into eight shares.' Lifting his hand for dramatic effect old Tom counted the participants on his fingers. 'It was plain that Dan must have been in that number. He had no comeback to that.' There were satisfied nods that at least Dan had framed himself as one of the robbers.

'There'd be one lie you will be glad he told,' continued Tom looking at O'Meally and then at me. 'He named everyone in the gang, except you two. He claimed he only knew you as "Billy" and "Charley".' For all his treachery and self-serving lies, some part of Dan had remained true to his childhood chums, or at least that was the only explanation I could offer. Tom puffed thoughtfully for a moment before delivering the bad news.

'Sadly, your mate McGuire wasn't so lucky,' continued Tom. 'Charters testified that Jacky was mates with the Darkie and had helped set the whole thing up.' My own relief was suddenly mingled with guilt for Jacky who was now staring at the hangman's noose.

'Tom Richards didn't do McGuire any favours either. Said he was working for McGuire at the time of the robbery and saw the Darkie, Jacky and Gilbert arrive at McGuire's for a meeting a week before the robbery. Others arrived later, but he didn't see them. He also said on the Sunday afternoon of the robbery that Jacky had looked at his fob and said to him, "The boys will be at it now." To his credit, Martin gave Richards a good roasting by asking if he'd been tried for rape in Adelaide and had run a brothel in Forbes.'

'What did he say to that?'

'Refused to answer and also kept quiet when Martin alleged that he had arranged to be arrested before making a confession in order to cover up the fact that he volunteered the information to get a slice of the fat.'

Seeing our mood had darkened considerably he laughed to himself and slapped me on the knee.

'This story has a ways to go yet. Dr Hans Slidell, the main defence witness, shot the prosecution's argument that Fordyce was one of the robbers to pieces.' As Tom again paused to spit a thick stream of brown baccy juice into the fire, we all pictured our neighbour, a large, bearded man in his late fifties whose heavy black cloth frock and dress coat announced him as a foreigner long before his heavily accented English. Tom picked up the story.

'Slidell told defence barrister James Martin that on the day Charters claimed Fordyce was being chased by police on Mount Wheogo he had been out looking for stray bullocks and met him between the Walsh and Nowlan places, miles away from the scene of the crime. By all accounts, Pottinger looked fit to burst.'

'So what was the result?' demanded O'Meally. Tom held up his hand and with a wide smile finished his yarn.

'The jury were still deadlocked at ten o'clock that night, so the judge ordered them to spend the night in court. The next morning, they still couldn't be split, so Judge Wise dismissed the jury and left it up to the Crown to decide whether to acquit the prisoners or re-try them. A great cheer went up in the public gallery when they realised Pottinger had been thwarted and journalists stampeded out of the court to file their stories. But the Attorney-General wasn't prepared to let it lie and asked the Judge to remand the prisoners in custody until they fixed a date for a new trial that would include Henry Manns.'

'So, it wasn't a win.'

'Nor a loss either. Public sympathy is with them. People in Sydney see Australia as a land of wealth and opportunity and want to see an end to the harsh convict rule. They've heard about the injustices of the land acts and how the police operate in bush areas. They know the world's changing and that Australia must change with it.' I had never been to Sydney, but the notion that people thought differently in a city a few hundred miles to the east seemed unbelievable. He might as well have been talking about another country.

'I hope that change comes quickly for the sakes of those boys,' I muttered.

While the trial occupied public attention, we used the absence of Pottinger and Sergeant Sanderson, who were in Sydney testifying at the trial, to good effect. The raid on the Pinnacle police station showed we didn't fear the traps and we proved it again by bagging three of the district's top policemen in quick succession.

We took the first one on a wet, drab day near my old station at Sandy Creek. We were alerted to the fact we were being tailed by a pair of rainbow-coloured wood parrots who shot out of the grass behind us trilling an alarm that sounded as if they had bells round their necks. They brought a rare dash of colour to the flat, rain-laden sky that seemed to merge into the lifeless grey karoo, making it hard to tell where the sky ended and the earth began.

We were aware that someone had been tailing us since we robbed Solomon's store, just outside Grenfell, a few hours before.

'Let's find out what we've got,' I said to the boys. We waited until we approached a narrow gully that dipped down sharply and had steep, wooded slopes on both sides – a perfect spot for an ambush. At my signal, Gilbert and I slipped from our saddles just before we reached the gully. O'Meally and Patsy went on with the four horses, so that whoever was following would see the same number of tracks.

Gilbert and I lay flat in the wet grass and watched the men file past a short time later. One was the blacktracker, Billy Dargin, who must have picked up our spoor back at Solomon's, and the other I took to be Trooper Hollister, the cove who tried to kill me after the Pinnacle police station robbery. *Now we'll see just who'll kill who.* I thought grimly as I watched our tails approach the gully warily, and then disappear from sight as they started their descent.

As soon as they were halfway down Patsy and O'Meally came around a tree and galloped at them at full speed. Borrowing the Darkie's old war cry, 'Bail up, you bastards!', O'Meally fired both barrels of his shotgun, forcing Hollister to dismount and use his horse's rump as a rest to return fire.

Meanwhile, Patsy, Gilbert and I stood up in the grass and used the distraction caused by O'Meally's charge to attack from behind. Realising they had been caught in a pincer movement, and that there was no way out, Hollister and Billy traversed and fired, trying to keep us at bay. Bullets sang through the air, along with shouts and curses as they failed to find their mark.

Seeing Billy had run out of bullets and Hollister trying to re-load, I charged in with my gun raised. Hollister threw down his gun and raised his hands, just as I squeezed the trigger.

At that moment I realised the man I had taken to be Trooper Hollister was, in fact, Sub-Inspector John Oxley Norton! He saw it coming.

My trigger clicked and Norton instinctively closed his eyes and turned his head away. I tried to pull my hand to the side. Desperately, I bade time slow just long enough to avoid killing the wrong man. The hammer hit the charge, the bullet exploded out of the barrel and smashed into the gum next to Norton, missing him by a whisker and spraying his face with hot wood chips. Such was the noise and the force of the impact on the trunk that he lost his footing on the wet grass and fell to the ground.

Billy Dargin used the drama of the mistaken identity to plunge into the bush. I went after him in hot pursuit. That bugger had already cost us the Eugowra gold and was far more dangerous than any trap. I vowed that if I caught up to him, I'd slice his hamstrings like a rogue bullock. That would put paid to his tracking days.

But Billy had other ideas. He was limber, but couldn't outrun Willy and sensing me coming up fast on his shoulder, he turned and flung his empty Navy Colt revolver. It hit me just above my right ear, stunning me momentarily. By the time I dismounted he had disappeared like a wisp of smoke.

Some believe the blackfellas are 'shape changers' and that they can turn themselves into a rock, a tree, a bird or an animal. A rustle of feathers drew my eye upwards. A big black and white currawong looked down at me with a steady yellow eye.

'Bugger off, Billy,' I muttered, picking up a stone to fling at it. But as soon as I drew back my arm, the bird lifted off the branch and lazily floated upwards to roost on a higher branch. I tried to unseat him a second time and it repeated the move. Billy and I would have to wait until another day. I had an important guest to attend to.

Covered by O'Meally, Patsy and Gilbert, Sub-Inspector Norton still sat under the stout gum where I'd almost nailed him, little caring that there was mud splattered on his splendid navy uniform and that the arse of his fine grey trousers was soaked through with cold, autumn rain.

His thin, fair hair that he had carefully arranged to cover his balding pate had gone awry and was plastered to one side of his head revealing his bald spot. The charge and shock of the gun going off so close to his head had deafened and shaken him up considerably. His china blue eyes were glazed over and he wore a look of shock on his face. He seemed to be fascinated by the ugly wound my ball had made in the stout ghost gum, which still fizzed with hostility and heat, fingering it and watching the red resin, which is as smooth to the touch as human skin, bleeding out onto the white bark.

This detachment is a common state for men who have taken the field, heard the roar of the cannon, looked death square in the face and lived to tell the tale. As I approached, my pistol hanging from my right hand, his eyes swivelled in my direction. I could see him wondering if I had just kept him alive for my own cruel pleasure, so I could pretend to give him life and then take it away.

Norton swallowed hard and he had to expend considerable effort to keep his voice steady, 'What do you intend to do with me?'

I said nothing, just continued to look down at him. I crouched down on my haunches and looked into his eyes.

'Why, nothing, Inspector Norton,' I replied coolly. 'I just intend to tell you a story. So listen closely.'

A puzzled look crossed his face. Was I just toying with him or perhaps, as had been rumoured, I was not in possession of all my faculties.

'Ben Hall's the name, and I'm no criminal. At least I wasn't until your lot drove me to it.'

Norton said nothing, but a look of disdain crossed his face.

Feeling my patience snap, I grabbed his chin and forced his face up. My return to menace got his full attention.

'I was a friend to the police, until they falsely accused me of being in Gardiner's gang and held me for a month, and then released me without charge. Although I have never been convicted of any crime, Pottinger burned my hut and left £2,000 worth of cattle stock to die of thirst, then Trooper Hollister tried to shoot me with no offer to stand–'

'And would you have stood if he'd asked you to?' ventured Norton, his pale eyes riveted to mine.

'No, I'd have fought him fair and square, and had he plugged me, I wouldn't have grumbled, that's the fortune of war. I'll tell you this much, Mr Norton, you'll never take me alive!'

I asked him if he understood. He nodded dumbly in reply. I stood up and held out my hand.

'Give me your watch.'

That snapped him out of his lethargy.

'What do you want with my watch? You already have one,' he protested, nodding at the fob chain slung across my chest.

'A trophy, Mr Norton. Some men would have taken your head, but I'm no murderer, so I'll settle for your watch. Otherwise, who's going to believe that Sub-Inspector Norton was really at the mercy of Ben Hall?'

He pulled out a big old turnip of a silver watch, handed it over and watched with a sour expression as I made it dance at the end of its chain. In matters of metal, I preferred yellow to white, but couldn't help admiring the way the sunlight glinted off its fine silver. Besides, its value was greater than any amount of money.

'I wonder if they'll hang those boys this time?' I said, referring to the second Eugowra escort trial, which was about to start in Sydney.

Norton shrugged his shoulders. 'It's in the hands of the jury,' he replied, his eyes following his fob watch as it disappeared into my pocket.

'It was my father's,' he said, an aggrieved edge to his voice.

'Then you have my word that I'll return it to you on the day you leave this district,' I said by way of consolation.

Having got over the shock of his near-death experience, Sub-Inspector Norton became his querulous old self. 'I'm not going anywhere,' he snapped back. 'The likes of you won't stand against the law.'

'We'll see about that,' I said cheerfully. 'Mr McLerie may rule the roost in Sydney, but this is our country. Out here, we're the kings of the heat and the dust and the flies. We're like naked savages on a hostile shore. If you land, we might just put an arrow in your eye.' I tipped the brim of my hat and turned on my heel.

It took a couple of hours for Billy Dargin to reach the nearest station and for a rider to raise the alarm in Forbes. Pottinger raised a civilian volunteer force of one hundred and fifty armed men, mostly squatters, storekeepers and assorted do-gooders who feared our menacing rise. Most ordinary folk had the good sense to stay out of it.

The largest armed force to have ever saddled up in the Lachlan arrived at the gully just after dark to find Sub-Inspector Norton sitting under the gum, unharmed, but minus his wallet, watch and horse.

The final act of the Eugowra escort trials was played out in late February, just a week after we bailed up Norton. We met Tom at the Tutils' again, but this time he didn't keep us waiting. He crossed the threshold shaking his head, 'Took the jury under two hours to come back with a "guilty" and that bastard Stephen laid the black cloth on his lambskin and sentenced them to swing.' He was referring to Chief Justice Sir Alfred Stephen who had the poisonous glare of a cut snake and whose opinion that bushrangers were 'the scum of the earth' was well known in the colony.

'Dan Charters sang again, stuck to the same story and named Henry Manns as part of the gang, who didn't help matters by making a clean breast of it.'

'What?' exclaimed Gilbert.

Tom nodded sagely.

'Aye, after Pottinger had been up, Stephen asked the accused if they wanted to cross-examine him. They all declined, Manns saying, "It was all correct, on Saturday last at Mr McLerie's office, I pleaded guilty to Pottinger."

'To make matters worse, between the trials your old mate Detective Lyons arrested Dr Slidell on a three-year-old warrant. Seems Slidell is not a physician, but some time back attended a sick girl who went under. The police arrested him, kept him in the logs and released him the day after the trial without charge.'

'Bastards!'

'What about Jacky?'

'That's the only good news. Jacky got off.' His grim countenance told us that any celebrations would be premature, so we held our peace.

'It came out that his wife Ellen was staying with that pimp Charters at the Harp o' Erin. His lawyer gave "Flash" Dan a good coating, claiming that Charters was only trying to lag Jacky so he could take up with his wife. I think it worked.'

I shook my head. *What is it with these Walsh women that they must throw over good men to take up with rogues? Are they she-devils in the guise of women who, in the end, must gravitate back towards their own kind?*

'Stephen pronounced the sentence of death on Bow, Fordyce and Manns with the words, "God have mercy on your souls – I advise you to look alone to Him for mercy, for I cannot hold out any exercise of mercy here and you, as condemned men, can scarcely expect it."'

There was a humble silence as we all imagined the moment of cold dread as they watched the black cloth being laid over Stephen's lambskin. *But for the grace of God* . . . I felt especially wretched as the idea of robbing the escort was mine. Not for the last time I would ask myself what started me down this crooked path. I would start with Biddy, but could never go past Pottinger and the burning desire for vengeance. Tom brought us out of ourselves by raising his glass and saying in that melodious rumble of his, 'No use dwelling on it, boys. It's just the fortune of war.'

We replied by bagging our second ranking officer. In early March we were working the Forbes road when we spied an approaching buggy. Watching from behind the willowy, yellow fronds of a wattle tree, whose thick summer growth made it an ideal hiding-place, we could see that two of the party were ladies and the other passenger was none other than Sub-Inspector Shadforth, identifiable by his blue uniform and squat, round-shouldered build. Gilbert reckoned the women were the wives of prominent squatters in the area and Shadforth had been asked to provide a personal escort for them to Forbes.

We listened and waited as the sound of clattering hooves and wheels got louder. When the buggy was about twenty yards away we burst out from our cover and positioned ourselves in the middle of the road. The buggy slewed wildly across the dusty road and came to a halt. I drew up alongside it, raised my hat politely and called out, 'Good afternoon, ladies, Sub-Inspector Shadforth. A lovely day for a drive.'

Shadforth's right hand instinctively went to his holster but fell away when he saw he was covered from all sides. I removed my hat and bowed all gallant like as if I was a Prince of the blood myself.

With my revolver in one hand, the other hand holding my hat across my chest in a courtly gesture, I said, 'Begging your pardon, ladies, Ben Hall, bushranger, at your service. In case Mr Shadforth has not explained it to you, it is something of a colourful tradition that when travelling in these wild, ungovernable parts, we relieve you of your money and valuables. I'm sure your husbands will have no trouble replacing them. Ladies, if you please.' With a sunny smile I held out my hat towards them, inviting them to place their valuables in it. The ladies looked nervously over at Shadforth who was obviously embarrassed by his failure to protect them. He nodded that they should co-operate, but the look in his eyes said he wanted to skin us alive.

As they parted with their loot, I took a moment to study them. Most Australian men would rather look at a horse, but I always had a keen eye for the doxies and studied them at every opportunity. Given my newfound profession, I rarely met them in agreeable circumstances these days. My romantic life had been reduced to brief, nocturnal interludes here and there, so this was indeed a rare opportunity. Both women were elegantly and fashionably turned out, as might be expected of women of their class and wealth. I could see that their husbands had not been spared any expense in importing the latest fashions and accessories from Europe.

One was quite short and plump probably around twenty-five years of age. Even though she wore her hair piled up on her head and covered by a silk scarf, a few rogue strands which were the colour of ripened corn had escaped and settled on the back of her neck. The lines around her mouth betrayed her sour disposition, most probably resulting from a life of boredom or an unhappy marriage. Her companion was quite a different proposition.

Tall and lithe, she sat in the buggy with a poise and grace not enjoyed by her rather heavy-boned travelling companion. I guessed her to be about my age, raven-haired, small, delicate features and the most bewitching hazel-coloured eyes. There was something of the exotic about her, Spanish or Italian perhaps, though her voice betrayed no foreign origins as I asked for the ornate locket around her slender neck. Her face clouded.

'It was my late mother's, a family heirloom,' she said with a clear English accent, uncluttered by that false upper-class accent that many of her 'colonial cousins' insisted on imitating.

I allowed myself a smile. 'And very fine it looks on you too,' I said softly. 'You may keep it, if only to see that radiant smile return to your face.'

Although bushrangers were constantly portrayed as heartless, unprincipled thieves, we did strive to follow a chivalrous path, in certain matters. She nodded demurely by way of a thank you, but I noted that our exchange had brought a slight flush to her cheeks. Since entering the bushranging game I had learnt that there were certain women who had a secret fascination for dangerous men who stray outside the law. Such women filled the bolter Martin Cash's cell with flowers before his execution and attended bushranger funerals to weep over their graves as if they were kin. This fine-looking doxy had clearly taken a certain pleasure at the thought that she was at the mercy of the notorious Ben Hall gang and confirmed my suspicions by lowering her eyes and allowing the faintest of smiles to play across her lips.

Our sport was rudely interrupted by Shadforth's feeble attempt to put a better face on the situation. Seeing Johnny Gilbert depositing a very respectable haul into my saddlebag, he piped up, 'Don't think you'll get away with this, Ben Hall. My men patrol this road and they'll soon be onto you–'

Not wishing to hear another word of his bluster, I cut in on him, 'Then it would be unseemly to involve these ladies in such unpleasant business.' Pausing to cover him with my pistol, I added, 'So best you hand over your pistol, watch and money without delay.'

Shadforth handed over the pistol and money without question, but thinking he might be given the same consideration as his travelling companion, he held back his watch, grumbling that it was his father's.

Offended that he tried to play upon my good and generous nature, I quickly put him in his place by snatching it from his open hand and admonishing him sharply.

'I've a good mind to take your father's trousers too! That would give the good folk of Forbes something to gossip about when you reach town!'

The ladies lifted their gloved hands to suppress a giggle as a look of horror passed over Shadforth's flushed face. Knowing the kind of wicked cove I was, he didn't say another word.

Indicating that the ladies should cover their ears, I discharged his pistol into the ground and handed his piece back to him. 'Ladies, Sub-Inspector, have a pleasant day. We've concluded our business here and I can assure you that your passage home will be without let or hindrance from us.'

Looking directly at the dark-haired one, I said softly, 'I hope we may meet again in more agreeable circumstances.' With a final lift of my hat, I motioned that they were free to move along. The dark-haired beauty afforded me a brief, flirtatious sideways glance and for the first time since I decided to take on the game, I felt a pang of regret for the life I had left behind.

The Ben Hall gang completed a notable trinity a couple of weeks later when we went in search of fresh horseflesh at Currawang station near Lambing Flat. By happy coincidence, Inspector Wolfe happened to be visiting the station's owner James Roberts, so I liberated his watch and two horses, including the champion hurdler Mickey Hunter. For a while afterwards I rode around with the watches of the three police inspectors on my chain and we worked up a little comic skit for our amusement. One of us would ask in a loud voice, 'What time is it?', and I would pull out my fob chain with the three watches, hold them all up and reply, 'Three o'clock!'. The questioner would then scratch his head and inquire, 'Would that be according to Norton, Shadforth or Wolfe?'

The press got wind of our skit and published it. We enjoyed a laugh at the traps' expense, but knew it would not be without cost.

A few weeks of heavy police activity around the Weddins and Mount Wheogo areas followed. From our vantage point, high up on top of Eualdrie, we watched their powdery dust trails move back and forth across the blue horizon. We knew it was them without ever putting the strong glass to our eyes – poking, probing, bullying and threatening known harbourers and telegraphs. They'd never find our crib unless someone gave them the office.

Once again, young Warrigal Walsh paid the price for Pottinger's incompetence when he was arrested for the second time in six months. The charge was that he worked for the Darkie as a telegraph and had supplied him with fresh horses after the Eugowra job. When Pottinger asked if he knew where the Darkie was keeping dark, Warrigal kept his own counsel. Gardiner had a good eye for the ones he could trust.

'You've nothing on me,' shouted Warrigal as the traps made a big show of manhandling him out of the Uoka homestead in front of the station hands.

'Then you've nothing to worry about,' smirked Pottinger smoothly. 'According to the law you're innocent until proven guilty.'

'Innocent until proven Irish more like,' retorted Warrigal giving Pottinger a good coating. The cheer from the onlookers dashed Sir Frederick's little victory – a wanton act that would not be forgotten.

We lost Patsy Daly in mid-March. Patsy and I were returning the fifteen miles from Grenfell to the cave and were passing the gold diggings at Pinnacle Reef when a rover patrol, led by Pottinger, came out of nowhere and started after us. We tried to lose them by dodging between the mounds of red mullock, disgorged from the ground by pick and shovel. Normally, we'd have lost them amongst the thousands of people digging, panning and sifting, but the workings were deserted on a Sabbath.

'Split up and hide,' I told him as we dismounted.

I ran into a luckless digger's bark hut that had started to go to ruin. I drew my pistol and watched through a gap in the wooden slabs as Pottinger's mob arrived. Patsy fled down a tunnel that burrowed deep into the hillside, but his faithful horse did him in by standing at the entrance, whereas Willy the Weasel had the horse sense to take off into the bush and wait until called.

'Come out, Daly, we have you covered. There's no way out.' Pottinger's gruff voice echoed down the hole. There was no reply, so Pottinger gave him an ultimatum.

'Fifteen minutes, then we smoke you out.'

Knowing they would have to go all the way, Pottinger struck a lucifer match and lit one of his cigars, which he held between clenched teeth. Meanwhile, his troopers gathered a pile of dry leaves and twigs, put them at the mouth of the pit and laid armfuls of green leaved branches on top. By the time they had finished Pottinger had smoked his cigar down to a glowing butt, which he held gingerly between his fingers.

'Last chance, Daly!' he called. 'Come on out, man, there's nothing to be gained by wasting any more time.' No reply. A minute ticked by, then another. With an oath Pottinger dropped the stub of the cigar on the bonfire. A few minutes of rising plumes of smoke, then yellow flame greedily consumed the tinder, crackling as it took a hold. Pottinger's men fanned the flames with cut green saplings, sending clouds of smoke drifting down into the tunnel.

A few minutes later, Patsy stumbled out of the pit half-blinded by the smoke, collapsing in a coughing heap. He couldn't resist as Pottinger clicked the darbies on. Afterwards Pottinger stood about shaking hands, laughing and congratulating his men. Patsy got fifteen years for robbery under arms.

Although he fancied he held the power of life and death in his hands, Chief Justice Sir Alfred Stephen didn't have the last word on the Eugowra escort robbery – Bow and Fordyce were reprieved, but for all the theatre of wigs and gowns, the conviction of Henry Manns on a dubious confession was allowed to stand. Although the police recovered most of the gold, they had no one to hang its theft on and two police constables had been wounded. Someone had to pay. James Martin, the defence lawyer at the first trial, summed it up best: 'It is only in revolutionary, semi-barbarous or unsettled times that criminals are offered not in vindication of the laws but as a sacrifice.'

Henry Manns was hanged at Darlinghurst Gaol on March 26, despite a spirited public campaign by prominent Sydney citizens and a petition for clemency signed by 14,000 people. Even prayers to Joe Samuels fell on deaf ears. He had gone to the gallows three times in 1824 and each time the knot slipped or the rope snapped. Samuels was given a Royal pardon. Although it appeared that some divine hand had decreed that Samuels should live, the truth was that his execution was bungled, just like Henry's.

We held a wake for Henry and Tom Morris brought out a copy of the *Sydney Morning Herald*. Their Lachlan correspondent was never slow to call for punitive action against bushrangers, but the sorry scene appalled even him:

When at length these [preparations] were completed and the bolt was drawn, there ensued one of the most appalling spectacles ever witnessed at an execution.

The noose of the rope, instead of passing tightly around the neck, slipped completely away, the knot coming round in front of the face, while the whole weight of the criminal's body was sustained by the thick muscles of the poll. The rope, in short, went around the middle of the head, and the work of the hangman proved a most terrible bungle.

The sufferings and struggles of the wretched being were heartrending to behold. His body swayed about, and writhed, evidently in the most intense agony. The arms repeatedly rose and fell, and finally, with one of his hands the unfortunate man gripped the rope as if to tear the pressure from his head – a loud guttural noise meanwhile proceeding from his throat and lungs, while blood gushed from his nostrils and stained the cap with which his face was covered.

This awful scene lasted for more than ten minutes when stillness ensued, and it was hoped that death had terminated the culprit's sufferings.

Shocking to relate, however, the vital spark was not yet extinguished, and to the horror of all present, the convulsive writhings were renewed – the tenacity to life being remarkable, and a repetition of the sickening scene was only at last terminated, at the instance of Dr West, by the aid of four confinees who were made to hold the dying malefactor up in their arms while the executioner re-adjusted the rope, when the body was let fall with a jerk, and another minute sufficed to end the agonies of death.

The executioner expressed his sorrow to the gaoler and under-sheriff for what had happened, assuring them that it was from no fault or intention of his but solely the result of an accident.

The body was lowered into a shell shortly before ten 'clock and it was with deep regret and indignation that some of the spectators saw the hangman attempt to remove a pair of new boots from the feet of the corpse. This revolting act was however blatantly prevented, and the body, which was decently attired in white shirt, moleskin trousers and a blouse, was removed to the deadhouse, where it remained untouched till the arrival of a hearse procured by the relatives of the criminal, to whom the authorities had decided to hand it over for interment.

Thus miserably and fearfully terminated the life of a man barely in the prime of manhood.

We sat round the fire and opened a bottle of grog to ward off the spectres that we could feel brushing past us. Henry Manns was the least deserving of such a fate. I had a grievance and acted out of vengeance. Darkie, Gilbert and O'Meally were already 'on the cross', and Charters did it for a lark, but like Bow and Fordyce, Henry was an innocent led down the path of evil and was the unlucky one that ended up kicking the clouds.

I fingered the little portrait Henry had given me just before we robbed the Eugowra escort. It showed a shy, smiling young man who had no idea of the brutal end that lay ahead. I tucked his picture inside my hatband as a remembrance and as a reminder not to stay in the game too long. Peace to his ashes.

There was worse news. A few days after Henry's burial, Warrigal Walsh went under in police custody, a result of Pottinger's neglect. A fever, brought on by the damp and cold of a winter in the logs, was ignored by the traps until Warrigal collapsed and had to be carried out each day by other prisoners to get clean air. There was a further delay before a doctor was called, and by then it was too late to save him. Warrigal was then moved to a nearby hotel where another doctor attempted to release the fever by opening some of his veins and bleeding him, but it was all to no avail. Warrigal never recovered consciousness.

There was a great gathering for his burial at Forbes. As was the custom on the day of a funeral, all shops kept their doors closed until the funeral cortege had passed. There was a great deal of public disquiet about the circumstances surrounding Warrigal's death and it turned a good many people against the police. Feelings were also running high amongst our supporters and the traps had the good sense to stay in their barracks and well away from the graveyard. This enabled me to attend, along with others of the brotherhood. Neither Kitty nor Biddy showed up at their brother's funeral. Ellen, Jacky and I were the only family present other than his father and stepmother.

I stood in the background as Father McCarthy conducted the funeral service. For all his fine words and all the lessons he read from the good book, we could not make sense of such a loss. When the time came I took a cord and helped lower the coffin. Warrigal now lay alongside his mother.

An epitaph rarely conveys a true sense of the life it recalls, but Warrigal's, which simply read 'died aged seventeen', said it all.

There was nothing more to tell. His was a life cut short and it was down to the man known as the Bastard Baronet Pottinger.

Jacky's recent release was the only good news in a black month. The funeral was Jacky's first public outing since his release. After being boxed up like a scrubber in a pound for nigh on seven months and surviving two trials, he looked pale and drawn. The cost of his defence had busted him and he had to sell his half-share of Sandy Creek. Despite the hardship he was determined to start again.

Over a beer at O'Meally's, he told me he was going to try his luck on the Pinnacle goldfields and had kicked over Ellen for dallying with Dan Charters whilst his life was, literally, hanging in the balance.

'I should have known what she was made of when I saw what Biddy and Kitty did to you and John Brown.'

I shook my head and took a sip of beer. 'I wouldn't have done any different, mate. We always hope we've got a good one.'

But Jacky had drunk from the same bitter well and said mournfully, 'Mate, where the Walsh women are concerned, there's no such thing. They're poison, the whole bloody race of 'em. I just hope the Darkie ain't resting too easy.'

Chapter Fourteen

We became victims of our own success. Mail coaches like gold escorts were getting tougher to bail up, so I decided that if the money wouldn't come to us, we'd go to it!

Close to the western goldfields, Carcoar had grown into an important commercial centre and the second largest regional town, after Bathurst. Sixty miles, or two good days' ride east, it was also a perfect target for us. The town is nestled in a valley in the crook of the meandering Belubula River that runs south-east past the town on its way to Lake Carcoar. We passed under the towering river oaks that line the river and glimpsed its brackish waters. It moved sluggishly, as did most things under the hot Australian sun.

Just as we reached the end of the stately colonnade of river oaks and were about to pass from their cooling shade, we drew level with a thin, dapper-looking gentleman, comfortably into his middle years, perched on a grey and white dappled horse. As our paths crossed, he looked down his long, thin snout at us, as if a caravan of queer-looking beasts had just happened past. I nodded at him, civil like, and tipped the brim of my hat.

'G'day, mate.'

He replied nice enough, but behind his cool front I could see his mind working, wondering what business these three shady coves had in town.

We let him go past for a minute, then I yielded to my gut instinct and called out to the others, 'Let's round him up.'

Hearing the drumming of hooves coming up fast behind him, he glanced over his shoulder, saw us and gave himself away by putting on a feeble spurt along the dusty strip, known as the Bathurst Road. His nag was all flash and no dash, and Willy had me up alongside him within a half-mile.

'Bail up!' I yelled over the noise of the rushing wind and the thundering of hooves on the earth beneath our feet. My pistol was out and in the gentleman's ribs before he could say jack. We pulled up in a cloud of dust.

'Let me be, I won't say a thing,' he pleaded.

The others came up and we guided him off the road into the dense scrub. I indicated with the point of my gun that he should dismount. Keeping him covered, I selected a shady tree and indicated that he should get under it. It wouldn't do if he got fried. With his shiny boots, soft white hands and neat suit he presented like a commercial or official, totally out of place in this rough setting. Nudging him in the chest with the cold steel of my pistol, I forced him backwards until his back was hard up against the rough crust of a big ironbark. It gave me a chance to size up our captive.

He was about six feet tall, a spindly specimen of a fella, about fifty, much too old for this lark. Beads of sweat glistened on his pale, freckled brow from which his sandy-coloured hair had long since retreated. Fearing he was about to breathe his last, he sucked in air greedily, his lips trembling behind the large walrus moustache. His bobbing Adam's apple betrayed his extreme nervousness. He blurted out his promise.

'I won't tell anyone. You have my word. Just let me go.'

Shaking my head, I looked at him. 'I'm afraid we can't take a chance on your good word, Mr–? Beg pardon, we haven't been introduced.'

'Hickles, Henry Hickles,' he said, swallowing hard.

'Well, Mr Hickles, we have some business to attend to in town and I think it would serve all our best interests if you stayed here a while.'

Hickles almost expired with relief when Johnny Gilbert pulled a length of rope from his saddlebag instead of a gun and, with the help of O'Meally, expertly lashed him to the tree.

'Don't worry, mate, we'll cut you loose on our way back,' I assured him. Hickles wasn't listening. He was transfixed by the procession of bull ants marching down the tree trunk and along the arm of his expensive suit.

'Don't move, or they'll start eating ya alive, bit by bit,' said O'Meally, taking a perverse delight in Hickles' discomfort.

*

We continued to Carcoar and sauntered down the steep main street. At the top end was the sloping slated roof of St Paul's Church, a gift from Thomas Iceley, its founder. I narrowed my eyes against the harsh glare of the noonday sun. The dusty strip of the main street was deserted. The sun's hot dazzle had chased the locals indoors, just as we knew it would.

We tied up our horses on the rail outside the Commercial Bank. I noted the canvas blinds had been drawn against the heat of the day. I put the flat of my hand against the heavy glass panelled door and pushed it open, the stiff hinges creaking ominously. We slipped inside and let the door close behind us. Our heavy bluchers echoed on the wooden floor as we crossed the large, musty-smelling room, the air inside as hot and still as it was outside. Silently I counted the twenty paces to the heavy wooden counter. It was unattended, so I picked up the bell and tinkled it. After a few moments the door leading to the back office opened and a young teller came out to greet us, dabbing at his perspiring brow with a handkerchief.

'Gentlemen, how can I help you?'

I presented him with a cheque I had lifted during one of our stick-ups. It bore the name of a man I had never heard of, and was dated a year ago.

'I wonder if you would cash this for me,' I said, smiling.

'Certainly,' he beamed, looking down to check the details. His brow furrowed when he spied the date.

'Excuse me, sir,' said the man who looked up to find himself staring down the barrel of my pistol.

'No, excuse me,' I replied, producing a calico bag and motioning him with my gun to fill it.

The shock on his face reflected the audacity of what we were doing. No bank in New South Wales had ever been bailed up before let alone in broad daylight.

'Tens and twenties now,' called O'Meally, cheeky as you like. But before the teller could do anything the door behind him opened. A short, balding man, who judging by the look of anger on his face could only be the manager, walked in on us.

In a voice that suggested he took our presence as a personal affront, he demanded, 'What's going on here, Parker? Who are these men?'

O'Meally brought up his shotgun level with his chin and snarled, 'Shut up, man, or I'll put daylight through you, quick as a wink!'

The distraction was enough for the teller to fumble under the counter for a firearm hidden for just such an emergency. As he raised it I was quick-witted enough to throw up my arm and deflect the barrel heavenwards. It went off with a deafening roar. As white plaster showered down on us, I floored Parker with the butt of my pistol. By rights, I should have holed him for his stupidity.

The manager was able to reach the glass panelled door and wrench it open, yelling out for help. O'Meally was on him like a ferret with a rabbit, threw a muscular arm round his neck and choked off any further cries as he dragged the manager back inside. Once O'Meally had locked the door, he gave the game old bugger a fat lip, threw him to the floor and bawled out, 'Stay there!'

It was too late. The sound of the gunshot and the manager's calls for help had roused some curious citizens from their afternoon dozing and voices rising in angry query could be heard out in the street. Johnny Gilbert turned to me from the window, anxiety written large on his face. 'That shot's stirred 'em up. Best we leg it, fast!'

Realising it was a lost cause, I reached over the counter, grabbed the calico bag and yelled out, 'Let's go, boys!'

As we came charging out of the bank, we almost cannoned into an old bloke and his daughter who were already on the scene. The bloke just stood there like a long streak of misery, unsure of what to do, while his daughter, a young blonde woman in a striped skirt and blue jacket, tried to undo our horses' reins from the rail, determined to stop our getaway.

'Leave them be!' I warned, but she kept tugging at the reins, undeterred by the presence of a gang of armed bushrangers.

As it has always been part of the bushranger's code never to harm a lady, I grabbed her around the waist, swung her off her feet and kissed her full on the mouth. The shock caused her to let go of the reins. I vaulted the rail and hoisted myself up into the saddle.

'Now, that was worth all the money in the bank,' I said with a wink.

She drew the back of her hand across her mouth and spat into the gutter, like a bullocky. Clearly outraged at being taken advantage of, she launched herself at Willy the Weasel, windmilling at his great head and chest with her dainty hands.

'You're an ignorant pig, Ben Hall,' she shouted furiously.

'And you have the most beautiful blue eyes this side of Bathurst,' I replied with a grin.

Firing my gun into the air, I wheeled Willy around and waded into the crowd that was pooling around us, more out of curiosity than hostility.

'Move aside,' I warned, kneeing Willy forward. 'We've finished our business and we're on our way.'

We knew there was a police station in the town and a couple of traps but, so far, they hadn't shown themselves. The crowd parted to let us push through.

As promised, we returned to free Mr Hickles who was by now well acquainted with the varied bird and insect life of the district. Other than having a few angry-looking bull ant stings on his neck, he had weathered his ordeal pretty well.

Our dreams of a big haul were dashed for the moment, so we decided to turn further inland and succeeded in making up for our disappointment with a £300 haul of clothing, blankets and tinned supplies from Hosie's store that same afternoon. It was a small consolation, but the raid on the bank had the desired effect of warning the powers that be that we were not playing by the old rules. Everything was fair game now. One thing was clear. If we were going to take on bigger jobs we needed to take more men, and needed to plan our every move, leaving nothing to chance.

I'd heard from our telegraphs of two Currency Lads who might serve our purposes. A few days later, I went out to meet them.

They made an odd-looking pair. John Vane was a thick-bearded, strapping six-footer who stood as tall and straight as a rush. Renowned as a horseman and cricketer, he dwarfed the angelic-looking Mickey Burke, who only stood five foot two, with his smooth complexion, neat brown hair and big brown eyes.

A wandering life had gradually led Vane into a life of crime and he had thrown his lot in with Mickey Burke, whom I had known since my boyhood days.

They went on the scamp together, lifting one hundred head of cattle, and shortly afterwards there was a warrant out for both of them. They had been keeping low for a while.

Vane's one weakness was cricket. He was a member of the Teasdale Cricket Club and he came out of hiding to hit a few sixes in a victory against local rivals, Caloola. He attended the party afterwards, but Caloola proved to be as poor sports as they were cricketers and turned him in.

The traps tried to arrest him. Vane managed to knock over the lamp and in the commotion Mickey escaped out of a window and Vane crawled between the scuffling feet and out into the night where he made off on a stolen police horse.

We needed that kind of pluck, so I had no hesitation in asking John Vane and Mickey Burke to join us. They jumped at the chance of action and now we were five.

The initial meeting with the others didn't go off too well. Mickey was a quiet sort of bloke, but Vane was a bluff, red-blooded Australian bushie. From the tip of his bushy beard that came to a peak well south of his prominent jaw, down to his red flannel shirt, cord trousers and heavy, ankle-length lace-up boots – there was not a scrap of flash about him.

His blue eyes, which stood out against the teak of his sunburned skin, widened when he caught sight of Gilbert's velvet-collared jacket, embroidered waistcoat, jewelled fingers and long hair.

He came out straight with what was on his mind. 'Strewth, I didn't reckon there were any sheilas on the cross!'

We all had a good laugh, except for Gilbert. His carefree nature had earned him the nickname of Happy Jack, but he wasn't amused at Vane's jibe. He muttered something about a 'ten-minute egg', which was how our North American brethren referred to someone who thought themselves tough or hard-boiled. Although only five foot seven and of slight build, I had seen Gilbert stiff much bigger blokes. He eyed Vane testily.

This'll be interesting, I thought to myself.

On that occasion, at least, Gilbert let it pass and after that early chaff, Burke and Vane showed themselves to be great horsemen and even better horse thieves. They were eager to show off their skills and as horses were an important part of our strategy, we were happy to oblige.

The bushranging business is all about the element of surprise. A bold plan, a brave heart and a fair wind are worth nothing unless you have the horseflesh to get you in and out of trouble. The traps could hardly raise a decent trotter between them so we took to stealing racehorses from surrounding stations to give us an edge.

Our spies would attend race meetings and relay back to us the names of the champions and their owners. We always made an offer to buy the horse, which would always be declined, so it ended up with us raiding the station and making off with them. Quite a few champions have worn our pigskins, I can tell you!

Being proper bushmen and rough riders gave us a big advantage in the mountain areas, but our policy of using racehorses paid handsome dividends as we also had an advantage down on the flat.

We started off by raiding Coombing Park, the station belonging to local Magistrate and member of the New South Wales legislature, Thomas Iceley. The night we did it I peeked in through the window and saw Inspector Davidson toasting his toes at a warm fire with a glass of French brandy in his hand.

The number of times we found high-ranking traps curled up with squatters tells you just how cosy they all were and who was calling the tune. This is where the *Free Selection Act* fell down. The Act gave the selector rights that they couldn't exercise because the squatters manipulated a system already heavily weighed in their favour. In a practice called 'dummying', the squatters used proxies to buy land in their names around the waterholes on their properties. The proxies would then transfer the land back to the squatters in a private land sale. The only land available had no access to water and no fool would select it.

Similarly, 'peacocking' was the practice of buying up all the waterfront property and waiting until those selectors on the backblocks realised they couldn't expand their runs and stock numbers without water, leaving them with no choice but to sell out to the squatters. These sharp practices were common, but the officers from the Department of Lands did nothing, and the magistrates turned a blind eye because they were the prime beneficiaries and had the traps tucked up next to them.

On this particular night, we not only made off with Iceley's prized stallion, Comus II, but bagged Inspector Davidson's grey gelding. The only downside of this operation was that some old dog called German Charley got shot in the mouth for trying to save his squire's horse.

Mickey and John were leading the horses from the stable and would have been clear in another minute or two, but the old bushie came out of the shadows firing. Before he realised who it was,

Mickey returned fire. Fortunately, the wound to his face was not fatal and we made him as comfortable as we could.

As we made our way home, Gilbert and Vane gave each other a gobful.

'Ya never should have fired,' Gilbert said to Mickey.

'And let some squatter plug ya? Nah, mate, you did good,' countered Vane slapping Mickey on the shoulder.

'Put a noose around ye're own neck, not mine,' countered Gilbert.

'Mibbe I will,' growled Vane.

'Shut it, and that's an order!' I snapped at the pair of them.

Some good did come out of our visit to Coombing Park. Saying that he feared for his life, Thomas Iceley moved to Sydney shortly afterwards to pursue his various business interests.

Vane approached me a day or two later with a troubled look on his face.

'What's up, John?' I said.

'It's me brother, Billy, me cousin, George, and Mickey's cousin, Jim. They've been pinched by the traps.'

'What for?'

'Harbouring and a bit of thievery at a pub.'

'Need some money to bail 'em out?'

'Nah,' he said scratching his bearded chin as he came to the point. 'They're being taken to Sydney for trial the day after tomorrow and I'd like to bail up the coach.'

'That's a big job for a bloke on his own,' I mused.

'Thing is, I'd like you blokes to help me.'

'Tell you what,' I replied, 'You can take Gilbert, Mickey and O'Meally, if they're game.'

Not wishing to see more of our kind locked up and keen for a bit of sport, they all agreed. The next morning they headed off for a coach stop called Waterholes, a few miles outside Carcoar, which they reckoned would be the best spot to set an ambush.

Any hope I had that such an endeavour might bond them together was cruelly shattered. They arrived back a couple of days later, a few hours after dark, Gilbert and Vane shouting and swearing at each other like sailors. They had barely dismounted before they were toe to toe. I pulled Mickey aside and demanded, 'What the bloody hell happened?'

'Cor, that was a rapid engagement,' said Mickey still breathless with excitement, his eyes shining in the flickering firelight. Snatching a breath, he related the events of that afternoon.

'The coach arrived on schedule and we went head-on at it full gallop and caught them on the hop. Vane tried to pull the horses over while Gilbert shouted, "Bail up, you bastards!" Inspector Morisset, who was sitting in the box seat next to the driver, refused and we let fly at each other. The coach pulled over and Gilbert had a pop at Morisset as he leapt down from the box seat, but the bullet smashed into the spot where he had just been sitting. The Inspector and the two guards used the coach as cover as we came galloping in for another go.'

'What about the prisoners?'

'They were still shackled together, but tried to push their way out of the coach in the confusion, but Morisset sent them back at the point of his pistol, warning them, "You'll go down before you'll go free".'

With two fingers and a thumb for a pistol Mickey described how they had ridden at the coach at a fast gallop from different directions, veering away at the last moment and ducking and dodging in their saddles as bullets fizzed past them.

'How did the boys perform?' I asked looking over at Gilbert and Vane who were still at each other.

Mickey shrugged, 'Vane seemed to be holding back, but Gilbert and I were in the thick of it and O'Meally was just wild. At one point, he threw out his arms wide, beat his chest with his fists and shouted, "Come on you bastards, shoot me if you can!" He took a bullet in the chest, but it hit a fob watch he was carrying in his top pocket. That woke him up and he went after a mounted trooper who had been scouting ahead, and came galloping in when he heard the shooting.

'"Come on, let's have a square go," O'Meally was bellowing as they circled the coach, each man looking to get a clear shot at the other. The trap's volley missed, but O'Meally caught him on the elbow, sending his iron clattering to the ground.

'We would've picked 'em off, but Gilbert's horse took a bullet in the rump and we were running low on ammunition. Gilbert ordered us back, had one more gallop up to the coach and gave the traps a good coating.

'"If we wasn't so low on bullets, we'd follow you to Hell and fight it out," he told them. "Sorry, boys!" he called out to the prisoners who were crowded together at the coach window hoping they'd be freed.'

So Gilbert's decision to pull out was the root of Vane's grievance. The two had been toe to toe all the while, neither giving the other an inch.

'Why d'ya pull back?' Vane demanded, 'those blokes are done for now.'

'I had two bullets left, O'Meally was trying to get himself shot and you weren't fit for the fight,' returned Gilbert.

'What?' roared Vane, his lips turning white with rage.

'I saw ya hanging back when it was getting too hot,' said Gilbert coolly.

'You calling me a coward?' said Vane, his eyes narrowing.

Gilbert shrugged, 'If the cap fits.' Both men put their hands on their pistols and waited for the other to make the first move. O'Meally, who had been in a strange distracted mood since his return, broke the stalemate by walking up to them with his hand outstretched as if he hadn't noticed they were about to draw on each other.

'See that?' Hardly trusting one not to draw and shoot when the other wasn't looking, Gilbert and Vane allowed themselves a quick downward glance. In O'Meally's palm lay the fob that had saved his life, completely flattened by the impact of the bullet, which left an ugly dent on the lid.

'See, it's a sign. Them bastards can't kill me,' confided O'Meally giving them one of his evil, rotten-toothed grins, which Gilbert later confessed he found quite unnerving.

It defused the tension, but this episode had done nothing to repair relations between Gilbert and Vane who continued to bare their teeth at each other at every opportunity. *Two cocks in the roost*, I thought to myself. *Best keep a cutty eye on the pair of 'em.*

Chapter Fifteen

The traps came in low and hard early one morning and caught us sleeping at Walter Tutil's place. We often laid low there when we'd been working the Bathurst road and the traps had never troubled us until that day.

From behind a picket fence they called out they had the hut surrounded and ordered us to come out. I recognised the voice of Senior Constable Haughey and I counted troopers Churchman, Kane, Pentland, Billy Dargin and a civilian volunteer called John Edwards. We made it our business to know all the troopers and those who supported them in the district. We'd go into town and memorise their faces in case they tried to mingle with the local population or set an ambush for us.

They were unprepared for the three-minute fusillade of bullets which reduced their picket fence to matchwood, wounded some of their mounts and sent Haughey spinning as a pill ripped through the soft flesh above his knee.

Exiting through windows, doors and the dunny we took off in separate directions pursued by troopers. Such was our haste that Johnny Vane had to go bush barefoot.

They were on horseback and I was on foot, so there was no chance I could outrun them. I spied a V-shaped hole in the bottom of the hollow shell of an old box tree that had been dead on its feet for years, which I enlarged with a few swift kicks before gratefully squeezing into its safe embrace. Through a split in the trunk I could see and hear them cursing when they discovered I had disappeared.

'Dismount and spread out,' ordered Haughey, his face twisted with pain clutching at his bloodied leg. He was out for revenge and with his throat ragged with pain he added, 'Search the area, he can't have got far.' Branches were snapped and bushes thrashed and at one point I was breathing in their tobacco smoke when they stopped for a pipe at the tree I was hidden in, little realising that only a few inches of wood separated us.

'Bloody waste of time, he's long gone,' I heard one grumble.

Seeing Haughey's horse about three hundred yards ahead grazing on a patch of scrub, I left my cover and moved from tree to tree and soon had the bay gelding nuzzling the palm of my hand. Unusually for a trap, he had a fine mount, worth a year's pay at least.

When they heard it break cover through the trees the traps ran back, guns drawn, but all they saw was a loose, riderless horse galloping past them. Haughey shouted to the troopers, who were lining up their shots, 'Hold your fire!' Then I heard him curse loudly when I suddenly swung myself back into the saddle and waved back at them as we sailed out of range.

I'd fooled them with an old circus trick we'd learned as kids to scare our parents, hanging on to the saddle and stirrups on the blind side to make it look as if we'd fallen off. Haughey's despair was echoed in the few stray shots he sent ringing through the thickly wooded canopy after me. Every missed chance added another verse to the legend of Ben Hall.

But they did have the consolation of bagging two of our oldest and most trusted harbourers, Walter Tutil and his mate George Slater.

We feared treachery more than the traps or the British redcoats and knew someone must have told them where Patsy and I were headed and that we kept dark at Walter Tutil's. In war there are no neutrals. You are either for or against. The traps exerted pressure and bribed people for information and so did we. Part of our program was to deal harshly with those who sheltered or gave the traps information and it was time to send those pimps a message, though we did things differently to the Sydney boy whose dark, violent moods had earned him the moniker 'Mad' Dan Morgan.

A criminal since his teens and with a six stretch on the hulks at Port Phillip under his belt already, Morgan had 'taken up a stand' between Wagga Wagga and the Victorian border. A £200 reward had just been put on his head after he bailed up and wounded a Wagga Magistrate and killed a shepherd he accused of being an informer.

We heard that a settler named Marsh, who lived out near Cal-oola, was cosy with the local constabulary. On the way out we were almost bowled over by a loose horse sporting police saddlebags and livery. Mickey Burke showed why he was one of the top jockeys in the district by chasing it down. We tied it to a tree and waited.

A half-hour later a heavy-boned, sweating trap with a head of black curly hair and that spindly cove Marsh came trotting along on the back of the same horse. They were relieved to find the runaway under the shade tree, but as soon as they dismounted, we showed ourselves and put up our guns at them.

'Hand over them irons nice and easy, or we'll drop you where you stand,' I commanded.

Constable Cummings showed little regard for himself or Marsh by going for his piece, but Gilbert settled him with the butt of his pistol, which made a hollow thump as it connected with his noggin. He went down like a felled heifer, his great bulk shaking the ground around us.

'No need for that,' he grumbled dabbing at the wound on the side of his head with bloodied fingers.

'I could have put daylight through you,' snapped back Gilbert.

I increased the discomfort shown by the wiry figure of Marsh by turning my full attention on him, 'We were on our way to teach you a lesson, but now you've saved us the trouble.'

Unfurling my stock whip, I nodded to O'Meally and Vane who slung Marsh face down over the uprooted trunk of an old ironbark whose girth was so wide that his feet dangled off the ground. I favoured the lash for such occasions because it was for so long the symbol of the squatter's power during convict times. Realising he was about to be flogged, Marsh tried to get his feet back on the ground, but Gilbert and Vane hauled at his arms, as though they were pulling a wishbone.

Vane taunted Gilbert, 'Keep him still, will ya?'

'Shut up!' shot back Gilbert. 'If I pull any harder I'll pop 'is bloody arm.'

I gave Marsh a sporting chance. 'Who will we find at your station?'

'No one, just my wife,' he volunteered a little too quickly. Marsh didn't believe I'd do it. Maybe he was the kind that refused to believe the worst in men until he saw proof of it himself.

Years of practice allowed me to bring down the greenhide with the full weight of my body behind it. There was an evil hiss as it sliced through the air and I landed it between his struggling shoulders, where I knew it would inflict the most pain. It sliced through his shirt and drew a bloody line across the pale, white skin beneath. A wave of intense pain escaped through Marsh's open mouth, his high-pitched scream chasing a mob of scavenging pink-crested galahs up out of the scrub.

'I've a stockman's arm,' I warned him as his cries subsided, 'and when I've cut the skin off your back, I'll give him a red shirt an' all,' I said nodding at Constable Cummings who regretted his earlier bravado.

I gave Marsh a repeat dose across the small of the back, which drew another agonised yell and caused more urgent rustling in the bush. He glanced over his shoulder, saw me winding up for another go and shouted, 'There's two traps at the hut with my wife.'

'Bugger you!' spat Constable Cummings from under the watchful eye of John O'Meally.

'Easy for you to say–' shot back Marsh, gritting his teeth against the stinging pain that was now crucifying his flesh. 'Why don't you do your own dirty work in the future?'

'That's the spirit, Marsh,' I called and fixing my eye on Cummings said, 'We'll have that uniform and not a word out of you.'

Cummings undressed and then we handcuffed them together to the upended ironbark.

A trail of soft, white smoke guided us down a fair beaten track to Marsh's slab hut, which stood in a stand of red gums. We spied two fat nags with the distinctive 'VR' livery on their saddles tied up round the back. Burke peeked through one of the windows and raised two fingers to indicate both were inside.

I raised my pistol and fired into the air. Gilbert and Vane did likewise.

Both troopers came out and made for their horses, but never got a foot in their stirrups.

'Back away from that screw, or I'll blow you to buggery,' I demanded as we stepped out of the bush, pistols levelled at them. Marsh's wife appeared at the door then ducked inside to hide her valuables.

We ordered the traps back into the hut where the scrawny, pinch-faced Marsh woman steadfastly refused to give up anything.

'We worked hard for what little we have,' she screeched, 'You aren't supposed to rob us poor folk–'

'Only those who cosy up to the traps,' Gilbert growled back.

'What have you bastards done with my husband?' she demanded,

'We shot him along with that other bloody trap,' I told her coldly and watched her rock backwards on her heels. The traps looked at each other, shock chasing fear across their faces wondering what we had in store for them.

I considered that Marsh's missus, who now sat slumped in the chair beside the fire, tears rolling down her careworn cheeks had suffered as much as her husband and told her the truth.

'He's not dead. We handcuffed him to that trap out along the Caloola road, but if we hear the traps have been round here again we'll come back and shoot him in front of your eyes. Now, get off your backside and fix us some tucker.' She wiped her eyes with her apron, sniffled a bit then started banging pots around.

After enjoying a proper set down meal, cooked by a woman, which was a rare treat for us, I ordered the traps to strip down to their drawers.

'Good God, man, there's a woman present,' huffed the older of the troopers.

His modesty drew an ugly sneer from O'Meally, 'You've nothing she hasn't seen before.'

We took their uniforms, pistols and handcuffs and in a final indignity we handcuffed them together and locked them in the chook pen before making for Grant's station at Belubula.

The well-upholstered figure of Mr Grant, the cove who heartlessly evicted and burnt the hut of the Irish woman and child we helped that rainy night some months back, did not fare so well. He was a known police informer, and although he denied it, we knew they had been out there just a few days before.

When I told him we were going to burn his house and crops, he began to plead, 'Please, don't. This is all I have.' I was tempted to ram my fist into his poxy face, but restrained myself.

'I imagine that poor woman and her bairn said much the same

that rainy day when Pottinger and his blue bellies burnt her hut at your request.' A shocked look crossed his face, but he tried to bluster on.

'But her husband was a duffer–'

I cut him cold. 'You told Pottinger that in order to break their lease, clear them off and broker a fat land deal for yourself.'

The frozen look of fear on Grant's sweaty face told me I'd hit the mark.

I gave the boys the nod. They lit brushwood torches, threw them onto the roof of his fine house and then set his fields of ripening corn alight. Grant spun around in horror as bright red and orange flames blossomed around him.

'No!' he cried hoarsely, as the smoke caught his dry throat, but his protests were drowned out by the crackling and roaring of the fire that quickly took a hold of his crops and house.

'Save your breath for opening your stockyards and stables,' I cautioned the white-faced Grant. Pottinger's patrol spotted the twisting column of acrid, black smoke rising from Grant's station, but arrived too late to save anything.

We headed south and repeated the dose in Canowindra at the store of Messrs Hilliar & Pierce. Mr John Pierce had been pointed out to us as a man who continued to speak out boldly against bushrangers, but we saw no sign of the brave crusader the day we walked into his shop, only a weeping man who begged us not to hurt him. His face was a mask of misery as we rooted around, helping ourselves to blankets, tinned food and other things we'd need for the coming winter.

'I hope you're going to pay for that,' he muttered.

'We'll pay all right, with a hook,' snarled Vane, ripping a couple of blankets off a shelf and stuffing them into his saddlebag to make the point.

When the till yielded little more than a few notes and small change, I turned to him, gun in hand and shouted,'Fork it over, Pierce!'

'That's all I've got,' he moaned, grinding his hands together in anguish.

Waving my arm across his wide emporium, which was stacked from floor to ceiling with goods of every description, I laughed in his face. 'D'ya expect me to believe that old flam?'

I joined him behind the counter and within half a minute or so I'd found a solid-looking safe hidden under the floorboards. 'What have we here?' I said looking at Pierce who shifted uncomfortably from foot to foot.

'Rich pickings I hope,' said Burke, rubbing his hands.

I gave Pierce a pat down and found a bunch of keys in his swag. There was a creak of rusty hinges as the heavy metal door opened. I pulled out what appeared to be bundles of money stuffed into faded brown envelopes and threw them on the counter. To our disappointment, though, there were only books and papers, no money.

'Where is it?' hissed Gilbert, turning on Pierce, his face flushed with anger.

'I haven't any money,' he wailed.

'Save your breath,' I told Gilbert. 'Everything he has is locked up safely in the bank.' While Gilbert and Burke continued to demand money with menace, I flicked through a thick leather-bound ledger filled with columns of neat little figures in red and black ink.

'What's this?' I said.

'Nothing,' said Pierce a little too quickly for my liking.

'It's your accounts book, details of the debts of all these poor selectors, isn't it?' I narrowed my eyes and stared him down. Pierce said nothing, which was all the confirmation I needed. There was so little in the till because he did most of his business on account.

I carried the ledgers over to the fireplace that Pierce kept behind the counter to keep his legs warm in winter, and carelessly tossed them onto the fire. The glowing coals were in need of fresh fuel and crackled greedily as they got to work on the paper. Pierce stood stock still for a moment, unable to believe what he'd just witnessed. Realising that hundreds of pounds owing to him was about to go up in smoke, he rushed forwards. 'No!' he screeched, trying to pull the burning books out of the flames with his bare hands.

'Hold him back!' I said sharply.

Gilbert and Vane wrestled him to the floor where he continued to struggle and shout out, 'Leave me be, you bastards!'

In the end, all he could do was watch in mute horror as the ink faded from the pages as they browned then curled into fine grey ash. He slapped his own face with his peeling, heat-blistered hands as if trying to awaken himself from a terrible nightmare.

'I'm ruined!' he moaned.

I felt no pity for him. He'd been sucking the poor folk dry for years. Now it was his turn.

Gilbert and O'Meally dragged Pierce outside into the fading light and tied him to a tree. They hoped for his sake that Mr Hilliar came out of hiding before it got dark and the bush rats started on his legs.

The razing of Grant's station and the burning of Pierce's ledgers sent a tremor through the local squatter community who, fearing they might be next, demanded action. The reward on our heads rose to £200, a sum that finally matched our infamy, or as Johnny Gilbert put it, 'a sum worth risking your neck for'. But it did little to quell the mounting fear that we really were taking over. The *Forbes Examiner* reported that five thousand people gathered in the streets of Forbes and burned a straw effigy of Pottinger, which flattered him greatly by all accounts. We kept up the pressure and soon afterwards there was another opportunity for a spree and to leave Pottinger to take the lump.

Chapter Sixteen

Our raid on Bathurst was said by many to have been the most audacious act we ever committed, but I cannot, in truth, claim it was my idea. The idea came from two young Bathurst surveyors, Mr Battye and Mr McHattie, whom we'd bailed up on the Bathurst to Young road late one afternoon.

Like Gilbert and I, they were flash dressers and they had a lot to say for themselves, as that class always do, but these well-bred, educated gentlemen had rotten mouths and used language that would have made a bullocky blush. Despite their cursing and their protests, we relieved them of their wallets, watches and two thoroughbred horses. Battye, who I later discovered was the son of Inspector Battye of the New South Wales police, wouldn't let it go.

'You're all cowards!' he burst out, the colour rising in his face. 'You'd never dare come into Bathurst and try this. The police and a mob of honest, upstanding citizens would soon make you turn tail,' he said, admonishing us fiercely.

'Hear, hear,' chorused Mr McHattie, showing us that he had some starch in him too.

Our usual policy was to give back stranded travellers enough loose change to help them reach their destination, but we fancied that a long walk in the hot sun might teach these two some manners. As we moved off, leaving them horseless and penniless, I tipped my hat, winked at Battye and said, 'Not a bad idea,' and watched his brow furrow as he tried to catch my meaning.

Not a bad idea,' I echoed later that night as we sat warming our hands round the fire recalling the barefaced cheek of those two young blokes.

'You're kidding!' said Vane, poking at the fire with a stick.

'Not where the game is concerned, John, you know that,' I reproached him.

'Its madness, mate,' he persisted. 'What if those blokes were setting a trap for us?' His was the lone dissenting voice. The sheer audacity of such a move was already beginning to overtake all reason. We had earned the distinction of being the first to target big squatter stations, storekeepers, banks and even traps, but we needed to think up fresh outrages, ways of undermining the shaky and corruptible forces of law and order represented by Sir Frederick Pottinger.

'It would shake them to their very foundations,' weighed in Gilbert.

'Bloody oath, it would!' agreed Burke. Vane still wasn't convinced.

'There are six thousand people and an army of traps stationed in Bathurst and only five of us.'

O'Meally, who was always ready for a good fight, sealed the argument. 'The odds are always against us, but only if they're sitting up waiting for us. I reckon those blokes we bailed up were just blowing off. There's only one sure way to find out.'

Three days and ninety miles later we sat up on a flat-topped hill overlooking the colony's first inland settlement, which was now the 'capital' of the western districts of New South Wales. Its prosperity came from the rich seam of gold that had been discovered in the surrounding district over the past decade at places like Ophir, Hill End, Turon, Lambing Flat and Forbes.

Gold had turned Bathurst into a bustling, prosperous town. The streets were thronged with carts and buggies, while its well-heeled citizens wore the latest fashions. The original ramshackle weatherboard shells of the pioneer era had given way to elegant stone Victorian façades. Expensive-looking shops displayed all manner of finery and were staffed by assistants and owners as flash as their customers. Bathurst was ripe for the picking but we were too well known to risk going into town. Wanted posters with our description and the rewards on our heads were sure to be on display, and the lure of fame and fortune might tempt some stout-hearted citizen to take us on.

I looked at Johnny Gilbert, with his long hair, slim build and fresh complexion, who had often been mistaken for a country girl.

We had discussed the idea of dressing him up like a woman and sending him ahead to find out the lay of the land. I knew it would appeal to Gilbert's sense of derring-do, but he would hold back as he didn't want the boys saying he had 'unnatural tastes'.

'It's our best card,' I explained when I announced the hour had arrived to put our bold plan into action. 'If it was good enough for the "ribbon men", then it's certainly good enough for us.'

This ruse had been used to great effect during the Irish Rebellion and had been well aired in the Lachlan, a district of strong Irish character. The British had decried the disguise as an act of cowardice, yet saw nothing wrong in masquerading in the clothes of liberators themselves.

Seeing the smirk on Vane's face, Gilbert said sourly, 'Fair enough, but I'll knock the block off any bastard who skits me.'

We bailed up a nearby store and held the owner at the counter. Not knowing anything about women's sizes, other than we liked them well rounded, Gilbert had to try on a few garments in the back room. We copped a few rum looks from the storekeeper, who wondered what manner of depraved creatures we were.

His modesty preserved by a wattle bush, Johnny brushed out his long hair and tarted himself in the dress, corset and brassiere we had lifted. When he emerged the transformation was truly astounding. His slim figure fitted neatly into the dress and with the aid of several pairs of socks, he had acquired a matronly pair of breasts.

'Strewth,' said Vane, tipping his hat back and scratching his head.

'Bugger me,' said O'Meally.

When the boys started jibbing him that there would be no more lonely nights without a woman's company they discovered that she might have the body of a goddess, she still had Johnny Gilbert's foul mouth.

'Not another bloody word, you bastards,' he warned, his cheeks crimson and fists bunched in a most unladylike manner.

With that he stomped, barefoot, over to his nag, hoisted himself up onto the gunny bag we'd put on the horse's back instead of a side-saddle and headed towards Bathurst at a canter.

We waited until he was out of earshot before the wisecracking began. Vane fired the first volley. 'I always thought he dressed like a doxy, but strewth, I could feel me manhood rising.'

This drew groans and protests from the rest of us, but Vane persisted.

'What? It's only natural, I haven't as much as caught sight of a bloody woman in months!'

As the laughter subsided, I added, 'One thing's sure, if any silly bugger sticks his hand between that doxy's legs, he'll get a lot more than he bargained for!'

Fluttering his eyelashes and brushing back his hair with one hand, O'Meally affected the demeanour of a maiden in distress. Grabbing his balls he shrieked in a squeaky falsetto, 'Unhand me, sir, I'm still a virgin!'

We rolled over on the grass and laughed so hard that we expected to see Gilbert returning over the rise with murder on his mind.

We were still lying around on the grass when Johnny returned a few hours later, his honour still intact. From the smirks we wore on our faces, he guessed what the main topic of conversation had been in his absence. He slid off his horse and began disrobing as soon as his feet hit the ground. He reported that everything seemed quiet and there was no sign of traps.

We waited until the sun began to dip behind the gums. The falling light would lessen the chances of our being recognised and our escape would be aided by the cover of darkness.

On a Saturday there was nothing unusual about five young men coming in for a night in town. We had chosen our two targets carefully. They were close to each other on William Street, one of the main streets in the town.

Our first port of call was at Pedrotta the gunsmiths. We had decided it was time to upgrade our arsenal. Johnny Vane and Mickey covered the street and kept the horses handy, just in case there was a need for a quick getaway.

Inside the shop, we eyed the rifles that hung on the walls, discussing their merits as we made our way to the front where the owner, Mr Pedrotta, stood in front of a glass case that held an impressive range of pistols. Pedrotta was a sober-looking man in his middle years. He nodded politely and spoke with a slight Italian accent.

'Gentlemen, I see you have a fine appreciation of armaments.'

'It pays in our line of work,' quipped Gilbert.

'Escorts, banks and so forth,' I added smoothly not wishing to arouse any suspicion.

Mr Pedrotta was the very soul of discretion. 'I see. How may I help you today, gentlemen?'

'I'd heard there was a new six-shot revolving rifle that would be ideal for our kind of work,' I said.

Pedrotta smiled and spread his hands apologetically. 'The Tranter revolving rifle, an excellent piece, but I'm afraid I sold the last one this very morning. It's a very popular item. Those bush-rangers have made everyone nervous, though I can't say it's been bad for business.'

Feigning shock and horror, Gilbert said, 'Surely, they'd never have the gall to attack Bathurst!'

Shaking his head Pedrotta's Latin tenor rose as he became agitated. 'They are mad dogs. Anything is possible with such men.'

'Then, may the good Lord protect us all,' said John O'Meally piously.

There was nothing we wanted here, so I tipped my hat and called an end to the farce. 'Thank you, sir. I bid you good day.'

'Please call again, Mr . . .?' Mr Pedrotta inquired.

'Hall. Next time we're in Bathurst we'll call again.'

Satisfied that Pedrotta had no idea he had just played host to the very people his guns were supposed to repell, we strolled a few yards further down William Street and entered McMinn's jewellery shop. The polite tinkle of a bell announced our entry, but the young male assistant, busy attending to some paperwork, didn't look up for a few precious seconds. By the time he did, he found himself staring down the muzzle of my police issue Colt Navy six-shooter.

The shock and fear I saw told me that he would not forfeit his life for the items of jewellery we were already scooping into a bag. I put my finger to my lips though I doubt he could have moved or screamed if his life depended on it.

Our shopping spree was brought to an abrupt end, not by the nervous assistant, but the owner, Mrs McMinn, who unexpectedly entered the shop through a side door. We were as surprised to come face to face with this formidable-looking matron with fiery-red hair, wound up into a fashionably tight bun, as she was to find a gang of armed men robbing her shop. She ran to the front door with a speed you would not credit a woman of her ample proportions, tore the door open with a violence that caused the previously discreet bell to jangle in alarm and throwing up her hands for dramatic effect, she 'cried beef' on us with a bellow that would have frightened a wildish cow, 'Help, police! Help!'

Seeing people looking over towards the shop, we decided it was best to scamper. We had to settle for what we'd already bagged, and raced out past the still shrieking Mrs McMinn. Realising we were about to vault onto our horses and edge it, she embroidered her cries for help with some choice profanities.

Tipping my hat to the screaming woman, who was urging reluctant bystanders to pull us off our mounts, I chided her, 'Madam, you are mistaken. My mother was a god-fearing Irish woman and my parents were not only acquainted, but wed long before I was born.'

With that we fired our pistols in the air to disperse the townsfolk who had begun to run across the road towards us.

'Five of us is good for fifty troopers' I yelled at the scattering crowd. Amid the shouts and screams I saw shock and confusion writ large across people's faces, as we wheeled and rode five abreast down William, Piper, George and Howick streets. To the locals, bushrangers were strictly rural creatures and the very idea that they might be found robbing shops, firing guns and galloping through the middle of Bathurst on a Saturday night was unimaginable.

Our daring mission accomplished.

Word that the Hall gang was shooting up the town reached the police barracks, and soon every available trooper was racing out of town down the Carcoar and Caloola roads leading back towards our stronghold. We knew this because we watched them racing past the front window of the Sportsman's Arms, while we were inside enjoying a beer.

We'd bailed up the pub, shouted the grog and yarned to the locals while we waited for the fuss to die down. Seeing how easily we'd gammoned the traps, a toothless old scourer, who told us he'd once been a government man, raised his glass to us,

'You boys will never be took,' he called.

'Not alive, anyhow,' snapped back O'Meally, glowering through half-closed slits with those green eyes.

A bushranger raid on a major regional centre certainly stirred the possum. It even made news in Sydney. Inspector-General McLerie was forced to leave his comfy perch and travel out west to personally lead the counter-offensive. He arrived amid much fanfare, but was as out of his depth as his protégé Pottinger. While the blue bellies were still out chasing shadows we kept dark in our crib and planned our next play.

After a week, we'd all had enough of the quiet life and agreed that it was time we pulled the Devil's tail again. Whatever our faults, idleness wasn't one of them. We chose Canowindra as our next target because it was a trap stronghold and would create the same stir as our raid on Bathurst. It was also a place I knew well as a cattleman having driven many a mob of cattle down to the southern markets. Canowindra was one of the few crossing points along the meandering Belubula River that runs between Forbes and Carcoar, the sort of place you pass through on the way to somewhere else. Our telegraphs told us that a party of traps, led by Pottinger, had been in town for a week waiting to see if we came south and which side of the river we would start working. They got impatient, crossed to the west bank of the river and headed south for Cowra.

It took us two days at a brisk trot to travel the forty miles southeast through rolling countryside to the sleepy little town of Canowindra where we arrived early in the morning on Sunday, October 11.

To describe Canowindra as a town is misleading, as it is no more than one wide, dusty street lined with weatherboard houses, stockyards, half a dozen shops bleached light brown by the punishing glare of the sun and a population of 67 at last count. It does have one unusual feature, though. The main street dog-legs sharply to the left for no apparent reason at the Canowindra Inn where, it is rumoured, the town surveyor enjoyed its hospitality to the detriment of his duty. But other than that quaint yarn there is little else to recommend it.

A stout hammering on the side door rudely awakened Mr William Robinson Esq., proprietor of the Canowindra Inn, from his usual Sunday morning lie-in. We had chosen Robinson's for our little show because the traps often stayed here when they were out on patrol. I could hear him muttering blasphemies under his breath as he stumbled down the narrow wooden staircase, no doubt half-dressed, half-asleep and hung over, on account of his propensity to have 'just the one' with his regular customers.

'Who's there?' he croaked, drowning out any possible reply with a hacking cough that told the story of too many whiskies and cigars the previous night. I used the words that opened more doors in this neck of the woods than 'Open Sesame'.

'Police!'

Over the metallic clanking of numerous heavy bolts that secured the heavy, bushranger-proof door, Robinson was heard to mutter, 'Bloody traps, will they never leave a man in peace?'

Robinson incautiously opened the door a crack and popped his head out into the harsh daylight. What had once been a magnificent mop of coppery-red hair stuck out at comic angles around his face.

An angry expression broke across his avuncular features when he saw we were not policemen.

'Bugger off!' he growled 'We don't open until eleven—'

He stopped dead as I stepped in from the side and cut him short by jabbing a pistol into his porky cheek. Keeping his head perfectly still, he moved his eyes in my direction as I smiled and delivered our calling card.

'Bail up, you bastard!'

His big shoulders slumped forwards.

'Aw, bugger it, boys, can't you see I'm just a working man?'

'And the owner of a fine establishment,' I chimed in. 'Don't play us for fools, Billy Robinson. Empty your pockets, please.'

No matter how hard we squeezed him the dry old skinflint only yielded £3. Threats to hole him like a sieve only yielded sixpences and pennies hidden in the most ingenious places – under candlesticks, behind clocks and even buried in the soil of a pot plant. He was either a damned fool or believed he led a charmed life.

'Is this it?' I said, feeling the weight of small change in my hand. With my pistol I shooed him upstairs, scolding him, 'Get a move on, you've got a bar to tend. Get yourself washed and shaved, or you'll be giving the Hall gang a bad name.'

The hotel opened at eleven o'clock sharp with some new staff behind the bar. In the locals came two by two – accountants, blacksmiths, clerks, draymen, stockmen, shopkeepers and the cockatoo farmers, in town to pledge a bit more of their selection to the storekeepers, in return for much-needed supplies.

We waited until the bar was full. I whistled and the three Johnnies covered the exits, and I climbed onto the bar.

'Gentlemen, the Canowindra Inn is under new management.'

There was a ripple of confusion. One short, stocky, tough-looking cocky, who was obviously a regular and no stranger to a blue, stepped forwards and puffed out his chest. 'And who are ya, ya bloody galah?'

'For a short time you will be the guests of Ben Hall Esquire,' shouted Johnny Gilbert from the back of the room. 'Along with Mr Johnny Vane, Mr Mickey Burke, Mr John O'Meally.'

'And all the way from Canada,' I chimed in, 'I give you, Mr Johnny Gilbert.'

As each name was announced we took off our hats and bowed like some music-hall act. The bar went quiet and the cocky took a couple of paces back, wishing he'd had the good sense to keep his head in. I put him at his ease with a broad wink, 'Not a worry, mate. It's business as usual and the grog's on us.'

That's one thing about your hardworking, downtrodden cocky, he knows you don't get much for nothing in this life, but when it's offered, he gets right on it.

'Well, in which case, I'll have a beer on ya, Ben Hall,' said the cocky, draining the glass he had been nursing for the past hour with a practised swallow and banging it down on the bar.

'Mr Robinson, if you please,' I said, producing a thick roll of soft and pointing down at the empty glass.

Everyone quickly lost their shyness and pushed towards the bar. With the regulars happily captive in the bar, we went out into the street and bailed up bullock carts, took their guns from them and herded them in. As the day went on we bailed up more and more passers-by. We ordered up some hearty tucker, put cigars and bottles of brandy on the table and paid for everything fair and square from our thick rolls of notes. Our large bundles were a sign that we had the power now.

One squatter, by the name of Kirkpatrick, made as if to resist until Johnny Vane gave him a sharp jab in the ribs with his pistol and I rifled his waistband, relieving him of his weapon.

'It's not that we need it, but we wouldn't want it to go off by accident,' I told him.

There was a flurry of activity at the far end of the crooked street and we watched the only policeman in the town, Constable Sykes, come round the bend in some state of disrepair, his tunic buttons still undone and without his kepi.

There had been some heavy spring showers and the road, which was rutted and pockmarked by bullock carts and horses' hooves, was now strewn with large, mustard-coloured puddles of unknown depth, which he had to step around.

I had posted John Vane further down the street to play the part of a concerned citizen. He pointed to a narrow lane that ran down the side of Sparkes the blacksmith's towards the cattle yards. 'They went that way, Constable. They're after the horses,' he called out to Sykes.

As our quarry rounded the corner, I stuck out my good leg and watched the feckless trap sprawl headlong into a brackish pool of water, losing his rifle in the process. Vane and I pulled him to his feet and when his eyes cleared Sykes found himself staring down the ugly muzzle of a Colt revolver.

We marched him back to the hotel and in front of the assembled townsfolk removed his ammunition and gave him back his rifle. Once Sykes got his wind back he quickly found his voice. 'Kidnapping a policeman is a serious offence. You'll rot on Cockatoo Island for the rest of your natural for this. Police will be swarming all over the district within hours.'

I smiled thinly in the face of his bluster. Sykes opened his mouth to speak again, but I levelled my pistol at his head, 'We've heard enough from you.'

Turning to the assembled throng, I pointed to the helpless trap at the end of my barrel. 'We're the power in this district now. We've marched into your town and taken over. We can stick up people on the roads at any time of day, rob banks, stations. And what can you do about it?'

I answered my own question by sneering, 'I'll tell you straight, nothing.'

I ordered Sykes to remove his uniform and march up and down the veranda in his long johns with his rifle over his shoulder.

'Your orders are to challenge any unsavoury characters that might try to enter this fine establishment,' I told him.

His brow creased and I patted him on the shoulder reassuringly as I pushed him towards his post. 'Don't worry, Constable, they'll be obvious to you. They wear blue jackets and may use the word "police" as they approach.'

A huge gale of laughter blew him out onto the landing to pound his miserable beat alone.

*

Having neutralised the forces of law and order, we set about giving the townsfolk of Canowindra an occasion to remember. As Mickey, Gilbert and I went outside for a breather the sun had already sunk behind the distant rise of Blue Jacket Mountain casting long evening shadows over the town.

The festive air created by a day of boozing and feasting was about to be improved by the appearance of a group of travelling musicians who informed us they had a wedding engagement at nearby Montague's station.

'Well, the newlyweds will just have to make their own entertainment,' quipped Johnny Gilbert, throwing back his head of long, girlish hair and laughing at his own joke. Then, sweeping back the front of his jacket, he selected one of the pistols decorating the waistband of his trousers and cocked the hammer, all in one practised movement. He gave them an altar boy's angelic smile and said, 'Bail up, you bastards!'

'Aw shite,' said the leader in a broad Irish accent and closed his eyes.

They just stood there looking awkward, so I pulled out my fat roll of notes, which spoke a language they all understood. Pushing the wad into his hand, so he could get a right feel of it, I said, 'You tell that Mr Montague you were paid handsomely, better wages than you'll ever get from them tight-fingered English bastards. Come on, I'll help you with that accordion.' They looked at each other, shrugged their shoulders and started lifting up their instruments.

As I pushed open the door to the crowded, smoky bar, which now had about forty townsfolk in it, the band were almost knocked backwards by the heady bouquet of tobacco, stale sweat and strong brandy. A great cheer went up as they made their way through the throng with their instruments above their heads.

Tables were pushed back and the band's repertoire of Irish and Scotch jigs and reels and new colonial favourites soon had everyone up dancing. I admit I'd lost some of my love of the free-spirited Irish since my lovely wife deserted me, but I had to admit, they and the Devil did have the best tunes.

The mood became more raucous as the grog and the music loosened tongues and people forgot that they were hostages to our fortune. Although we observed a vow of strict temperance, some of the boys got up and danced when they struck up *Whiskey In The Jar*, the old Irish ballad about a lusty highwayman:

As I was goin' over the Cork and Kerry mountains
I saw Captain Farrell and his money he was countin'
I first produced my pistol and then produced my rapier
I said 'stand and deliver, or the Devil he may take ye'

Musha ring dum adoo dum a da
Whack for my daddy-o
Whack for my daddy-o
There's whiskey in the jar-o

Gilbert took the floor and did a combination of a Yankee barn dance and a jig with a local girl, showing off some nimble footwork. Not to be outdone, Vane stomped his big feet around. Old Slasher had put paid to my dancing days long before, but I could never say no to the attentions of a pretty girl and stole a kiss from one of Billy Robinson's pretty daughters.

Well past the witching hour, the only lights on in Candowindra were at Robinson's hotel, which was guarded by the tireless Sykes who was still marching up and down in his long johns. We allowed the ladies and children to sleep in the hotel rooms upstairs and took their word that they would not try to escape. The men remained downstairs with us, as we took it in turns to have a nap, though I doubt anyone was sober enough to stand up, far less able make a run for it.

I was awoken at first light by the drumming of heavy rain on the hotel's tin roof. The leaden skies that passed overhead the day before had now opened.

The mood amongst our 'guests' was more subdued than the previous day, due to the copious amounts of grog consumed, but they perked up once they smelt breakfast on the go. These country folk had eaten and drunk their way through a small fortune already as could be seen from the smile plastered across Robinson's phiz. If this went on, we'd be back in his quarters looking for loose change.

The rest of the day passed with hands of cards for the men, charades and piano for the ladies.

'Will ye not play a hand with us, Ben?' asked one of our captives.

I shook my head smiling, 'Gentlemen, I've staked more than enough on this lark and have no taste for the cards.'

After lunch we put on a show of target shooting in the back garden. The men and children crowded round as Johnny Gilbert drew his pistol, which he called a 'barrel', a Yankee word I'd heard on the goldfields. He stuck his finger through the trigger guard and spun it round and round before popping a grog bottle. He and O'Meally went bottle for bottle for almost two dozen and we had to resort to showmanship to separate them. We had them standing on one leg, putting a hand over one eye, shooting underarm with their backs to the target and firing with the other hand, before 'Flash' Johnny Gilbert carried the day with a fine exhibition of marksmanship.

The festivities came to an end on the morning of the third day when a Mr Hibertson came to me and asked if he could leave urgently.

'What's wrong, mate? Not enjoying yourself?' I asked him.

'No . . . no,' he explained. 'It's the river. It's been rising with all the rain we've had these past couple of days and if we don't cross soon, we'll be stuck here for a month.'

Looking out of the rain-splattered window I could see the river had already risen well up the timber marker and the fast-flowing, muddy waters were dragging sizeable lumps of dead wood downstream at a fair lick. I also saw a police patrol on the far bank pacing up and down, wondering if it was still safe to cross.

'No worries, Mr Hibertson,' I said, 'We were going to call time on this little gathering anyways.'

Far from relief, there was disappointment when we announced that we were calling it a day. People followed us outside and continued to mill around buzzing with excitement.

For generations to come, they'd be telling their neighbours, family and friends about this. Everyone will know someone who danced with Johnny Gilbert, played poker with John O'Meally and stole a kiss from Ben Hall. A hundred years from now, even if Canowindra is still a small town with a crooked left turn in its main street and a ferry crossing, it will still be remembered as the place where the Ben Hall gang had its greatest victory.

We fired our pistols in the air, alarming the police patrol on the other side of the river. They could do nothing but seethe and wait for the water levels to subside. I shouted out at the top of my voice, 'They'll never hang Ben Hall,' and we rode out of town with the cheers of the townsfolk ringing in our ears.

The new telegraph wires connecting Sydney and Bathurst fairly hummed as news of our party in Canowindra produced headlines and hysteria in the newspapers. No one had ever heard of bushrangers bailing up entire towns and then being given a heroes' send-off by the townsfolk. We had graduated from small-time villains into a formidable enemy. Everywhere we went we were given a heroes' welcome. Girls would ask us for a kiss and men ride for miles so they could say they shook our hands. We knew that had public sympathy not been with us, we wouldn't have lasted a week. Where would we appear next, wondered the press: Forbes? Goulburn? Sydney? The *Bathurst Times* summed up our manifesto perfectly:

> *Bushranging by this gang is not followed as a mere means of subsistence. Every new success is a source of pleasure to them, and they are stimulated to novelty of actions by their desire to make history. This has become their great ambition. They aspire to a name. They combine the desperado and the gallant and feel they have built up a superiority which defies the power of the Government. The sympathy which they get from a section of their public builds up their vanity in which they indulge.*

The traps were in a spin and our magisterial informant, Tom Morris, told me that Inspector-General McLerie received offers of help every week. There were proposals to recruit a private army, train a team of savage hunting bloodhounds, manufacture exploding mailbags and even a specially armoured escort coach. McLerie rejected them all, but a Victorian shipping owner, eager to show the police how it should be done, commissioned the armoured coach privately.

A regular Cobb & Co. coach was refurbished using iron cladding and had firing slits cut into the sides. The anonymous coach ran up and down the Bathurst road to its own timetable. The plan ended in disarray when the traps, thinking it was some strange invention of ours, attacked it and arrested the occupants when they stopped to relieve themselves. It's the fortune of war.

Chapter Seventeen

It came to our attention through newspapers and word of mouth that there had been men lifted in places as far apart as Bathurst, Murrurundi and Queensland on the suspicion that they were Ben Hall. They would be dragged all the way to Sydney where their true identity would be confirmed before being released. When I caught my image in the window of Hilliar & Pierce's Canowindra store, where the staunch storekeepers had hung a 'Wanted' poster, I saw the description bore no resemblance to the feral creature that stared back at me.

Described as 'About 28 years of age, 5 ft 9 inches high, stout build (would weigh about 13 stone 7 lbs.), figure erect, flash appearance, fair wavy hair, short light beard, grey eyes, nose inclined to be hooked, and thin, compressed lips that curl upwards into a pronounced sneer,' they'd never identify me now from that description, I thought.

Here I was in all my shabby majesty with an unkempt beard of biblical proportions, which once again hid my legendary lip, and the rigours of the game had thinned me down. My hair was a wild, tangled mess that almost touched my shoulders and my days of 'flashness' were long behind me. The tailor had more genteel pursuits in mind when hand-crafting these fine garments of mine. Worn by a man who sleeps on a damp swag in a cold, dark cave with a pistol for a pillow, they now looked much the worse for wear.

The Darkie had always been immaculately turned out, but he had divided his wardrobe between every doxy in the district and he rode from one to the other to take his pleasure, have a good feed and change his clothes. These were duties the redoubtable Kitty Brown would now be expected to perform. I wondered idly if such domesticity had cooled her romantic ardour.

If you live as an outlaw and steal for a living it is generally understood that you are entitled to dress with some style. So, after prevailing on Gilbert to cut my hair and shaving off my straggly beard, I rode into Forbes and inquired as to who was the finest tailor in town.

Conveniently, his small glass-fronted shop was at the bottom end of the main thoroughfare. The sign outside said 'Manfred Zink Bespoke Tailor'.

A tinkling bell announced my entrance into his dimly lit Aladdin's cave. It was packed from the ceiling to the floor with rolls of cloth of every colour, texture and shade. Finished suits, trousers and coats shrouded in white cotton hung behind the counter awaiting collection. Busying himself with order books and dockets was a short, elderly, bespectacled man who I took to be Mr Zink. Without looking up he called out in a thin, reedy voice, heavily accented with German, 'I'm sorry, we are closed.'

I ignored him and made my way to the counter. He looked up, the light reflecting off the round, thick lenses of his glasses. The watery eyes behind them told of too many late nights cutting and stitching by the pale light of a single, spluttering lamp. Before he could repeat his apology, I thrust out my hand in greeting, 'Mr Zink?'

'Yes,' he replied, a note of uncertainty weighing heavily in his voice. I felt the leathery tips of his fingers brush my open palm as we shook hands.

'Ben Hall,' I said with a smile. The name clearly did not register with the tailor. I drew aside my jacket, making sure he saw the Colt and the other pistol stuck in my belt.

He swallowed once and inquired politely, 'How may I help you, Mr Hall?'

'An emergency fitting, Mr Zink,' I replied.

In his tiny attic cum living quarters, we burned the midnight oil. The elderly tailor's fingers danced like a pianist as he measured, cut and stitched a creation befitting a gentleman – a single-button jacket and matching trousers in a lightweight, pale grey material. A white shirt, black ribbon tie and a sash of red silk completed the outfit.

As I stood before the mirror, I noted with satisfaction that being held at gunpoint by a notorious criminal had not resulted in an unsteady hand or an inferior cut on Mr Zink's part. The finished article hung beautifully. Mr Zink was a true artist.

To complete my sartorial transformation, I helped myself to his own Panama hat and tipped the brim with my fingers as I left.

'When they ask, what does Ben Hall, the bushranger, look like, your reply will be "you'll know him by his finely tailored suit". . . I'll be a walking advertisement for your tailoring skills.'

I suspect, as his tinkling doorbell announced my departure into the night, my final comment probably caused him more despair than his unpaid labours.

The next day I visited the local photographer, William Lennox, who also dedicated his time and services to a special, after-hours sitting.

Dressed in all my new finery, I sat in a chair in front of a fancy background. Forbidden to move a muscle and staring into the lens till my eyes started to water, his powder tray flashed periodically as he took shot after shot.

Lennox, in search of artistic perfection, forgot the nature of our relationship and busied himself making minute adjustments, first to the lens and then under the black hood where he disappeared to fiddle. He muttered to himself all the while and his hair stuck up from his balding pate at ever more ridiculous angles each time he emerged.

Finally, he proclaimed himself satisfied and I had to endure another long wait while he disappeared into what he called his 'dark room', leaving me waiting in the studio that was still thick with the noxious fumes of his last assignment.

Just as I felt as though I might drop off in one of his overstuffed armchairs, a coughing, spluttering Lennox appeared from his dark room, the tang of sharp-smelling chemicals reviving me at once. In his hands were a dozen sharply defined images of a flash, youthful-looking Ben Hall.

I wrote 'Ben Hall' on the back of each one and posted them to all the main newspapers in the district with the following hand-written note:

TO WHOM IT MAY CONCERN

It has come to my attention that in recent months police have mistakenly arrested a number of citizens on suspicion of being the bushranger Ben Hall, for whom there is a £250 reward for robbery under arms and other crimes.

Recently, a stockman from Murrurundi and a salesman from Forbes were arrested and dispatched to Sydney for identification. Both were released, once it was established that neither man was Ben Hall, but the delays resulted in considerable inconvenience to both parties.

It is clear that these cases of mistaken identity stem from the descriptions displayed on wanted posters, which are as inaccurate as they are unflattering. Therefore, I am taking the liberty of supplying you with an image of myself captured within the past week, in the hope that the New South Wales police might consent to publishing an accurate description.

I am hopeful this might prevent any further inconvenience to innocent citizens in the future.

I remain, your faithful servant,

Ben Hall

What was described as a 'proper piece of impudence' by the press quickly paid dividends when we bailed up the Bathurst mail and found a heavily perspiring gent sitting inside. I motioned with my gun that he should get out. Blinking as his eyes readjusted from the gloom of the carriage to bright sunlight, O'Meally stuck his pistol in his ribs, but the traveller didn't react. Instead, he looked him straight in the eye forcing John to snarl, 'Get your hands up.' As he did so, slowly, I took a good look at what we'd caught.

Amply proportioned, his receding, rust-coloured hair and neatly clipped beard, both tinged with grey, put him somewhere in his fifties. He was dressed like a city dandy in a fashionable tweed suit with a rounded black velvet collar and had a pair of fashionable Cuban-heeled boots on his feet. I pointed at his upraised hands with my pistol and said, 'You'd make better use of them by turning out your pockets.'

By now, we'd normally be halfway through a tough yarn of sick mothers, grinding poverty and how we were robbing them of their last shilling in the world, but this one gave up his watch and wedding ring without protest.

Having parted with his valuables, he spoke for the first time in what I'd call the Queen's English, crisp and undistorted by any accent or burr. 'Ben Hall, I presume?' he said, staring intently into my face.

'And what would a gentleman like you be wanting with the likes of me, unless you are a representative of Her Majesty, of course?'

'My name is John Kaye, the editor of the *Bathurst Examiner*, and I'd like an interview,' he replied evenly.

My eyes narrowed. 'Interview?'

'I want to find out who Ben Hall is and what he wants.'

'What he wants?' I echoed. 'Isn't he just some wild, raggedy-arsed bushranger tryin' to make some easy coin? Isn't that what all "gentlemen of the press" think?'

Kaye bit his lip thoughtfully. 'I don't think so. He chooses his targets too well. Policemen, magistrates, squatters, storekeepers and even whole towns. Why do all that if he were only in it for money? No, I think there's more to Mr Ben Hall than meets the eye and I aim to be the first to publish his story.'

Looking at my fob watch, I motioned for him to climb back into the carriage. 'Half an hour.'

He greeted the news with great relief and a humorous aside. 'Thank God! I've been up and down this road three times this past week in the hope of meeting you and it's cost me a watch, £20 and two wedding rings.'

'We live in troubled times, Mr Kaye,' was my riposte.

So, I had my say in the comfort of a mail coach, under the shady umbrella of a cypress pine, midway between Bathurst and Young, while my partners-in-crime set about ripping open letters and packages in the shade. Knowing the sharp eye of the newspaperman was monitoring their every move, they took every opportunity to try on ladies hats and discuss the merit of the various dresses they found in parcels. To his credit, Kaye wasn't fooled by their larrikin behaviour.

Producing a notebook and a lead pencil, he settled back in the creaky leather upholstery and asked what got me into the game in the first place.

I told him what I had told Inspector Norton, the plain truth. 'I was driven to it.'

'How so?' replied Kaye, his interest piqued and pencil poised.

Kaye started scribbling furiously as I told him how Pottinger had imprisoned me for a crime I did not commit and destroyed my station at Sandy Creek. I waited until the scratching of his pencil stopped before I continued.

'The Colonial Secretary of New South Wales, Charles Cowper, said Pottinger was justified in burning down my hut because I was "one of the greatest villains in the country". I had not been convicted of a single crime, far less "one of the greatest criminals in the country". Pottinger claimed he acted at the request of the owner, Mr John Wilson. Wilson bought Jacky McGuire's share of Sandy Creek six months after Pottinger razed my station, but doesn't own my share. Furthermore, a police officer is only entitled to raze private property if it was built on Crown lands. How can I respect a law that chooses its enemies at will and sets out to destroy them by any means at its disposal?'

'So, you took up the game after Inspector Pottinger burnt your station?' asked Kaye looking me in the eye for confirmation.

'When a man's situation becomes unbearable he has a choice – submit or rise up.' I nodded at the boys who were still sitting on the grass ratting the mailbags. 'Perhaps, in the end, all that awaits us is death and dishonour, but it's time someone drew a line in the sand for the tyrants who rule this country. I can read a newspaper, Mr Kaye, and I know the world is changing and that Australia will have to change with it.'

He nodded and then pressed me for what he called my 'manifesto'.

'Manifesto?' I exclaimed.

'Your declaration?'

This, then, is the gist of what I told him, though I may not have spoken it so eloquently at the time.

'A pox on all squatters. This colony is not yet fifty years old and twenty-nine persons belonging to just four families own the best land in New South Wales. They are the "squattocracy", our new colonial nobility. The Free Selection Act entitles the selectors to 2,500 acres of "free selection before survey", but they thwart any selection of their lands by using crooked practices such as "dummying" and "peacocking" and nothing is done to prevent it.'

His pencil kept scratching and I kept talking.

'A pox on the traps, the hirelings of the squatters, paid to uphold their laws and do their dirty work. Despite the Police Regulation Act they are still rotten to the core. Between a quarter and a third of the force are dismissed each year for drunkenness, corruption and cowardice.' I noticed that the boys were silent, their work laid aside, as they listened.

'A pox on all storekeepers. They hold the poor selector to ransom, keeping the title to his land whilst he battles drought, flood and the fluctuations of the market to provide for his family.' I jabbed my forefinger at him. 'If you look in their ledgers, you'll find the names of all their debtors and what they owe all carefully entered. The storekeeper sits and waits for Providence to break the back of the selector so he can take his land. Nature has its bloodsuckers in leeches, ticks, cow flies, but none are as practised as the storekeeper.'

'So, is Ben Hall out to change the world?' he pressed.

'Just my little bit of it,' I shot back. 'The rest of the world can look after itself.'

There was much more that I could have said, but the half-hour had passed more quickly than I thought. A sharp whistle and an agitated wave from Gilbert warned me that the traps were approaching. I stood, returned his personal items and looked him in the eye. 'Your liberation is at hand, Mr Kaye,' I informed him, returning his wallet and valuables. 'I trust I won't be disappointed by what I read in your paper. Remember, Bathurst holds no fear for us.'

He returned my even stare. 'You have my word, Mr Hall.'

But whether Mr Kaye was as good as his word, I never found out. When it was discovered that he had spent a cosy half-hour in the company of Ben Hall and that he intended to publish an interview with the brigand whose gang had recently terrorised Bathurst and Canowindra there was outrage amongst the squatter types. The owner of the *Examiner* dispensed with Mr Kaye's services and he was run out of town. I heard he moved to Charters Towers, in Queensland, where I hope their commitment to truth and free speech is more steadfast than in the small-minded town of Bathurst.

Our feeling of invincibility reached a peak one Sunday early in October 1863. We had collected a good crowd of about thirty under a big shade tree on the Bathurst road, just a few miles out of Forbes. As it was a hot day, we bailed up a passing dray and served them some refreshments.

The distant drumming of hooves caused me to look east towards Bathurst. Through clouds of fine red dust and waves of shimmering heat, I saw an approaching police party with the distinctive figure of Sir Frederick in the lead.

They'd obviously missed the Forbes to Bathurst mail coach we'd bailed up earlier in the day. The vehicle in question was still at the side of the road where we were still ratting the mailbags.

The patrol looked flash enough in their blue uniforms and hats, riding six abreast, the sun glinting off their drawn firearms, but their old daisy kickers were so slow across the ground that I still had time to rob another poor cove of his watch, wallet and wedding ring. I lingered even though I sensed Pottinger nearing and his finger tightening on the trigger he no doubt held in his outstretched hand. Why I decided to take him on that day, I can't say, except that when you live with constant danger you eventually get curious about how close to the flame you can go without getting burned.

'When his lordship gets here, tell him we'll be at The Pioneer,' I told my victim as I tipped the brim of my new Panama hat and dug my spurs into Willy's grey granite flanks. I swear I could feel Pottinger's rage brush my shoulder as I pulled away out of range.

Our speedy mounts meant we had plenty of time for a leisurely beer and a nobbler of whisky at The Pioneer before the blue bellies got within cooee of the pub. Fearing we'd set an ambush they were seen circling the pub for ten minutes before bursting into the empty bar, their pistols cocked. Martin Bradley, the landlord, nodded at the five empty glasses that sat on the bar and the six full ones next to them. I thought as the New South Wales police were recruiting bad Irish drunks, they'd enjoy a beer on a hot day. But they'd stood there so long the beer had lost all its vim.

'Been and gone,' Bradley informed them. 'Said he'd get another round in at the Prince of Wales. Pottinger's face flushed an angry red and he cursed openly in a manner quite unsuited to a knight of the realm. He led his troop, who looked longingly at the beers, back outside.

They pulled up outside The Prince with a clatter of hooves and again found six beers awaiting them. The same happened at The Brown Cow, The Union, The Cockatoo and the Bush Travellers' Inn, as we took them on a tour of the local hostelries.

As word spread of our little game, the locals lined the dusty roads to watch the spectacle and salute Sir Frederick as he went past. At first, he'd taken it as a mark of respect and local approval and saluted back, until he found out we'd put it about that failing to salute a titled gentleman could lead to a flogging.

By the time we'd got to The Peacock, we'd had our fill of grog and it must have slowed us up because there was no time to get the beers up before Pottinger's mob pulled up outside, their screws all wild-eyed and steaming. Having long since thrown caution to the wind, they burst in and finding no beers on the bar and the locals crowded at the back of the room, the traps fancied they had caught up to us.

Seeing a storeroom door adjacent to the bar slightly ajar, Pottinger drew his pistol, cocked it and edged towards the door, his eyes fixed intently on his target. The hotel owner, a timid little creature by the name of Yorkshire Jack, who had been standing motionless behind the bar suddenly piped up, 'Er, Sir Frederick.'

Irritated by the disturbance Pottinger hissed, 'Quiet, man! Take cover!' Jack tried again, 'But there's—'

'Do as you're told, man!' he boomed, ordering one of his men to cover him.

The sight of a loaded barrel traversing in his direction caused the barman to bend his knees. Pottinger sidled nearer to the store-room door.

'Ben Hall, come out now, or we'll shoot you up!'

There was no reply.

'Last chance!'

He motioned to his men to present arms and barked the order, 'Fire!' There was a deafening roar as six guns went off blowing a hole the size of a bucket clean through the door. Before the thunder and smoke had died away, Pottinger had kicked the splintered door off its hinges. But as he lurched through the doorway he found himself looking not at the bullet-ridden corpse of a bushranger, but at the shredded remains of a scarecrow we'd lifted from one of the surrounding fields, standing in a leaky bucket, dressed in the tatters of what had been one of Flash Johnny's Crimean shirts.

Realising he'd been done over again he emerged from the smoke-filled storeroom. 'Bugger it!' he yelled venting his anger on the piano that stood against the wall by thumping the butt of his pistol down on the keys with a discordant crash. With comic timing the pale-faced hotel owner popped up from behind the bar.

'I did try to tell you,' he chimed in.

'Shut up! Shut up!' roared Pottinger, rounding on him with menace.

The man stammered, 'Yyy . . . yes, sir!' and in a nervous reflex reaction saluted and disappeared again. Sir Frederick had endured quite enough ridicule for one day.

'And stop saluting! I will not be mocked.' A stale, acrid smell caused him to stop. With a furrowed brow he began sniffing the air, quickly tracing the source of the odour to the pool of brackish water that leaked from the bucket and was eddying round his Wellington boots. His proboscis was doubtless more used to the bouquet of fine wines and brandies, but he had no trouble identifying this particular vintage. He jumped back in horror, as though he'd had a sudden vision of us all standing round laughing as we pissed into the bucket not ten minutes before. A catcall came from the back of the room, 'That's about as close to Ben Hall as you'll ever get, mate.'

Pottinger swung round, but the gallery of grinning faces that greeted him protected the identity of the wag. A big fellow, over six feet and powerfully built, Sir Frederick grabbed the nearest grinning cocky by the front of the shirt, putting a stop to the merriment as quickly as it had begun. Pushing his face close to the farmer's rough, grizzled phiz, he said evenly, 'I'll have my day with Ben Hall. And if I find any of you are in league with him, I'll make sure you hang alongside him.'

After looking up and down the line for a good half-minute, as though he was memorising their faces, Pottinger motioned for his men to follow him outside with a violent jerk of his head.

Had he done his job and searched the hotel properly he would have found us in the kitchen all warm and cosy with the hotel owner's wife, just to make sure the cove wasn't tempted to give us away.

Where Pottinger had made enemies of the locals, we made friends with them by paying the score for the door and a few rounds of drinks for all present.

Even before a low whistle from the crows outside told us that the coast was clear, the drinks were flowing. The little cocky who had skited Pottinger was quickly sniping at him again. 'He's gentry all right. He's an "arch duke" if ever I saw one!'

The crowd exploded into laughter.

'What?' mouthed Gilbert, puzzled.

'Old English slang for a funny fellow,' I explained.

'He's that all right,' chortled Mickey Burke, as we raised our glasses.

In honour of the occasion, someone banged out a verse or two on the piano. It was combined with other yarns to become the folk ballad, *The Bloody Field of Wheogo*. Performed in the stop-start rhyming style made popular by London music-hall entertainers, it ended with the lines:

But the 'ranger proud, he laughed aloud,
And bounding rode away,
While Sir Frederick Pott shut his eyes for a shot,
And missed in the usual way.

From that day on, Frederick Pottinger was known as 'Blind Freddy', on account of his inability to tell the difference between a broom handle and a bushranger, and it soon became a common saying. I doubted that scapegrace will be remembered for much else.

Leaving the cheery, tobacco-filled bar where the piano player continued to thump out his songs, I went out the back to the dunny. I was on my way back when a female voice stopped me in my tracks.

'I wouldn't have thought there was a drop o' piss left in ya.'

I turned and saw a young, raven-haired girl sitting on a chair near the woodstove warming her long legs. Without another word, she rose and closed the distance between us with several swaying movements of her slim hips, put her arms round my neck and kissed me full on the lips.

'So, it's true what they say, Ben Hall–' she said, in a low, husky voice, her dark eyes darting back through the open doorway to the shot-filled bucket, which now had pride of place on top of the piano.

I realised with a grin that she'd probably been watching while we had filled the bucket, but her face betrayed no hint of shame.

'Well, it would never do to have it said that I promised more than I could deliver,' I replied with a grin.

She led me by the hand down a darkened corridor to the laundry room. As I said, there are certain women with fascination for dangerous men who stray outside the law. This was one of them.

We lay down on a pile of unwashed sheets and bedclothes, and she proceeded to loosen her hair clips, allowing a stream of jet-black hair to cascade over her shoulders. I reckoned she wasn't a day over seventeen, her face still unlined by the cares of the world, her supple body a just reward for a brave knight.

She unbuttoned her white cotton blouse and unfettered two wonderfully proportioned breasts, into which I instantly pressed my face.

Well, mate, I thought to myself, *this bushranging lark has its moments, there's no denying that.*

'Your mother must be very proud of her little girl,' I grinned up at her.

'My mother is a god-fearing woman,' she replied primly, but her cool front was betrayed by the wicked twinkle in her eye. Hitching up her skirt, she pushed me back further into the tangle of laundry and leaning over me, those firm young breasts pushing against my chest, she blew softly in my ear and whispered, 'And she *did* warn me you're a very bad man, Ben Hall.'

'Very bad,' I agreed and rolled her over. Fornication is a great comfort to the lower classes, God's compensation for the many hardships we have to endure.

Later, we rode back to our mountain lair across the wide plains, strung out five abreast recalling the derring-do of the day just ending.

A soft trail of cottony cumulus stretched out across the panorama of the open skies. It was fringed with golden light and shot through with what poets call 'a hectic red', a fitting backdrop for the heroes who had just carried the day.

I looked at the faces of my gang, young, fearless and drunk with the power and excitement of it all. The excitable Mickey Burke declared that it had been a good day for the underdog and, as I remembered the warmth and smell of that maid's supple young body, I thought that it had also been a very good day for Ben Hall.

O'Meally pulled a blood-red fogle from his pocket, tied it to a bit of stick he'd picked up along the way and held it aloft like a standard as we galloped for home.

Johnny Gilbert raised a clenched fist and roared out into the sunset. 'See you in Hell, or in California!'

We howled like dingos in reply. For that one moment we were on top of the world, indestructible. Nothing could touch us, or so we believed.

Chapter Eighteen

The traps and the squatters would never give in and watch us take over. Our successes made them resolve to cut us down to size, but judging by the 'Letters to the Editor' in the local newspapers, the squatters had lost faith in the police and started calling public meetings to organise their own protection. At these gatherings, they called for 'public spirited' men, or any gung-ho drunk with a gun who was game for some live target practice, to volunteer to defend the town and hunt down bushrangers. They had been assured, on the quiet, that even if they shot us in cold blood, no Magistrate in the district would gaol them.

Out of curiosity, I attended a meeting in Grenfell, though, truth be told, I watched through an open window along with the other curious onlookers who'd put up with the stink of fresh horseshit and having their skin tattooed by whining mozzies before they'd share a seat with a squatter.

In the small, dimly lit wooden hall the odour of stale sweat was only mitigated by the smell of decent tobacco that rose in a cloud from the ranks of assorted storekeepers, squatters, bank managers and 'good citizens' who were crammed on the long wooden benches that ran to the back of the room.

It was one of those hot, still nights in the bush when men's blood ran hot and angry shouts and harsh words drowned out the eerie discord of the cicadas.

Flanked by his father-in-law, the Honourable Henry Rotton, a successful horse breeder and stagecoach operator and a member of the New South Wales Legislature, was Henry Keightley, the assistant gold commissioner and a police Magistrate for the Rockley area. What a peacock!

Keightley was a crooked bastard who was investigated for theft and dishonesty when he was Clerk of Courts in Tamworth and found guilty. As is always the way with his class his indiscretions were dismissed as 'carelessness' and his punishment was to be 'sent to the goats', that is, exiled to the outlying Lachlan district.

Keightley stood up on stage, his well-tailored Panama jacket draped casually across the back of a chair. He was immaculate in a white starched shirt and moleskin trousers the colour of clotted cream tucked into his polished Wellington boots, a fat fob chain slung low across the belly of his tan waistcoat. Punching the air with a clenched fist, he shouted, 'Damn these bushrangers and those who harbour them. They are the enemies, not the saviours of decent hardworking folk—'

There were shouts of agreement. They stood as one and shouted that they would 'never surrender to the lawless reign of those raggedy-arsed bandits', 'God save the Queen' and other blandishments. Grogged up and feeling the safety of numbers, they were all lionhearted defenders of the noble cause. In my experience they'd be the first to raise their hands or turn tail if they ever saw a bushranger. I looked on with disdain. The bedlam subsided for a moment and I decided it was time to spice things up. I leaned forward and shouted through the window, 'Keightley, you'll be getting a visit from Ben Hall one of these nights.'

A flush came to his cheeks as he looked around, his head twisting from side to side in a desperate effort to see who the voice belonged to.

'Who said that? Stand up and declare yourself, like a man,' he shouted, his voice betraying his anxiousness. He staggered like a Friday night drunk as my words hit home. He tried to regain his balance and his sense of moral superiority, but cruel, judgmental smiles were already playing across the lips of the cockies and townsfolk who'd turned up. They knew his type. When he said 'we'll stand and fight them', what he really meant was 'when we give the order, you lowly types get up and fight them'.

Satisfied, I saddled up and slipped back into the darkness before anyone recognised me. Not a mile up the road, a galloper overtook me, travelling faster than the fox who has just heard the huntsman's horn. I smiled at the knowledge that there would be no more night rallies for Mr Keightley. He would spend tonight and every night dozing in a chair by a darkened window, gun on his knee, waking up in a sweat every time the dogs barked, waiting for us to come roaring out of the wild colonial night with fire and vengeance in our hearts. One night we would come, but it would be at a time of my choosing.

The morning of October 16 dawned clear and bright above us with no hint of the tragedy that lay ahead. It had been another cold night at the 'Star hotel', so we brewed up some coffee and sat at the fire watching the pale dawn sky turn a deep, impossible blue that looked as though it had been rendered by the hand of an artist. Its perfection was spoiled by an ugly twist of black smoke that suddenly appeared like a dirty smudge to the south-east. Realising it was coming from the direction of his father's home, Arramagong station, O'Meally went racing off. He returned a few hours later, fizzing with rage. Dismounting like a circus rider, we could see he was cut up pretty rough.

'They've burned the shanty, the house and broken me old da's heart,' he said, his voice wavering between grief and anger. Knowing drastic action was needed to restore public confidence Pottinger had struck the first blow. A few weeks before, the Weddin Inn, another shanty run by another of the Lachlan's pioneer families, the Thurlands, was also torched and a police station built on its ashes. John told us that morning, while we were having our coffee, Pottinger had arrived mob handed at first light with a warrant to evict the O'Meallys and raze the infamous shanty.

'He said it was a favourite watering hole of bushrangers and criminal types and that we ran sly grog and allowed gambling,' raged O'Meally. 'But he's never managed to pin anything on me ol' da, Paddy, or any of his boys.'

'Does Paddy own the lease?' I asked, having experienced the rough end of Pottinger's justice myself.

'Paddy sold the lease to the local undertaker, Miles Murphy, a while back and just paid him rent. It was a fine enough arrangement.'

'Pottinger must have had something over Murphy and forced him to sign an eviction notice. That allowed him to evict your kin and burn anything they left behind them.'

The traps were tightening their grip on the area, but at a price. Each burning might have rid them of one sympathiser, but it garnered us ten more.

The sight of police evicting people and burning homes revived dark memories of the treatment of their forebears in Ireland where the police and landlords used eviction and fire to drive people to starvation, rebellion or emigration. Old grievances were not my concern. Before I left for California I would settle up with Pottinger for burning my station and John O'Meally would be a useful ally and a relentless hunter.

'We'll pay that bastard back in his own coin, you have my word on that, John,' I told him. 'I'll keep after him till he's finished and if he pops me first, you'll square it.'

'Yer on,' he snarled.

I should have known that he wasn't the sort of bloke who could keep his vengeance warm for another day. The O'Meallys were a quick-tempered family from a quick-tempered race. After John had kicked a log or two out of the fire, the red and orange sparks matching his fiery mood, he started in at the grog. I told him several times that it was time to put the peg back in the keg, but he wouldn't stop until he'd cursed the Queen and every member of her family all the way back to Adam. After sleeping it off for a few hours, he seemed to recover a bit and we decided to go out and do a bit of road work.

We whipped a few assorted citizens along the Bathurst road and the rest of the day passed without incident, until a storekeeper called John Barnes, and his assistant, John Hanlow, came along. O'Meally and Barnes seemed to know each other and were at it right away.

'Barnes,' said O'Meally, 'just the man I've been looking for.'

'I've nothing for you, John,' Barnes shouted back.

Whatever dark business they were transacting the storekeeper's horse was in the middle of it.

John held onto its bridle, whilst Barnes tried to be off, digging his spurs into its flanks. It was never going to be a close contest. The bridle was torn from O'Meally's grasp and Barnes showed his back as he wheeled round and galloped off.

John set off after him yelling, 'Pull up, Barnes!'

Barnes had no intention of stopping, so O'Meally sent two shots after the fleeing storekeeper. It seemed he had pulled clear, but fifty yards on, the bullets suddenly took effect. Barnes lurched forwards out of his saddle like a felled tree and hit the road with a solid thump. As Barnes didn't throw out his arms to break his fall, I feared he was dead before he ever hit the ground.

We all stood in stunned silence gaping at the still figure as the dust settled on him. I knew we'd have to clear out quickly, so I jerked my thumb at the shocked travellers and told them to 'hook it'. They didn't need a second invitation and took off down the road running; little caring that it was nearly five miles to the nearest station.

Although no one had said anything, I noticed the boys were all glancing anxiously down the road half-expecting to see Barnes staggering to his feet. I distracted them by saying, 'Let's get the loot in the saddlebags.'

By the time we'd packed up, the storekeeper still hadn't moved a muscle. As we approached him the bush flies buzzed and settled, covering his whole shirt, and we knew we were looking at a dead man. He was sprawled in the dust on his right side, his arms and legs jutting out at strange angles, which told me he'd broken bones when he came off his horse. The fall didn't kill him, but the ugly, black hole the size of a shilling in the middle of his back did. The blood had flowed out of Barnes like a blind creek in a thunderstorm and drained away into the thirsty ground. All that remained was a brown sticky smudge the colour of burnt toffee.

I stole a glance at the unrepentant O'Meally, who was putting up a defiant front.

'Serves him right,' he snarled, breaking the spell the shooting had cast. 'He was minding my share of the Eugowra loot and when I asked him about it, he laughed in my face and rode off.'

I nodded at O'Meally and told him straight, 'Fair enough, John. I hope you carry the reward on your head as well as you carry that pistol on your hip.'

O'Meally had acted rashly, but had been off his pannikin after seeing his da's shanty burnt. I had no right to judge him. Vengeance was a feeling I knew well enough. I didn't think he meant to kill Barnes, but it was done and like it or not, 'We're in this to the death now,' was Johnny Gilbert's grim postscript.

If we were ever taken it wouldn't matter who shot Barnes, they'd hang us all in a row.

When Henry McBride got bitten by the snake, O'Meally had made no move to help him and now did the same with Barnes. I could never leave a man lying in the road, whatever he'd done, so

I rolled Barnes onto his back, closed his startled eyes and open mouth, crossed his hands across his chest and straightened his legs.

'Leave him for the crows,' grumbled O'Meally.

I stared him down, 'We might have to do the same for you one day, John.'

Muttering that 'the stupid bastard shouldn't have run for it', he stomped over, grabbed a booted leg and then screwed up his face. In the oven-like summer heat, Barnes' lifeless body had begun to swell like an overripe fruit, releasing its noxious gases and fluids.

'Breathe through your mouth,' I told him.

We carried him into the shade of a clump of eucalyptus and left him as decent as we could.

The next day, the police posted a £500 reward on our heads. Shortly afterwards, we suffered our first loss.

To keep the pressure on Pottinger we needed to claim a big prize and they didn't come much bigger than assistant gold commissioner Henry Keightley. One of our sympathisers complained that he had stolen a claim on Lambing Flat from him and to keep him happy we agreed to take it up with Keightley. He had spoken out against bushrangers many times and had led the chorus that night at Grenfell when I'd shouted through the open window. I had intended to keep my promise to visit him and this hot, still night was as good as any.

The double V roof of Keightley's station was silhouetted against the darkening sky that had been bruised pink, orange, red and blue by threatening black rain clouds colliding in the heavens.

As we came over the rise the station came into full view and we saw Keightley and a mate standing on the covered verandah, drinks in hands watching the spectacle of changing colours in the sky. We picked up speed and as the fields of corn began to whizz past us in a blur, I saw them jump to it.

We were so close that I heard the tinkle of breaking glass as they dropped their drinks on the flagstones at their feet. Keightley and the other man I recognised as the habitual drunk and busybody, Dr Pechey, fled indoors.

Drawing my pistol, I called on them to stand, but they slammed the door shut just as I fired and my bullets gouged huge splinters out of its stout wooden panels.

Sending Vane and O'Meally round the back, Gilbert, Burke and I stayed on horseback in the rose garden in the front. I cupped my hands to my mouth and shouted at the darkened house, 'Keightley, you're surrounded and outgunned. Come out, for the sake of yourself and those with you.'

His response was to lift his rifle and fire at me through the netted window of an upstairs room. I felt a deadly draught as a speeding bullet whistled past my right shoulder. We were forced to dismount sharpish, and take cover amongst rose bushes and behind the picket fences. We crawled around on our bellies, peeping through windows trying to see who was inside and how many men we were up against.

To keep us cautious, Keightley kept the lights off and moved from window to window, discharging his shotgun at anything that moved. Having got the lay of the land, we agreed that the only men inside were Keightley and Pechey.

We decided to draw Keightley's fire by rushing the front door. Vane would stay at the back in case they tried to run for it. On my signal, Burke and Gilbert took out the front windows with a volley of fire, which enabled O'Meally and I to reach the door. There was no returning fire. I shot the lock out and John hit the door with a few powerful wide arm swings of the slegehammer he found in an outhouse, but it wouldn't budge an inch.

'Barricaded from inside,' he puffed.

A sharp crack from the house broke the silence. There was a shout and I saw Mickey Burke fall from behind a wooden cask. Keightley was determined to finish him off and released another shot, which splintered the barrel.

I heard the crunch of heavy feet on the slates above my head, and realised the mongrel was on the roof! I stepped back and sent up a burst of fire at him, forcing Keightley to flatten himself on the roof with a grunt.

Mickey was in pain, groaning and clutching at his stomach. Blood oozed between his fingers. Gilbert crawled over to him and confirmed our worst fears.

'It's a gut shot.'

There was no need to say more. It was the wound we all dreaded. Even if we left now and let Dr Pechey tend to him, Mickey would die from a loss of blood before morning.

Vane, who came running from the back of the house when he heard Mickey cry out, was close to tears. 'Let's get that bastard!' he snarled through gritted teeth.

'You won't take me alive!'

Half turning I saw the pistol in Mickey's hand and heard the sharp crack of a gunshot. I screwed my eyes shut in horror, but not quick enough to blot out the sight of Mickey's head being blown apart in a shower of fine, red spray. Mickey knew he was done for and a slow, lingering death or a dance at the end of the hangman's rope was all that lay ahead of him. He'd chosen his own way out.

John Vane's grief turned to anger when he saw his little mate lying in the dust, a stream of blood running out from beneath him.

'That bastard's killed my mate.'

'Come on, let's have 'im,' spat O'Meally. We renewed our assault on the front door, which finally buckled like paperbark, while Keightley fired at Gilbert and Vane and called urgently to Pechey that he needed more bullets.

Pushing back the mountain of heavy wooden furniture that was piled against the door, we cautiously made our way into the large hallway, where a large grandfather clock stood guard ticking patiently. In front of us was a sweeping horseshoe-shaped staircase that led up to the shadows of the upper floor. To our right and left were darkened corridors with rows of closed doors. O'Meally went towards the stairs, but I shook my head and pointed, indicating that we should check the ground floor first. Warily, we moved through each of the empty darkened rooms, until we came to a solid-looking door at the end of the passage.

I opened the door of the adjoining room, which was Keightley's study judging by the bookcases lined with rows of leather-bound tomes and the official-looking papers sprawled untidily across a large writing table. Making sure we had a wall between ourselves and whoever was in the next room, I reached through the doorway of the study and gently turned the handle.

It was locked.

I nodded to O'Meally. We ventured into the corridor where we applied a few vicious booted kicks to the door panels, before ducking sharpish back into the library. Though the wood had split, the lock still held firm. A moment later, a booming shotgun blast finished what we started, smashing two holes in the timber door.

We returned fire and followed our bullets in after kicking open the shattered door.

In the haze of blue gunsmoke we found a Keightley, all right. No less a person than Mrs Keightley herself.

Caroline Keightley's beauty was well known throughout the district. She was known as 'the Belle of Bathurst', which was no understatement. Her dark brown tresses were drawn up behind her head to reveal a fine slender neck and elegant sloping shoulders. There was beauty in the shape of her face and the contours of her body underneath the sweeping lines of the pale silk dress with its ribbons and flounces, its ridiculous crinoline hoops. This picture of new colonial refinement and sophistication was spoiled by the smoking shotgun she held in her manicured hands and the shocked expression that now creased her fine features. The wooden panelling on each side of her had been reduced to charred matchwood.

I despise this new fashion for women carrying pistols and powder flasks in their bags next to their Scripture texts and turning out to defend their homes. Such unruly business should be conducted between men, as is tradition. I took the gun gently from her soft, trembling hands, sat her down on her husband's well-padded, leather armchair, and motioned for O'Meally to pour her a brandy from one of the crystal decanters on the sideboard.

Keightley continued to be a game cove, dodging about on the roof like a frightened opossum. Hearing the shots coming from inside had started him shouting for Pechey again, little knowing that Gilbert had located that useless drunk cowering under a cabinet in an upstairs room. He had been sent to get more ammo, but couldn't reach it without exposing himself to our gunfire. So, he'd taken cover and allowed a woman to defend him.

In disgust, Gilbert had pulled the thin, ferrety-looking Pechey downstairs by the roots of his thinning, curly grey hair and thrown him at our feet. If his reddened cheeks and cherry nose only hinted at a life blighted by grog, then his sour breath confirmed it. He begged us not to hurt him. I didn't, but John Vane was Mickey Burke's cousin and wanted revenge.

'This one's a spineless coward, not worth wasting good boot leather on,' I said, prodding the still cowering Pechey with the toe of my boot. I nodded upwards at the ceiling, 'Time we brought Keightley down off that fuckin' roof.'

Knowing he'd no bullets left to fire at us, we lit some oil lamps and went outside where Gilbert shouted up to him, 'Come down, now or we'll burn down your house, and then you'll dance to our tune, good an' proper!'

Keightley kept his own counsel, hoping we'd give up and go away, but it had gone too far for that.

I then played our trump card and shouted up, 'Keightley, your wife, Caroline, is our hostage. No gentleman would abandon such a lovely lady to the whims of bushrangers.'

There was a silence while he agonised over my threat. He'd killed one of ours, and now he feared the consequences. The alternatives didn't bear thinking about. I heard all of it in his voice as Keightley shouted back down, 'If I surrender, promise that you won't hurt my wife?'

'Promise.'

'Honour bright?' he pressed me.

A strange concept for a crooked cove like Keightley, I thought to myself, but shouted back, 'Honour bright.'

There was a scuffle in the darkness above and one of the Tranter revolving rifles we had been after at Pedrotta's in Bathurst and two police issue six-shot Colt Navy pistols sailed out of the darkness and landed heavily in front of us.

'I'm coming down,' he warned in a voice heavy with anxiety.

There was more scuffling before the shadowy figure of Henry Keightley dropped down from the tiled roof at the front of the house. His apprehension proved to be well founded. A furious Vane lunged forwards and was on for shooting Keightley there and then.

Keightley was about thirty-five, stood six foot three in his socks and was known as a gutsy bastard, but this night he was scared for his life.

In between bouts of sobbing for Mickey, Vane drew his piece three or four times pointing it at him, all the while sucking in air through barely opened lips making sharp hissing sounds. To complicate matters, an elderly servant woman called Mrs Baldock appeared out of nowhere and bravely stood between Vane and her master, pleading that Keightley had a wife and two children.

Vane waved her aside with his pistol, 'Missus, I don't want to shoot you, but I will, if I have to.'

It's a brave soul that comes between a beast and its meat, but the old dame stood steadfast, her grey hair plastered to her forehead with sweat. Were it not for her, I'm sure Keightley would have been breathing in dirt.

'Mickey was only twenty-three,' stammered an emotional Vane, still trying to line up a shot at Keightley. 'He was my cousin and that bastard is going to pay the debt in full tonight.'

Caroline Keightley grabbed my sleeve and pleaded with me to save her husband. Over the din of shouting, screaming, swearing people, Johnny Gilbert stood beside me looking hard at Vane. 'He's gone,' he hissed, jabbing at his temple with his index finger. Pulling out his pistol he said, 'Let me take him out. He's a liability. We should never have brought him in.'

I knew there had been some chaff between the two, but had no idea it was as bad as this.

With emotions running high on all sides, it was a dangerous situation, which could end in more bloodshed. *What would the Darkie have done?* I asked myself. He'd told us about his duel with Johnny Connors while we waited for the Eugowra escort, so I already knew the answer. I took a deep breath, and nodded at Gilbert, who still had his hand on his pistol. 'No, it's down to me.'

Reluctantly, I drew my piece, sighted Vane down the barrel, curled my finger round the trigger and slowly increased the pressure.

Out of the corner of my eye, I saw a cruel smile play across O'Meally's face and tried to comfort myself with the thought that it was the least of all the evils that faced me.

Fortunately, Mickey Burke who lay in a little pool of spill light behind the struggling knot of people chose that moment to let out a loud groan, stunning everyone into silence. I eased the pressure on the trigger as his dead fingers twitched once and then again. *Holy Christ, he was still alive.*

Vane turned away from Keightley, crying out Mickey's name as he rushed over to his mate's body still crumpled on the grass where he'd fallen. I grabbed one of the oil lamps and brought it over. It was the most gruesome sight I'd ever seen.

Most of the top of his head had been blown away and the clumps of wispy grass around him were stained red with blood and flecks of grey and white, bone and brain through it. He'd also been shot through the body. His hands were clenched over a gaping hole in his stomach and I could see the pink of his guts sticking out between heavily bloodied fingers. The only mercy was that he didn't appear to be conscious.

'Good Christ!' swore Gilbert, his face ashen in the flickering lamp-light, 'that's twice he's come back from the dead, poor bastard.'

'Let Dr Pechey have a look,' I said pulling Vane aside and motioning for a wary-looking Pechey to come forward.

The doctor kneeled and placed his fingers on his wrist and then on the neck. Unable to find a pulse he looked up at me and shook his head, 'That was the last of him, he's gone.'

I watched a fresh wave of emotion sweep across Vane's face, as his last faint hope that Burke had somehow survived was cruelly dashed.

'This is on him,' he said making another lunge at Keightley, determined to finish what he had started. I reached out and caught Vane by the arm and as he turned to look at me I saw the red, naked savagery in his eyes and knew I still might have to shoot him.

'He shot our mate,' he growled trying to rip his arm from my grip. 'I say we even it up. "An eye for an eye", just like the Good Book says.'

I kept a hard grip on him. 'There was a lot of shot flying around. It could have been anyone's. Christ, I could have done it myself!'

He turned his head away, drawing his sleeve across his nose, fighting back the tears, his anger rising again. 'What did we come here for, then?' he demanded.

'To teach him a lesson, not to kill him. I don't want a murder on my hands.' To kill Keightley in a fair fight was one thing, but to shoot him after he had surrendered was another. But Vane was beyond reason. He wanted revenge. Blood for blood. I had to offer him some redress and Mickey's final intervention had bought me a few minutes to think.

'What good will killing him do us? Mickey's gone, but we can still get something out of this.' That had the desired effect and I felt him relax below my fingers.

'Keightley will get the £500 reward for Mickey and I reckon we send his good lady wife to get that same amount from her father, the Right Honourable Henry Rotton. We give her twelve hours and if the money's not delivered, we shoot Keightley and call it quits.'

Vane stopped pulling against my grip. He fixed me with those cobalt eyes and nodded, his face set in a grim mask. 'Twelve hours, then it's him or me.'

We marched back to the veranda where the Keightleys stood clinging to each other, wondering what was going to happen next.

The ordeal had taken its toll on Caroline Keightley's previously immaculate appearance. Her eyes were red from crying, her bell-shaped crinoline had been crushed into a shapeless mess and strands of long hair had escaped their clip and spilled untidily down her neck. She paled further when I started telling her what she had to do.

'Go upstairs and get changed into something suitable for travelling. You're going to get us a ransom from your father.' I stemmed the protest already forming on her lips with an ultimatum.

'You'll be back here with £500 by noon tomorrow. If you fail to deliver or alert the police your husband will be shot,' I warned, pulling out my timepiece for emphasis.

Showing a cavalier spirit sorely lacking when the shots were flying, Dr Pechey interjected, 'I'll happily go in your place, Caroline.'

'She's twice the man you'll ever be,' cut in O'Meally with undisguised contempt, knowing Pechey's offer was motivated by self-preservation rather than any sense of chivalry.

As soon as she started up the stairs, I ordered Keightley to put his hands behind his back. Seeing that I was all that stood between him and a shallow bush grave, he did as he was told, with military briskness. I produced a set of darbies we'd taken from the traps some months before and snapped them on his wrists. Making sure Vane heard me, I told O'Meally to take Keightley up to Dog Rock, which overlooked the Bathurst road. 'If he tries anything fancy, or you get a sniff of the traps, put a bullet through his skull, and get out of there.'

In the ten minutes it took Caroline Keightley to change, we'd harnessed up a buggy to one of the skittish horses we'd found stabled in the barn. As I handed her the reins I could see she was no equestrian, but drawing deeply on her last reserves of courage she shook the reins, and the horse, glad to be clear of the madness, shot off down the bumpy track into the darkness.

We spent the rest of the night making sure that Mickey Burke got a decent funeral. As penance for his cowardice, we set the wretched Dr Pechey to work digging Mickey's grave under a tall stringybark, while we gouged the initials 'MB' into the trunk with a Bowie knife.

The good doctor was unused to hard yakka and had to stop to spew a couple of times before he'd dug a decent hole.

The sun rose in a final tribute and garlanded the bush setting with a vivid array of pinks, reds and golds. We wrapped Mickey in his blanket and lowered him into the earthen vault. We took our hats off respectfully with no one sure quite what to say. In the bush, men revealed as little about their feelings in death as they did in life. Consequently, the tributes were short, but heartfelt. 'Bye, Mickey, you were a good mate,' was about the sum of it and that's about the best you can say of any man. It'll do me, when my time comes.

Pechey then applied his blistered and bleeding hands to the shovel handle once again. When he'd finished filling in the hole I ordered him to place slabs of flat stone over the grave to stop the dingos getting at the body. We filed back to the house in sober silence, Mickey Burke's requiem the scrape of Pechey's lonely shovel.

We sat in silence in the Keightleys' spacious living room as the minutes ticked by loudly on the large grandfather clock in the hallway. The only other sound in the room was that of Johnny Vane preparing for his moment of vengeance by painstakingly cleaning and loading his piece. When the clock struck eleven he looked up. In an hour Keightley's fate would be decided, one way or the other, and Johnny Vane was counting the minutes.

'Looks like Dog Rock will be Keightley's last resting place. Seems a fair enough place for a bloody mongrel,' he growled poking at the dozing Dr Pechey with the toe of his boot. 'Stand by your shovel, Doctor, we'll have another cadaver for you within the hour.' The waiting hadn't cooled his temper. If the money didn't arrive, I'd have no choice but to let Vane have Keightley.

When the hands of the old clock were only ten minutes away from noon, a cooee came drifting over from Dog Rock. We all jumped to attention. Was it the traps, or Mrs Keightley? There was nothing for a few minutes and then the rattling of wheels on the rutted track.

'Careful, boys, it might be a trap,' I warned, as we went out the front and took up defensive positions. When the buggy finally pulled up, it carried a single passenger, a short, grey-haired figure. As he came closer I saw that our delivery man was sporting a neatly trimmed goatee and was none other than Keightley's father-in-law, the Right Honourable Henry Rotton himself.

Fashionably attired in a blue, velvet-collared, one-button coat, tan-coloured cords and brown knee-length Wellington boots, Rotton dismounted and tied off the reins. He merely raised an eyebrow when he saw he was covered from all sides.

'Easy, boys, I have your money. I'm alone, no tricks,' he trilled as I patted him down to ensure he had no weapons about him.

'What are you doing here, Rotton? This wasn't the deal,' I said coldly.

Rotton looked disdainfully down his long nose at the man who had disturbed his Sabbath.

'Your instructions have been carried out to the letter, except that I had to go into Bathurst and persuade the manager to open the bank on a Sunday morning without asking too many questions,' he answered caustically. 'In any event, Caroline was overwrought and in no state to make the return journey.'

As the old clock chimed twelve o'clock, Rotton produced the bulky calico bag. But before we had even counted the money, he was nipping at our heels like a cattle dog, insisting that we keep 'our side of the bargain', calling us 'good chaps' and suggesting we be 'on our way', as though he was talking to servants, not the people who held his very life in their hands. To remind him who was running the show, I stuck my piece under that long nose of his, grinding the barrel into the bone and cartilage.

'Shut yer yap, Rotton. Unlike you money-grabbing mongrels, we'll keep our word. If we were half as notorious as is made out, we'd have taken the money, then shot you against the barn. Remember that next time you've got some poor bloody selector up in front of you.'

Rotton wisely kept his English trap shut as we saddled up and headed out.

Just before we gained the Bathurst road, we turned off and headed for Dog Rock. John O'Meally was there, with a rumpled-looking, handcuffed Keightley kneeling in the dirt in front of him. His smart tweed jacket and cream-coloured breeches were stained and torn, and his fine mane of hair was dishevelled. Keightley was also sporting a couple of angry-looking purple bruises on his forehead, and there were smudges of blood at the side of his mouth. O'Meally smirked, 'Fell off his 'orse.'

I gave O'Meally the 'eye', so he knew his childish yarn didn't fool me, but, all things considered, Keightley had got off lightly with a few thumps. I jerked my head towards the assistant gold commissioner and said to O'Meally, 'Cut him loose.'

As soon as the bracelets came off the man's wrists, I pulled him to his feet by the front of his shirt and shoved him off into the bush. I shouted after him, 'Let that be a lesson to you. Don't interfere in our business and we won't interfere with yours.'

Keightley looked back at me dazedly, but wisely said nothing and stumbled off into the dusty scrub.

We rode in silence back to the cave. The shock of Mickey's death was beginning to sink in. I had plenty to think about.

It was the first time we had come under serious pressure and Vane had proved himself a liability. You never really know a man until you're in a tight spot with him.

Once we had lit a fire and boiled a billy, I divided up the loot. I only split the £500 we got from Rotton into three shares, put one in my jacket and handed a bundle each to Gilbert and O'Meally.

'Hey, what's going on?' asked Vane, a look of surprise crossing his face.

'I've decided you won't be getting a share for this job, not now, not ever again.'

'I did my bit!' he said defiantly.

'No you didn't, you bloody fool,' spat an angry Gilbert. 'You nearly cost us the loot and nearly had us shooting at each other. Ben was about to pop you when Mickey let out that last groan. He was a true mate. He saved you with his dying breath.'

Shocked, Vane looked over at me, and saw from my expression that Gilbert was telling the truth. His face went scarlet and he bunched his fists, 'That bastard killed my mate!'

'He was our mate, too,' O'Meally reminded him.

'Then you should have let me even the score,' insisted Vane looking at each of us with a frustrated look on his face.

'This is a war, John. Men die. We salute them and we go on, get up and do it again. We took the loot and lived to fight another day. He'd have done the same if it was you. It's the fortune of war.'

Vane jumped to his feet, yelling, 'Ye're a bunch of cowards.'

Gilbert was up in a flash, and they were toe to toe, nose to nose, eyeball to eyeball.

'Who're ya calling a coward?'

'I saw ya. Wouldn't go in after Keightley when the shot was flying. Ya stayed back and that's when Mickey got hit–'

Gilbert cut him off with a swing of his fist, catching Vane full in the face. He might have been six inches shorter than Vane and much lighter, but he still packed one of the best punches in the district.

'Bastard,' Gilbert shouted as the blow sent Vane sprawling. Vane tried to spring to his feet, but Gilbert stopped him with a hefty kick to the ticklers, which made a cracking sound as Vane went crashing back to earth. This time he didn't move, but lay there holding his side, groaning in obvious pain.

'My ribs! You broke them, you bastard!' he wailed. Blood from a heavily bleeding nose was smeared across his face.

'Piss off before I do the other side for you,' growled Gilbert.

Vane, realising he'd run out of friends and sympathy, lurched unsteadily to his feet and holding his side, disappeared into the darkness.

'Don't go barking to the traps,' I called after him, although I doubted he would turn dog on us. He knew what a traitor's pay was.

That was the last we ever saw of John Vane.

A week later, we got a telegraph saying that he'd surrendered to Father Timothy McCarthy, the priest I'd known since I was a boy, who had accidentally come across Vane hiding out in a bush camp. Father McCarthy went directly to Inspector-General McLerie and brokered a deal. Vane was told that if he gave himself up he wouldn't be charged as an accessory to the murder of Barnes, but would do fifteen years hard labour. A few days later Vane went in under the protection of Father McCarthy, to the frustration of Pottinger and the squatter press. These types needed a big win, to stick a bushranger's head on a pole. They feared they would never get one if McCarthy kept guaranteeing them an easy way out.

Smarting after our first defeat and two men down, we needed a quick win ourselves.

I decided to keep turning the screw on the squatters with a raid on Goimbla station, which belonged to David Campbell. It was a mile off the Orange road, just past the Eugowra Rocks, which we hoped was a good omen. Like Keightley, Campbell had spoken out against us on many occasions and had hunted us with various citizens' defence committees.

The night of November 19, 1863, was still and peaceful. We crept across darkened paddocks past cattle who'd sensed our menace and stood motionless. The moon had slipped behind a thick bank of cloud, as if she preferred not to witness what was about to unfold.

As our shadows flitted noiselessly across the yard, a passing hand or two went out to calm a dog's raised hackles and quell the low rumble forming in its throat. The sticky closeness of a hot, airless summer night had plastered the shirt to my back and as I crouched in the front yard, a rivulet of sweat ran down from my armpit to my belly.

One dull glim burned within the recess of the dark, silent house. A clock chimed eleven times; its cheery call at odds with the nervous tension that was building up outside. I nodded to the dark shapes of Gilbert and O'Meally, who were crouched beside me. Silently, we moved forward, reaching the veranda without drawing fire. Following on so soon after our attack on Keightley, Campbell was ready for us inside the house. His wife was crouched by his side, ready to feed him ammunition. Sensing our presence, Campbell let fly from a downstairs window. We replied in kind, but the bright flashes of our gunfire revealed our vulnerable forward positions and he cleared us off the veranda with another volley. The boom of gunfire that rolled across the open, darkened fields was as loud as thunder, but Goimbla was ten miles away from the nearest station or settlement. We knew we had time to flush them out.

I threw myself headlong into a flowerbed, raised myself up on one elbow and yelled, 'We've got you covered, Campbell! Come out!'

Campbell answered with bullets, causing us to flatten ourselves against the ground again.

After doing a quick reconnaissance, I realised that the big Dutch barn was our best chance of forcing them out quickly. I called out again, 'Last chance! Come out, or we'll burn you out!' My threat received the same short shrift. 'Bloody tight-arsed Scotchman,' I snarled. 'He'd give up his last breath before he'd give up a penny. Right, let's show 'em we mean business.'

We found some bales of hay, piled them against the side of the great wooden barn, then set them alight. A few minutes later the horses inside began to whinny, but there was still no movement from the darkened windows. The summer heat had made everything tinder dry, and within five minutes one side of the barn was completely ablaze. The horses began kicking desperately against the door.

'Let the horses out, O'Meally!' I shouted. 'Just lift the latch and stand well back, they'll do the rest themselves.'

Flames blossomed as the roof caught alight with a great roar unleashing a wave of furnace-like heat, forcing us back. Over the savage spit and crackle of the fire and the neighing of horses, I heard the sharp crack of a single shot.

I crouched down, relieved that bullet didn't have my name on it. Through rising waves of heat I saw the shimmering image of John O'Meally reeling around drunkenly and Campbell turn and retreat back to the house. When the barn went up Campbell must have caught sight of O'Meally in the firelight and crept out to have a go at him. I sent a couple of shots winging after him. They tore great lumps out of the door, but missed their mark.

O'Meally was lying on his stomach, hands clutched below him. By the time, Gilbert and I reached him, crawling on our hands and knees, our smoke-reddened eyes were streaming with tears from the smoke. Every moment I expected to hear the rattle of Campbell's gunfire and feel the bullets thudding into my flesh.

'Is he dead?' asked Gilbert anxiously. As I rolled O'Meally over I saw he'd taken a single shot to his right side. Around the ribcage, blood oozed, black in the reddish light. I put my finger to the side of his neck. There was no pulse. I nodded in confirmation.

A terrible high-pitched screaming from inside the barn shocked us back to the terrible reality. The whole barn was engulfed by the snarling flames and with the smoke, the noise, the acrid smell of burning horsehair and flesh and John O'Meally's still warm body lying nearby, it was a preview of Hell itself. But even the terrible sound of their prized horses burning to death hadn't dislodged the Campbells.

'Let's smoke 'em out,' I said to Gilbert.

A few tense minutes followed. While Gilbert shot out all the windows, I threw more bales of hay along the veranda. Campbell dodged from window to window, piercing the darkness with short, sharp bursts of fire, hoping more of his bullets would find their target.

This time I didn't waste words on a warning and lit the hay. We were positioned, one at the front of the house and one at the back. We knew it wouldn't be long before Campbell and his wife were forced out.

But it was to be Campbell's night.

First, came the thunder of hooves. Through the smoke and fire I caught sight of a mob of six horsemen galloping across the darkened paddocks. As they neared I made out the towering figure of Pottinger.

'Traps!' I yelled out to Gilbert. The blazing barn would have stood out like a beacon in the darkened countryside. I reckoned we only had a few minutes to make a getaway.

We won't make it if we try to run for it,' I hissed at Gilbert. The light from the fire would have made us into targets that even a trap couldn't miss. I pointed down at O'Meally's lifeless cadaver and said, 'Come on, let's hoist him over the saddle. I'm buggered if we'll leave him behind. Wouldn't be right.'

As the police started pulling the burning bales off the veranda and dousing them with buckets of water, Campbell and his wife struggled out of the house holding wet towels over their heads.

'Are you all right?' called out Pottinger, catching the arm of an emotional Mrs Campbell. The Campbells' first thoughts, however, weren't for their wellbeing.

'Hall's hereabouts,' I heard David Campbell yell, between fits of coughing, 'I think I got one of them.'

'Spread out!' roared Pottinger, drawing his pistol. I lifted my rifle and sighted him down the barrel. He was framed nicely by the firelight and I had a clear shot. If I pulled the trigger I could shut his yap right here, but not without exposing the safe position we'd taken up in a stand of dark trees just to the side of the house. I remembered the bushranger's code, 'live to fight another day', and eased the pressure on the trigger.

The traps started rooting around like cattle dogs and soon found O'Meally's gun, hat and his blood splattered across the grass. Sensing we might be carrying a wounded man, they split up into pairs and started combing the surrounding area.

There was no way we could escape dragging a dead weight behind us and the smell of blood was making the horse nervous.

I looked at O'Meally's dark, lifeless shape and thought back to the day that he'd tried to rescue Vane's relatives from the traps. I pictured him, arms outstretched, urging the traps to shoot him and then holding the fob watch flattened by a bullet in his palm saying, 'See, it's a sign, them bastards can't kill me.' But they did.

'Looks like we'll be seeing you in Hell before California, John,' I muttered pointing his horse east towards Orange and slapping its rump hard with my open hand. It bolted from the cover of trees and shouts went up from the mounted traps as they gave chase. Gilbert and I slipped away across the darkened fields in the opposite direction with heavy hearts.

After the loss of Burke, O'Meally and Vane, Johnny Gilbert and I decided to split up and keep dark for a while. Gilbert left the district and weary from months on the move I went 'holidaying in the Bermudas', as the old English lags used to call hiding out at a harbourer's spread.

After a spell I teamed up with a rum pair called Gordon and Dunleavy and went back to the game. Short, stocky and barely out of his teens, Dunleavy was 'from Greenland', as we said in these parts, while the tall, thin and balding 'old man' Gordon had been on the cross before we were born and would have been about sixty. It wasn't a successful partnership and so we split. Like John Vane, Dunleavy turned himself in and got fifteen, but Gordon thought he was too wily to be caught. The traps found him in a hut on the Fish River and the judge sent him to prison for the rest of his natural.

Chapter Nineteen

Late February 1864, I got a telegraph saying that Father McCarthy wanted to see me. My first thought was that it had something to do with my family, or Biddy and Henry.

I agreed to meet him in an abandoned hut left for the rats next to the lazy, brown eddy of the Abercrombie River. I knew the lay of the land and could stake it out beforehand. I trusted Father McCarthy, but I didn't trust Pottinger not to use him to trap me.

I hid myself and watched Father McCarthy approach the hut. I then waited a good half an hour, and seeing no signs that he'd been followed made my way down to the hut, with my gun drawn, just in case. I pushed open the door with my boot. The smell of rotting wood, damp and of nature reclaiming what belonged to it was sharp on the nose. There was also the faint medicinal smell of eucalyptus leaves. The back wall of the hut had already succumbed to the elements. In the shadows, framed against a backdrop of gum tree branches reaching through the roof, was Father McCarthy.

He came forward to greet me, dressed in his familiar black cassock. The last time I'd seen him was seven years ago on my wedding day. I noticed that he'd greyed a lot since. But I had also changed. I could see he was struggling to reconcile the nervy, fresh-faced groom with the unkempt creature pointing a gun at him.

'Should I raise my hands?' he asked politely, nodding at the weapon. I stuck it back in my belt and managed to look suitably shamefaced. A smile creased his leathery face and he offered his hand again. 'Ben, my boy, it's been a long time,' he said warmly, his thick Donegal brogue unaffected by thirty years in Australia. I shook it warmly. I could see that it had hurt him that I thought he might allow the police to use him as bait.

'A lot of water under the bridge, right enough, Father,' I said, coming straight to the point. 'How's our ma?' I added, guessing that she was the one who had sent him on this mission.

He looked a little chastened at how easily I had seen through his blind, but realising there was no point in denying it, he smiled broadly. 'They're all fine, Ben, and they send their love and best wishes. Your mother is worried about what's going to become of you.' He paused and then came right to the point. 'She wants you to give yourself up before it's too late.'

If anything could have given a man's heart a turn the right way, it was the image of our ma's worried face that appeared in my mind's eye. I closed my eyes and silently asked for her forgiveness.

'Tell her I'm sorry for the way things turned out, but it's too late for turning back.' Father McCarthy took hold of me by the arm. 'No, no, Ben you mustn't speak like that,' he said, earnestly. 'You've not killed anyone, yet, but as the risks get greater, it can only be a matter of time.' He was agitated and started pacing, shaking his clenched fists at me as he used to do when he got to the main point of his sermons. His voice rose as he pressed his points home.

'You're no killer. I know that, and so do the police.' Seeing the question in my eyes, he sighed and held out his hands in silent appeal. 'I went to see Inspector-General McLerie. He gave me his word that no harm will come to you, if you surrender now. You can name the time and place.'

'What's the deal?' I asked quietly.

Father McCarthy looked at me quizzically, 'The deal?'

'How much time must I do?'

'Twenty years,' he answered bluntly.

I gave a low whistle and shook my head. 'That's a long time to be branded with the broad arrow. I'll be an old man by the time I get out. If I ever do.'

Father McCarthy looked at me, bewilderment clouding his blue eyes. 'But you will be all straight and square, and you can start again.'

I smiled sadly at his innocence and told him the plain truth, 'Even if I did fifty years, they'd never leave me alone. That's the rub, Father. God might forgive me, but the New South Wales police never will. Once the traps have got a nailer on you, they'll crush you and your kin for generations.'

'Taking vengeance on Inspector Pottinger won't bring you peace, Ben.'

'Maybe not, Father, but it'll rid this district of a tyrant.'

'And they'll put another as bad in his place. There's too many of them,' he said gently, trying to appeal to my reason. I smiled as I remembered our secret pilgrimages to Bathurst to get one of us baptised whenever our da went bush. On a Sunday our brood would take up a whole pew at St Michael's, our arses going slowly numb on those hard parish benches, while Father McCarthy told us Bible stories.

Gently I reminded him of those long ago days. 'Remember David and Goliath, Daniel in the Lion's den? Have a little faith, Father,' I added with a grin.

But Father McCarthy had no intention of letting me off that lightly. His mood suddenly changed, and he gave me what the Irish call the hard stare, which usually comes before a brawl. He admonished me in a voice that was sharp with concern, 'Those were stories for wee boys! You're a grown man. Look at the trail you've left behind you! Friends shot down or in prison, your family lost to you, and the police and every blowhard in New South Wales out raking the bush for you.' His Irish temper was well and truly up.

'John Vane will do his time and begin his life again. Come in with me, or it can only end one way.' He sighed, and shook his fist at me. 'I know this isn't the time or place to be preaching to you, but I can think of no better words than Deuteronomy 30:19: "I call heaven and earth to record this day against you, that I have set before you life and death, blessing and cursing: therefore choose life, that both thou and thy seed may live."'

I didn't answer him. It was too late to renounce the Devil and all his pomps. Father McCarthy was a priest and a father figure whom I was taught to look up to. The rules of such relationships rarely change. A flock of crimson-breasted rosellas fluttered up into the river gums. More concerned with their own territorial issues than the grave affairs we were debating in the hut, they noisily disputed the tenure of one of the upper branches. We watched them for a moment or two, and when I looked back to Father McCarthy, he had regained his composure.

'Will you at least think about what I've said?' he implored.

'Tell our ma I will, anyways,' I said. Suddenly I felt fidgety. When you live life on the run, you become conditioned to never settling too long in one place, never getting too comfortable. Suspicion is a constant companion and fear is your best mate.

Seeing I was ready for the off, he made the sign of the cross and said, 'Go safely, Ben, wherever fate and your wild life may lead you. And if you need me–'

'I'll find ya,' I said, finishing his sentence. I made a parting request. 'Look after our ma, Father.'

Like some terrible biblical premonition the dramatic news that Darkie Gardiner had been taken by the traps raged through the district like a bushfire.

Despite being warned against contacting her family, Kitty wrote to Biddy, giving every detail of their aliases and whereabouts. The treacherous mongrel that intercepted the letter knew there was a £500 reward for Gardiner on offer and Detective McGlone of the Queensland police received a tip-off as to where he might find the notorious Frank Gardiner.

From the pimp's information, McGlone found the Darkie and Kitty living openly as Mr and Mrs Christie at Apis Creek near Rockhampton. Gardiner had become a respectable citizen and had a share in a pub and store.

On the morning of March 3, 1864, fourteen police surrounded the pub and although he fought like a man possessed, they were soon clicking the darbies on his wrists.

Kitty Brown saw what was happening and came out of the house screeching at them to leave him be.

'Thanks for your help, Mrs Brown,' said McGlone, salting her wounds, as they led the struggling Darkie away. Those Walshes are cursed people. Three daughters, all bloody whores, and young Warrigal dead before his time. Little wonder that God felt moved to strike old man Walsh down with a bolt of lightning.

The traps were cock-a-hoop at the capture of their great nemesis, and there was no shortage of froth in the papers reminding the public that crime never pays and justice will prevail in the end. A guard the size of a royal escort met him at Sydney and took him to Darlinghurst Gaol to await trial.

However, the Attorney-General soon discovered that it was going to be hard to pin a capital offence on him. Any thoughts of trying the Darkie for the Eugowra escort robbery were soon dashed. Dan Charters refused to testify. Some said Kitty Brown had given him some garnish to keep quiet, but the truth was somewhat different.

Informants, or fizgigs, narks, snitches, splits, peelers, pimps and so on, were the lowest form of life on this earth. While we respected human life, no such rules applied to men like Dan Charters who had broken the first rule of the game. He had been discovered living in Bathurst under the alias of Mr Thompson and working as a horse-breaker for Captain John McLerie, son of the Inspector-General himself. It was put to us that if Dan testified at his trial the Darkie would soon be wearing the Tyburn collar. Let me be clear, they wanted us to knock him off his spot, to kill him.

Though my pact with the Darkie ended when he left for Queensland, that speech he gave at O'Meally about bonds of 'fellowship' and being 'comrades in arms' was more than just words. Word reached me that Gilbert had returned so I arranged to meet him at a harbourer's hut. Gilbert was in right away as he owed the Darkie a debt for rescuing his brother and had a score to settle with Charters too. He had brought along a high flyer who he introduced as 'Johnny Dunn, one of the finest riders and bravest blokes in the district'.

Dark-haired with fresh-faced features and a short, nuggetty stature, he reminded me of the late, great Mickey Burke. Gilbert swore that Dunn was as good as Mickey at picking out a good horse and riding one. Remembering the fate of our previous recruits, I was naturally wary of taking on anyone else.

'The hardest shilling ever earned is "on the cross". It's never yours and the traps are always waiting to collect,' I cautioned him. 'There's no men sharper looked after in this colony than us. So, are you still ready to get into the game?' I pressed.

'I'm already in it,' he replied flashing me an infectious smile. 'There's a warrant out for me for robbery under arms. I've known Johnny a while and he's told me a lot about the Ben Hall gang – as if I needed telling.'

I countered sharply with a bold statement of fact rather than a question. 'Then Johnny's told you how we play the game. This is no regular brigade.'

Realising the moment to either declare himself or leave had arrived, the smile faded from his lips, but the twinkle never left his eye. 'Aye, I'm ready. Just like you told Inspector Norton, "They'll never take me alive!" Beneath all the blarney, I could see he was serious. I squinted across at Gilbert who gave me a barely perceptible nod. I offered Dunn my hand.

'If you'll do Johnny Gilbert, then you'll do me. Welcome aboard.' We raised our glasses and I added, 'It's good to have two Johnnies in the team again.'

Honest sweat and toil were not qualities known to the 'Flash' Dan of old, but when we cornered him in a smoke-blackened blacksmith's hut just outside of Bathurst he was preparing to shoe a fancy-looking horse.

'Hello, Dan,' I said, 'or is it Mr Thompson these days?'

He spun around like a scalded cat, the heavy blacksmith's hammer in his hand, but Dan had lost none of his shine during his spell of being in service to the police.

'Come on, boys, I had no choice,' he said, shrugging his slim shoulders. 'The traps had me . . . Ben,' he said fixing me with those big blue eyes brimming with innocence, 'I kept you and O'Meally out of it. Pottinger wanted you, but I couldn't–'

Dunn had heard enough of his fancy palaver and cut him cold.

'I say we spread his brains right here,' he snapped, his pistol already levelled at Charters. Dunn knew nothing of our past lives, just that this pimp had cost a mate his life.

'No, let's find a stout overhang and make him dance like Henry Manns did,' growled Gilbert, coiling the thick rope he'd brought with him round his fist. He had known Henry Manns as a boy, got him involved in the Eugowra robbery and now assumed the role of his avenger. The blood drained from Dan's face. He knew that baby-faced Gilbert was a cold cove and would finish him.

He threw me a despairing look.

'Ben,' he pleaded again. This was a matter of honour, but I still couldn't stand by and watch a man shot down in cold blood and I did owe him something.

Although I had no plan in mind, I heard my voice shouting over the others, who were working up the rage and courage to kill their former gang member where he stood.

'Shooting is too good for this bastard!' I yelled.

The shouting stopped. Dunn's finger eased off the trigger a little and Gilbert looked at me out of the corner of his eye, 'What do you have in mind?'

I desperately cast about me, looking for inspiration. Then, I saw it hanging there. I felt the sweat pricking my brow at the very thought of it, but knew it had to be done.

'Hold him down!' I yelled. Dunn and Gilbert rushed in, blocked his swinging hammer, got him down and pinioned his arms and legs.

'Turn his head away,' I ordered as I took the branding iron the traps used to mark their horses down from its hook. It bore the letters 'VR', *Victoria Regina*. I stuck it right into the red-hot heart of the fire. Although Dan couldn't see what I'd done, the others did. Not a word was said in protest.

As I watched the brand change from black to the colour of a ripe cherry I looked down at Dan who was on the ground on his side, and spoke my last ever words to him. 'You've always been a "flash" cove with a pretty conceit of himself, but from this day on everyone will know the cold-hearted treachery that lives inside of Dan Charters.'

I had branded plenty of horses and cattle, never a man, but it was either this or death for Dan, though he may yet prefer the latter. I pulled the glowing iron from the fire and knew that I had to get it over with before my nerve failed. I closed my eyes and plunged the branding iron downwards. He didn't feel the intense heat until the three of us could barely hold him.

I planted the branding iron onto the side of his face and heard his skin sizzle like a rasher in the pan. As I pulled the iron away, I saw his skin was blistered bright red and that he now wore the badge of his masters, or his royal mistress, if it came to that.

Dan let out a raw, animal wail that chilled me to the marrow. His screams and the stomach-turning smell of singed flesh and hair also made the horses whinny and rear up.

We left Dan writhing in agony and clutching at his face. 'Glimming' or 'lettering' was common back in old England where they branded criminals on the face or hands to warn honest people of their thieving nature. Dan had spared my life and I his. *May we never meet till we be in Hell's darkest pit.*

*

With Charters no longer willing to testify, the traps offered Jacky McGuire £300 to name Gardiner as the leader of the Eugowra gang. He was never going to lift a finger to help the Bastard Baronet and they also drew a blank with Fordyce and Bow.

In the end, the only case they could try him for was the attempted murder of Sergeant Middleton and Constable Hosie during the skirmish at Fogg's hut three years before.

In Sydney, the Darkie's 'Knight of the road' image had caught the public imagination. The jury adjudged that evidence offered up was circumstantial and based on no more than the word of two policemen against the Darkie's and quickly returned a 'not guilty' verdict. There was much rejoicing in the Lachlan, but after the Eugowra trials, I thought the celebrations might be premature, and so it turned out.

A second trial began on July 7, with Chief Justice Sir Alfred Stephen, the judge who'd consigned poor Henry Manns to the gallows, presiding.

It was alleged that Gardiner had attempted to murder and do grievous bodily harm to Constable Hosie, the other officer involved in the shoot-out at Fogg's hut. Knowing that it would be hard to gammon the twelve a second time, the court was told that the Darkie had pleaded guilty to a lesser charge of robbery under arms. Without missing a beat, Stephen sent the Darkie down for 32 years, with the first two in irons. Kitty Brown screamed when she heard the sentence and had to be bodily removed from the court. The normal tally for wounding a policeman was five years, which is what our harbourer George Slater got a few months back, but Stephen had decided to also punish him for all the crimes they couldn't prove against him as well.

'Thirty-two years! I'd rather hang than serve that,' muttered Dunn when he heard the verdict, but Johnny Gilbert reckoned that the ghosts of Warrigal Walsh and Henry Manns were looking out for him as, by rights, he should have danced on air.

Though Gardiner would be well over sixty the next time he took a stroll down Sydney's George Street, Kitty vowed to wait for him. The last I heard, she was trying to whip up public sympathy for an appeal, and bribe some traps into springing him from prison. Women are as bad as peelers and I'll travel much easier without one.

Chapter Twenty

Powerful forces were now pulling me in opposite directions. Dunn and Gilbert were keen to go on with it, but unsettled by the deaths and imprisonments and Father McCarthy's sermon, I wondered whether it was time to give the game away? Bushranger tales do not, as a rule, have happy endings and the fact that even the great Darkie Gardiner was now rotting back in his old crib on Cockatoo Island should have told me it was time to quit, but betrayal, guilt and vengeance are powerful forces. To leave would be to betray Henry Manns, Mickey Burke and John O'Meally, all lost in my quest to settle the score with Pottinger. So, uncertain how or when it would end, I decided to carry on.

Dunn, Gilbert and I went about our business as usual, roaming up and down main roads at will, bailing up an impressive array of mail coaches, assorted diggers, travellers, chinamen and drays. We also went cross-country to raid stores, squatters and visit retribution on those we knew to be consorting with the traps.

The traps soon heard we were on the grass again and started bothering the local population in the hope they'd manage to drop on us. A party of six traps had a poke at us on the Eugowra trail. We didn't like the odds, so we left the road and careered through green paddocks soaked through by the winter rains that made everything smell fresh and earthy. We weaved in and out of stands of spindly mallee and mulga trees to prevent the traps getting a clear shot at us, and, as usual, our thoroughbreds started to pull us clear. That is, until we came to Mandagery Creek.

Dunn and Gilbert forded it easily and topped the other side into saltbush, but Willy got stuck in a flat bog on the other side, and presented the traps with a clear target.

'We've got 'im now,' I heard one shout. On the other side, I saw the troopers kneeling on the bank by the fast-flowing water so I slipped down off Willy and promptly sank up to my knees in the quagmire, which sucked noisily at the top of my boots.

Throwing me a greenhide, which Gilbert lashed to his pommel, he tried to pull us free, while Dunn provided covering fire. The wet red clay stuck to us like glue, and soon the bullets started fizzing around me, but even with their fancy new rifles, they couldn't turn a trick. A couple of bullets burrowed into the mud two feet from my left leg, the hot metal hissing angrily as they failed to find their mark.

'Ben, leave the damn horse,' shouted Gilbert, knowing that they'd soon get their eye in and start picking us off, one by one.

'I never leave a mate behind,' I yelled back and continued hauling at the greenhide. Finally, there was a wet slurping noise and Willy was able to lift one foreleg, then another and gain firmer ground.

Having hit nothing at the shooting gallery, the traps re-mounted and started fording the creek, still firing from the saddle.

Dunn and Gilbert returned fire while Gilbert's horse continued pulling me clear, literally dragging me through the mud towards firmer ground where Willy stood waiting, mud plastered to him clear up to his haunches.

I scrambled up onto his back and, keeping my head low, drummed my knees urgently against his solid trunk. He responded immediately and was off like a shot out of a barrel. I yelled to the others, 'Let's get out of here!'

I still had time to look back ruefully. We'd got clear, but our little escapade had not been without its price. Marooned in the middle of that ocean of mud was my best pair of Napoleon boots! A poor return for the traps, as *Bell's Life* later remarked:

> *Police are getting closer to snaring their nemesis, Ben Hall. Despite getting bogged whilst fording a creek, with police in hot pursuit, he still managed to escape. However, police did take into custody a pair of Napoleon boots, which the Sandy Creek Pimpernel left sticking in the mud. Despite intensive questioning, they have so far refused to reveal the whereabouts of their owner.*

We drifted a few days south-east and started doing some cross work around Goulburn where we found the travelling natives to be plumper in the pocket than the Lachlan folk who were determined to thwart us by ripping bank notes in half and sending them by two separate mails as well as using bank cheques and drafts. With a population of about three thousand, it was Goulburn's turn to wonder if we'd strike them next, but with only three in the gang, we preferred to operate just out of town. We bailed up the Yass and Gundagai mails six times in quick succession.

Dunn proved to be a perfect foil for Gilbert. He shared the same reckless devil-may-care attitude, and brought the fun back to robbing the mails and leading the traps a merry chase. He was like O'Meally in his willingness to take on a fight, but seemed to have Mickey Burke's gentler nature.

We also paid Captain Francis Rossi, a Magistrate and one of the wealthiest men in the area, a visit, but he was away escorting the Bishop of Goulburn around the district. It would have made for an entertaining dinner party had we caught them all at home.

Rossi, like all these squatters, was always braying about law and order, but played it fast and loose with the rules himself. He took advantage of the lack of fencing in the district to impound cattle, and claim them as his own or demand a hefty ransom for their return. His father was an infamous flogger of convicts, earning himself a line in Frank MacNamara's well-aired poem, *A Convict's Tour to Hell*, as one of the figures 'destined for Satan's fold'. We had intended to give his son fifty lashes, as atonement for both his and his father's sins, but in the end, we had to content ourselves with a few horses from his stables.

Seven is said to be a lucky number, but November 17, 1864, the day we held up our seventh mail coach, didn't turn out lucky for us. It started off quietly enough. Before the sun was over the treetops we already had five drays, thirty chinamen, teamsters, a squatter and his wife all lined up along the road near Jugiong. It was high tide again for us. We'd already whipped £100 plus assorted watches, rings and jewellery.

It was like a carnival and, as was our custom, we raided passing drays and offered our guests some refreshments. We were enjoying a drink of lemonade when a lone blue belly came round the bend in the road.

He was as surprised to see us as we were to see him. The only difference was that we were quicker on the draw. He was called to stand, but pulled out his Navy Colt revolver instead. The travellers we had bailed up were forced to throw themselves on the ground as the trap let loose half a dozen wild shots before we forced him to surrender.

'Shit, shit,' he screamed in frustration as the barrel spun, and the firing pin clicked on empty chambers.

We came out from behind the Wilga trees and drays with our pistols drawn, and soon found out McLaughlin was an advance scout for the Gundagai mail, which we'd planned on stopping later that day. Johnny Gilbert, who was about the same size and weight as McLaughlin, relieved him of his uniform, then rode out and sat on the horizon so the mail coach and the two guards heading our way would think the way ahead was clear.

Going by the sun, I reckoned it was about two o'clock when we saw the mail coach come rattling around the bend, the bright sunlight reflecting off the familiar red Cobb & Co. livery.

The driver sat up top and Constable Roche sat inside with the mailbags. Bringing up the rear, on horseback, were two police guards, Sub-Inspector O'Neill and Constable Parry.

As we'd done at Eugowra, we pulled a couple of the drays across the road so that the driver only had moments to pull across the road to avoid a collision. We just had enough time to see the stricken look on the driver's face before he was forced to drag on the reins so hard that the bits in the horse's mouths turned red.

The coach hit the bank on the other side of the road, lifted up on two wheels and wobbled dangerously before crashing back to earth, ploughing to a stop just short of the drays.

When O'Neill and Parry saw the coach skidding across the road they knew it was a bail-up and put on a spurt to get to it before we did. Like medieval knights, we charged at each other at full gallop, pistols raised. Dunn and I took on O'Neill, while Gilbert took on Parry. O'Neill fired at me with his carbine, but missed. I returned fire, one bullet passing through his shoulder pad and the other through his coat-tails. Miraculously neither hit him. O'Neill's horse lurched sideways as it took a bullet, flinging man and horse against a tree, which caused him to drop his revolver. As he fumbled for the other gun in his belt, I put my gun to his head.

Meanwhile Gilbert and Parry were trading bullets and curses

with equal venom. Parry, having used up his six shots, threw his empty pistol at Gilbert's head, wheeled away, and started to unsling his carbine from his saddle holster. Gilbert called on him to stand, but was ignored as Parry struggled to unsheathe the rifle. At that fateful moment, Gilbert caught Parry square in the back. There was no more than thirty paces between the two men and the bullet passed straight through Parry, exiting out of his chest.

Parry pitched forwards heavily, landing lifeless in the dust. A cold feeling in my stomach told me the Ben Hall gang had claimed its second victim. We turned on Constable Roche. He was the only one who hadn't yet fired a shot. His gun had stayed in his belt on the orders of the only passenger in the coach, a Magistrate called Rose, who wasn't willing to die for the sake of a few letters. Having seen his colleagues captured and cut down, Roche took his chance and hightailed it into the bush. We let him go, but as the tall scrub closed behind him, I remarked to O'Neill, who stood with hands raised next to McLaughlin, 'You both fought well, but you should sack that coward.'

Gilbert was in shock and his feelings running riot behind his wild stare. He rode up to McLaughlin, looked into his face and roared out, 'Christ Almighty, why didn't that bloody fool stand? I didn't want to kill him, but he gave me no choice. It was him or me.'

McLaughlin averted his gaze and said nothing for a moment.

Nodding towards the body of Parry, McLaughlin asked, 'Can I see to him?'

I shrugged my shoulders. 'If you want to, but I reckon you're too late.'

McLaughlin turned Parry over and searched for signs of life. I saw the haunted look in Gilbert's eyes when McLaughlin looked up at O'Neill and shook his head.

Whilst we ratted the mailbags, the two traps, with the help of Magistrate Rose, carried Parry's body to the side of the road and covered him over with an oilskin poncho from his saddlebag. We'd come up with a tidy sum, but I felt no sense of triumph. Before we took off, I had one last look at Parry, his boots sticking out from beneath his waterproof, the humming bush flies milling around the sticky brown smudge in the dust, and realised that everything had changed. I could no longer surrender to Father McCarthy and hope to atone for my sins by doing gaol time. That particular door had slammed shut forever. I had become an accessory to the killing of a policeman. If I was caught I'd dance a jig at the Sheriff's ball, sure as apples is apples.

Gilbert had now earned the mantle of murderer and for the crime of murdering a policeman there is only one verdict. Death. Gilbert didn't deserve it. The late John O'Meally, on the other hand, had a reckless disregard for human life, as did 'Mad' Dan Morgan who'd just been on another spree.

On what became known as 'Bloody Sunday', he killed three cattlemen and two traps near Albury. The *NSW Police Gazette* announced that the reward on his head had been lifted to £500 to match the price on ours.

The police called for the government to act decisively against the bushranger menace. Sydney newspapers, which were mostly owned by squatters, the *Sydney Morning Herald* in particular, demanded action before the bushrangers fomented a full-scale rebellion in the western districts.

We found out through our informers that Constable Parry was buried two days later with full honours at Gundagai. Constable Roche, the trooper who'd fled the scene without firing a shot, was found guilty of deserting his post without obtaining permission and was fined £5. O'Neill was also investigated for only firing one barrel of his carbine, but he'd fought bravely until he was outnumbered.

Inspector-General McLerie sent out orders that from this point on all mail coaches would carry constables armed with the latest revolving rifles. They would receive three shillings extra per day for performing this hazardous duty. Never again would there be such easy pickings from mail coaches.

Early in December, Tom Morris sent out a telegraph to tell me that he needed to see me urgently. I could tell from the grim expression that met me at the hut door that it was not good news. He told me that Pottinger had been summoned to Sydney for an audience with Inspector-General McLerie.

'How did you know that?' I asked.

'Walls have ears, or they'll grow 'em if there's enough sparkle around.' He'd obviously gone to some lengths to get the details of their secret meeting, which he proceeded to tell me.

*

Pottinger stomped his way up the two flights of 'the gallows', and was ushered into McLerie's well-appointed office. The Inspector-General was at his desk. Without looking up from the letter he was writing, he indicated a chair on the other side of the desk.

'Excuse me for a few moments, Inspector.'

Pottinger took the chance to study the short, stocky, barrel-chested Scotchman sitting opposite him. An unmistakeable air of melancholy surrounded McLerie who looked more gaunt and grizzled than the last time they'd met. It was as though a light frost had settled on his hair, sideboards and eyebrows. Gone was the jocular man who'd appeared from behind a sliding bookcase and given him a whisky.

Not two months before McLerie had buried his son, John, a Captain in the New South Wales police who was only twenty-five years old. He died of rheumatism brought on by exposure to the elements, which he contracted whilst in pursuit of the Ben Hall gang. As McLerie lifted his head to look at the bushy bearded Pottinger, ten years his junior, the dark shadows under his eyes spoke of long, sleepless nights. Before the Inspector-General could speak, Pottinger lowered his head and said, 'Sir, may I express my sincere condolences to you and your wife. John was a fine officer.'

'Thank you, Inspector,' said McLerie dryly. Like most men in the services he had little time for outward displays of emotion. Such matters were personal and must be strictly divorced from duty and he abruptly changed the subject.

'As you know, the issue of bushranging has been weighing heavily on the minds of the Governor and both Legislative bodies.' It was business as usual. Pottinger lost no time in airing the strong feeling of grievance he had been nursing these past months.

'With respect, Sir, not so heavily as to persuade them to sanction the deployment of the extra troopers I requested.' This was a pointed reference to the Legislative Council's recent decision to vote against deploying more police in the Lachlan district.

'I understand your frustration–' McLerie began.

Pottinger was in no mood for platitudes and cut in, 'If Sydney was under attack they would not hesitate–'

Feeling the need to remind Pottinger that rank, not birthright, carried sway in this room, McLerie interrupted sharply, 'Inspector, if you would permit me to finish.'

Seeing that he now had his Inspector's full attention, he lowered his voice to a more civilised level. 'I fully appreciate your frustration and applaud your sterling efforts to bring these barbarians to heel, but we are bound by the decisions of our political masters. However, there are other ways in which we can impress upon the criminal class the desirability of discontinuing such a hazardous profession, if you get my meaning?'

'Shoot the bastards!' growled Pottinger expecting to be shouted down. To his surprise, McLerie remained silent. Pottinger looked at McLerie for confirmation. He'd always thought of his superior as weak and lacking the strength of his own convictions. McLerie's thin mouth stretched into what Pottinger took to be a grin. His normally inscrutable face showed no less than total agreement with Pottinger's sentiments.

'The words came from your lips, Inspector. A week ago I was summoned by the Colonial Minister, Cowper. In short, he has given me six months to end the bushranging outbreak or he will be seeking my resignation. He made it clear that if I fail to resign at such time, he would sack me along with most of the senior officers in the New South Wales police force.'

McLerie got up from behind the desk and walked over to the window and stared down at busy Macquarie Street below. On the harbour, a few streets further down, a ship's siren hooted mournfully. Without turning round, he continued. 'Frankly, Inspector, I'm buggered if Ben Hall is going to have my job. We will engage the enemy on all fronts, and need not be overly concerned if we bring them in dead or alive. There will be little open public sympathy for their passing, other than in the rural press and the criminal fraternity.'

'Easier said than done,' Pottinger huffed.

McLerie swung round to face him, the bitter resolve clearly stamped on his face. 'In light of recent events, the time has come for drastic action. Chief Justice, Sir Alfred Stephen, has said that it is time we declared Hall and his like outlaws and came down hard on his harbourers.'

Pottinger could hardly believe what he was hearing.

'The Chief Justice has drawn the Colonial Minister's attention to a piece of medieval English legislation known as the Outlawry Act, which, by all accounts, has not been enacted since Robin Hood roamed Sherwood Forest. The Crown lawyers have re-named it the Felon's Apprehension Act and if they can get it through the Legislative Council, it will give us more power than we had under the Bushrangers Act. In brief, once enacted it will allow the police or public to shoot bushrangers on sight. The Act will also give us the power to crush their bush telegraphs and informants with imprisonment, and the confiscation of land and property.' McLerie allowed himself another rare grin, seeing that for once Pottinger was lost for words.

Clearing his throat, Pottinger asked, 'Will the public not expect that we would do everything to bring them in alive and subject them to the due process of justice?'

'Truth and justice are often uneasy bedfellows, Inspector,' answered McLerie. 'We will call on the outlaws to surrender them-selves by a certain date. Of course they won't, and after that they will be presumed to bear the wolf's head, and we will declare them stateless, lawless and fair game. Furthermore, I have approved your requests to arm citizens' defence forces with modern firearms, and to form special police patrols to track down the bushranger gangs. The reward on their heads will also be raised. Men who rob and kill for the sake of gain will betray each other for the sake of gain. All we need to do is make it worth their while.'

McLerie leaned over his desk to look deep into Pottinger's eyes. It was his turn to challenge Pottinger, 'We go all out to nail them. Do we understand each other, Inspector?'

McLerie indicated the interview was at an end by returning his attention to his papers. Without looking up he said, 'Carry on, Inspector. I trust you appreciate the need for me to speak to you in person.'

Pottinger stood, brought his heels together and saluted his superior officer.

Tom Morris looked at me. The strong white moonlight emphasised every line that long experience had etched into his face. In a soft voice he said, 'Ben, the forces of your destruction are now in motion. They mean to take you down and they don't much care if they bring you in dead or alive. It's time to give serious thought to California.'

I nodded, 'Thanks, Tom. I've a plan in mind to square the ledger with Pottinger and then we'll be off.'

'Don't leave it too long,' said Tom, his voice rising with sharp emphasis.

Our telegraphs informed us that McLerie proved to be as good as his word. Within two weeks of their meeting in Sydney, new Spencer rifles were being unwrapped from their greased paper wrappings and handed out to citizens' defence committees that had now formed in many towns to help police. These new American seven-shot, repeat loader carbines took metal bullets with no need for powder or shot. For speed of re-load and accuracy they were far superior to anything ever seen in Australia.

We also learned that Pottinger had formed two new police patrols whose sole task was to hunt us down. One was to operate from the west, under Sub-Inspector Roberts, and one from the east, under Sub-Inspector Brennan. Each party would be well armed, mounted on first-class horses and consist of a blacktracker and two troopers with knowledge of the bush.

The traps nearly had no need of either the patrols or the *Felon's Apprehension Act*, as a week from Christmas they almost bagged me.

We had been waiting all day to bail up the mail coach on the Yass to Binalong road. It was delayed and night was falling fast, when we heard the familiar sound of a wagon bumping down the road, moving much faster than normal carts or drays. We also heard two horses approaching ahead of it about one hundred and fifty yards away.

'Who are you?' I shouted, once whoever it was got within earshot.

'Police!' came the reply.

We answered with three blasts from our double-barrelled shotguns. The flashes briefly illuminated the darkness, revealing two traps on the road with the mail coach following behind.

The traps answered in kind, and not knowing how many were escorting the coach to the rear, or how many armed men might be inside it, we decided to take off. They chased us into the bush and I felt a couple of bullets whiz past my head. I had to turn sideways in the saddle to fire at the rider on my tail. He was so close that when I fired, the flash of the powder must have blinded him, as he swore, put a hand up to rub his eyes and slowed down, swerving off course.

At that moment, the normally sure-footed Willy the Weasel stood on the lip of a rabbit hole. It crumbled under his weight, causing him to stumble and lurch sideways. Normally I would have been able to right myself, but I was facing the wrong way, with my eye fixed on the pursuing trooper, my grip on the reins slackened. I didn't see the fast-approaching tree and the hanging low branch. A solid thump on the side of the head sent me catapulting out of the saddle. I hit the ground, one foot still caught in the stirrup. The breath was knocked out of my body and I was being dragged along the ground over every stone, hillock and thorn bush. Frantically I reached up and tried to free my leg. I felt the heel of my boot come free from the stirrup and I skidded to a halt. The last thing I remembered was rising nausea and the feeling I was falling into a black pit.

I came to with a thumping headache. Gingerly, I moved my head an inch or two and very carefully looked about. Two blurry figures hovered, peering down at me. I recognised Dunn's voice, then Gilbert's.

'The bugger's still alive,' said Dunn.

'What hit me?' I said, feeling the side of my head, which was now covered with a bloodied bandage.

Gilbert smiled. 'A branch. Knocked you clean out. We thought the traps had shot you, but when we saw them striking lucifers and hunting around in the bush we chased them off. Believe it or not,' he said nodding at the angry red scratches, stained yellow by Holloway's ointment, which were beginning to rhythmically throb all across my arms, legs and back, 'you're lucky you were dragged away from the place they found your hat and gun. It probably saved you.'

As I was going to be laid up in this warm corner over Christmas I sent a telegraph into Forbes to find out what the go was. He returned with the news that the traps were claiming that they'd knocked me off the spot and with Christmas only two days away, the squatters were shouting drinks in all the hotels.

Apparently the traps had returned to the scene at first light and recovered my bloodstained hat and shotgun. The police report fuelled gossip and speculation. I found myself reading the headlines in the *Forbes Examiner.* 'BEN HALL DEAD!'

'Well,' I said, 'if Ben Hall is dead, then I'm sure my mother would have a wake for me in the best Irish tradition. God bless her.'

*

To the dismay of the traps and the gentlemen of the press, I returned from the dead on Boxing Day, before they'd even had time to digest their Christmas turkey.

Christmas in the bush is nothing like the Christmases our parents told us about back in the old country. Here, you could cook the plum duff out in the sun and the closest we get to snow is the white blossom on the flowering gums. But it was a time for celebrating, so Dunn, Gilbert and I decided to flash up and have a night out with the Monks sisters, Ellen and Margaret, and Christina McKinnon, the girl I was enjoying a bit of heels up with at the time.

As we passed the Flagstaff store at Binda we saw the owner, Edward Morris, watching us through the window. His balding pate suggested he was in his middle years and a thin, wiry moustache decorated his top lip. He wore the sour disapproving look of a penny pincher whose store is always open, ready to prosper from the sweat and toil of the common man.

Christina said she had worked for Morris and when she told us he had been a trap, I said to the girls, 'You go along to the inn, whilst we pay Mr Morris a visit.'

Dunn, Gilbert and I went into the shop, pretending to be customers and after looking at various goods approached the counter. His face broke out in a welcoming smile.

'Gentlemen, Merry Christmas. How can I help you?'

He never got an answer, just a row of pistol barrels, with not so much as a grin between them.

'We'll help ourselves,' I said dryly. The others began poking about the shelves helping themselves to anything that took their fancy.

'But it's Christmas,' he protested.

'It certainly is,' I said, as I lifted £100 from the quart pot on the shelf, a stash Christina had told us about.

A small, dark-haired woman appeared through the curtained doorway that led out to a back room. I took this to be Mrs Morris. She clutched at her husband's arm.

'Edward, what's going on?' she asked, startled as she watched Dunn and Gilbert helping themselves to their goods. Her husband knew to stay silent, but she turned to face me, her initial apprehension replaced with annoyance. 'It's Christmas, for God's sake,' she seethed at me.

'Then in the spirit of Christmas allow us to invite you to a party,' I said, a wide grin spreading across my face. They looked puzzled as we escorted them across to the local pub, the Flag Inn, where a Christmas Ball was being held. It was here that I had intended to announce my resurrection.

The band stopped mid jig and a great murmur cut through the haze of tobacco smoke as we entered the pub. I approached the tight knot round the bar and called out, 'What does a bloke have to do to get a glass o' grog, come back from the dead?' and won myself a glass of some warm, villainous-tasting brew.

Whilst Dunn and Gilbert stood by the doors, I hoisted myself up onto the bar and addressed the sea of expectant faces. 'I've got two things to celebrate. I have miraculously risen from the dead, and, as Mr and Mrs Morris have reminded me, it's bloody Christmas!'

A great cheer went up as I held up £30 of the money we had taken from Morris, placed it on the bar and announced, 'Drinks for everyone, courtesy of Mr Morris!'

Evidently, these were words never before heard in this district and the locals sent up another rousing cheer as they stampeded towards the bar like wild cattle during a muster. The locals seemed very comfortable with the idea of being bailed up and made to enjoy themselves. The band started up and everyone began dancing.

A few hours later, with everyone the worse for the grog, two of our captives started a fight. It was a total mismatch. There was a skinny cove like a ratty terrier, up against a heavyset bloke who looked to be twice his size. They were weaving around waving their fists at each other, unable to land a decent punch. They were spoiling the atmosphere, so Gilbert and I pulled them apart.

'Gentlemen, gentlemen, we're having a nice evening here. It's not every day that a man comes back from the dead, especially one that buys you a nobbler or two!'

Despite my gentle good humour, the heavyset man wouldn't let it go. At my nod, Gilbert landed him a punch right between his lamps, and knocked him stiff. Gilbert then showed his gentle side by playing an old lament on the Jew's harp, whilst someone accompanied him on the accordion. I watched his long shapely fingers, which had minutes before been bunched into an ugly fist, dance nimbly across the strings and thought, *He's a rum mix, but I wouldn't have anyone else at my back.*

Whilst the fight distracted us, Morris decided to make a run for it. At about two o'clock, he left the party through a window. Dunn, who had gone outside to give the gums a drink, saw him running across a paddock and sent a few shots after him.

Alerted by the gunfire we raced outside.

'He's after the horses!' I yelled. Cursing we went after him. Seeing we were on his tail, he detoured away from the horses and headed off into the bush.

'Come out, Morris, or it'll be the worse for you,' I shouted, 'I'll burn your store down to the stumps.'

'Do it, Ben,' Christina urged. 'He's got a ledger in there with debts of more than £500 owed to him by selectors. He bleeds them dry and threatens to take their deeds if they don't pay, I've heard him at it.'

'Bastard!' said Gilbert. 'Let's do it.'

'Yeah,' agreed Dunn.

'This will be my Christmas present to the folk of Binda,' I announced as a crowd from the pub began to gather.

Mrs Morris, who had followed us, watched with horror as we piled dry twigs and branches onto the veranda.

'Let me save my dresses,' she pleaded, but I was having none of it. 'Your husband's got plenty in the bank. Let him buy you new ones.'

The crackling of the fire drowned out the sound of Mrs Morris' wailing about their ruin.

Gilbert and Dunn danced around the burning store like demons, flailing their arms as they urged the flames higher and higher. Knowing Morris was still out there, I wandered to the edge of the bush and called out into the darkness, 'Merry Christmas, you bastard!'

A week later when the church bells rang out to greet the New Year I vowed 1865 was the year I would settle the score with Sir Frederick Pottinger.

Chapter Twenty-one

For all the bristling menace of the traps' new weaponry and increased patrols, the Ben Hall gang took the first honours of 1865. Just after New Year we decided to go to the Wowingragong races. Going to a place where folk would instantly recognise us and the traps would be thick on the ground might seem an act of folly, but we had the element of surprise. It was here, three years before, that Pottinger had first arrested me for the Bacon dray robbery and it was here that I intended to get square with Pottinger for ruining my life.

We exchanged our usual gallopers for plainer mounts, nothing too spicy, and with our coats pulled up around our noses to keep out the early morning chill we looked no different to the steady stream of wraiths looming out of the cold grey swirl of mist. We arrived at the race ground at sunrise, the chilly mists still rising off the dew-filled grass.

The smell of sizzling sausages spiced and warmed the frosty air, the calls and whistles of the cross-biting cullies, coggers and card-sharpers adding a shrill excitement as they tried to tempt the foolish and the unwary to chance their arm at roller sweat, pea and thimble, the spinning wheel, three card trick or have a roll at the dice.

'Roll up, roll up! Try your luck, here, now! Come on, ladies an' gents . . . step up. It could be your lucky day!'

We took a beer for our early morning constitutional, making absolutely sure we were seen by the country folk milling about in their Sunday best. Word spread quicker than a bushfire that the Ben Hall gang was about. The reward on just one of our heads would be half a lifetime's wages for most people and just associating with us could see them sent to gaol. But far from avoiding us, people pushed towards us waving their hats, calling out 'Good on ya, boys' and holding out their hands so they could say they had shaken hands with Ben Hall or Johnny Gilbert.

Knowing Pottinger's desperation to capture us, I waited until someone asked, 'What ya up to, boys?' and spread some loose talk.

'I've a good mind to cut Pottinger out, if he dares to run a race here,' I declared loudly. We were careful to say it within earshot of 'Scabby Harry'. This old scourer had a taste for hard grog and had been living 'on the ribs' for years from the odd scraps of information that came his way. We sat back and watched our stratagem unfold.

Sure enough, Harry sidled up to Pottinger at a booth where he was enjoying a lemonade, and pretended to engage him in a casual chat. We could see his twisted lip movements and furtive whispering a mile off.

'Sir Frederick, I have some news,' Harry would be saying. 'Ben Hall's here, and he's planning to capture you.'

Pottinger, still trying to retain some modicum of composure, shot up off his stool by the bar, uncoiling his powerfully built frame to its full height of six foot and more. Towering over Harry, we watched as he demanded answers.

'When?' asked Pottinger, anxiety and desperation written all over his face. This was his chance to nail the bushranger who had mocked him for almost three years. Sir Frederick may have been an arrogant fool, but he was no coward. Threats to make Harry spend the rest of his natural life in prison were of little consequence to an old man who had already done his living. Harry didn't need to be threatened, just paid. I saw Pottinger fumble in his pocket, hand the money over and Harry surrendered everything he knew, just as we had intended.

'Ben Hall is planning to cut you out of the race, if you dare ride.'

Pottinger's expression remained impassive, and he quizzed him further.

'How did you hear this?'

'By standing in a place I had no business being.' Scabby Harry then melted back into the milling throng of people.

Sir Frederick's face was a study of a man torn between professional duty and a success that would end the ridicule that had plagued him ever since he had been made Inspector.

To make sure that Pottinger did race, I set a honey trap, which I knew he could not refuse. I spotted one of the aromatic ladies of the district with whom I had enjoyed a bit of under before she landed herself a rich, fat squatter. The miniature top hat, trimmed with feathers and lacy ribbon balancing on top of the pile of blonde hair accentuated the tall, stately figure of Mrs Susan Thorsbury. Her sculpted cheekbones and milky complexion drew as many admiring glances as the striking light blue and pearl grey silk dress adorning her shapely figure.

'Cor, she's a right sort. I wouldn't mind tippin' 'er the velvet,' moaned Dunn longingly as she swept past.

'She'd 'ave you for breakfast, mate,' I said, following in her fragrant wake as she cut a confident swathe through the crowds. Even the Victorian obsession for layered skirts and overskirts worn over yet more layers of underskirts and petticoats had not spoiled the sweep of the long, shapely legs that led up to her splendidly rounded arse.

I waited until she was alone, then pulled her by the hand into an empty tent. 'Lovely as ever, Susan Sweeny,' I said, using her maiden name and kissing her gloved hand with a low bow.

'Ben!' she exclaimed. The surprise of seeing me here caused her blue eyes to widen, and brought a light flush to her porcelain cheeks as she recalled the passionate affair, which we'd conducted 'under cover of moon' due to the disapproval of a belligerent father who could have given our da a run for his money, any day of the week. Looking at me tenderly, her eyes filled with concern as she said in a lowered voice, 'Should you be here?'

'Probably not,' I replied, 'but I aim to settle the score with Sir La-di-da Pottinger, and I need your help.'

Susan arched her neat eyebrows as I handed her a big pink rosette I'd just lifted from a prize-winning heifer in the show paddock.

A short time later, Susan skilfully waylaid Pottinger and surrounded him with her fragrant entourage of country wives. Knowing that few men can resist female flattery, she opened with a flirtatious smile. 'Sir Frederick, how very handsome you look in your uniform.' Laying a gloved hand on his arm, and leaning slightly forward so he had a good view down her décolletage, she whispered. 'In fact, we were hoping you might wear our colours in the Ladies Bag.'

Traditionally, the last race of the meet was the Ladies Bag, so-called because the prize was a bag of handmade goods and gifts donated by the ladies of the district. It was an open invitation race, which gave local riders a chance, and was always fiercely contested.

A great smile cracked Pottinger's face. 'Ladies, I'm flattered, but I'm not sure it would be appropriate for an officer of the law,' he protested weakly.

A chorus of disappointment from the brightly coloured butter-flies cut him short, and Susan squeezed his forearm, allowing him to bask in the full radiance of her ample breasts in their froth of lace around her neckline.

'Oh, Inspector,' she pouted. 'It's just a bit of harmless sport. Your predecessor represented us with distinction on many occasions.'

'Well, I'd have to think about it,' he blustered, unable to tear his eyes away from her breasts.

Susan wouldn't be denied. 'Say you will, Sir Frederick,' she said breathlessly in his ear.

'Oh, yes,' chorused the fragrant ladies.

'Oh, very well, then.' Pottinger bowed his head in submission.

'Well, I'm flattered that you should choose me to wear your colours. To refuse such lovely ladies would be ungracious, and deserving of a night in the logs.'

While the other ladies clapped, Susan pinned the huge pink rosette to his lapel.

'Why, er, thank you,' he said, looking at the rosette uncertainly, then glaring at the grinning larrikins and cockies who were making a few choice remarks about his manly demeanour. He fought back any show of temper with the thought that it would be a small price to pay if he could land Ben Hall. Pottinger then completely forgot his social graces, normally observed by men of his social rank, and began bragging to all and sundry that he would be racing in the 'Ladies Bag', convinced now that he was the hunter and not the fox.

By the time the stewards began pushing back the crowd to clear a corridor of rough, patchy ground for the racing, the rumour that we would try to take Pottinger had been passed from lip to lip, and decanted into every ear. You could feel the anticipation in the air.

The saddling bell ordered the riders to their gallopers. Pottinger elected to ride in his uniform rather than racing colours to distinguish himself from the other riders. Whatever else could be said of him, he was a fine horseman and the 'black legs' took a late rush of heavy betting on his horse, which he had named Bushranger.

The starter, holding a shotgun aloft, called the horses and riders to the line. The noise of a thousand grogged-up locals baying for the nag with their hard-earned coin on its nose was making the horses a bit skittish as they raked at the dry dirt with their hooves, nervously straining at their bits.

Pottinger and the local favourite, Scrammy Jack, bumped and barged for position at the starting line. As well as the kudos of winning, the prize was worth about £40 to the winner. That was big money in these parts.

The crack of the starter's gun released the nervous, pent-up energy of crowd, runners and riders alike. A great roar came as the horses exploded forwards in a blur, sending clods flying into the air. The riders emerged from the great cloud of dust that obscured them for the first hundred yards, all except Pottinger, who made no effort to chase down the fleet-footed Scrammy Jack, who had taken off like a bullet.

Ignoring the howls of derision and insults, which flew from the blur of faces that lined either side of the course, he cantered well behind the pack, giving us ample opportunity to cut him out, if that was ever our intention. We made no attempt to take him and Pottinger trotted home a country mile behind Scrammy Jack and every other nag in the race.

If his reputation stank before the race, it was rank now. He looked around with a puzzled look, that said, 'Why didn't Hall make his move?' A chuckle, that then became a ripple, then a roar of laughter as the crowd realised that we'd towed him out. Like the pink rosette nailed to his chest, it had all been a big joke.

The newspapers and squatter community expressed great disquiet that the Ben Hall gang was able to attend the races and embarrass Inspector Pottinger, but also claimed our supposed cowardice as a moral victory for Pottinger. The trap had already been sprung. The real reason why we didn't cut him out of the race became clear when a letter from a concerned citizen arrived on the desk of

Pottinger's patron, Inspector-General McLerie. It demanded to know why one of his officers had ridden at a public race meeting? This was a clear breach of the police code of duty, which expressly forbade police officers from having anything to do with racing matters.

Our spies told us about the day the innocent-looking dun-coloured envelope bearing McLerie's crest arrived. Thinking it concerned nothing more than new regulations or a request for information an unsuspecting Pottinger ripped open the envelope and the colour drained from his face as he read the contents.

Dear Inspector Pottinger,

It has come to my attention that on January 3 of this year you attended the Wowingragong race meeting in your official capacity as an Inspector of the New South Wales Police.

It has been alleged that during that meeting, you entered and took part in a race in which the purse was £40. I'm sure I need not remind you that police regulations expressly forbid any such activity.

Therefore I must consider this a serious disciplinary matter, but before I decide what action to take I would ask you to submit a full report on the incident.

I will expect to receive your reply within fourteen days of receipt.

John McLerie
Inspector-General
New South Wales Police

By all accounts, Pottinger had a dark fit and went roaring round the barracks like a wounded bullock. The purpose of our deception was clear to him now – vengeance.

McLerie's letter and Pottinger's reply, which ran to fourteen pages, practically a novella, were widely published and discussed. He insisted that he was aware of the regulation and had only raced to provide bait for Ben Hall, after receiving information that he would try to capture him if he raced. He had also been asked to race by the local ladies and felt that had he refused, it would have reflected poorly on his character, both personally and professionally. The rest merely recounted his many sterling deeds and his colourful rantings and ravings about the menace of bushrangers.

However, the politicians and police had their fill of the so-called Bastard Baronet. His appointment hadn't brought any results, only controversy and driven a wedge between the police and the ordinary folk of the Lachlan district. McLerie informed Pottinger that he found his explanation highly unsatisfactory and suspended him from duty with immediate effect.

When we got the news we went on the rip for three days straight, but your greatest loss often comes hard on the heels of your greatest triumph.

The sky that greeted us on the morning of January 26, 1865, was a portent of what lay ahead. Rain clouds as black as a witch's hat rolled overhead.

A mob of crows prowled the windy heavens and we all heard the ominous rumblings of God's displeasure.

We ignored the warning signs.

The heat was oppressive; the cicadas droned in the heat – a sleepy, hypnotic rhythm that dulled the senses. The normally inquisitive kangaroo dogs knew to lie still and wait for the storm to break, but a lost day to a dog is of no consequence. With the police rudderless after the departure of Pottinger, we decided to make the most of it.

We started the day bailing up ten travellers, south of Goulburn, until the traps came galloping along and spoiled our party. We then headed north-west towards Collector and bailed up five people, including a young boy of about ten years old who went by the name of Henry Nelson. Afraid that they would alert the traps to which direction we were headed, we brought them along with us.

We arrived in the town of Collector at about six in the evening where we bailed up Kimberly's Inn leaving the boy outside with the horses. Little did we know that as soon as we'd gone inside and started helping ourselves to a couple of pistols, £30 in cash and other sundry items that the boy would desert his post, run home and tell his father.

It turned out that, not only was young Henry Nelson a native of Collector, but the youngest son of Constable Samuel Nelson, one of a trio of traps assigned to the town. That day, however, as luck would have it, the other two mounted police were away on patrol looking for us.

The stocky, red-haired Nelson took his son by the hand and sat him down in his armchair so that he might understand the great importance of telling his father everything he knew. Kneeling down, Nelson looked into his son's eyes and asked gently, 'Can you tell me what the men looked like?'

Five minutes later, while we were standing our hand at the bar, Constable Nelson was buckling his gun belt round his waist, pulling his coat round his shoulders and putting his cap on his head. His distraught wife grabbed onto his sleeve, begging him not to go, 'Leave, it Samuel, let them be.'

But he looked at her and said quietly, 'I can't. It's my duty to stop them.'

Unlike the two that were away on patrol, Constable Samuel Nelson took his responsibilities very seriously. Normally, he was just a turnkey, but this day he decided to be a hero. His wife realised there was no stopping him, so she gently let go of his sleeve, and kissed him goodbye. He stepped out of the house, his carbine in his hand, and started walking up to the High Street towards the Kimberley's Inn. When I noticed the boy had deserted his post, I sent Johnny Dunn outside and told him to give us the griffin if the traps were sighted. Our youngest and most inexperienced recruit had the misfortune to be there when Constable Nelson came into view.

The locals, who had fled indoors when they saw us arrive, watched fearfully from behind their curtains as Nelson made his way up the middle of the dusty main street.

Dunn had taken up a position behind a water barrel at the corner of the hotel and warned Nelson to stand.

'Stop . . . or I'll nail you where you stand.'

Nelson kept on coming.

'Have you family?'

'Aye.'

'Then stop, for their sake.'

'I can't do that.'

Dunn looked round at us to get the nod, but we were still ensconced in the bar bailing up the customers, so he raised his shotgun and fired from twenty-five yards, hitting the trap high up in the ribcage.

Nelson was probably dead on his feet after that first shot, but his brain hadn't yet told his body, and even though his knees were wobbling, he kept staggering towards Dunn through the gun-smoke. This spooked Johnny, who was sure he'd hit him. Determined to stop this phantom in his tracks, he ditched the shotgun, pulled a pistol from his belt and shot Nelson square in the face. This time he went down and didn't get up.

Hearing the shots, we rushed out onto the veranda of the hotel to see Dunn in the middle of the street holding a smoking gun, the trap, Nelson, sprawled at his feet, blood running out into the dust around them.

Finding no pulse, I confirmed with a shake of the head that Nelson was a hero all right, a dead one.

We cleared out sharpish and a heavy silence hung about us all as we rode home with the thunder rumbling in the heavens above us. This time there was none of the usual banter and wisecracking.

If only Nelson would have taken cover and engaged Dunn, we'd have pulled out once we'd robbed the hotel, I thought. But like us, Nelson felt bound by duty and the oath he'd taken. He died for what he believed in and his wife would now be crying over his cold, still body in the back room of the Collector police station. Her three children had lost their father and they had nothing more than a widow's pension to come and go on.

The southerly finally broke the back of the heat. A biblical rain fell from the skies, but all the tears in heaven could never wash away our sins.

It was Dunn's turn to endure that endless night of sorrow and self-loathing as we all sat there listening to the fire hiss in angry disapproval. As he raised umpteen cups of tea, laced with Old Tom, to his lips I saw his hands shake. We heard it was being said in Forbes that we had shot Nelson to even up the score and that Parry and Nelson's deaths were payback for the shooting of Mickey Burke and John O'Meally.

A day or two later, we came across a poster nailed to a tree offering a reward of £1,100 each for Ben Hall, John Dunn and Johnny Gilbert. Dead or Alive.

'Things must be bad,' said Gilbert sourly. 'We're now worth more than Dan Morgan.'

'God rot Morgan's soul, we're nothing like him,' I thundered. 'He was born bad and got worse.' I remarked to the boys that

Constable Kennedy only got £10 when I turned in my da, so at least I'd outdone him on that score.

The newspapers said the magisterial inquests had returned a verdict of 'wilful murder' against Gilbert and Dunn who were wanted for the murder of Sergeant Parry and Constable Nelson. I was wanted as an accessory to both murders, but I knew that if they caught us, we'd all dance a jig at the Sheriff's ball.

The death of Constable Nelson had brought us to a turning point in the history of the Colony of New South Wales. On March 16, the *Felon's Apprehension Act* had its second reading in the Legislative Council. So harsh were the measures proposed that it was rejected the first time, but on its second reading, it was swept through the House by a wave of popular opinion after the death of constables Parry and Nelson. I learned all this on the last occasion I met Tom Morris. As he had done the last time we met, he left his usual good humour at home so I might understand the gravity of my situation.

'So, McLerie got his way?' I said.

'Aye, after the death of Constable Nelson there was no stopping it, but not without a fight. Some of the members of the Legislative Council have been in the police and don't trust them with such powers. The President of the Council, himself, stated that the New South Wales police was built, drilled and operated on the Irish model like an army of occupation. Unable to perform the tasks of a civil police force and having lost the respect of the general population it was now proposing to declare war on the very society it was supposed to protect.'

I gave a low whistle, 'So, it's war they're preparing for.'

'Nothing less, Ben,' said Tom quietly. 'The Felon's Apprehension Act is a legal invitation to murder. Rather than have to bring you in and go through the bother of a trial, police and citizens can shoot you like cattle with no fear of condemnation or prosecution. Even the Kings of England, as cruel as they were, stopped that practice in 1329.'

'But it's still good enough for Australia in 1865,' I said with a shake of my head.

'Justice doesn't always belong to those who claim to represent it,' said Tom firmly. 'All men should enjoy the same justice and freedoms. It should not be a privilege of social rank. This very day there are white men fighting and dying so that black men may be freed from slavery.'

'I hope we see that day here too.'

'We will, Ben, but not before they've spilled your blood.'

Realising that his words had mirrored my own deepest thoughts, Tom stared at me closely. I felt a stab of dread deep within me. I knew it myself, but somehow it was more shocking to hear someone else say it. I smiled grimly and said, 'I promised Inspector Norton that they'd never take me alive and maybe that's where it's headed.'

Tom was in no mood for my self-pity. 'Your mates believe in you and would follow you to Hell. Get away from this evil life or you will bring ruin and sorrow to them all.'

I recognised the truth of his words, nodded, turned from the window and accepted Tom's outstretched hand. 'This will be the last time we meet. They'll know someone tipped you the wink and there will be an investigation.'

'Thanks, Tom,' I said, returning his firm handshake.

'Godspeed, Ben.' There was a flash of the old Tom as he cracked an easy smile. 'When you land in California, be sure and lift a glass to your old friends in Australia.' With that he turned and slipped through the door and into the night.

For the first time since I came to the game, I felt the Ben Hall gang were on the back foot. At least we were forewarned.

On April 8, 1865, the *Sydney Morning Herald* announced that the *Felon's Apprehension Act* would shortly become law in New South Wales. They did not see that they were resorting to the same barbarism and despotism the British Empire claimed it stood against, despite its admission that in order to see the law as useful the public must cease to care whether bushrangers are brought in dead or alive. Its editorial ended with the fateful words:

> ...*The Legislative Council will not say that the present law would justify a Constable in shooting bushrangers without challenge, but they intimate that no jury would convict and no Judge condemn.*

That same day, the *Government Gazette* published a summons calling on Dunn, Gilbert and myself to surrender to the gaoler at

Goulburn by midday on April 29, so we might stand trial for the murders of Parry and Nelson. Failure to do so would see us declared the first outlaws in Australia under the new Act.

The kind of animal savagery that the *Felon's Apprehension Act* would unleash was quickly demonstrated as the sensational news that 'Mad' Dan Morgan had been shot at a station at Peechelba in Victoria appeared on the front page of every newspaper. Morgan was a mongrel, who showed no respect for human life, but the desecration of his body would have chilled the blood of a Spanish Inquisitor.

First, those 'decent folk' who shot him souvenired locks of his hair, placed a gun in his hand and took photographs of his corpse. Then Superintendent Cobham put the cadaver on public display at Wangaratta police station to satisfy the ghoulish curiosity of the so-called 'gentlemen of the press', before flaying off Morgan's bushy beard, which he pegged out on a sheet of bark like an opossum skin. Dr Dobbyn, the local coroner, announced that he wanted to make a death mask. He ordered the town physician to decapitate Morgan and had the barber shave the head.

After the impression was taken, the head was placed in a hatbox and addressed to Professor Halford, the Professor of Anatomy at Melbourne University, to further the cause of medical science. I had read that scientists had caught onto some European voodoo called phrenology, which claims that criminal tendencies can be discerned by the size and shape of the brain and head. The reading of 'bumps' has become a popular fairground attraction and by my reckoning that is where it should remain.

I almost underwent a late conversion to religion when one of our loyal bush telegraphs came with the dramatic news that Pottinger was near death.

After his dismissal from the police service, he fell into a deep depression, but was buoyed up by a show of appreciation from his supporters who wrote petitions to the authorities in Sydney and all the leading newspapers. The Lachlan correspondent of the *Sydney Morning Herald* spouted some rot that:

> *Sir Frederick had the misfortune, it seems, of being the best abused man in New South Wales . . . selected by small wits of the country press as a butt for their abuse and ridicule.*

Richly earned ridicule, I'd say! '*Kind ... gentlemanly ... and urbane*' were not qualities most folk would remember him by in the Lachlan where he almost committed as many offences as he cleared up.

In any event, the petitions had no effect, but they persuaded Pottinger to go down to Sydney and seek redress. He resolved to climb 'the gallows' at McLerie's office again and tackle him face to face. The Governor of New South Wales, Sir John Young, was a friend of his family and he also hoped to persuade him to intervene with McLerie on his behalf.

Tragedy occurred during a routine stop at Wascoe's Inn in the Blue Mountains. Pottinger went into a nearby orchard to relieve himself. Seemingly, he spent too long playing with his pizzle and the coachman took off without him. Pottinger ran alongside the coach and jumped aboard, but the violent motion accidentally discharged the four-barrelled service pistol he was carrying in his waistband. The bullet entered his body around the ribcage, travelled upwards and became embedded among his offal. It didn't kill him, but he was gravely injured.

When I heard the news, I thought, *Ah, well, that's one back for Henry Manns and Warrigal Walsh!* and recalled the night Pottinger had lain in wait for the Darkie at Kitty Brown's. He had pointed his carbine right at him and without a word of warning pulled the trigger. Luckily for the Darkie, the shot stayed in the breech. God was saving that bullet for Sir Frederick.

I said nothing to the others about my meeting with Tom or quitting the game, but with Pottinger on his deathbed there was nothing to keep me in Australia. We had spent sleepless nights round the fire, painfully aware that time was passing and we'd soon be outlaws. Perhaps we'd all been thinking it was time to quit, but no one had been game to say it. As Tom rightly said, they'd follow me to Hell if I asked them to.

I waited till after we'd eaten and had a couple of nobblers. I drew in a deep breath and laid it out for them, 'It's time for some plain talking, boys. We'll soon have to choose whether it's Hell or California we're bound for.'

They looked at each other, as if to confirm they had heard me correctly.

'Our warrant is up at midday tomorrow. The traps will soon declare us outlaws and raise the country on us, and if they have their way the bullet will get us before the rope. We've done what we can, but in the end it's gonna be the three of us against the whole bloody British Empire. Can't say it plainer than that.'

We looked into the flames of the camp fire and listened to the crackling of twigs. Gilbert spoke, 'There's no competition. It's California for me.'

Dunn raised his hand. 'Aye, California for me an' all.'

Our course of action decided, we slept soundly for the first time in weeks.

When we woke the next day, April 29, 1865, we boiled the billy and raised our mugs of tea laced with Old Tom to the three men who would shortly be declared the first outlaws in Australian history. It was a distinction that came with no reward, except death. With over £3,000 in reward money for the taking, all the fortune hunters, mercenaries and madmen would now burst out into the bush armed to the teeth with everything from rifles to pikes, eager to show the traps how it should be done. We decided to keep dark, pay up all our scores and in a week, if we were all still above ground, meet at Billabong Creek, just north of Forbes.

There was a strange, unearthly feeling that maybe we would never meet again, but we hid it under bluster and bravado as we clasped hands. In those few moments before we parted, again we travelled the many miles, celebrated our triumphs, mourned the mates we had lost and felt the mist-laden rush of wind on our faces as we galloped helter-skelter down the side of a mountain with guns blazing all about us. We all felt the force of the moment.

As we rode off in opposite directions, we let rip one last time.

'See you in Hell!' Gilbert called over his shoulder.

'Or in California!' I yelled back, hoping I was closest to the mark. There was still ten thousand miles of heat, dust and deep blue sea between us and California, not to mention Her Majesty's constabulary.

Chapter Twenty-two

The decision made, I went to the hut of Coobang Mick Connelly, which sits at the bottom of the Nelungaloo station about twelve miles north-west of Forbes. He was known as Coobang because he lived in a hut by the southern half of a ribbon of water known as Coobang Creek, which meandered gently northwards until it became Billabong Creek. He was a fencer, a trader and a duffer. Mick had also been my banker since I started in the game. At that moment he was holding about £6,000 of mine in a bank account in his name, for safety reasons.

I stopped in at Mick's and told him to have my money ready when I returned in a few days and to expect Gilbert and Dunn.

'S'trewth, Ben,' he said, 'that's a lot of spare change to be carrying around.'

'I'm going to need it to get me started in California,' I said. His eyes widened with surprise.

'You hooking it, then?'

'I've had me fill of the game,' I said. 'They're out to finish us now, Mick, and it's going to take more than three of us to stop 'em. I'll need something up front.'

'How much?'

'A thousand ought to cover it,' I replied. He regarded me solemnly, out of eyes the colour of burned toffee, the worry lines etched into the side of his mouth suddenly deeper. 'You can take it out of my money when you draw it out of the bank.'

Nodding, he went inside and a few minutes later re-appeared with five fat rolls of notes.

'Thanks, Mick.'

'I'll start into Forbes tomorrow, then.'

'See you in a few days.'

*

I made my way west across bleak, treeless back country on a brittle carpet of Mitchell, and mallee scrub bleached grey and white by the merciless sun. It was strange, bad country, which looked all burnt out. I found out, courtesy of Scabby Harry, that Biddy, Taylor and my son Henry were living out here in a hut on Humbug Creek. He had come across Taylor during one of his periodic appearances in the Forbes court for giving Constable Kennedy a well-deserved poke on the nose. Jim Taylor had come up after Harry on a charge of robbery under arms, that was dismissed when the witnesses failed to show. Scabby Harry, knowing I wanted more information on him, followed Taylor and saw a woman and a boy run out across the paddock to meet him. Harry let our telegraphs know he had some valuable information, and after hearing him out I gave him thirty quid for finding them plus an extra ten to cover the fine he got for neddying Kennedy.

I took my time getting there as I knew the bush was thick with traps. I heard they got together in groups, agreed go whacks on the reward money, and spent their Sundays raking the bush, hunting us like roos.

It took a couple of days in the saddle to cover the forty miles to Taylor's isolated hut. I kept well back out of sight but he must have seen my approach, because Biddy was waiting for me on the doorstep, arms folded. It was the first time I'd seen her since that day I'd left for the Goulburn cattle run almost four years ago.

I flicked my eyes over her body with an intimacy permitted only to former husbands and lovers. I noted that her thin dress strained to contain her breasts, which had remained much fuller after childbirth. Her waist was as narrow as ever, her hips just as rounded. Biddy was still the wild, beautiful untamed country girl who had first beguiled me, but she no longer inspired any of the old stirrings or foolish bravado that made me want to fight jackeroos or take on Slasher the brumby. I had buried that part of my past so deep that I may as well have been describing someone else's life.

I noticed that the world of worry and disappointment Taylor had delivered her into was etched on her young face. Those telltale lines were nature's own little betrayal. Mind you, they do say a woman loses her looks quicker than a man when she goes to the bad. Taylor had been charming enough during those secret liaisons, the deceit only adding to the excitement. It was easy for him to tempt her away with extravagant promises. Now she found herself marooned in Humbug Creek, tethered to a drunken drongo whom she realised wasn't good enough for her.

Biddy had remained here with Taylor, instead of returning to the man who would have forgiven her.

Whatever goodness she still had in her, she wasted none of it on me. After cruelly betraying my trust and taking away my son, I searched in vain for a shadow of sorrow on her face, a downward glance – or some gesture to acknowledge the hurt she had caused. Despite her misfortune with Taylor, no sorrow, no acknowledgement of betrayal, there was nothing, just that defiant Walsh stare, full of centuries of Irish belligerence that cared little for rights or wrongs.

She cast a disapproving eye over my wild, unkempt appearance and my tattered clothes, and said coldly, 'You look a fine state.'

'Well, we know who's to blame,' I said cuttingly. I was surprised at how easily the bitterness came.

She shot me back a look that would sour a quince. 'What do you want?'

'Where's Taylor?' I replied, barely able to spit out his name.

'What do you want with him?' Her arrogance quickly dissolved into fear of what I might do to her lover. I realised with a stab of regret that she'd never worried about me like that.

'I need to speak to him,' I said coolly. 'Ask him to step outside.'

'You leave him alone, Ben Hall!' she shouted, tears flooding her eyes. She spoke my full name as though I was a stranger.

Our raised voices produced a scuffle of feet from the darkness behind Biddy. Thinking it was Taylor, I had my pistol drawn and cocked by the time I saw a small face peeking out from behind Biddy. It was Henry.

He was eight now. He had grown into a fine, strapping boy with a swipe of his mother in him. I could see it in the way he pouted at me, but with his blond hair and grey eyes, there was undoubtedly something of me in him too. Forgetting all about Taylor, I kneeled down to get a better look at him. Biddy tried to push him back inside.

'Henry,' I said, but before I could even remind him who I was, he yelled out fiercely, 'You leave my da alone. Don't you kill him!'

'Henry!' I said, as shocked by the idea I'd gun any man down in cold blood as by Henry thinking that mongrel Taylor was his father. Biddy pushed him back inside and closed the door firmly behind her, but he continued to hammer on it with his fierce little fists.

'What have you told him?' I demanded, a great wave of sorrow welling up inside of me. They had poisoned him against me.

'The truth!' she said, her lips drawn back in a disapproving and sanctimonious line.

'The truth?' I roared back, 'You don't know the meaning of the word, just like you have no idea what being faithful means.'

'You never loved me,' she cut in.

'*Never loved you?* Everything I ever worked for, the farm, everything I built was for you, for us.' But even the truth plainly spoken wasn't enough to silence her.

'You go to hell, Ben Hall,' she said in a shrill voice.

'I have looked that gentleman between the eyes on many occasions and feared him less on each occasion,' I said with a confident grin. My outburst brought the crimson to her cheeks, which always happened when she got raised.

'What do you want here, Ben?'

'I'm only here to tell you I'm leaving the country and I won't be back. I've got some money to help you bring up the boy, but I won't hand it over until I see Taylor.'

She hesitated, knowing I'd wait all night if need be. After a moment she nodded and said, 'I'll get him, if you swear, in front of your only son, that you won't hurt him.'

Without waiting for a reply, she opened the door and brought Henry outside, holding him in front of her, so he could bear witness to the promise she knew I'd have to make. *She would do anything, use anything to save Taylor*, I thought sadly.

'You have my word. Go and get him.' It was all I could manage, my voice was beginning to fail me.

She left me by the door, took Henry by the hand and the two of them walked down the paddock. Once she got near enough she started calling out.

'Jim! Jim!'

Henry took his cue from her. 'Da! Cooee, da!'

I felt sick to my stomach. I knew why I had avoided this day for so long. The familiar pain twisted in my guts as this return to the past opened up all my old wounds.

The gutless bastard finally emerged from his hidey-hole, brushing burrs and grass from his clothes.

A gangling, dark-haired bloke about my age, who had clearly let himself go since he left the police. Gone was the smart, short-haired, clean-shaven man I remembered coming up to Sandy Creek. He was one of those raggedy-clothed, long-haired feral creatures that inhabited this remote corner of the Lachlan. I wasn't too flash myself, but at least I had good cause. He shambled up, his eyes downcast for fear that he'd see his own death in my eyes.

In his presence, I took five fat rolls of bank notes from my pocket and held them out to Biddy.

'We don't need *that* kind of money,' protested Biddy weakly.

I brushed her words aside, 'Don't go putting yourself above me, lady. I'd remind you that this cove has been up in front of the magistrate for robbery once and he'd do more cross work, if he could find anyone to go in with him. This money isn't for you, it's for my son to give him a decent start in life.'

I turned my attention back to Taylor. 'If I hear you've touched a penny, I'll come back and I'll shoot you where you stand, and that's a promise!' I let the threat hang over his bowed head a moment longer, then drove home the point. 'You got it?' I growled.

He mumbled something. I grabbed his chin with my left hand, which caused the boy to clutch at Biddy. Both of them retreated a step or two, eyeing me fearfully. I uncurled my fingers slowly and let Taylor go.

Taylor wore the sly look of a dingo who knows when it's time to roll over. This time he said clearly, 'I hear you.'

'Best you do,' I said, with as much menace as I could force into three words.

He nodded sullenly, and Biddy hesitantly took the money from my hand. The uneasy silence that followed was broken by the inquisitive Henry.

He looked up at me, his face full of childish curiosity, and said, 'Where are you going?' I knelt down in front of him, looked into his cool grey eyes, and smiled at him.

'California,' I answered. 'That's where I'm headed.'

'Where's that?' he pressed.

'In America. Far, far away, son, away over the sea.'

'Will you ever come back?' he said.

I thought my heart would burst as I looked into that innocent, trusting face. Determined that my last words to him wouldn't be a lie, I answered, 'No, son, I never will.' I couldn't bear to look at him another moment, so I stood up quickly, pulled him close, kissed the top of his head and turned sharply on my heel.

As I strode towards the ever patient Willy the Weasel, who had carried me unquestioningly through all the turmoil, I sensed my boy's confusion and the questions forming in his mind, but I had no answers for him. *May God, such as he is, keep you safe from harm and never let you follow in your father's footsteps.*

Somewhere between Humbug Creek and Forbes I toasted my twenty-eighth birthday and almost three years in the game with a nobbler.

Using an old bushman's trick, I spread a heavy cotton blanket over the low-hanging arm of a mulga bush overnight. By early morning it was heavy with dew. Wringing it out, I got enough water to fill the billy. To my coffee I added a caulker of brandy, the common stuff, nothing special or foreign like. Savouring the fiery glow the amber liquid left in the pit of my stomach, I mused that it was only the fourth of May and I was celebrating my birthday five days early. I knew I'd have no time to tip my elbow on the day as Tom sent me a telegraph that the *Felon's Apprehension Act* would become law on May 10. I had decided that by then Dunn, Gilbert and I would be in the saddle riding hard for the Queensland border.

I had checked the shipping pages and noted that a ship sailed from Brisbane to San Francisco on the fifteenth day of each month. I decided Queensland would be our best dart as all the ports in New South Wales would be so closely watched that a strange rat wouldn't squeeze on board without being noticed. It was 600 miles as the crow flies, but if we went hard, we could be onboard when the next ship weighed anchor in June. Strange to say, having been boxed up in the bush all my life I'd never seen the sea, nothing except green trees and sunburnt country.

On the rare occasions I got a chance to read a newspaper, my eyes always searched out news from America, where for so long I'd hoped to start a new life. I read that the last Confederate army had surrendered in the American Civil War. Tom Morris was right, soon there would be no more slaves in America, but the British were still sending white convict slaves to Australia and the police would keep on persecuting them and those born to them. The struggle was not over yet, but I noted with grim satisfaction that Sir Frederick Pottinger's was. A report dated April 10 announced he had died in Sydney from complications arising from his self-inflicted gunshot wound. I felt no sense of triumph or joy, just an odd sense of unfinished business. Perhaps we would have our go in the great hereafter, the Bastard Baronet and I. Pottinger had played out his hand, but, as the circle of betrayal, guilt and vengeance tightened around me, I had yet to play mine.

I arrived at Billabong Creek, where I was due to meet up with Gilbert and Dunn and start for Queensland. I went up to Native Cat Hill to meet Mick, but he didn't show. Perhaps he was still on his way back from Forbes. I came down, carefully covering my tracks, and set up camp under a big old yellow box surrounded by a thick stand of cypress pines in a paddock at the bottom end of Nelunga-loo station near Billabong Creek.

The sun, now just a glowing ember, slipped behind the distant Weddin Mountains and hundreds of starlings rushed into a large pine tree and started kicking up a terrific din. I sensed an ill-wind had blown them in and shivered, as darkness and the night chill closed in around me. Summer had gone and the mornings and nights had grown sharp again. I cooked up a bit of tucker, lay on my swag and watched the stars glitter through the gum branches a while and fell asleep.

As instructed, Coobang Mick went into Forbes and withdrew my £6,000 from the Oriental Bank telling them he was intending to buy some land. The sudden withdrawal of such a large sum of money by a 'person of interest' was quickly reported to Sub-Inspector James Henry Davidson whose eight-man patrol had been tracking us through the bush for the past two weeks. The traps had expected all along that I might try to leave the district once I was declared an outlaw. They put two and two together, and, for once, came up with an even four.

Davidson, Sergeant Condell, Billy Dargin and Constables Bohan, Buckley, Caban and Hipkiss set off north for Coobang Creek with fresh hope in their hearts. Many such parties had ventured out full of purpose and hope and had all returned empty-handed. But Davidson vowed this sortie would be different.

After spending another uncomfortable night crouched in the bush, they were rewarded just before dawn by a flicker of light from inside Connelly's hut then, shortly afterwards, wisps of white smoke rising from the chimney. Uncertain how many were inside, Davidson's men took up positions around the top of the gully where Coobong Mick's hut nestled. Their orders were to spare no one if the shooting started.

Davidson and Condell crept down into the gully, onto the veranda, which ran round three sides of the house, and waited until the sun skirted the tops of the trees. Sweat prickling his brow, Davidson rapped on the crude door three or four times with the butt of his rifle.

'Who's there?' came a muffled voice from inside.

'Police,' called Davidson loudly.

'What d'ya want?' asked the same voice, irritably. Davidson detected no nervous tremor in the abrupt question. Either Connelly was a bloody good liar or there was no one in there with him.

'You're surrounded, Connelly, come out now.' There was a scuffling of feet on the earthen floor, a snap as the bolt shot back and a creak, as a bare-chested, bleary-eyed Mick opened the door and peered out. He stepped out onto the veranda, raising his bushy eyebrows when he saw the two heavily armed traps crouched on either side of the doorway. Instinctively, he crossed his arms across his chest to ward off the early morning chill settling on his naked skin.

'Any guests inside?' asked Davidson, motioning at the gloomy interior where the smell of yesterday's gravy and wood smoke mingled with the sour odour of Connelly's unwashed body.

'Nah,' said Connelly, running a careless hand through his woolly crown of hair. He completed his morning ritual by stretching his heavyset frame and noisily dredging up the phlegm from his nose and throat and releasing it over the rail in a thick stream of spittle.

Davidson nodded to Condell. Both policemen stood up and flattened themselves on either side of the thick beams supporting the doorway. Remembering how the Darkie had outmanoeuvred Hosie and Middleton at Fogg's, they darted in through the door, one after the other, with pistols drawn.

Looking up at the surrounding hillside, Mick saw that the other troopers had their carbines trained on him. He grinned, knowing their bullets would be staying in their breeches. His confidence was borne out by a disappointed Davidson and Condell, who came back out onto the veranda.

'Told ya,' muttered Connelly sourly as he stuffed his hands into the pockets of his cord trousers.

With his thinning red hair, neatly clipped beard and moustache, and finely appointed features, Davidson had the look of a fox. As the wiry Scotchman looked at Mick's surly, distrustful expression, he realised he would need all the native cunning and ruthlessness of Reynard himself to get anything on Ben Hall.

'Coobang, we hear this place is something of a jackdaw's nest. D'ya reckon we might find a bit o' sparkle if we looked, boys?' ventured Sergeant Condell.

'I'd say,' chimed in Trooper Caban.

A confident smile split Mick's bearded face, as he looked Condell square in the eye. 'Go on then,' he challenged, stepping aside to let the blue bellies enter the hut once more. Davidson's eyes narrowed as he calculated the odds. *Either he was a good poker player or a bad liar, but if we turned up nothing we'll never break him.* Trusting his instincts, the sub-inspector changed tack.

'Connelly, can ye read?' he asked.

'Course,' snorted Mick.

'Then you'll have heard about the Felon's Apprehension Act?' he asked.

'I have,' replied Mick evenly.

'Well, now, section four says that any person who aids and abets bushrangers will forfeit all their property and goods and do fifteen years hard yakka on Cockatoo Island.'

Mick spread his arms out in feigned innocence, and looked across the veranda, left then right, and said in a cocksure voice, 'Well, as you can see, I'm aiding and abetting no one, Inspector.'

'We know you're Ben Hall's banker,' cut in Davidson.

Mick eyed him warily for a moment, then showed him a set of bad yellow teeth that would have made a dingo turn tail. He gave a short, nervous laugh. 'Where d'ya hear that bulldust? Ask for yer coin back, mate.'

'We know what you were doing at the Oriental Bank,' sneered Davidson, 'and if you don't spill your guts here and now, we'll get Ben Hall without your help. And, what's more, mate, you'll be the first man in front of the Judge under this new Act. I'd bet my pension he'll want to make an example of you.' Leaning in towards him, so his lips were almost touching his ear, Davidson whispered, 'We'll see to that, mate.'

He paused to let the poisonous threat take its full effect and grinned as Coobang Mick swayed slightly and held onto the door-frame for support as his knees threatened to buckle.

Suspecting the conflicting emotions and loyalties that must be raging through the man, Davidson magnanimously allowed Mick to slump onto the rough slab bench on the narrow veranda before continuing to pile on the pressure. 'It's up to you, Connelly. Each of these bastards are now weighing in at eleven hundred pounds and you get to keep your freedom. Or there's prison and you lose every-thing. Doesn't seem much of a call to me.'

'But you're not me, are you?' spat Connelly in his own defence.

'No, I'm not,' retorted Davidson, viciously, 'and bloody glad of it too.' To emphasise his point, he stepped out into the yard, scooped up a handful of coppery red dust and let it run through his fingers like a time glass.

Mick Connelly saw the remaining years of his life blowing away like that wisp of sand across the arid waste of bushland he had clung onto by his fingertips for twenty years or so, for precious little return. Lowering his head, Mick sighed and thrust his hands deep into his pockets in a gesture of acute discomfort and embarrassment.

Sensing he was weakening, Davidson's men circled Connelly like predators smelling blood. 'Here Mick, is it right that Ben Hall rooted your wife?' asked Trooper Hipkiss. Mick didn't react, but the trooper had hit a tender spot. Whilst he had been courting Mary, she'd had a fling with Ben Hall . . . nothing much, just a bit of 'heels up'. Later, Mary and Mick married, but he'd always felt second best to 'Flash' Ben Hall and had sometimes taken it out on his wife.

'Where's Mary, these days?' pressed Hipkiss.

'Gone,' said Mick dryly. She'd tired of his jealous moods and gone off to Brisbane a year back with a digger who'd done well out at Lambing Flat.

'I wish I had a mate like you. He roots your wife and gets off Scot-free whilst you do his time for him.'

Mick stayed silent, the only sign of his agitation the relentless drumming of his fingers on the bench.

Sergeant Condell picked up from where Hipkiss had left off. 'I hear them blokes on Cockatoo Island like a new chum, especially a young bloke.'

He was immediately backed up by Davidson's mocking Caledonian burr, 'Aye, they reckon once you've been out in the hot sun breaking rocks all day, you don't have the strength left to fight them off.'

Condell continued the assault. 'Like flies on horseshit, they say. Lots o' blokes can't live with themselves after a while. Jump in the briny or the wardens find them hung up by their own belts.'

Mick winced as he pictured himself in each scenario. He didn't have much, but it was better than spending the rest of his days fighting off molesters. It was obvious that the traps had the upper hand now and neither Ben Hall nor Johnny Gilbert could protect him anymore. The jig was up and it was every man for himself. Mick knew in his heart that he was beaten, and my whereabouts was all he had to bargain with. His shoulders slumped as he leaned forwards and looked down at the ground in silent despair.

'Billabong Creek,' he said, suddenly. 'He'll stay there tonight before moving on to meet Dunn and Gilbert tomorrow.'

Sub-Inspector Davidson, excited at the prospect of bagging the prized scalp of Ben Hall, lifted Coobang Mick up off the bench and slammed him back against the rough bark wall of his hut. The bang sent a startled mob of lorikeets screeching skywards in a flurry of green, red and yellow feathers. Their racket caused his nervous troopers to lift their rifles and scan the horizon, half-expecting the Ben Hall gang to appear. But there was only silence out there, except for Connelly's ragged breathing and the fading noise of retreating birds.

Mick was transfixed by the big jewelled beads of sweat oozing from the roots of Davidson's receding coppery hair, but the trap could smell the biggest opportunity of his career and a fat slice of reward money and kept his hands and eyes on his quarry and let the droplets roll unchecked. Davidson leaned in close to his quarry, smelling the gravy and beef Mick had for breakfast on his sour breath. He was now sure Mick could be bought. 'Time's up, Mick. You and your class have had your gallop, now it's our turn.'

Breathing heavily, as if speaking required some great physical effort, Coobang Mick completed his betrayal of the remaining members of the Ben Hall gang. 'I don't know about Gilbert and Dunn,' he said, dully. 'They were here the other day, but some stockmen spooked them and they lit out, but Hall will be at Bill-abong Creek tonight.'

Davidson stared intently into Connelly's face as if he was trying to read his mind. 'If I find you've lied to me, I'll put it about the district that you're a peeler and there won't be a warm corner for you in the whole of New South Wales. Don't be going behind our backs to warn Hall neither. We have an account to settle with him.'

Davidson's instincts, honed by his years in the police force, told him he'd knocked at the right door. Mick had caved in and committed the worst sin of all in the eyes of these people, giving up a bushranger to the traps. Like it or not, they were both on the same side now. Letting go of his shirt and allowing him to slump back down on the bench Davidson warned him, 'Best you clear out for a while and lie doggo until it's all over.'

Mick mumbled back, 'I'll be right.'

Davidson shrugged and nodded at his patrol to saddle up. A foot in the stirrup, Davidson turned back, 'Have it your way, but if folk ever suspect that it was you who betrayed Ben Hall, we'll be finding bits of you from here to Bathurst.'

Connelly looked suitably admonished as he stood, hands in his pockets. Gnawing his lip a moment, head down, he suddenly said, 'A word to the wise, Inspector. If you get all three of them together, shoot them where they stand, because if they get a yard start, you'll be chasing their shadows till Doomsday.'

His betrayal complete, Mick lifted his head and, without meeting Davidson's eyes, inquired, 'We'll be going whacks on this, will we? I've risked my neck and I want a slice of the fat.'

Davidson curled his lip, his disgust for the mercenary Mick undisguised in the expression on his face, 'If we bag Ben Hall at Billabong Creek, you'll get your half.'

Using a trembling hand to shield his eyes from the harsh glare of the sun, now risen well above the trees, Coobang Mick could only stare at the retreating silhouettes of Davidson and his troopers as they climbed out of his gully and melted away into the black trees beyond.

A rustling noise in the bush brought me bolt upright with my gun drawn and my head full of demons and betrayal. I half-expected to see the face of a trap staring at me down the length of his barrel. It turned out to be nothing more threatening than a fat, old opossum clinging to a paperbark tree, as startled by my sudden movement as I was by his. He knew I had him covered and stayed there, frozen in the moonlight awaiting its fate. The stand-off lasted a good minute as my befuddled mind cleared and I realised I'd been dreaming. I saw the humour of the situation and had a good chuckle as I lowered my arm slowly. I was showered with dry paperbark as the startled creature made good its escape into the upper reaches of the tree from where it continued to peer down at me until I lay down and went back to sleep.

I was woken a few hours later, the sun just starting to rise behind the trees, by a black and white curlew perched high in the old yellow box above me. It let out a mournful *Hoo-Hoo-Hoo* that sounded like a sad lament. My life as a stockman and a bushranger had conditioned me to go down with the darkness and rise with the first light. As any good bushman does, I first went to see to Willy, who was hobbled in the nearby scrub, before taking a mug of tea from the black arsed billy to see off the morning chill.

I hadn't even shaken the cold and stiffness out of my legs when I heard the sharp crack behind me, and felt the burn as the ball found its mark just below my right shoulder. I never saw the bastard mongrel that fired that first shot, but as it came without warning and caught me in the back, I was sure it was the dirty work of some gutless trap.

The force of it knocked me sideways into a growth of young wattle. Ignoring the sharp pain and the sticky wetness, which was already spreading quickly under my jacket, I grabbed at the saplings and swung round to face my attackers. Through numbed senses, I peered hard into the greyness, but there was nothing there. The gunshot had come like a thunderbolt out of the blue from some angry, avenging God.

In the mornings, a bitter south wind comes straight across Lambing Flat, which rustles the treetops and chases the thick clouds of pre-dawn mist out of the hollows and gullies. It all transpired to give an otherworldly aspect to the skeletal trees that flanked me on all sides, and raised the hairs on the back of my neck.

My heart leapt as several shapeless silhouettes suddenly materialised out of the swirling fog like spectres emerging from some sinister netherworld. They flitted as soundlessly as shadows between the gnarled stumps of the dead trees that littered the hollow between us like tombstones. I took this to be some phantasm, a trick of the early light, but the illusion was ruined by the first, earthly crunch of brittle, rain-starved Myall grass beneath cloddish, frost-numbed bare feet. These 'ghosts' were mere flesh and blood mortals who had taken off their boots to aid their stealth.

The element of surprise now gone, they came on boldly, shoulder to shoulder, their carbines levelled at my upper body. If I was mistrustful of their intentions, then their guns spoke the plain truth. Tongues of fire leapt from booming barrels as they let rip at me. The reddish flashes of gunpowder cast a sinister light on the forces of law and order that called on me to stand, while they dispensed their own brand of rough justice, sanctioned and supported by the law.

I once looked Inspector Norton in his eye and told him, 'You'll never take me alive.' Now his troopers were determined to take me at my word. They'd come armed with double-barrelled shotguns and revolving rifles and intended to use them. It was bodies, not prisoners, they'd come to collect.

I was fair set to give them a hot reception, a blast or two from the shiny, new revolving pistol I had stolen from a squatter who had intended to use it on me. I fumbled with my gun-belt with fingers that were suddenly clumsy but somehow it slipped away and was swallowed up by the grey mists that seemed to be swirling around my boots, rising up to meet me.

Though unarmed, I expected no quarter and none was given. It took a few more shots to put me down, and as I lay sprawled on the ground my blood soaking into the earth, I could smell the sweet scent of fresh, young wattle as the traps' bullets gouged and splintered the green wood. My fate was sealed. Death was on its way.

A rustling caused me to turn my head and I saw Billy Dargin staring at me. He was sitting back on his heels in that wide-legged Aboriginal squat, as comfortable as if he were in an armchair. His forearms rested on his knees and a pistol hung limply from his right hand. *Had he, in some final, bitter irony been sent to finish me off?* I wondered. As soon as I saw him I knew Mick had given them the office. Billy was a tracker, not a magician, and he would never have found me here unless he had help.

'Was it Mick who turned dog on me?' I asked him.

He looked at me a long minute with those keen, black eyes of his, and then spoke. 'Yair, they dropped on 'im after the bank fella tell Mister Davidson about Mick collectin' yer money.'

I nodded. That's the bushranger's strength and weakness. You rely on men whose silence and co-operation you have paid for, but once a man's loyalty can be bought, it can be bought again. It's just a matter of knowing what price will make him yours. This arrangement suited Mick very nicely. What was mine would now be his, along with a share of the reward on my head.

Billy nodded towards the trees where I'd seen the ghostly shapes of the traps. 'Them police fellas bin watchin' you the whole night. They want Billy come shoot you dead when you sleepin'. I send warnings. 'Tis time to run away fella, but you forgot what Billy teach you long ago.'

I stared at him, mesmerised, my brain refusing to function. *Warnings? What warnings?*

Seeing the confusion in my face, he said, 'First, I sent ya the scare birds and then a dream 'bout that Mick fella.' He waited patiently and nodded as he saw the realisation that he was right break across my face. *He sent me the starlings and the dream.*

Once again, I saw Billy and I as young boys sitting cross-legged in a bush clearing with our faces painted with mud. Billy is drawing in the sand with a stick. I heard him say, 'Opossum means someone's coming. Beware.' *It had been Billy who had sent the old opossum that visited me during the night.* Then I remembered him saying, 'If curlew call three times, death close by . . . someone is gonna die.' My mind flashed back to what had wakened me this morning. *Billy sent the curlew to warn me.* He didn't want to shoot a man in his sleep and had tried to give me a sporting chance. *I had been too blind to see them, too far down the track from where and what I had once been.* I'd like to think he did it for old time's sake, but Billy had no fond memories of the past.

'I grew me up with big shame. Billy poor bugger long time. Whitefella all same liar. Too much gammon blackfella,' he said bitterly.

I looked at him and felt sorry for what I'd done and that it had all come to this. But it was much too late in the day for all that, so I did what I'd long intended to do. 'Billy, I'm sorry, sorry for everything, mate.' And with those simple words the circle of betrayal, guilt and vengeance that had snared our da, Billy Dargin, Dan Charters, Mickey Burke, Henry McBride, John O'Meally and then Jim Taylor, Biddy Walsh, Sir Frederick Pottinger and myself, finally closed. We had all allowed too much of its poison to seep into our lives and had each paid a high price.

With some effort, I raised my head and looked down at the ragged, bloody mess that was my chest. Thankful that the worst of it was covered by dark red blood I slumped back and looked up at Billy. I had no right to ask anything of him, but the pain was now intense. With what little strength I had left, I lifted my hand and struggled to form the words.

'I'm done for, Billy,' I wheezed between heavy gasps. The gunfire had stopped. *Was that the sound of boots on the ground, coming for me?* I reached up, clutched at Billy's hand. 'Don't, don't let them take me alive,' I croaked.

Billy just sat there looking at me.

'Please, mate,' I said and nodded at him, pleading, 'For the old days, Billy. We put our hand marks in that cave. They'll be there long after we've both gone.'

He continued to stare at me for a few more minutes as if lost in a trance. Then, he slowly raised the gun, looked straight at me and fired a single shot which hit me with such force my whole body jumped.

The pain, noise and the roar of the guns all disappeared and a calm I had not felt for a long time washed over me. Up in the sturdy, gnarly branches of the old box tree, the rising sun tinged its green leaves with gold. Beyond them I saw a cloudless expanse of early morning sky, which promised to be blue and clear. A strange elation crept upwards through my shattered body and blossomed as a smile on my dried, cracked lips. A currawong soared overhead, riding the currents of warm air, and I shared the thrill of its freedom from all earthly bounds. *Was the sky just as blue in California?* I wondered. *Did that woman we helped and her family ever make it? Ah well, I'll never know now, but that's the fortune of war.*

Regrets? I had a few, but my final thought was of the motto of those poor bolters who took to the bush blindly searching for China, 'Better dead than living in Hell.'

*

Before he left for England, the explorer and statesman, William Wentworth, Pretender to the convict throne of Australia, said that he feared that gentlemen in Australia are now like the 'last roses of summer'. If that is so, then we were the first breath of autumn.

Australia was a blank page of history where we might have started again without the injustices and mistakes of the past, but it was not to be.

From afar, England is greener and fairer than ever she was and the British transplanted their traditions along with the seedlings they'd brought from home. They claimed their roses, lilac and lavender smelled sweeter than our Banksia, Waratah and Wattle. But out beyond the black stump, where the natives still grow tall and strong, the English rose does not smell so sweet and its perfidious perfume cannot poison.

When I grasped the thorns of that English rose and pulled at its root with all my strength, the people raised their hats and cheered from the heart.

I know this to be the truth, for I had heard them, and seen them, myself.

Epilogue

The remnants of the Ben Hall gang, Johnny Gilbert and John Dunn, lived long enough to be declared outlaws, but not much longer.

Following the death of Ben Hall they fled south. On May 8, a Proclamation was issued declaring Dunn and Gilbert to be outlaws. They could be shot on sight by police or any member of the public who spotted them.

Early on the morning of May 13, 1865, Gilbert and Dunn arrived at the hut of John Kelly, Dunn's grandfather. But if they thought they were safe in the soft bosom of family, they were much mistaken.

While they were asleep, Kelly went into Binalong, and, fortified by alcohol, visited the police station asking what the reward on Gilbert and Dunn was. When he discovered it was over £2,000, Kelly told them that they were hiding at his hut.

A four-man police patrol, headed up by Senior Constable Hales, rode up to Kelly's. As they approached the hut on foot the dogs started to bark, which woke Dunn and Gilbert. Both sides exchanged fire and Dunn was hit in the arm and Constable King in the foot.

The bushrangers fled from the hut, split up and tried to escape down a paddock and along Binalong Creek. The police followed and in an exchange between Constable Bright and Gilbert, the bushranger received a fatal wound.

Dunn escaped. He remained at large for another seven months, but was finally arrested on Boxing Day, 1865, at a harbourer's hut in the Macquarie Marshes after returning to the Wheogo area to search for his loot. Although he took a bullet in the foot and back, to Dunn's account was added the charge of wounding a police officer, Constable McHale, and that of killing Constable Nelson.

Thinking he was close to death, they put him on a bed in the police station, but during the night he escaped. His freedom was short-lived, however, and he was re-captured the next day. After surgery to remove the bullets, he was found guilty of killing Constable Nelson and hung at Darlinghurst Gaol on March 13, 1866. And so ended the story of the Ben Hall gang, almost.

Driven by that unquenchable human thirst for freedom and a better way of life, the convict bolters dreamt of escaping to find 'China' and some bushrangers, like Ben Hall, dreamed of starting a new life in California. 'China' did not exist, except in the imaginations of desperate men, and the Ben Hall gang never got to see if California was the Shangri-La they believed it to be, because by the end of 1866 they had all been shot, executed or imprisoned, all except one.

Frank 'the Darkie' Gardiner whiled away the years in Darling-hurst prison making coir mats and reading newspaper reports detailing the death or capture of the wild colonial boys he had once ridden with.

Gardiner may have been a wild man on the outside, but on the inside he had always behaved impeccably, even stopping a prison riot. After serving only ten years of his thirty-two year sentence he was released from prison, thanks to a public petition raised by his loyal sisters and the support of influential Sydney liberals who argued that prison had taken the steel out of him and that he was a reformed man.

Blinking, he emerged from the gloom of Darlinghurst prison into the light of civilised society once more. Now forty-three years old, he was older and greyer, but the man they couldn't hang still had his swagger, even though there was no Kitty Brown to meet him.

After Gardiner had gone to prison she went to stay with her sister, Biddy, who was still living with Jim Taylor, and took up with his brother, Richard. In 1868, they went off to seek their fortune on the Otago goldfields in New Zealand, but Kitty found out too late that like his brother, Richard was a notorious drunk. After only a few months she could take no more, put a gun in her mouth and blew her brains out. She was only twenty-five.

A condition of Gardiner's release was that he leave the colony forever, a sanction he would gratefully have accepted a decade before. Police officers escorted him to Newcastle and put him aboard the *Charlotte Andrews*, which, ironically, took him to China on the way to California.

Under the alias Frank Smith, he settled in San Francisco and just as he said he would years ago, before the Eugowra robbery, he opened a bar. The Twilight saloon was on Kearny Street, near the corner of Broadway, in the notorious 'Barbary Coast' area. For a decade after the gold rush of 1848, it had been known as 'Sydney Town' after the Australians who poured in and ran the rackets.

In a final historical irony, the Darkie had Detective McGlone, the officer who had arrested him at Apis Creek, working behind the bar. McGlone had been removed from the police force following the assassination attempt on the Duke of Edinburgh during his 1868 visit to Australia, which started an anti-Irish backlash.

Gardiner married a rich American widow who bore him two sons. They later visited Australia in the guise of surveyors looking for radium.

They returned to their father's old stamping ground at Mount Wheogo, where the gang had hidden after the Eugowra escort robbery, dug a huge mysterious hole there, and were said to have carried away some of their father's 'possessions'.

The Darkie outlived all of his old bushranging mates, and the so-called 'Ned Kelly generation' that came after them. He died at home in his own bed in San Francisco in 1904 at the ripe old age of seventy-five.

It's said that he had an Irish band play all the old tunes at his saloon bar every day, proving the old adage that the Devil and the Irish did have the best music.

Author's Postscript

This book is a work of 'faction', a mix of history and fiction. Nothing else is possible if the story of Ben Hall is to be told from his perspective. The newspapers of the day and the New South Wales police archives give us a rough chronology of his life, but only folklore and oral history offer some insight into his character. Although these latter sources sometimes yield gems of truth, they are generally dismissed as myths by historians. During my research for this book, the story of Ben Hall featured three such myths.

The first myth is that police drove Ben Hall into becoming a bushranger. This has been repeated in newspapers, local histories and reminiscences dating back to the nineteenth century. The main source of his grievance was always the same – the police burned his hut and left his cattle to die. It led to Hall's famous quote, 'I might as well have the game as the blame'.

That Pottinger razed Sandy Creek is beyond dispute. In a letter to Inspector-General John McLerie, Pottinger justifies his actions by saying that Hall and Jacky McGuire had sold Sandy Creek to a John Wilson who wanted the criminal fraternity evicted. Pottinger wrote:

'I accordingly deemed it my duty to at once interfere and conclusively show Hall and those of his class in the district that at any rate, as yet, they could not have everything exactly as they thought fit.'

Pottinger later arrested Wilson for harbouring Hall, making it hard to believe he would have evicted Hall, even had Wilson owned the land. Local land records reveal McGuire sold his share of Sandy Creek in 1862, but Ben Hall's share was only sold a year after his death. Clause 32 of the *Crown Lands Occupation Act* of October

1861 empowered police to seize lands and evict people from Crown land, but there is no mention of burning property on private land.

The second myth is that Ben Hall was ambushed by police on May 5, 1865, and never fired a shot in self-defence. From the widely published police statements it is clear that there was ample opportunity to capture Hall before a shot was even fired. According to Sub-Inspector James Davidson, leading the patrol, the night before the shooting the man they thought to be Ben Hall 'passed very close to where we were standing', and according to Edgar Penzig in *Ben Hall: The Definitive Illustrated History* '. . . so close that they could have touched him with their guns'. Penzig also speculates that they were tempted to open fire, but held off until daylight so as to be positive of his identity. So why didn't the police grab him and establish his identity? Arresting citizens on suspicion and holding them until their identity or guilt was established was standard practice at that time.

At first light they shot him. Davidson made the following statement at the subsequent magisterial hearing:

> '. . . About half-past six in the morning (5th May) I saw a man with a bridle in his hand about 150 yards from where I was, approaching the horses. By this time the horses were feeding on a plain, bordering a scrub and when the man was about half-way from the border to the scrub to the horses, myself, Sergeant Condell and Billy Dargin ran after him.
>
> After running about 50 yards the man became aware of our presence and ran in the direction where the five men were posted. By this time I identified the man as Ben Hall. I several times called on him to stand. After running about 100 yards, I got within 40 yards of Hall and fired at him with a double-barrelled gun. Hall after my firing jumped a little and looked back, and from his movements I have reason to believe that I hit him.
>
> Sergeant Condell and Dargin the tracker fired immediately afterwards: they were running a little to the left of me and not far away. From the manner of Hall I have every reason to believe that Condell's and Dargin's shots took effect. From that time he ran more slowly towards a few saplings. The five police who were stationed beyond him, immediately ran towards him and

fired. I noticed Trooper Hipkiss firing at Hall with a rifle and immediately afterwards the belt holding his revolvers fell off him. At this time he held himself up by a sapling and upon receiving Hipkiss' fire he gradually fell backwards. Several other shots were fired afterwards. There were about 30 shots in all.

Hall then cried out, "I am wounded, shoot me dead." I went up to the body and noticed life was extinct.'

Sergeant Condell stated he shot the man before he even knew who he was:

'. . . I then covered him fully in the back with my rifle and fired; I then saw it was Ben Hall. I believe my first shot took effect between his shoulders.'

Constable Hipkiss, also present that day, told quite a different story to Davidson, as reported by the Lachlan correspondent of the *Sydney Morning Herald*:

'. . . Mr Davidson repeatedly called on him to stand, but to no purpose. The next moment a bullet was sent after him, which took effect in the back. Here his pace slackened, and he was observed convulsively clutching at his revolvers, but his arms appeared to have lost their office. Sergeant Condell next fired and planted two balls between the shoulder blades.'

Significantly, Hipkiss testified that Hall was disabled by the first shot that hit him and could not reach his guns, which is far sooner than in Davidson's account, which mentions he was disabled by Hipkiss after quite a few more shots had hit him. So, why keep firing?

During a stormy debate on the *Felon's Apprehension Act* in 1865, Mr Terrence Murray, President of the NSW Legislature and a former commandant of the mounted police, stated the strong opinion that the New South Wales Police operated like an army of occupation, had lost the respect of the general population and was now proposing to declare war on the very society it was supposed to protect. He was supported by another member, Mr Docker, who said:

'. . . One might think he was reading the manifesto of an invading general, the bill teemed with legalised murder, and legalised plunder and confiscation.'

The Act was passed and the *Sydney Morning Herald* maintained that in order to see the law as useful the people of New South Wales had to cease to care whether bushrangers were brought in dead or alive. The editorial ended with:

'. . . They [the Legislative Council] will not say that that the present law would justify a Constable in shooting [bushrangers] without challenge, but they intimate that no jury would convict and no Judge condemn.'

Again it should be noted that Hall did not fire one shot in his own defence and had no history of killing policemen or civilians. The *Sydney Morning Herald* conceded this point and noted:

'. . . the dead bushranger was not so bloodthirsty as his two companions in guilt, Gilbert and Dunn, is perfectly true, and there are good grounds for believing that he has, on more than one occasion, prevented the effusion of blood when but on his intervention blood would have been shed.'

In his version of the shooting, Penzig has Hall reaching for his gun *before the police opened fire*. This is a contradiction of the accounts given by Davidson and Hipkiss, who both have him running away and not reaching for his gun until *after he was shot*. A bullet in the chest of a man with a gun in his hand is quite different to a bullet in the back of a man running away. But even if Penzig failed to make this important distinction, the subsequent magisterial inquiry, conducted by the Police Magistrate of Forbes, William Farrand, should have. On May 12, 1865, the *Sydney Morning Herald* boasted:

'. . . The magisterial inquiry held upon it elicited evidence suffi-cient to show that every precaution had been taken with regard to Hall's identity, and that the observances of the law, even as it existed previous to the passing of the Felon's Apprehension Bill, had been respected.'

However, as the *Felon's Apprehension Act*, in which Ben Hall was actually named in the formal proclamation along with Johnny Gilbert and John Dunn, did not come into effect until May 10, 1865, five days after Hall was shot, Ben Hall *was not an outlaw* when he died and police were not entitled to execute him in a summary manner. Farrand should have established whether the police were justified in killing a man when, by their own admission, they could have easily arrested beforehand. Even in 1865 the police were required to take their quarry alive, if possible. It is difficult not to be drawn back to the comment in the *Sydney Morning Herald* that '. . . no jury would convict and no Judge condemn'.

The third myth is that police riddled Hall's body with bullets to show the general population that bushrangers were not invincible and would be harshly dealt with. The number of bullets that reportedly took effect on Hall varies from 15 to 32 'from the crown of his head to his feet'.

To hit a moving target 15 to 30 times whilst running from distances of 40 yards, at first light with weaponry that was notoriously inaccurate, makes the Sub-Inspector's claim that '. . . nearly every shot hitting that was fired at him' hard to believe, unless Hall's body was used for target practice after he was dead. This story still circulates in the Forbes area to this very day. I heard it, first hand, from a local squatter whose family once owned the Nelungaloo station, where Hall was shot.

Although the yellow box that Hall spent his last night under was destroyed in a bush fire in the 1920s, the squatter's father had told him about the tree, which was riddled with bullet holes. The police had apparently put Hall up against it after he was dead and used him for target practice. Although there is no hard documentary evidence to support this charge, Trooper Bohan, a member of the patrol that shot Hall, later alleged Hall's body was used for target practice. He claimed he was ostracised and dismissed from the police force for refusing to join in the carnage of Hall's dead body. The same story was told by Billy Dargin, who became a miserable drunk after the shooting, and went about saying that Hall took most of the bullets after he was dead.

This issue was also raised immediately by the likes of the *Maitland Mercury* who posed the question:

'The death of Ben Hall in itself is a matter for public congratulation, but the manner is certainly no cause for joy ... What ground for satisfaction is there in the fact that by the eight men who surrounded the robber some thirty shots were fired and about half the number, as is reported, took effect ... Not a word is said to indicate that Hall offered to return the fire. Hit by the first shot, severely wounded by the second, his chances of escape were gone. Where then was the need, where the excuse for these volleys we read of?'

The 'need' was revenge for the three years of ridicule Ben Hall had subjected the New South Wales police to and the loss of constables Parry and Nelson. The mood of savage vengeance is conveyed in a private letter written by Sub-Inspector Davidson to his father. He says that after the first shot his men went 'perfectly mad', that the air was filled with the 'yells and shouts of frantic Irishmen' and that they gave Hall 'a fearful riddling'. Sergeant Condell confirms that overkill took place by stating that:

'Hall ran to a cluster of timber and laid hold of a sapling, and said "I'm wounded, I'm dying." The men fired again and he rolled over.'

But whether or not this third myth is true, the shooting of Ben Hall, I believe, was a cold-blooded execution and nothing less. The man who once told police 'you'll never take me alive' was taken at his word. The fears expressed by members of the NSW Legislative Council about the dangers of police abusing the new powers that would be granted under the *Felon's Apprehension Act* were well-founded.

Far from ending the bushranging outbreak, the 'roaring 60s' were only just getting started and the echoes of their ill-fated decision could still be heard more than a decade later when Ned Kelly rode through the streets of Deniliquin shouting, 'hurrah for Ben Hall and Dan Morgan'. Ben Hall was more than a mere boyhood hero to Kelly – he was an inspiration. Kelly's career mirrored Hall's in many important respects: robbing banks, burning storekeeper's ledgers, terrorising whole towns and bailing up pubs and entertaining his hostages. Sadly, Hall has been completely eclipsed by his contemporary whose better documented struggle against the establishment and epic last stand at Glenrowan has burned itself indelibly onto the nation's consciousness.

For better or for worse it is time that Ben Hall took his rightful place in Australian history. In his celebrated history, *Ned Kelly: A Short Life*, Ian Jones says that perhaps Ned was 'the only real Robin Hood who has ever lived'. Not only did Ben Hall come before Ned Kelly, but he displayed daring, chivalry and derring do that Ned never did. As the only landowner to turn bushranger he pulled off some of the most spectacular and celebrated robberies in the colony's history, avoided bloodshed wherever possible and never killed anyone. More importantly, he was part of that first generation of native Australians who took on the powers that underpinned a corrupt system of justice no better or fairer than the one that transported their fathers and determined that Australia was not England and nor would it ever be.

Glossary

a bit of a gull – a fool
a bit of under – sex
a blind – a trick
a fill – to tell a lie
a mag – a chat
a nailer – a grudge, a down on someone
bairn – baby, child
best dart – best course of action/ plan
black arse billy – a pot used to boil water on a camp fire
black leg – illegal bookmaker
blind hole – a dump, a terrible place
bluchers – a popular make of boot
blue bellies – police
bracelets – handcuffs
branded by the broad arrow – to be in prison
breast it – to climb
Bunyip – creature, monster
bush it/go bush – to hide in bush
campaign coat – second hand army issue coat
cattled – roughed up, treated like cattle
caulker – a measure
chook – chicken
cockatoo farmer (cocky) – poor selector
cocky's joy – golden syrup
coggers – card cheats
cove – man, bloke
crib – hideout
crook – sick, bad

cross-biting cullies – dice cheats
cross work – bushranging, stealing
crow – lookout
daisy kicker – horse
dance at the Sheriff's ball – to hang
darbies – handcuffs
darby roll – the rolling gait after wearing leg irons in prison
dill – fool
donahs – girlfriends especially of larrikin types
doubling – to inform on
doxy – woman
drop a few bob – bet a few shillings
drop on – to arrest, detain
dumb leg – physically impaired leg
dummy – a person who bought land on behalf of someone else in order to get round the law
edge it – to leave in a hurry, flee
feel your oats – to spread your wild oats
fizgig – police informant
flam – a scam, sham
flash a roll – show off a roll of bank notes
flash jack – a fancy dresser with the attitude to match
flash up – dress up
fogle – silk hanky
from Greenland – young, naïve
gammon – to fool, to lie to
gammon the twelve – to fool the jury
garnish – bribe
give the griffin – to warn someone
give the office – to give up a criminal's hideout
glim – candlelight
glimming – to burn, or deliberately mark with a hot iron
go under – to die
gone to the bad – become a disreputable character
got the gruel – to be killed, or die
grapple the rails – whisky
hard trot – tough times
have a mag – have a chat
heels up – sex

hempen cravat – hangman's noose
high flyer – adventurous young man
high tide – to be flush with money
holidaying in the Bermudas – a safe haven for a wanted man
irons – pistols
jocking – having sex with
jugged – put in prison
keep dark – to keep a low profile, hide
kick the clouds – to be executed by hanging
knock off the spot – to kill
lamps – eyes
larrikin – a wild, free-spirited character
lettering – letters branded onto the skin of a criminal
lie doggo – to hide, stay out of sight
long-tailed notes – notes of a large denomination
moke – cow
mongrel – the wild, hard, dark side of a person's character
moxie – guts, courage
muzzle – beard
neddied – beaten
Never-Never – the wilderness, remote area
nobbler – a measure of grog
notch – vagina
nugget – an unbranded calf born in the wild, which is of great value
    as it can be claimed by anyone.
off his pannikin – out of his mind
on the burst – on a spree, high spirits
on the chain – in prison, a convict.
on the cross – to make a living from criminal activities; working as
    a thief or bushranger
on the grass – back in business, out and about
on the hip – a prostitute
on the raw – unawares
on the ribs – scavenging, living hand to mouth
on the rip – out thieving
on the square – honestly, come by honestly
palaver – smooth talk
patter – flash talk
pay with a hook – to steal

peacocking – a practice employed by squatters to keep selectors off their land, which involved securing the best land, normally on water frontage thereby denying others direct access to precious water; can also mean expanding a landholding using dummies (see dummy)

pigskin – saddle

plumbs – good quality livestock

plump in the pocket – rich, wealthy

roll of soft – bank notes, money

root – to have sex with, to tire out

rooter – wild, untameable creature

rough trot – bad time

royal spread – the biggest lie imaginable

scourer – scoundrel

screw – horse

scrubber – a wild horse

selector – a small, speculative landowner who selected small runs under the various land acts

sharper – trickster, cheat

skit – to poke fun at

sleep in the Star hotel – to sleep outside under the stars

slice of fat – a share of a reward

sparkle – jewellery, money

spell – to rest up

spicy – lively

split – police informer

squatter – a large, wealthy landowner, a person who occupied large areas of Crown lands before the issuing of licences

stand the steel – to bear being arrested and put in irons

starch – backbone, courage

stick to the square – stay honest

stir the possum – cause trouble, stir things up

strong glass – powerful telescope

sundowner – old, derelict man

swag – sleeping roll or pocket

sweeten – to bribe, induce

take the lump – take the blame

the game – bushranging

ticklers – ribs

tip the velvet – to slip your tongue into a woman's mouth when kissing

to be given a coating – to be given a good talking to, or taught a lesson

to be in it – to be involved in a crime, robbery

to be sent Bay side – transported to Botany Bay

to go whacks – to share, divide reward money

to keep a cutty eye on someone – to watch them closely

to pink someone – to kill someone

to rat – to rip, to tear into

to tow someone out – to fool them

to turn dog – to betray someone

to turn out – to go out to rob or steal

to weigh in at – to be worth a certain price in reward money

to whip – to rob

tough yarn – hard luck story

trap – policeman

turnkey – a gaoler

Tyburn collar – hangman's noose

Vandemonians – a roving band of marauders, criminals

walloper – policeman

warm corner – safe place for a wanted man to hide out

Warrigal – a wild, untameable dog/creature

white in the eye – to be fearsome

Acknowledgements

A book does not write itself and an author is invariably indebted first to those who help compile the myriad detail required to make historical fiction come to life and then to those who ensure all that detail does not overwhelm the story.

In Forbes I'd like to particularly thank Olly and Rob Willis for their kind hospitality and local knowledge, which really helped me get inside Ben Hall. The archive at Forbes Library was informative and their Ben Hall file gave me a lot of great background material, and many thanks to Mayor Alister Lockhart and Richard Barwick at Forbes Shire Council for their kind offer to help launch the book.

I'd also like to thank Graham Seal, Professor of Folklore at Curtin University, for his insights into mythology and outlawry, and Anthony O'Brien for sharing some of his research material on nineteenth century policing, which will form part of his thesis. Thanks also to University of Queensland Press for permission to reproduce the 'Ben Hall Country' and the 'Weddin–Wheogo Area' maps that appear at the front of this book.

The original manuscript was many times larger than the finished item and I'd like to thank my mother, Iris Bleszynski and Courtney Prince for their valuable input into the early drafts, my agent, Margaret Gee, for her unfailing support and guidance and Jody Lee for her commonsense editing suggestions. Once again, Jeanne Ryckmans and Lydia Papandrea at Random House kept me honest and gave me the latitude to fully render this epic yarn. Above all, I must thank my long suffering wife, Jill, and my young son, Stefan, whose first full sentence was, 'Daddy, turn off that computer.'